# BADLANDS
## NOVEL BY THOMAS EDWARDS
### D Good Thief Multimedia Company, Inc.
### Bronx, New York

Good Thief Multimedia Company, Inc
http://www.dgoodthief.com
ISBN: 978-0692222560

## Dedication

In memory of my mother, Evoniza Edwards, who demonstrated to me that women are indeed magical beings that deserve much better
treatment than they usually receive, especially from their sons
and fathers, the two places where they should always be loved, protected, honored and cherished.

In memory of my sister, Dylette Edwards, who, although less than two years my senior, often mothered me and always attempted to protect her little brother.
In memory of Diane Solomon, whose choice to be my spiritual mother touched my heart and perhaps saved my life.

R.I.P. Hezekiah G. (1959-1979), Sydney F. aka Pearl (1968-1993), Marko W. (1974-1994), Howie Z. (1959-1995).
Life on the street often ends in death there. We all chased fool's gold and truly believed crime would pay off big…what big fools we were to sell ourselves so short. I'm sorry I couldn't figure out that there was a better way for us before you all departed. Not to worry, I'll pay off all the debts we created by living *the life*.

## Acknowledgments

Writing a novel is very similar to raising a child and to do so correctly, you need all the assistance you can get: it takes a village to raise one child and no story can be told by just one person. There's always more than one account, with at least two sides, and that's without the different versions from all the participants and bystanders. Without the input, feedback, support and assistance from so many people *Badlands* would be incomplete.

Therefore, my thanks to, Ro-Ro Brown and Big Game Born, who laughed at my efforts to write a book, often asking if I was still working on that "bullshit book," which was as good as any encouragement I received. On to more positive support: Rashan Smalls aka Amenta, Tyrone Anderson aka Big Ty, --thanks for the route to Jamaica Estates-- and Chima were all sounding boards, offering feedback and/or information on locations, scenes or anything else needed to improve the story. Their interest in my creation showed me I wasn't alone in believing that I was a real writer. In addition, Black, at the Points, read the first completed draft and loved it, which kept me on the grind toward the finish line—good looking, my brother. Trigger aka Kendell A. and Troy R., who each read it twice, and with such enthusiasm. Rahson Johnson and Douglas Duncan, thanks for the support and interest toward the book and my evolution. J. D. P., although the book didn't catch your attention, your support over the years is greatly appreciated and I pray that life brings you everything you desire.

Although I have a lot of fun at his expense, Inf aka Kenneth B. has to get his due for his editing prowess and knowledge of any and every subject. He's definitely an editor, though I had to edit behind him because he lacks my great vision and creativity (smile). My son, Marquet, has always been an inspiration, whether I see him or not. My daughter, Shenita (has been the best part of my life), and showed interest and provided support throughout the project, seeing my vision and pushing it along with her love. Dumitru Alexandru designed the cover and produced the graphics lifting the project to the next level. Danyell Guyton, created the cover art and is a talented writer as well as artist, read the story and immediately believed in it, offering her time, talent and funds to get it out there, but more importantly her faith. Stephany Jones, whose organizational skills are as creative as any artist's, brought it all together with her support, can-do attitude and goal driven li'l self. Both shared my vision for *Badlands* and fought for it as hard as I did and without them, I'd still be in a fight.

Lastly, L. A., my brother, stay up and know that you're not forgotten. To anyone I forgot, I apologize and thank you for your assistance.

One last mention, though definitely not the least, Mohaman Gueka Koti who has been imprisoned for more than 35 years, continues to be an inspiration to my evolution as well as to other men that have chosen the path of redemption. He is on the Jericho list of political prisoners. His story is one from the Black movement of the 1950s and '60s and after all this time behind bars, and at 86 years of age he deserves the chance to spend his last years beyond the walls of prison. Since you have taken the time to read this, please go another step; find out whom Mohaman G. Koti is and what you can do to have him freed.

# CHAPTER ONE

The rain had come and as the last drops pounded the sidewalk, Billie Holiday's, *Willow Weep For Me* poured out of the two speakers in the room. Billie's sad lyrics and pain filled voice combined with the rain to create a cloud of melancholy.

As much as he wished them gone, the sad images played in his head like an old Blues singer who had no idea his time on stage was over. Try as he might, Man couldn't force them out.

*Walking out of the old tenement building, the only home he'd ever known, he heard the sobs. Wounded and wretched sounds that was more animal-like than human. As he slowly moved toward the awful sounds, his heart ripped with each hesitant step—he was sensitive like that. Someone else's pain became his own as soon as he witnessed it. Leaning forward to see who was huddled under the dark stairwell, he couldn't believe his eyes.*

*"Rita?" Man breathed her name, making it sound more like a denial. It couldn't be. She was naked; clutching what looked like a bloody rag to her chest. Her face was battered and bloody—one eye swollen shut, her nose smashed. Bruises covered her face and body. He went to her without hesitation now, scooping her up in his arms.*

*"I tried to stop him but he beat me so bad. He kept hitting me," she moaned as blood flowed from her nose with each word.*

*"Why did he beat me so bad? Why?"*

*"Don't worry. It's okay now. I got you," he said, carrying her as fast but as gently as possible, to the apartment they shared with his mother. Tears welled up in his eyes, but he held them back*

*"Mama! Mama!" He shouted, kicking on the door.*

*The door opened suddenly. "Boy, what is wrong with yo...Oh-my-God," his mother gasped. "Rita?" She didn't want it to be true anymore than her son had. It broke her heart to see the young girl her son loved beaten and bloody. "My poor baby," she said, as she led them to the couch.*

*Rita whimpered, "Mama Willie, he beat and raped me. Oh, Mama Willie, why did he hav'ta beat me so bad? I told him to stop. I tried to fight 'im back. But he . . ."*

*Mama Willie looked at her son, "Call 911 and tell 'em we need an ambulance right away." She took the teenager in her arms and rocked her back and forth, afraid to do anything more. "You poor baby. Its gonna be all right." Ms. Wilona Soleil tried to hold back the tears as she saw the look on her son's face, but couldn't, they streamed down her cheeks.*

*Rita's eyes seemed to go blank—the one eye that wasn't swollen shut, that is. "No, Mr. Fuddy, please don't hit me no more. I'll do what you want. No, get off. Man, help me. Please, Man, please..."*

*"Hush, baby, its gonna be okay," Mama Willie whispered. She didn't want Man to hear anymore. She looked up, their eyes met and she knew he'd heard the name.*

Man shook the images from his head and stood up. The rain had stopped. It had cleaned the street, washing the trash down the sewer. If only the images and memories could be washed away as easily, he thought.

Billie was singing, *No Good Man*, now. The irony made him smile; however, there was no joy in it. Looking out through the glass door onto the dark street, he knew he should deal with the present but the past refused to let him go.

The cool October night was perfect for a jacket. He preferred to wear a jacket because it made it easier to conceal the large, blue-black, 45-caliber Colt semi-automatic and extra clip he usually carried. Gazing around the game room at the three pool tables, nine video games, shelves of books and pictures covering the walls, his mind wandered back to how he came to own the place. He snapped himself out of it. Enough with the memories, he thought as he slipped on his jacket. He was late for the first of his two meetings.

Since he'd been sitting in the dark, letting Billie's words paint the picture of both their souls, he didn't have to go behind the counter to turn the lights off. He preferred the dark, for the same reason he preferred to wear a jacket, they both had the ability to conceal things: one, his weapon, the other, emotions that he'd rather not face.

He stepped out into the night and inhaled deeply, as if picking up a scent, and let his eyes take everything in before he started up the block. He didn't bother to lock the door or pull the gate down. Man wasn't afraid of anyone entering the game room. Who would be fool enough to mess with Badlands?

As he walked up the block to Blue Seal's headquarters, the neighborhood crackheads put the touch on him. The crack addicts knew Man would drop a few dollars on them, even though he couldn't care less about supporting their habit. But it was worth a try for their next hit. More times than not, he'd buy them something to eat.

Everyone spoke to him, even the working folks. They all knew him, some since he was a child. Dope fiend, crackhead, working square, welfare mom, hustler–they all gave him his due. And why shouldn't they? He had earned it. There was no doubt how he carried it. He had always stood up.

Man stopped in front of 442, the largest tenement on the block. The two lookouts nodded. He returned their nods and continued up the steps, passing the runner. He looked around for the pitcher. Blue Seal crew was doing it in a big way–two lookouts on the street watching for the police and the stickup kids, and a runner to keep the supply of $5 caps of crack on hand at all times, and finally, a pitcher to serve the customers. Oh yeah, they was doing it—a real business and a very profitable one at that.

Tonight, the pitcher was Ramsey, a kid from the hood. He had Terry, a young cutie from down the street, hemmed up in the corner. Although neither one of them had seen their seventeenth birthday yet, they thought they had all the answers. After watching them for a few seconds, Man's eyes locked on Terry. "Get to gettin', Shortie," he commanded.

Startled, both teens jumped. Terry recovered first. "Hi, Man. I was on the way to the store for my mama, and—"

Man cut her off," Ain't a store in here. So, see ya' and take yo' butt straight to the store and back home," he said, with a paternal stare.

"Okay, okay. I'm going, Man," Terry said. She waved to Ramsey and added, "See you later, Man." Then, with a smile, she threw an extra twist in her hips and left.

Watching her go, Man thought the smile and walk was too grown for her young ass. He shook his head and turned his attention to Ramsey. "Boy, if you working, how you playin'? What kind of fool is you?"

"Awh–Man, I was just kickin' it with Terry. You know, tryin' to get my swerve on. And anyway, any fool can pitch," Ramsey said, looking confused.

Man nodded in agreement. "You got that last part right 'cause only a fool would be selling crack hand-to-hand, risking his life and freedom for a few dollars over lunch money," Man said, as Ramsey dropped his eyes. He thought he knew what he was doing, so he hated Man's lectures. But out of respect, he figured he'd let Man finish.

"But what you don't get is that even this petty shit ain't no game. Anything can happen when you slinging poison. Stickup kids can roll, a crackhead can go off, and what about Po-Po? It's they job to put your young ass in jail. You gotta stay on point."

Ramsey's sixteen years of life told him he knew what was what, and he shared it with Man. "Ain't none of these fools crazy. Stickup kids and heads know Blue Seal protected by you. And I know what time it is with Po-Po. Fuck 'em!"

Man stared into the kid's eyes. The admiration he saw there made him as sad as Billie's songs. Sadder, because at least Billie had known hard times had a hold on her.
Man started to say more, but realized it wouldn't do any good, so he started up the stairs. Ramsey had dreams of fly cars, jewels and getting paid. Man couldn't remember how many times he had told the boy to stay in school and leave the streets alone. He had chased him away more times than he could count. Still, here he was pitching—selling drugs for a salary of $600 a week—and thinking that he's a real hustler. Hell, I know a few hustlers and the boy sure ain't one of them, Man thought.

***

Ricky sat motionless, listening to José. The tall, skinny, half Black and half Puerto Rican pretty boy, from across town, was going on and on about the time being right for changes. He talked about expanding, blowing up in the game. He was saying all the right things. His rap was full of big plans and major loot.

"We gotta flood the whole fuckin' hood. More drugs, more money," José said with passion. He had everyone's attention— money could do that.

The three drug crews were meeting to discuss business. Although José was on a roll, he paused to look at Ricky. Ricky's small black eyes gave away nothing. As the boss of Blue Seal, the biggest and most profitable crew, Ricky didn't need to say much. Getting paid made you important in the hood—just like in the rest of the world; money was power.

Ricky's dark brown skin, medium height and weight were all ordinary. That is, until you noticed his deep-set, narrow eyes that hinted at his shrewdness. He prided himself on being a true *Machiavellian.* Although he wasn't a thug, he was dangerous just the same. A thug was more straight up with his intentions, aggressive moves and hostile ambitions. While he didn't have much heart, Ricky was intelligent and manipulative, with a mean streak. He'd kill a kitten just because he could, but only if he was sure he'd get away with it.

And with the power drug money gave him he was someone to fear. Most people were cautious around him, including José. While Jose's crew was getting paid, Ricky's was clocking twice as much, close to $30,000 a day. Plus, he had a new spot downtown that no one knew about, pulling in another $15,000. With two houses, a hide-a-way condo, sneaker store and barbershop/ beauty parlor, Ricky could throw his weight around.

Ricky settled his hard gaze on José. "So what you sayin? I mean, you making a hell of a speech but ain't sayin' shit."

José squared his slender shoulders and met Ricky's stare. "I'm sayin' it's time for a change. Why we gotta shut down every morning from 7 to 10, and from 2 to 5 in the afternoon? There's paper to be made all fuckin' day," José said with a smirk.

With the radiator in the corner hissing and pumping out heat, the eight young men felt the tension. José had two of his boys with him, and Sammy and Mack from the Green-Top Crew were there. Ricky glanced over at his two lieutenants, Chill, and ShortDog. He had to show them all how he got down. He grunted and said, "It's the rule. That's just how shit goes—"

José exploded, "Fuck that! It ain't my fuckin' rule!"

Ricky steadied himself – he hadn't gotten this far by jumping into shit –and continued as if he hadn't heard Jose's outburst. "It's how shit goes down around here. Since I got down with the program I made more money than ever, and that's what it's about for me–stacking paper. "And we can cut to the chase. We know who made the rule. It's the same muthafucker we pay every week. Shit, I knew Man since I was a kid runnin' numbers in this same hood, and I ain't got no problem doing shit his way. He handled his business, did a bid for it, came home and put shit together," Ricky said, pausing and smiling at José. "So, if you got somethin' to say, say it." Before José could respond, the apartment door opened, and Man stepped in. From where he stood he could see everybody in the room. Nobody moved. His eyes held them in place.

With a stoic expression, Man spoke, "Good evening, gentlemen, and I use the term loosely. My apologies for my tardiness, I was otherwise detained."

"What's up, Man? Have a seat. We been waiting for you," Ricky said in a rush. Man remained standing. His brown eyes locked on José, who quietly took a seat.
José might not like the way shit is, but he ain't trying to fuck with Man straight up, Ricky thought as he took in the scene.

Man let his eyes slide from José, who was meekly checking out the floor, and pinned everyone in the room with a quick stare. After a moment, he said, in a resonant baritone, "I took the liberty of showing myself in. Although the young fellows working the door wished to announce me, I had to decline their cordiality."

Short-Dog sat back and quietly observed Man work the room, and thought, *Muthafucker talks like he's writing a book sometime, but pity the fool who let that smooth talking shit get his ass played out. Everybody knew Man could flip without warning.* Short-Dog watched Man's every move, mesmerized like a little kid seeing his sport hero in person.

At 6' 1" and about 200 pounds, Man's size wasn't intimidating but his presence was. Built like an NFL safety, Man moved with the grace of a dancer and the confidence of someone extremely dangerous.

The stories told about him made most people nervous. Like the one about how he came to own the apartment building and game room–Old Man Coby supposedly signed it all over to him after being tortured. However, there wasn't any way to be sure about that one. After all, ain't nobody ever seen Coby's perverted ass again. Not that he was missed. Coby had used money and threats to pressure the neighborhood kids for sex.

Whatever happened, his ass was history, and Man had the building. He'd hooked up the game room, named it Badlands, made sure the building was clean and safe, and that the apartments had plenty of heat and hot water. The whole building stayed spotless, even the crackheads respected it. Of course they did. Who would fuck with Man's shit? Oh, it wasn't like no one had tried Man, just none lately. Smiling, Short-Dog thought of the few he'd witnessed and nodded his head.

"How are you my jocund friend? You seem in high spirits."

Realizing that Man was speaking to him, Short Dog's smile widened as he replied, "I'm cool, Man. You know, just chillin'." He wasn't really scared of Man, as much as he was careful around him. He knew Man was a hard mutherfucker and would make hell yo' home quick, fast and in a hurry. But he also knew that Man liked him. And Man didn't like many people, at least not grown ones.

Short-Dog thought it was because at 5' 1" and 120 pounds, the average thirteen-year-old was bigger than him. Whatever the reason, Short-Dog didn't plan on getting caught doing anything to fuck it up.

"Short-Dog, you're an amiable fellow. Though small of stature, you're ample of character and, as always is the case, it's a pleasure to be in your company," Man said with a smile.

Short-Dog laughed. He loved it when Man talked that slick shit, especially since he knew Man learned it in a damn prison cell. Man had told him about being locked-down, sometimes 23-hours a day, and using books to escape. Damn, Short-Dog thought, I gotta read that book Man gave me. The crazy muthafucker had more than a thousand books in the game room, and said that he had read every one of them.

"Without further ado, let us proceed with the business at hand. I take it you have some concerns. Well, you have my full attention," Man announced to the room, as he gracefully slipped off his brown, butter-soft leather jacket, the shoulder holster in plain view.
The room became quiet—even the noise from the radiator seemed subdued. A baby was crying next door while a dog barked on the street below and other street sounds — traffic, an argument over the price of *ThunderBird* and laughter — drifted up to the third-floor apartment. But, the room itself was silent.

"Come, come, my outlaw associates. Voice your grievances so that we can get outta here," Man said, before pointing to Ricky. "You put this little party together so why don't you get it started."

Ricky looked around nervously. Shit, everybody had agreed to kick it with Man about shit. Now it was on him. He cleared his throat. "Uhhh. Aw . . . well, we just been sorta' worried about this new Neighborhood Watch and the way they gonna be snitching to Po-Po. It's gonna be bad for business."

Man spoke to everyone present while looking at Ricky, "Yeah, I can see your point. Here you are tearing down the community. Mind you, the same community you come from, and folks who live here have the audacity to object and want the drug dealing to stop." Man snapped his fingers. "Ricky, wake up. You a drug dealer. You spread poison and death. I guess you could call it an occupational hazard," Man said, with a chuckle, before continuing. "But it's a hazard to the people living here and they want the shit gone. And the fact that you was born and raised here probably makes it worst to them. One of their own, killing them!"

Man looked around the room. "I digress. I'm speaking of morals and integrity, which are as out of place here as a black man at a Klan rally. All we care about here is money. So, you sell drugs and I protect you for a reasonable fee. I can deal with the Watch or whatever they call themselves this week. I grew up here, just like you, Ricky. I know how these old folks get down. Talk, that's what they do. Understand?"

Ricky nodded, and Man continued, "By the way, citizens ain't snitching when they call the police. Those codes don't apply to them. Hell, with all the so-called gangsters turning state's and taking the witness stand it seems like they don't apply to us anymore, either. Anyway, if y'all keep the buildings clean and don't fuck with folks, they'll look the other way for the most part. And cut out the beat-downs. Crackheads got people that love them too. Give everybody a li'l room and shit'll run smooth."

Man exhaled. He didn't have much use for most of the young men in the room. The youngest wasn't yet twenty and the oldest a few years shy of thirty. But all were without hope or much chance of making it through the prison and death traps that awaited them. He shook his head. "Now, is that it?" he asked, as he turned and faced José.

It took José a minute to collect himself. "You right, Man. But we was kinda wondering about the no-work hours. You know, like, maybe shortening them to—"

Man cut in, "Ain't no need to keep going. The first problem is that wondering is too close to thinking, Ze … You don't mind if I call you that do you? I hear all your friends call you that, and since we gettin' all cozy and shit ... I mean, you thinking for me and all."

José opened his mouth, but Man raised his hand and stopped him. "Ze, don't think about what the fuck I do. The hours stay the same," Man said, as if he was giving someone the time of day.

Although afraid, José didn't want to look like he was bitching up, especially after all that hot shit he had popped. So he tried a different approach. "There'd be more money if we worked some of those hours and expanded closer to the game room. More money for *everybody,*" he finished quickly.

Ricky just watched. He knew José had fucked up. His dumb ass was waving money at Man. Didn't he realize Man didn't care about money? Not like that anyway. Man was on some other shit– honor, loyalty and some other bullshit codes.

The muscles of Man's jaw flexed, his gaze narrowed and settled on José. Feeling the tension, José involuntarily looked at his two boys for backup. Carlos, the bigger of the two, at 6' 4" and 250 lbs, started to get up.

"Sit the fuck down," Man said in a calm voice, without taking his eyes off José. Caught halfway up, Carlos didn't know what to do. He peeped at the big holstered .45 under Man's arm, and then at José, –who looked away–before he dropped back in his chair.

Man waited. Seconds went slowly. When he finally spoke, his voice was like steel: "Ze, check your boy. And if I catch a muthafucker slinging shit near Badlands God won't be able to help him." Man seemed to drift for a second, his eyes had a faraway look, then he was back. "Even ghetto kids oughta' have a place. Now if we're finish here I'll be on my way. I have another engagement." He slipped on his jacket and said, "Ricky, I read *The Prince* by Machiavelli, too. He was a fraud and coward. And Short-Dog, that book I gave you, *Manchild in the Promise Land,* by Claude Brown, is a book you really should read."

## CHAPTER TWO

Gazing down at the traffic on the Cross Bronx Expressway, which was sparse at ten o'clock on a weeknight, Man walked slowly up 174th Street. The occasional headlights passed like phantoms moving between the living and dead. The fleeting lights reminded Man of his lost salvation, and of how it all started. He thought of the first murder he had committed. Instead of being sorry, he wished that he could bring the piece of shit back to life and kill him again.

The images pounced on him: *The little gun was like a toy in his hand. He didn't remember how it had gotten there. It was the gun his mother kept hidden in her bedroom closet. He'd gone in the room to call 911, and now he was making his way through the basement of the building next door. He moved along... trance-like... unsure of what he was doing but unable to stop and think about it.*

*He entered the back room. Fuddy stood shirtless, with his back to the door. His back was broad, muscled, and scarred. The scars and muscles had prison stories to tell. Although they were about the same height, 5'10", at 240 the older man outweighed Man by eighty pounds. Seconds passed as slowly as hours, but Man stood there. Was it indecision or fear? He didn't know. But he couldn't leave. He had to make things right. But how? Fuddy spun around. "What the... Oh, it's yo' bitch-ass. I knew that li'l ho'd tell how I gutted her hot-ass. That's right! I fucked the bitch. So what?"*

*He stared into Fuddy's eyes and saw the amusement mixed with contempt there. He wanted to say something but couldn't. Nor could he move. Maybe he didn't breathe, either. Fuddy smiled "Boy, what the fuck you want? You know you ain't gonna do shit." Fuddy laughed. "Wait a'minute, maybe you want old Fuddy to fuck you too? I don't mind a little boy pussy every now and then. Then I can go try yo' mama out, huh?"*

*When Man didn't move or speak, Fuddy took it for fear and took a step toward the seventeen-year-old. Man fired from the hip. Two shots: Bang! Bang! Both shots found Fuddy 's chest. He looked down at the wounds, then at the gun in Man's hand. He hadn't noticed it before. Fuddy staggered, steadied himself, then took another step forward, "You fuckin' faggot." Bang! Bang! The shots hit Fuddy in the groin. He fell to his knees, still cursing. The manchild walked up to Fuddy and put the little gun in his face and fired the last two shots.*

Man fought his way out of the past and readied himself for his meeting with the good law-abiding folks of the neighborhood. Although he didn't have much use for them, he'd listen out of respect. He knew it was a waste of time, though. The only thing the Neighborhood Watch was going to do was sit around and watch, he thought.

He was a man of action, and the images that haunted him confirmed it. He didn't waste time judging his actions. Whatever law he had lived by prior to the, as he called it, damnation of his soul, did nothing to save the people he loved. So he created his own.

He had learned to live by his own rules. Rules that protected him and the few things he still cared about. And if someone was caught breaking one of his rules, he wouldn't hesitate passing and enforcing the appropriate sentence. Whatever it might be.

Though he could count the men he had killed, he didn't bother. He slept good. And despite the memories that raided his head like refugees, he liked to say that it was him who haunted the dead and not the other way around. In his mind, he carried a sword of righteousness and had no qualms about using it when necessary.

\*\*\*

*The Neighborhood Watch* waited for Man inside of Sam's Cleaners. Five of the people there had lived in the neighborhood for over 30 years.

Mr. Sam Keys and his wife, Mary, owned and ran the cleaners. Mr. Bob owned the barbershop down the street, even if he couldn't cut hair anymore because his hands were no longer steady. Also present was Ms. Judy who still owned and operated the diner around the corner and Ms. Nez, who had been one of the first people of color in the neighborhood 45 years earlier.

The rest were relative newcomers, except for Nicki. Though she was three years younger than him, at 28, Nicole Porter had grown up with Man. They'd gone to the same schools and she recalled the sweet older boy she'd had a crush on throughout her childhood. Her father — God bless him — had thought the world of Man; just knew he'd become famous. She remembered how proud her father was whenever Man accomplished something in sports. He used to say Man was the best athlete he'd ever seen—a star running back and third basemen in high school. In a way, Man was the son he never had.

Man had made it easy to be so highly thought of—he respected his elders, looked out for the younger kids and worked as hard on his schoolwork as he worked on sports. Colleges were showing interest in him. Every adult in the neighborhood loved him. And, with his rich brown color and build, the girls loved him, too. He was as nice as he was handsome, Nicki thought. Looking back, she thought, Man had everything going for him. As difficult as it was to make it out of the ghetto, Man had seemed a sure bet to do just that. But, then, everything changed with the rape of his childhood sweetheart, Rita.

It was a shame. Rita's rape and everything was bad enough, but then what happened to Mama Willie and the baby . . . The whole neighborhood had been devastated. So, Nicki could imagine what it had done to Man. So much pain was unnatural. But, oddly enough, Man seem to take it all in stride. Mr. Sam's voice shook Nicki out of her thoughts.

"Now, where is he? He's almost thirty minutes late. Maybe he ain't coming," Mr. Sam said as he stared out the window.

"Sam, you know if Man said he'll be here, he will," Mr. Bob said.

"Well, he shouldn't keep us waiting."

"My God, Sam!" exclaimed Ms. Judy. "You think all Man has to do is listen to us complain. He's probably busy and running a li'l late."

"Yeah, that's the problem. He busy messin' with them damn drug dealers."

Ms. Nez twisted up her lips and shook her head. "Oh, hush up, Sam. You always find a way to say the wrong thing at the wrong time."

"I'm speaking the truth and y'all know it. The boy done gone bad. He ain't the kid we seen grow up. He done change into somethin' none of us knows."

"The chile loss Rita, his mama, and the baby. He was forced to kill and then put in some damn prison, when he should've been treated like a hero. Of course he changed," Ms. Nez responded with a wave of her hand.

"I agree that that low-down Fuddy Ray got what he deserved. But look how Man done it ... like he enjoyed it. And if he hadn't turned around and killed that other Ray boy in jail, maybe his mama and the baby'd be alive today. 'Cause then the oldest boy, Larry Ray, might not'a done what he done."

Mr. Bob jumped up. "I can't believe you said that foolishness. I know you don't believe that. You know what them Ray boys was like: all three of them was bad. Bad through and through. Nobody was safe with them around. Man did what we shoulda' done a long time ago. Killing was too good for 'em if you ask me."

"Ain't that the truth," Ms. Nez threw in.

# CHAPTER THREE

Short-Dog stood in front of 442, the building Blue Seal worked out of, sharing a blunt with Carlos. He was in a good mood
– in the last two days Blue Seal had pulled in over $70,000. So he listened graciously as Carlos told war stories, tales of his exploits in the hood.

The physical contrast between the two hustlers was comical. Carlos was as big as a linebacker and Short-Dog was smaller than the average sixth-grader.
Still feeling the residual effects of his encounter with Man, Carlos, by recalling his more daring adventures, was putting batteries in his own back. He was pumping himself up to step to Man, and he wanted to do it in front of everybody who witnessed his humiliation.

Man had been on his mind since that night, but seeing Terry come out of her building in skin-tight jeans gave Carlos something else to think about. "Damn, check out Terry's bad ass. Shortie's holdin'."

Short-Dog watched Terry cross the street and said, "Yeah, she proper. Body and all."
"You know I can hit that, right?" Carlos boasted.
Short-Dog laughed. "I hear that slick shit. Terry ain't thinkin' 'bout yo' big ass."

"Oh, and you think she thinkin' 'bout yo' li'l ass?" Carlos retorted, as they laughed and slapped palms.

As Man's gold Towncar went by, Short-Dog waved as Man beeped his horn. Carlos' mood soured. He followed the car with his eyes. "Fuck Man," he said.

"Yo, don't sweat that shit, Lo."
Carlos balled his huge hands into fists. "Like I said, fuck him. I ain't about to forget that punk shit he did."

Short-Dog looked up at him and said, "Leave that shit alone. You don't wanna go there. Trust me, homey."
"You must think that muthafucker's superman or something. And if he is, bet I'ma' find some Kryptonite fo' his ass."

"Yo. I know he ain't superman, but I wouldn't fuck with him even if was. See, I know the real deal 'bout Man."

Carlos made a face as if Short-Dog's words smelt like monkey shit left out in the sun too long. "What's that suppose to mean?"

Short-Dog glanced around, and said in a conspiratorial voice, "Don't say shit about what I'ma' tell you." He stopped and looked in the direction Man had gone. "I was only about five when the shit went down but I'm hip to it anyway. You know how muthafuckers always talkin'."

"Yeah. Like what you doin' right now," Carlos answered with a chuckle.

"Fuck you, Lo. You wanna hear the shit or not?"

"Chill, Dog. I was just fuckin' with you. Kick it."

Short-Dog took a deep breath. "Back in the days, Man and his shortie, Rita, had a baby. And they was—"

"Yo, Dog. I ain't tryin' to hear no fuckin' love story," Carlos interrupted.

"Oh, this shit is more like a horror story," Short-Dog said with a nod of his head. "Anyway, these three brothers had the hood on smash–everybody was under pressure. Mean muthafuckers too, robbing and dissing everybody. Well, one of 'em raped Man's girl—beat the cowboy shit outta her too."

"So what Man do?" Carlos asked, his interest obvious.

"Well, that's where the shit with the "four-fifth" got started. Man strapped up with that pretty-ass .45 and blew the muthafucker's dick off. Two shots in the joint, then two in the heart, and two more in the mouth." Short-Dog paused for effect "Now, is that some rough shit or what?

"But that ain't all. Man took the shit to trial even though he could've copped out and got probation. He went up north – I 'on't know what prison – and found another one of the brothers and stuck a knife through his neck."

"Damn, that is some shit," Carlos said, rolling the story around in his head.

Short-Dog nodded. He liked telling the story, even though he'd gotten it all secondhand. "Yeah. But that still ain't all of it. You see, Man fucked up because there was one more brother, and he killed Man's moms and li'l daughter. So, even though word is that Man's boys from prison came home and cut dude's head off he still gotta live with that shit." Short-Dog paused again and rubbed his hands together before adding, "Now, you see why he ain't the one?"

Carlos glanced down at the game room. "No wonder he on some gun-ho shit. But what happened to his girl that got raped?"

"Oh. She killed herself when Man got knocked for that first body," Short-Dog answered matter-of-factly.

***

As he cruised along the F.D.R. Drive, Man lost himself in Guy's, *Piece of my Love*. He rocked to the beat and lyrics while thinking how true the words were. He wasn't totally free and there were a lot of things he couldn't tell.

Rocking with the beat, he reminded himself that it was time to quiz Peter-Gun and Kid on the setup in Queens. It was about ready and should be a huge payday.

In the five years he'd been out of prison, Man had made over a dozen moves. It averaged out to almost three a year, which was too damn many, he thought. Sooner or later he'd catch a bullet or a bid, and prison sounded the worst of the two. Nevertheless, he didn't know if he could live any other way. He was just playing out the hand he had been dealt.

He figured that if the breaks in life balanced out, he wasn't due for another bad one in this lifetime. He'd went to prison, not for killing a rapist, but because he refused to plead guilty. Guilty? Fuddy's death was justice: nothing more, nothing less. Still, he'd gotten three years for it. And while Mike Ray's death had been ruled a justified homicide, Man had come to believe it was more luck than justice that he was alive and Mike Ray was dead.

Man ejected the Guy cassette and put in Curtis Mayfield's, *Superfly*. He sang along with the first song, *Little Child Runnin' Wild*. "Watch awhile, see he never smiles." What was there to smile about, Man thought? It was like the song said: "Didn't have to be here." But, here he was. He had killed two of the badass Ray brothers and became a ghetto legend for it. What a joke – Fuddy hadn't given him a choice and Mike would've killed him if he hadn't got a hold of the knife when he did.

Trading Mike's life for his own hadn't cost him any more time in prison. But he had gotten an additional 3 to 6 years for breaking the jaw of a racist guard, who attacked him first. And the state had gotten everyday of the nine year maximum out of him.

Everybody wanted his or her pound of flesh, and the state prison system was no different. Prison was full of poor fools, and those same fools spent their time preying on the weak. It was the same in the street. The cops'd beat an unarmed man half to death for sport, and crack dealers'd beat a crackhead to death for a $2 debt. But, both dealers and cops would plead for mercy when the tables were turned. Man wondered if it was human nature to take advantage of the weak.

As the song came to an end, Man popped the cassette out, and got off at the Water Street exit. He had an appointment with his financial advisor, Tyrone Jenkins, a sharp brother who had graduated from Howard University with a B.A. in finance and then went on to get a M.B.A. from Harvard. Mr. Jenkins — as he insisted his white colleagues call him — graduated "magna cum laude" from both schools. He was the truth when it came to the stock market; knew when, and what to buy and sell. Man dug his style because he knew for a brother to make it on Wall Street he had to be better than everyone else. And Tyrone was honest, all the way legit. Man smirked at the irony: there were more crooks on Wall Street than there were in Sing Sing.

At 1:57, Man walked into the eighth floor offices of Whitman, Brown and Pauls at 60 Broad Street. His appointment was for two o'clock. Within a couple of minutes, Ty came out and led him back to his office. "Man, good to see you," he said, extending his hand. "You're looking well, as always."

Man smiled and shook Ty's hand. "Thanks. But you don't have to flatter me. You already have my business."

"It's only flattery when the man's not worthy," Ty said, as he returned the smile.

"Ah, true. But as the English playwright, George B. Shaw, said: 'What really flatters a man is that you think him worth flattering.' So keep it coming," Man said, his smile growing.

"You're on a roll, huh?" Ty replied. "By the way, nice suit." They both laughed as Man did a slow three-sixty. He was wearing a two-piece, brown and olive, hound's tooth Italian wool suit tailored perfectly to fit his wide shoulder and tapered waist. Over his arm he carried a light Gore-Tex trench coat, in a slightly darker brown, that matched his leather wing tips. His .45 was secured in its shoulder holster; otherwise he would have felt that his outfit wasn't quite right.

"Thanks, and your attire is equally as stunning," Man said, before turning serious. "Now that we've completed the male bonding thing, let's get down to business."

Ty opened the folder on his desk. "I researched a few annuities like you asked. You mention that you were looking to invest $500,000 to $700,000, right?" Man nodded. Ty looked up from the folder and continued, "And the eventual return will be going to the Village Day Care Center?"

"That's right."

Ty was quiet for a moment. "You must really love kids. In the last three years you've donated more than $200,000 to this place," Ty said, questioningly. When Man didn't offer an explanation, he went on, "And each donation has been anonymous."

Man gazed out the window for a second, then said, "Even poor ghetto kids ought'a have a chance, and what difference does it make where it comes from?"

After they finished discussing the business at hand – annuities, stock and bond valuation and taxes – Man asked Ty to give him a quick overview on a few international investments he'd been considering. They discussed some new opportunities before ending their meeting.

After Man left, Ty wondered about him. When he'd first taken him on as a client four years ago, Man had one commercial property, a thirty-two-unit apartment building with a storefront. At that time, Man was looking to set up a diverse portfolio with $250,000. The money was accounted for on his tax returns as gambling proceeds.

Everything was in order too, the deed for the property as well as the property tax. Man had acquired five other properties over the last four years. Together, the six properties were worth, $2.6 million and Man's stock portfolio was valued at close to $1,000,000.

Four years of prudent investments had created a steady increase of income. Still, Ty was perplexed by Man's altruistic nature, and now his sudden interest in the international market. Each item was another piece of the puzzle that constituted Man Soleil. Ty knew that he'd been to prison for killing a man, and that he'd killed another one while there. A lawyer friend of his had provided the information and when his friend delivered the story he added: "This is one bad hombre." And Ty had agreed with him, for different reasons, though. Ty knew the circumstances behind the story, which caused him to wonder about his own survival instincts. Man had once said: "Desperate times calls for desperate measures." Maybe he was right; who knew what they would do when tested? A select few did whatever they had to do to survive and an even smaller number did it without excuses or pretense. In any event, *Man's story would make a hell of a movie,* Ty thought.

Man stood on the corner of Williams Street, pretending to use the pay phone as he observed the Federal Reserve building. Whenever he was in the area he cased the joint. Wouldn't it be something to jack the joint for $50 or $60 million, he thought? His smile was playful, yet cunning. He'd been inside the place once, as a Xerox repairman. His cover and phony I.D. were always impeccable; he had even worked on a copier that day.

He glanced around, giving the building a last look — his eyes taking in everything — before he strolled off. He moved up Williams Street and turned onto the first deserted side street he came to.

The three young thugs who'd watched him while he was checking out the Reserve, hastily followed. The young men were out looking for easy prey and had foolishly chosen Man for a robbery victim. Spying a construction scaffold ahead, Man walked directly toward it. Once beneath it, he slowed down.

His three pursuers picked up their pace — they couldn't believe their good fortune. Man dropped his newspaper as they approached, and heard one of them laugh as he bent to retrieve it. A quick glance confirmed the lottery-winner smiles plastered on the faces of the other two men. The three of them thought it was their lucky day–they had found an unsuspecting victim.

When the first guy reached for him, Man suddenly brought his right elbow up, the force of it catching the man flush in the testicles and lifting him off his feet. The guy howled in pain, dropping the knife he held alongside his leg.

The second attacker ran into the first, and Man's left hand was crushing his throat before he could recover his balance. A dull thump echoed in the tight space, as Man slammed the guy's head against the iron railing of the scaffold.

The third mugger broke to run, but he was too slow. Man caught him with a straight right to the jaw that dropped him — face first — to the pavement. The guy was out like a George Foreman knock-out victim.

The two other men lay on the ground whimpering, begging for mercy– mercy they hadn't intended on showing their victim. Man considered killing them, but since there were a couple of onlookers–witnesses—he killed the thought instead. After all, he thought, the punishment should fit the crime. It would've been different had he caught them committing rape or abusing a child. Standing over them, Man said, "The next time, there might not be a next time," then he walked off.

*Everybody wants to hunt the bear, but it ain't never funny when the bear hunts back, is it,* Man thought as he turned the corner, putting distance between himself and the wounded men. He headed for his car. He was meeting Pete and Kid uptown, at the *Cellar,* a bar and restaurant, to discuss their next job. And, just that quickly the three would-be-robbers were pushed aside.

# CHAPTER FOUR

Nicki and Ms. Nez sat at the kitchen table where Ms. Nez had laid out one of her famous Creole meals–gumbo and teacakes. Nicki enjoyed her visits with the older woman. Ms. Nez had become a surrogate mother since Nicki's mother had died six years ago. With similar features and the same café au lait skin tone, the two women could easily be mistaken for mother and daughter.

Inez LeNoir was exceptionally beautiful, and though a tiny woman at 4' 11", she had an enormous personality. She was a difficult woman to forget. The same was true of Nicki, who was only two inches taller, and just as beautiful and vivacious.

"How's Man doing?" Ms. Nez asked, with a little smile. "I guess he's fine. I haven't seen him since that night at Mr. Sam's," Nicki answered, without taking her eyes from her food. After a few seconds of awkward silence, as she smiled slyly, "But then you was there too, Ms. Nez."

"Oh, I just thought … He did take you home, right?"

"Ms. Nez! You're too much. Man took us both home. We just dropped you off first."

"Well, I'm sure he walked you to your door."

"Uh, huh. Just like he walked you to yours," Nicki replied with a giggle.

Ms. Nez's eyes grew wide in disbelief. "I know you didn't let him go back out in the cold, wet night without offering him some warmth and comfort, or *somethin',*" she said, moving her slender neck to match the implication of her last word.

"Man and I are just friends," Nicki said, as she dropped her eyes to avoid the older woman's inquisitive gaze. "And Man knows he's welcomed at my house. But why didn't you offer him *somethin'* yo'self Ms. Nez?" She asked, regaining her confidence and sass.

"Now, if I was twenty-five years younger and didn't have to compete with you, I sho' woulda offered him *somethin'!* Ms. Nez exclaimed, with sass to match Nicki's.

Both women laughed. They enjoyed each other's company. Nicki was comfortable with Ms. Nez, and she felt a special connection to her, one that stretched back to her childhood. Because of her deep spirituality, some people were uncomfortable around Ms. Nez. But the fact that she set out a plate for the ancestral spirits – Egun – whenever she ate didn't bother Nicki. And while some people called Ms. Nez's beliefs black magic, Nicki knew it was "Orisha" worship from the Yoruba culture of Western Africa, the region now called Nigeria.

After the meal, they moved to the living room. Nicki admired the African and Oriental art for the thousandth time as they talked and reminisced about the "good old days."

The admiration was mutual between the two women. Ms. Nez thought the world of Nicki, who had studied dance and had dreams of becoming a famous dancer. However, her love for children caused Nicki to become a teacher, instead.

She came back home to teach, and then opened the Village Daycare Center where she also taught dance – African, modern and jazz – three nights a week.

"Nicki, what did you think of our little community meeting the other night?"

After thinking for a moment, Nicki responded, "I thought it got off on the wrong foot. Mr. Sam can be … well, a little overbearing at times."

"Oh, no. That's too nice. He can be a damn fool," Ms. Nez said with a shake of her head.

"I don't know how Mary put up with him for forty-three years. The woman's a saint."

"Ms. Nez!" Nicki exclaimed, feigning shock. "It's true though. When I was little I used to avoid him like the plague, though Ms. Mary has always been a sweetheart."

"That's probably why she's so sweet—to make up for his sour butt," Ms. Nez said with a laugh. "But Sam might have a point about Man forcing the dealers out. They sure stay outta his way. And he didn't have much to say during the meeting."

"Man can only do so much. And to put a stop to the drugs would start a war where people get killed. At least he makes them stop when the kids are around, and he keeps the game room safe," Nicki said in a rush.After catching her breath, she went on, "Plus, the ones selling drugs are from this neighborhood or one just like it. It's not like they're the real problem either. It's the lack of education and opportunities, along with their lack of vision that leads them to the street-life. There's only so much Man can do."

Ms Nez turned her head slightly, pretending to examine something or another, while hiding the smile on her face. She'd known Nicki would defend Man. And why not, he was a good man. *And the chile' was in love with him,* thought Ms Nez.

*\*\*\**

Even though it served food and offered live entertainment on weekends, the Cellar, on Ninety-third Street, between Columbus Avenue and Central Park West, was more of a bar than a restaurant. Man liked the ambiance of the place, it suited him—the crowd was made up of hustlers and entertainers for the most part—and the dark interior was easy on his senses. The jazz performers that usually played there were another plus.

Man sat in the last booth, drinking cognac from a snifter and relishing the aroma of the aged brandy. He drifted into a contemplative mood, as he waited for Pete and Kid: *Why had his life taken the road it had?* He'd studied theology and philosophy in search of answers. Still, he had none, neither Christianity, Islam, nor Buddhism had provided explanations. Nor was there any edification to be had from philosophers like Aristotle, Locke, and Nietzsche. Was it all left to chance or was it preordained?

He thought about karma – the Bible's "A man reaps what he sows." Did that mean he had brought it all on himself ?
He'd read *The Egyptian Book of the Dead,* Hindu, Buddhist and Taoist texts, and looked to Santeria, yet, he'd discovered nothing to explain what he'd been through. Perhaps he was searching for divine meaning when there was none to be had.
But, did he even have a right to answers? Or to complain? He was alive and healthy wasn't he? Sometimes, on the inside, he felt dead. But with babies dying, children homeless, and women being raped and beaten, how could his pain warrant special attention? How could soldiers slaughter whole villages? Or fathers murder their own families? Life was what it was. That was the only answer he had come up with.

Once he saw Pete and Kid walk through the door, Man snapped himself back. He'd perfected the art of drifting on his thoughts while remaining conscious of his surroundings. He watched them approach –wondering which one was more dangerous. Both of them moved with an easy confidence born from their well-conditioned bodies, and having been tested in battle. Each had proven his self under fire. Man brought out the best in them. Or maybe it was the worst?

In the four years that they'd been rolling with him, Man had taught them about weapons, small arms, and minor explosives. He'd taught them that sticking up was a profession, not a desperate act. He'd also influenced them to workout regularly, maintaining a high level of fitness. Man had become their mentor, and the model of what a gunman was supposed to be. Pete and Kid were petty stickup-kids when he'd first decided to put them to work. He'd raised the stakes for them. He'd elevated their game to major crime. And to their credit, they'd excelled at it. At the age of twenty-two, they were hardcore hoods.

Man worked well with them and more importantly, he trusted them. It was crucial that everyone perform their job just right, because any mistake could cost them their lives. Man led by example. He stayed on top of his game and in top shape, and the same diligence went into the preparation for all their criminal undertakings.

As the two younger men slid into the booth, they exchanged greetings with Man. Once their drinks arrived, Kid took center stage, as usual, with one of his stories. "Check it, Man: Me and your boy here had a couple of hookers last night. You know, high class pieces," he said with a big smile. "We got us a suite at the Miford Plaza, over on the west side, and called the agency Black June put us on to, for three girls. They get there, all three fine as a'muthafucker too. I get right with it, you know, laying pipe like a fuckin' plumber. And while I'm banging two of 'em, I look over at Pete and the boy is kissing the ho'." Kid laughed, looked from Man to Pete and waited for one of them to respond.

Looking puzzled, Man said, "I don't get it."

"Man, he was kissing a hooker," Kid said as Pete sat quietly, amused. He was used to Kid's bullshit.

Man looked from one to the other. "I'm missing something. All you said so far is that he was kissing a woman."

Kid made a face. "It was a damn hooker," he said with a smile.

"Okay?" Man responded with a questioning look.

"Well, you ever kissed a hooker'?" Kid asked, scratching his head, and grinning. Man looked into Kid's face, noticing how perfectly groomed he was. His eyes locked on Kid's. He exhaled deeply and said, "Fuck kissing a hooker. I loved a hooker."

He let his words hang, and as they settled he added, "The second week I was home, old man Shine decided that I needed a piece of ass. So he got me a high priced call girl, paid her a gee to spend the night with me. The next morning, she gave Shine back his gee, went to the bank and took out three-gees of her own money and took me shopping.

"For the next seven months she took care of me, and loved me just for love's sake, 'cause I sure didn't know how to return it. She fed and clothed me. She did all of it from her savings too, because she stopped hooking. For the first time in nine years a woman loved me; cared if I lived or died," Man stopped, then nodded slowly.

After a moment he continued, "So, forget the question about me kissing a hooker. I loved a hooker. And you know what? I still do. Now you know I don't love much, and you know what I'll do for what I do love. So, the next hooker you meet, treat her right 'cause she could be that one."

Although it had all been said in Man's easy way of speaking, his passion was unmistakable. While the three men sat in introspection, Kid recalled, almost three years ago: After the three of them had robbed some Colombians in Marble Hill and Man saw a guy beating a dog with a broomstick Man asked him why he was beating the dog? The guy said, "Cause he's mine." Man's response was to cut the guy's throat and take the dog.

Kid looked in Man's eyes now and thought about his reply when he'd asked him why he'd killed the guy like that: "Cause I love dogs. And I don't love much."

Pete finally spoke, breaking the mood. "We made the pickups. Everybody's shit was correct, no shorts. We took our ten and left the other forty-five with Bigum."

"Good. I know Bigum got his and put Eddie's and B.E.'s aside," Man said.

"What's up with Eddie, and Bad-n-Evil," Kid asked; his playful smile back in place.

Man smiled too. Kid had shaken off the somber mood–nothing fazed him for long. "The God's name is Born Equality, and him and Eddie should be in town soon. Perhaps, on his return, you and him could build. You know how the God likes to share the knowledge of the Five Percent Nation."

Kid laughed, "I ain't messing with Born."

Pete joined in, "That's just what you need, Kid—knowledge of self"

They all laughed. To the regular citizens in the place, the three men in the back booth were just three guys out having a good time, enjoying each other's company. They could even be brothers. But to the regular customers, who also happen to be a part of the street-life, they were dangerous men. It was evident in their manner and movements, even if you didn't know exactly who they were. And, they were armed, of course—Kid and Pete carried .9 millimeters, and Man had his .45.

Man said, turning to business, "What's up with our job in Queens?"

"We delivered the flowers three houses down. The woman was so happy to get them, even if the return address was her job's. You was right; every woman wanna get flowers. And like you said, it gave us a chance to check out the block."

Kid jumped in, "I drove through the block with a U-Haul van for another look after Pete went through again on foot. It's ready," he said. There was no play in him now.

"Word. It's a go," Pete backed his partner.

"Good. This is the biggest move we ever worked together. So we gotta be on top of our game, cause ain't nobody trying to lose that much paper."

Pete finished off his drink. "Eddie and Born in on this?"

"We'll see," Man said as he signaled the waitress for another round. "They may not be back in time. Once the money is dropped off, it'll only be there a day or two."

"Whatever. I'm ready to get paid," Kid said with a smile.

"Fo' sho' and the drinks are on me," Man replied, as the waitress brought the fresh drinks over. They laughed and ordered their food. The Cellar was known for its soul food.

After a good meal and two more drinks, Kid felt relaxed. Outside on the street, he hesitated for a second then asked: "Man what happened with shortie? The one you loved, why'd you only stay with her seven months?"

Man answered in a low, reflective voice as he shoved his hands in his pocket, "I walked out on her because I didn't deserve her." For a long sad moment no one spoke. Then Man embraced each of his young partners. His love for them was obvious as he watched them drive off in Pete's blue Acura Legend.

He considered stopping at Under the Stairs, a nice spot around the corner on Columbus Avenue. But he decided to check on the game room instead. Man turned right on Broadway, and headed back uptown. He was listening to *Street Life,* by the Crusades. Thinking about Pete and Kid, Man wondered if either of them would get the chance to grow old as Randy Crawford sung about playing roles and growing old in the game. Man knew the truth of each word she sung about life on the street. Was it possible for them to make it out whole and intact, and not damaged like him?

He hadn't assigned either Pete or Kid their roles. He was just another character in what he hoped wouldn't become a tragedy for either of them. It was already too late for him.

# CHAPTER FIVE

While Man was driving back uptown, José was on his way downtown. José needed a couple of shooters. The first step was to establish a bond with another crew. The barrio was the perfect place to start; he could use his Puerto Rican heritage to his advantage, not that he cared about it.

All he cared about was blowing up in the drug game. Fuck Man, Ricky, and anybody else who stood in his way. It was only a matter of time before he'd control the whole hood and flooded it with drugs. Then, who knew what was next? He just had to plan for the future, his future.

His cousin, Peto, was doing it in a big way. Getting paid. *Dog food,* heroin, was where the real money was, maybe he could just get down with him. No, he thought. He was a boss, not a worker. He'd call the shots, and he'd figured out a way to use Peto to his advantage.

*** 

Man walked into the game room where a few of the older kids were playing pool or video games. A couple of kids were reading. Books were a big deal in the game room. Authors and subjects varied from O'Henry to Donald Goines, and from mysteries to autobiographies. Whatever your interest — philosophy or archaeology — there was a book on it in the game room.

Though always an avid reader, Man had discovered the true power of books while in prison. Malcolm X said that because of books he'd been freer than he'd ever been while in prison, Man knew that books could take you out of one place and to new and exciting ones. So as long as the books were read and discussed, the pool tables and video games were free. No reading, no playing, was another one of Man's rules. The kids could choose what they read, but sometime he gave them certain titles to read. Man had started book clubs and reading groups. In the game room, reading was mandatory as well as fundamental.

Bigum stood behind the counter in deep conversation with the Smith brothers, Joseph and Kevin. The two teenagers hung on his every word.

Man nodded at Bigum, who returned his nod while continuing his conversation with the boys. At seventeen, Joseph was older by two years. Kevin worked hard at emulating his brother in every way. That's why it was essential to keep Joe on the right path. Two for the price of one, Man thought with a smile.

Though it was shameful that their father wasn't around, it was a blessing that they had Bigum. Man was pleased that he'd brought the big man in to manage the game room and apartment building. In the three years he'd been there, Man had nothing but praise for him. At 6' 6" and more than 300 pounds, Bigum was true to his name: Big. You'd think that because of his larger than life dimensions, children would be afraid of him. The opposite, however, was true. They gravitated to him; it was as if their child's radar system confirmed that it was a safe place to be. It seemed that Bigum was born to work with children.

Children loved the big man, but no more than he loved them. It was a match made in heaven. At least that's what Man would've thought, if he believed in heaven. Nonetheless, he felt good with Bigum there for the kids and knew they'd be protected, even if it meant Bigum's life.

Man talked sports with Danny, who swore that the Giants were going to win the Super Bowl again. Man disagreed, said it'd probably happen the next year. Lisa came over and joined them. Man always got a kick out of her. She knew more about basketball than any of the fellows, –Man included–something Danny didn't like at all.

Lisa, Terry's younger sister, was starting to attract the attention of some of the older guys in the neighborhood as well as the ones Danny's age. Although only fifteen, her body was already showing signs of womanhood. *Why couldn't they have their childhood without all the pressures?* But then, he guessed, that's what growing up was all about.

The conversation moved from sports, to growing up in the hood. Man knew exactly what they were going through. His childhood had been spent on the same streets. They'd have to navigate their way through the desperation, crime, and drugs just to have a chance. He knew it was possible, but hadn't been able to accomplish it for himself.

Man took two books from the bookcase. He gave Maya Angelou's *I know Why the Caged Bird Sings* to Lisa and Danny got Richard Wright's *Black Boy*. Man wanted them to realize that there were successful people who had struggled early in their lives. He hoped that the eventual triumphs of other people would inspire Lisa and Danny to believe in their own dreams. "After y'all finish them we gonna talk about them," Man said.

"Man, you read both of these?" Lisa asked, examining her book.

"Of course. How else could I discuss them with you? And if I didn't, you and Danny'd know more than me and I ain't about to let that happen," Man replied playful.

"Yeah, you know she thinks she knows everything already," Danny said, with a smirk.

"Well, it's a known fact that women are smarter than men," Lisa quipped.

"Yo, Man, don't let her get that off, Danny urged.

"Danny, as men we have to know better than to argue with a woman—even a young one," Man said with a smile.

"That's right," Lisa said, while punching Danny softly in the arm.

A little after ten o'clock, Man announced that it was time for everybody to go home. "Home, not hanging on the corner or in the hallway" he commanded, hoping that their homes were safe.

After the kids left, Bigum and Man sat in the back room with a bottle of Remy. They shared a quiet drink. Bigum yawned; it was getting near his bedtime. Both were early risers, testament to their time spent in prison.up

With his clean-shaven head and huge frame, Bigum looked like a jet-black genie, Man thought, smiling to himself. Maybe that was why the kids loved him so much? They could relate to the idea of a genie–especially one so gentle and quick to grant their every wish. Man smiled again and shook his head. Life was strange: Children knew right off that Bigum was okay. Yet he'd spent 27 years in prison for killing two men with his bare hands when he was only 20 years old. At 50, he was Man's senior by 19 years, but had no problem deferring to the younger man.

"I see you're in a good mood tonight"
Man replaced the smile with a questioning look, but said nothing.

Bigum smiled now. "Even without the smile, its obvious you're feeling good. What? You got a big date or somethin'?"

"Did you have a chance to get the $20,000 to Shine?" Man asked, abruptly changing the subject.

"Yeah, he got it. He said, he'd meet with his man from the four-seven later tonight and let us know when them boys gotta shut down. Cops ain't shit; they get paid to stop crime, then get paid to keep crime going. Either way, they get paid cause of crime."

Man nodded, "Your assessment of our esteemed officers of the law is not only accurate but colorful as well–They ain't shit."

"They getting' a nice piece of change. But so am I–$5000 every week. And I don't deserve it either. Shit, I don't even need it."

"Bigum, you worth every dime you get. You got this place running like a blocking fullback that finally got to carry the ball."

"Anybody could do what I do," Bigum said, waving his huge hand.

"Don't believe that. These kids'd drive anybody else crazy in a week."

They both laughed.

"I put the rest of the money up," Bigum said.

The bathroom had a stash built into the doorframe. There were quite a few hidden stash spots in the game room, as well as a hidden passageway to the basement.

"What's up with the Smith boys?" Man asked, changing the subject again,

"Troy took them down to Howard's campus last weekend. They loved the school and the city. The capital is a slick city. Joe wants to enroll once he graduates next year."

"That's good, because Kevin'll probably follow him," Man said, obviously pleased.

"I have to admit, Troy is doing better than I thought he would. You did right getting him outta here and enrolled at Howard. He was heading for trouble, but now he's showing other kids the way out."

"It was Ty's connection that made that happen. Tyrone Jenkins is the man at Howard."

"Oh, I know he hooked that part up, but you put it all together. Got the boy to give up the street, and you pay the tuition. You done good, Man. That's all there is to it," Bigum said with conviction.

Man shook off the praise and peeked at his watch. Bigum smiled. "What's so funny?" Man asked as if he really didn't want to know.
"Oh, nothing. When you get old you just smile at living."

The two men talked a few more minutes before Man left. It was one of Nicki's late nights at the center–her dance class–and Bigum knew Man would be there to make sure she got home safe. He poured himself a small drink and smiled.

*****

José and Peto sat in the back room of the bodega on 103rd Street, off Lexington Avenue, smoking a Blunt. The weed chilled them out.

The room, in contrast to the bodega and building it was in, was lavishly decorated with plush leather furniture and the latest home entertainment equipment. All the comforts of home, for the successful drug dealer, that is.

"Cabron, you must really want somethin' bad to come down here." Peto said, stating the obvious. Laid back on the recliner, his dark features gave testimony to his Taino ancestry. He knew his history and thought of himself as a "Boriqua".

"Why I gotta want somethin'? Maybe I just came to check you," José responded with an attitude.

"Look, I been getting money long enough to know that when family show up, they want something."

José felt self-conscious and hated Peto for it. Who the fuck did Peto think he was? If he didn't need him ... But he did, so he checked his temper. "Well, I do need a li'l help, but I got *paper*. I ain't come looking for no handouts," José said with more force than he actually felt.

Peto stared quietly at his cousin. After a few seconds, José continued, "I got a li'l problem uptown, and I'll pay ten gees to have it taken care of."

"I'm listening."

"I want this Moreno hit. The muthafucker's pressing me and holding up my business." Peto showed interest for the first time. "Who is he, the Moreno?"

"Punk muthafucker named Man. He got a game room called Badlands. And once his ass is gone, I can blow the fuck up," José exclaimed with renewed confidence. "All I need is ..." Peto cut him off, "Check it. I know 'bout homey. My boy, Ice, did a bid with dude. They did like four joints in the box together –23-hour lockdown. Ice said dude killed some bad-ass bootybandit, cut the puta's throat. Anyway, the way Ice tell it, he ain't somebody you fuck with."

José was heated, and he exploded. "Fuck what your boy Ice says. Man ain't all that. I got loot to pay and that's all—"

"Hold up, muthafucker– Ice'll tear yo' ass up. And that little ten gees ain't shit."

"I ain't tryin' to dis your people. I just want this taken care of. I'll even go thirty," José said in a submissive tone.

"Hear me – you might need to go double that, and that still might not be enough."

"What . . ." José started, but stopped when Peto silenced him with a hard look. "Check it, I'ma' tell you a li'l story Ice hit me with 'bout dude. 'Bout three years back, some hick-ass Dominican from the Heights opened up a weight spot up the street from that game room selling keys of coke and shit. So homey steps to him, tells him he got to pay to do business. Well, the hick said 'Sure, you want money, I pay'.

"But, he brought in two hit men. They sneak in the basement while dude is in the game room and wait for him. They get in smooth as shit too. Well, after awhile Man come walking in, just like always. Alone and everything. The driver down with the shooters saw the whole thing. He was waiting on them to come out. Muthafucker's still waiting. They ain't make it out. As a mater of fact, they ain't been seen since. And the hick who paid them was found the next day with two in the head."

José didn't speak. Things weren't going the way he'd expected.

"So, that li'l thirty grand ain't shit, Homey's the real deal. And he got a crew that get busy. What, you gonna hit 'em all? Peto laughed. "You might as well keep paying off or you can come work for me."

José left disappointed, and later that night Peto tried to reach Ice, to let him know what was up. But he was out of town.

Blood didn't mean shit in the drug game, it was all about who was holding you down. He sure didn't trust José, he knew the fool had cross in him and his heart was suspect.
Ice was standup and if he said that this cat, Man, was too, it was enough for Peto. And if Ice wanted to pass the information on, that was all right too. Peto knew that only the strong survived in the street, and one day he might need some extra strength. Fuck José, his money was on the Moreno.

## CHAPTER SIX

Nicki sat behind her desk. She'd been working on some paperwork, before her mind drifted to Man. She knew he'd be there to pick her up shortly. It was an unspoken arrangement between them. Without a word, he was there. And when he wasn't, Bigum just happened to be out for a walk and made sure she got home safe.

She'd taken a quick shower after the class and from the moment she undressed thoughts of Man crept into her mind like nightfall sneaking up on daylight.

The thought of him made her warm and tingly, recalling his touch brought her to a boil. Plain and simple, Man gave her a sweet, sexy fever. He was so … She needed to snap out of it. Man and her were just friends, she reminded herself. Ms. Nez was to blame for her mind running wild, Nicki thought as she shook her head and giggled. Her shoulder-length black hair bounced with the movement.

She thought about the night's class, it had been the advanced class' turn to receive the bulk of her attention. She would focus on one group during each lesson, beginners, intermediate or advanced. Since it was the advance class' night, she got to do as much dancing as teaching. The group consisted of only five girls, ages 13 to 17, and was her smallest group.

Tonight, with the emphasis on jazz, it was an opportunity for self-expression. Dancing to Duke Ellington and Cab Calloway's swing music, the dancers' energy created spontaneous expressions, within the choreographed moves.

Nicki loved to dance, and she loved to teach. So she had the best of both worlds. She'd chased her dream of becoming a famous dancer and it hadn't eluded her either. She'd just decided that there were more important things in life, like coming home to teach, then opening the center.

It was what she wanted. No, she hadn't come up short. She'd won the real prize. She'd found her dream. Initially, the center struggled financially. As much as people needed quality daycare, they just couldn't afford it. Charging the lowest rates possible that first year, she'd barely been able to pay the rent. She hadn't figured out how she would make it through the second year when two incidents changed that. First, new ownership took over the building and cut her rent by 60% - they called it a tax write-off. Then, the center received the first of what became an annual grant of $75,000 dollars.

She hadn't meant to look a gift horse in the mouth, but she'd wanted to know something about her new benefactor and had investigated the source of the grants. She discovered that the money came from the *We Raise Up Foundation* that was chaired by a Mr. Jenkins, an investment banker for Whitman, Brown and Pauls' Water Street office. The foundation was a client of his, and Mr. Jenkins assured her that everything was in order, and that the money was hers. Well, actually, the center's.

And on top of all of that, Man donated $1000 dollars each month. He'd also donated a brand new twelve-passenger van last year, to replace her old station wagon. He also had fresh flowers delivered weekly and supplied sport equipment, regularly.

Man had been her biggest supporter before the grants started, and remained someone she could count on. And the children loved him. Nicki sighed: Just when she'd taken her mind off him, he forced his way right back. She thought, with a smile of admission, *I have Man on the brain.* She slipped into her coat, turned off the last of the lights and headed out.

Man stood with his back to her, staring off into space. She loved the stately way he stood, like a champion of some kind. His shoulders square, back straight and his head cocked slightly to the left.

Her heart skipped a beat as he turned to face her. Damn, he was handsome, she thought. "Hey, li'l lady," he said playfully.

Nicki came down the steps, walked over to him and looked up into his face. "Hey, big *Man.*" They laughed. He hugged her like he always did. For a moment, she rested her head on his chest, enjoying the contact.

She'd always felt comfortable and safe around Man, even as a little girl. But now that she was grown, those feelings had a sensual aspect to them.

Breaking the embraced, Man asked, "How was the class?"

"Well, had you came in you would've saw us in action."

"And interrupt expressions of art?" Man replied, with a big smile.

"Although I'm sure your majestic presence would have created a stir among my young and naive students, I'm also sure that they'd have been inspired," Nicki said with a straight face, amusement in each word as well as in her eyes.

"But, my lady, it is not I who inspires. For under your tutelage, your students can't help but be inspired."

They laughed again. Since they'd grown up together, Nicki and Man had a lot in common and laughter came easy. Though reserved, Man usually relinquished his hard edge in Nicki's presence. He liked her sassy manner and quick wit, as well as the repartee they shared. Although he'd be hard pressed to admit it, her beauty and salacious nature captivated and evoked strong desires in him. Which was something he wanted nothing to do with.

Of course, he satisfied his sexual need. But he didn't want or need love. He'd killed out of love, and it had cost him everything that he'd loved. Man believed that love had died because of him. So, he'd let it die inside of him. He had no dreams of love or of the future. The walls were in place to help him survive, but the foundation of those walls were the sorrows of his life, and in turn, they kept him from truly living. Yet, Nicki touched a part of him that screamed for more, love and the sweet dreams of life. As much as he enjoyed being around her, he knew he had to limit their contact. He had nothing to offer her.

As they came to her house, Nicki asked, "Man, what were you thinking about? You got quiet all of a sudden."

"Oh, just stuff. Nothing important," he answered, with a sad look in his eyes.

"I guess that means you're not going to tell me, huh?" She was sympathetic. She could feel his pain, but she could also feel him shutting her out.

"There's nothing to tell, really," Man said with a disarming smile.

As they walked up the front steps, Nicki debated with herself about asking Man in. Maybe she could offer him a drink or *somethin'.* Instead, she said, "Thanks for walking me home."

Man nodded and reached for her. She stepped into his arms and wrapped hers around him. The embrace lasted only a few seconds, though to each of them it seemed to last and move in a unique rhythm made just for the two of them–provoking hidden emotions lasting an eternity.

"My pleasure." Man said as he stepped back. He slipped quickly back into his self-contained mode, holding his feelings in check.

Nicki was at a loss for words. The distance Man had placed between them frustrated her.

"Well, why don't...I mean., ...Good night, Man."

"See ya' later," Man called over his shoulder, as he hurried down the steps. Nicki watched him for a minute. She still didn't know what to say. He refused to let her get close.

After leaving Nicki, Man walked down to the subway station, as he often did around this time of night. It was his way to discourage muggers. Some of the neighborhood folks came home between 10 and 11 o'clock, and he wanted to make sure they were okay. The token booth clerk waved at him. She felt better whenever she saw the guy who'd stopped a couple of muggings.

## CHAPTER SEVEN

Ricky was feeling good about life—the last few days had been profitable. Blue Seal was clocking major paper and his licit businesses were also doing well. He had over $300,000 in the bank, every dime taxed and clean. Another $800,000 sat in his stash. On top of all of that, and quiet as kept, his new spot was turning into a gold mine. He had every reason to feel good. José and his crew had been checked by Man, which in turn gave Ricky an advantage over him.

So, the $25,000 he paid Man every week was worth it. Sammy and Mack didn't have a problem with the $15,000 they put in. Only José had a beef about paying.
So what, Man got $55,000 a week; they didn't have to sweat the police or stickup kids. Man let them know if Po-Po was due on the block, ahead of time and the stickup kids stayed away because of him. The way Ricky saw it; Man really worked for him–he just didn't know it. The thought made Ricky smile.

***

Man watched as Bigum sank the 8-ball in the far left-hand corner pocket to win the game. He couldn't figure out why Bigum got a kick out of beating him. Bigum was a pool shark and Man was merely average at the game.

But he enjoyed Bigum's glee. It allowed Man to picture the big man as a kid, albeit a very large one.

"I ain't never seen nobody as happy as you when they getting whupped," Bigum said with a chuckle.

"It's not like I expect to beat you. And since you get so much joy from beating me..."

"That's right. Somebody gotta beat you at somethin'," Bigum responded lightly.

"Bigum, life been beating me so long it's a natural thing now," Man said without humor. Bigum watched Man drift off in thought for a minute. But then he snapped himself back and asked, "Did Eddie and the God check in?"

"They gonna call the pay-phone on Boston Road tomorrow night, at ten," Bigum answered.

When they couldn't talk face-to-face, their conversations took place from one pay-phone to another; let the Feds tap every payphone in the city.

"I wanna give them the info on Ricky's new spot. It's ready to be had. After they bag `im, I'll make him an offer for protection," Man said.

They moved to the office. As Bigum eased his bulk into his huge chair, he thought about the bond Man shared with Born Equality and Eddie King. Man was fresh in the joint and in a fight for his life, a fight he had no chance of winning–Mike Ray was literally beating him to death. Then, Born and Eddie stepped in. While Eddie pulled Mike off Man, Born slipped him a shank. It still didn't seem like Man had a chance. But, somehow the shank ended up in Mike's throat.

Bigum understood Man's connection to them, yet he realized how different Man was from Eddie and Born. While Born and Eddie were children of the streets, who became men of those streets, Man came from a loving and nurturing background. Although Man came from a single parent home, it hasn't been a broken home. Man's mother had given him support and guidance, and set her son on the right course. Fate had just work to change it. No one could have foreseen what happened to him.

Bigum understood that, because his life had taken a similar path. He came from good, decent people, but one night of fun and drink had changed his life forever. But, wasn't that true of Eddie and Born as well? He was sure neither of them chose to come up the way they had– in the streets, hard and without love. Hadn't fate set their course too?

Maybe what they all had in common was fate, itself, Bigum thought. Still, the bond the three younger men shared troubled him–they were too dangerous for their own good. Individually, each was a formidable force. But together, anything could happen. Anything! In truth, Bigum knew the three of them didn't spend much time together. But that was mainly because if something happened to any one of them, the other two would be there to make it right. It was another thing that bothered Bigum–they were prepared to die violent deaths, just as long as some payback was dished out.

All three were well read, intelligent and in top shape. They pushed their bodies hard, and not because of vanity but because they wanted every edge when shit hit the fan. At 6' 1", Man was the tallest, with Eddie just a shade shorter. Born carried the most bulk on his 5' 8" frame. At around 200 lbs, Eddie and Man were leaner, but far from small.

At 33, Eddie and Born were two years older than Man. But, they'd all lived beyond their years. They were hard men, living hard lives. Bigum shuddered at the thought of how many men the three of them had probably killed. And this from a man with blood on his own hands. Bigum was concerned. He liked his life, the calm of it, and being around the children. The kids were his family now. They were all he had. He knew Man's actions had made it all possible, but he also knew those same kinds of actions could destroy it all. In any event, his loyalty was to Man and whatever course was set by it, he'd follow.

"Maybe they'll be able to find Ricky's real stash. I know that that chump's holdin'." Man said, breaking into Bigum's thoughts.

Bigum looked at Man. "You'll take all his loot."

"Without a doubt. Everything he got is fair game. The boy got four cars and all that other shit. But his mama, brothers and sisters live in the building he sells drugs outta. And the more money he gets, the meaner and more sneaky he is."

"Yeah. The boy ain't shit," Bigum said.

\*\*\*

Shine's was an old-time bar, a throw back to the 60's with its real oak bar and brass stools that were padded with dark brown leather. The different ornaments and cardboard advertisements in the window limit the view from the street.

The interior was dark and secretive, with low hanging, dim lights. Located on the corners of Tremont and Third Avenues, Shine's had actually been there since the 50's. Most of the bar's clientele went back as far as the bar.

Shine owned the place with his longtime partner, Black June, both old gangsters who'd come up under the legendary Bumpy Johnson. Shine and June was a dying breed. In their late sixties, they lived by the code of the game: always stand up and hold your own. They'd gotten the game straight from the man himself, Bumpy, who'd been college educated, and from a well respected family in South Carolina. He'd come to New York with his degree and a dream of working in the banking industry in the 1920's.

But after encountering the same racism he'd left the south to escape, he became a force in the policy game — the numbers racket — and stood up to the likes of Dutch Schultz. So, having been fortunate enough to have had Bumpy as their mentor, the two aging gangsters were men of honor.

Man respected Shine and June, and picked their brains every chance he got. He also had no problem giving them $20,000 every week. He didn't know how much went to the cops, nor did he care. It was the price of doing business, and it was only right that Shine and June make something out of the deal.

They had called for him. So he figured the thing in Queens was ready. Well, he was ready too. He'd planned and doublechecked as much as he could, and was ready to do what he did for a living–get paid.

As he parked, Man nodded his head to E.P.M.D.'s *Strictly Business.* The song was still getting airplay. Although his taste in music ran more towards jazz and R&B, he was cool with some of the rap pieces the young brothers were putting out. He remembered the early stages of the music, before he'd went to prison in 1972, so he felt connected to it. Good music was good music. He reluctantly turned the car off killing the music.

Man entered the bar and gave it a quick, but effective onceover. He nodded at the barmaid; a buxom reddish colored woman, with hair to match, in her forties. She waved Man to the bar — she was sexy and full of play — leaned over and whispered in his ear as he got a nice view of cleavage. Man cocked his head back and smiled.

"I'm serious, Man" she added, in a husky voice, with her breast pushed out. The sounds of Marvin Gaye's *Sexual Healing* coming from the jukebox added spice to her proposition. Man gave her an inquisitive look, before moving off to Shine's office in the back. Shine and June stood up when Man came through the door. After shaking hands, the men took seats. Shine got a glass and poured Man a drink of the cordon bleu cognac they were drinking.

After a quick toast, Black June got right to business. "We just got the word, the money is being dropped off between five and eight tomorrow morning. But, it'll only be there until noon." Man studied the old gangster, who was tall and rail-thin with a deep blue-black color. A thin scar ran from June's left earlobe to his chin. After settling into his face for the last forty years, it looked more like a crease than a scar. Black June's manner was easy, but conveyed a sense of strength and danger.

While June was like a big cat –quiet and observant–, his partner, Shine, was like a big dog–full of growl as well as bite. Though short and kind of portly, it was obvious that Shine would get down. He claimed to have sported his shiny bald pate since his sixteenth birthday, and usually wore a smile that could become a sneer quicker than a $2 dollar ho' could bend over.

"That's good news," Man finally answered. "We ready."

A couple of minutes later, Man was on his way out the door. "Don't forget what I told you. I mean it too," the barmaid called out,
Man smiled and wondered if she could really give him head while singing to him.

Once on the sidewalk, he realized he was hungry and decided to walk up the block to the Big Four Restaurant, a family owned and operated soul-food spot. He could beep Kid and Pete from there. Plus, the fact that one of the daughters in the place was always extra nice to him, and just as nice to look at, meant he'd enjoy his meal that much more.

# CHAPTER EIGHT

Pete watched with amusement as Kid slept. Although it no longer amazed him that his partner was able to sleep anywhere and at any time, it still amused him — Kid was a fool. They'd been friends since first grade. Pete recalled that their first encounter had resulted in a fight after Kid had joked about Pete's clothes. As far back as the first grade, the fool was snapping on people, and about anything that came to his crazy mind. Life was a joke to Kid, he laughed his way through it. And he was funny, Pete thought.

Even with all of his bullshit, Pete knew he couldn't have a better partner than Kid. They worked well together. Where Kid was usually talking shit and laughing, Pete was quiet. They made a good team, complimented each other. With the taller Kid playing shooting guard and Pete running the point, they'd made a hell of a backcourt on their school's basketball team. They both played hard, and what one lacked the other had. Because they'd been through battles together, on and off the court, the trust was there. Each knew the other would come through when shit hit the fan.

Pete looked at Kid, and wondered what he was dreaming about. Something crazy, Pete thought with a grin. When they were young, they had dreamed of playing in the NBA. Then later on, they'd wanted to be cartoonists—Pete doing the art and Kid writing dialogue. The stuff they created was pretty good, too– they just hadn't pursued it. No one had pushed them, either; not at school or at home.

Without fathers around, there was only so much their mothers could do. And most of the teachers didn't care. As long as you didn't cause too much trouble, the teachers left you alone. The schools in the hood were over-crowded and under-staffed. Nobody had time for two bad-assed kids; especially the men who'd fathered them. Pete didn't know his pops and didn't want to. Actually, from what he'd heard about the man, he wasn't missing anything. Kid's father wasn't worth shit either, although he did show up occasionally.

So, of course, they'd ended up running the streets. They'd started out working for Ricky, but he tried to play them because they were a few years younger than him.
After cutting Ricky loose, they'd tried to do the drug thing on their own. It didn't take long for them to figure out that it wasn't for them. So the next step was to pick up the steel: guns. In a few short months, they became the worst nightmare a street level dealer had. They had more drama over short money than a brother with four baby-mamas.

Then, Man came home and they'd been all over him. But Man had changed, stayed to himself. It wasn't like when they were kids and he'd take them everywhere. Prison had changed him. Before he'd went to prison, Man was the big brother every kid wanted–he'd play sports with them, talk to them and just listen. That was when all the adults were saying, "Be like Man." And, the thing was, all the kids wanted to be like him. Man was cool. He made sure all the little kids in the hood were all right.

But when he came home it hadn't been the same. It wasn't anything bad, just different. The first few months he was home, he hardly came around. When he did, he didn't have much to say. He just kind of watched everything. Pete knew it was because of what happened with the Ray brothers–everybody knew about that. And Kid and Pete had wished that they'd been old enough to kill all three of them. That way, Man would've just stayed Man.

Nevertheless, they'd hung around Man every chance they got. Man would question them about school and the shit they were doing in the street. He kept at them about staying in school and getting jobs. But they didn't want to hear that.

In time, Kid and Pete convinced Man that they were going to live the street-life. Though he'd tried to discourage them, Man eventually started to put them down. He started them out slow. He'd have them dress like school kids, then he would drop off a knapsack full of guns and money for them to disappear with on a city bus crowded with school kids. He let them know it was serious, and taught them how to blend in with their surroundings.

He schooled them, and when they were ready he raised the stakes. He took them from petty stickup kids to professional gunmen. Yeah, Man had changed and he had changed their lives. He had put them down. Only now, the old folks in the hood were no longer saying, "Be like Man."

Pete came out of his reverie, as Kid stirred, and laughed as Kid woke up with a huge smile on his face. Without knowing the cause of it, Kid joined in the laughter.

"What's up? Man ain't get at us yet?" Kid asked, on his way to the bathroom. Pete waited for him to come out. "Nah, but he said to stay on point and be ready to move."

"I'm getting tired of laying low. You know I got ho's to get at," Kid said slyly.

"Man done told you about talkin' slick," Pete said jokingly.

"I love the shit outta Man, but he's crazy as a muthafucker. He got some shit with him," Kid said with a smile.

"Kid, you know Man ain't hardly crazy."

"Not like crazy – crazy, but he got some shit going on," Kid said, laughing again.

"What you talkin'bout?" Pete asked, with a look that said they both knew who was really crazy.

"That's what I mean. Man can't be all there 'cause he fucks with us. Yeah, that right. Both of us," Kid replied, busting out with laughter.

Pete laughed with him. "Yeah, Man got love for us. We rolling with the big dog."

"Ain't no doubt. We the truth," Kid add, as he turned the radio on and started rocking to Eric B. and Rakim's *I Ain't No Joke*.

# CHAPTER NINE

Born and Eddie sat in the old car deciding on their next move. It was obvious that they'd wasted enough time tracking the chump sitting in Fish, Wings and Things – a Caribbean restaurant in North-West D.C. — enjoying his meal. It wasn't going to jump off. Oh, they had him dead to right–knew where he laid his head and had the location of a couple of his stash spots. But the problem was that the Feds knew all this too.

The 'Bama was hotter than fish-grease, and didn't even know it. The police were on his every move. It was a shame because the 'Bama was moving 40 to 60 kilos a week. It hurt to back off, but that's how the game went. Although it would really be something to rob the 'Bama with the Feds all over him, it was too risky.

"Ain't no sense in watching this fool no more," Eddie said, his voice thick with disgust.

"You right about that," Born said with a sad shake of his head. "This fool getting ready to fall and he don't even know it. What kind of hustler is he?"

"Word. Feds following this fool everywhere and he ain't peeped shit," Eddie said as he started the car. "It's time to move on to something else. I hope Man got something for us."

"That's a good bet. You know how he do," Born responded.

"That thing he been working on probably jumped off already."

"Eddie, you know Man keep somethin' on the fire."

Thinking about all the time they'd invested in this move, Eddie guided the car down Georgia Avenue passing the Penthouse, a hot strip joint. Four months of watching and waiting. Four months of following Lenny Campely from joints like the Penthouse and Foxy's Playland – another strip joint – to hotels in Prince George and Silver Springs. All for nothing. Eddie was disappointed, but not as much as Lenny would be when the Feds put his dumb ass in cuffs.

Although he had checked with Man about some work, Eddie wasn't hurting for money. He had done well for himself in the 6-1/2 years he'd been home. The 10 years he spent in prison were still fresh in his mind, the memories kept him sharp. He had gone from the street to juvenile joints, and finally to prison. So life had never been easy for him.

That's why Eddie King lived and played hard. He'd learned to take all the shit life threw at him and use it to his advantage. So, if prison had been hell, Eddie thought of himself as the devil. More importantly, he'd created the only bonds that mattered to him in prison.
Eddie and Born went back to their days on the street as kids struggling to live past childhood. But their time behind the wall had sealed their bond–then they'd added Man. Eddie's bond with both of them had been forged from surviving battles.

As an orphan, the idea of family created conflicting emotions in Eddie–he just couldn't understand what it meant. After all, his own mother hadn't wanted him. But after years of embracing loneliness and proclaiming it solitude, he was no longer alone. He had Born and Man, and he'd gladly give his life for them, though he'd much rather kill for them.

Actually, Born and Eddie had already killed for Man. No, not Mike, they had only given Man a little help with that. But when they got out before Man, they'd hunted down Mike's brother and killed him slowly for the foul shit he'd done. Likewise, Man had caught a body or two in their defense, over the years.

Although the three of them were killers, they possessed a twisted humanity, as well as a sense of honor. They lived by a code: self-discipline, bravery, justice and loyalty. Like a Bushido Warrior, it was their thing and they didn't need anyone to sanction it. They didn't have a need to discuss it–they just lived it.

*At least me and the God knew the score early on,* Eddie thought, looking over at Born. Born came out of an abusive home and had been in the street almost as long as Eddie. It had been hard for them right out the womb, and maybe that was best. At least they'd known from the start that life wouldn't be a rose garden. And if it was, the thorns would still be there. But Man had known a life filled with love and dreams, so he felt the pain of loss.

Born broke into Eddie's thoughts. "What you thinking so hard on."

"Nothing," Eddie answered.

"If it ain't nothing, why you been driving in circles for the last twenty minutes?" Born said, looking out the window.

Eddie turned left on Clifford Avenue, but didn't answer. He followed Clifford to Sixteenth Street, where he made another right. Still, he didn't respond.

Born laughed. "So now you going home? But that don't mean your mind is clear."

"I ain't like you and Man, always needing to know the answer to shit. I just live this shit the way it comes," Eddie said, with a shrug of his shoulders.

Born knew it was more to his partner than he let show. "So why you always reading them books and—"

"You mean the books I get from you and Man," Eddie cut in. As they laughed, Eddie added, "You know I need to read all that shit to keep up with y'all."

"Eddie, you know you want life to make sense," Born said as he locked his eyes on his partner.

"Life just ain't like that. Shit just kinda happens."

"So you don't contemplate why and try to reach a semblance of truth and reasoning?" Born asked thoughtfully.

"Hell, no. I ain't got time for all that shit. Plus, I might start sounding like you and Man," Eddie said with a smile.

"I hear that, but I see all them philosophy books you got in the crib. And I already caught you talkin' like Man."

Eddie couldn't stop the laughter. "Well, at least I ain't kicking today's lesson, God."

They both laughed again. Born Equality was part of the Five Percent Nation, and their lessons were based on mathematical truths.

Eddie slipped a Rare Essence Go-Go tape in the car's radio and bounced with the funky beat. Born didn't understand what Eddie got out of Go-Go music– but that just made their bond that much stronger. While they all traveled their own path, they stayed connected through what tied them to one another.

They worked together whenever the opportunity arose. They also steered jobs to one-another, and when one got paid they all got a piece. Though their bond consisted of criminal acts, it was founded on righteous principles, or so they believed.

***

Once they got Man's call, Kid was pumped up. Things were in motion, just the way he wanted them. It was time to get busy. Pete was quiet, his mind on the next few hours to come and how they might affect his life. Kid paid him little attention. Actually, it was Pete's mood that Kid overlooked. He was too caught up rapping with Big Daddy Kane's *Ain't No Half Stepping,* and shouting that it was time to step the game up.

"Yo, Peter-Gun, it's on boy. We 'bout to get paid," Kid shouted over the music.

Pete nodded, and wondered if anything bothered Kid. The laughter and jokes were always there, but Pete knew some of it was Kid's way of hiding his true feelings. But even he, as long as he'd known Kid, couldn't tell where the cover ended and the real feelings started.

More than anyone else, Man forced Kid to be serious. Kid couldn't figure Man out. Man didn't react to Kid's antics. Man usually gave him a blank look when he made one of his jokes or burst out laughing. Kid always expected a reaction of some kind, but Man had his number, Pete, thought with a smile.

Observing Pete's smile, Kid laughed and said, "Its good to know you're alive. Because we 'bout to get paid."

"We should be out in the next half. Man said to be at the warehouse at two."
Kid clapped his hands together, "I'm ready now. Shit, I been ready for weeks."

"You and me both."

"I feel good about this shit. I know shit gonna go just like we planned," Kid said with confidence.

Although he wasn't as sure as Kid, Pete nodded in agreement. Man had them study Sun Tuz's *Art of War*. So they understood the importance of stratagem, the application of ruse, precautionary maneuvers and reconnaissance.

Their years with Man had been well spent. Before, they had reacted to situations, now they controlled them by being prepared for the unexpected as well as the expected.
Under Man's guidance, they'd graduated from opportunists to topflight gunmen. They'd studied the battles of Hannibal, and knew that a Black man had fought the largest army ever fielded by the Romans in 216 B.C. They were familiar with Attila the Hun and Genghis Khan's nomadic warriors, and the manner in which they'd wreaked havoc on Europe and Asia. They even had the U.S Armed Forces, "Special Forces" manuals. They studied warfare, because it had become a way of life for them.

Pete knew they were ready, but each job gave him a case of butterflies. He wished that he could be more like Man, Eddie, or Born. They were emotionless and professional. Come to think of it, he'd settled for being like Kid, right now, he thought with a deep chuckle.
"Damn bro. You feeling good, huh?" Kid said.
"Like you said, 'Its time to get paid.'"

***

Seated in his black 735i, Ricky bounced to the sound of Soul to Soul's *Back to Life*. Chill sat up front with him, nodding his head to the beat, while Short-Dog rode in the back seat.
The car was "kitted-out," and the admiring glances from the people traveling along the Grand Concourse made Ricky smile. His triple-black Beamer was the shit, and he knew it.
He was wearing all black, with his gold on onyx jewelry and his black reptile kicks with the gold bar across the front. Chill and Short-Dog were just as fly–Chill in some hot Gucci gear and Short-Dog playing the latest Polo styles.

They were headed to the Castle, a hot new club. Things were going well and Ricky wanted to let the world know it. He wanted to shine, just like the star he was. After paying their way in the spot, Ricky ordered two bottles of Moet Red Star, since they didn't have any Don Perrignon. Once the champagne was opened, Ricky made a toast: "To gettin' money." He laughed and continued, "I wanna thank Man for making it so muthafuckin' easy. And to the city where all it takes to be king is some money and a little brains."

They clicked their glasses and drained them. The party was officially on now. The honeys were out and wearing that shit that made even Ricky, tight as he was, want to spend some money. The Moet was attracting attention, too. The place was packed, and the sound system was pumping Al B. Sure's *Night and Day.*

"Yo, check out shortie in the blue dress. She holding," Chill said, with thirst in his every word.

"Word. She's bad," Short-Dog said, following Chill's gaze.

Ricky gave the girl a casual glance and said, "She's a'ight."

Chill smiled at Ricky's words. He knew Ricky was on some shit when it came to women, mainly because his wife was a bitch, and to make it worst she wasn't much to look at either. Chill checked the girl out and thought: *Ricky's wife, Pat, can't see shortie.* So, that "a'ight" shit didn't mean a thing to him. He got up from the table and made his way toward the girl.

While Chill was busy trying to talk the girl into leaving with him, Ricky and Short-Dog drank and talked shit. Ricky was basking in the glory of being a *Big Willie*— money-getter. He was young and successful, and had the money and toys to prove it. He was ghetto fabulous and all that his eyes could see was his for the taking. Damn, he thought: *I could have any ho' in the spot. Shit, any two if I wanted.*

It wasn't hard to figure out—If you were shrewd and willing to take chances, the world was your playground. Ricky nodded to the music; he had it figured out too. His mama ain't raise no fool– which was ironic, because she was one herself. A bottle of cheap vodka and any worthless man to warm her bed was all that mattered to her. He didn't owe her shit, and whatever she got from him was more than she deserved.

His brothers and sisters weren't much better–always wanting and needing. How did they think he'd gotten where he was? It sure wasn't by giving away his hard earned cash. His whole family wasn't worth shit. No wonder his father hadn't stuck around– whoever he was. His mother sure didn't know. She had seven kids by six different men, all losers except for Ricky's pops who'd had the sense to get away from her trifling ass. And, that's just what he was doing, staying away from his sorry ass family, unless, of course, he needed them for something.

They were lucky he stashed his drugs in the filthy apartment, because the $100 a day he paid his mother was more than it was worth. It didn't seem to matter how much he gave her, she drank up whatever she got or spent it on whatever loser happened to be slipping his hand under her dirty bathrobe.

"Yo, Ricky, look at them two young cuties checking us out," Short-Dog said, pulling Ricky away from his mind trip.

Ricky scrutinized the girls for a few minutes; they couldn't be more than seventeen years old. He liked them young– they were easier to impress and control. And control was important to Ricky. "Dog, get them hos'," he said, without taking his eyes off the girls. "I'm ready for some fun and games."

\*\*\*

Man sat at the desk with his feet up, listening to Miles Davis' *Kind of Blue*— the greatest jazz session ever recorded. The music touched him, he felt as if he'd been there during the recording itself. Actually, he could feel the scene: The dim lit, smoky room with an easy but powerful energy flowing. Man flowed on the music, traveled with it through his memories, through space and time. The sound out of the speakers was flawless.

From the outside, you'd never imagine that the old warehouse had a high tech sound system, or that it had a topnotch surveillance unit in place. The building was also soundproofed, with a shooting range.

There were six older model vehicles inside the warehouse. Although the three cars, two vans and pickup truck were six to ten years old, they were all in perfect condition. In fact, they all had high performance engines as well as police scanners and secret compartments inside of them. The warehouse was located in a deserted industrial area on Park Avenue off 184th Street. The building didn't get many second looks. The location was perfect, little or no traffic and very few neighbors.

When the last selection on *Kind of Blue* ended, Man put on Aretha Franklin's *Sparkle*. The song *Giving Him Something He Can Feel,* caressed him. It was as if Aretha was singing to just him. He wondered what it would be like to feel again. Then he reminded himself that he knew — he felt the pain. He thought of Rita. She'd given him something he could not only feel, but something he could love and hold in his arms—their daughter, Utopia.

He'd loved them both, but he'd still let them down, along with his mother. Creating a foundation in their memories did little to fill the emptiness he felt. He'd taken the first letter from each of their names and came up with the *We Rise Up Foundation,* but it didn't help him rise beyond the guilt he carried.

As much as he blamed the Ray brothers, he blamed himself more. Why did he kill Fuddy, and then Mike? Maybe if he hadn't... Goddamn it, he chided himself, they'd both needed killing. He hadn't sowed any of the misery that fate brought him. Man knew he wasn't really to blame, and he knew it wasn't fate either. It was three cowards, the Ray brothers, who'd lived to prey on people weaker than themselves. The more they got away with, the more they tried. And maybe the Rays couldn't be held responsible either. They were just what they were. The fault rested with those who stood by for years, allowing the brothers' deeds to go unpunished.

Man stood and walked to the window, he stared down at the empty street. Although the street was empty of traffic so early in the morning, his mind was jammed with the traffic of his past. Aretha's sweet voice, bearing witness to her own suffering, was a personal invitation to memories he'd rather forget. But they came anyway, with the force of a hailstorm beating on his brain and heart.

Though he continued to stare down on the street, he no longer saw it. The past was back: *The two officers came to his cell. He 'd been on Riker's Island for nine days. He sat in his cell in C-74, the adolescent facility. The guards called his name, "Man Soleil. "*
*He didn't bother to look up, just stared at the floor.*

*"Man Soleil, "the guard shouted now. Still, Man didn't move or respond "Boy, what 's wrong with you? "*

*Man remained motionless.*

*"Boy, the chaplain wants to see you."*

*Man didn't respond.*

*The second guard spoke, "Son, you might want to see him, okay?*

*Man continued to stare off into a world only he could see.*

*Finally, the guards gave up and left. Man didn't move. In a few minutes they were back with the chaplain.*

*The clergyman, an older white man, said, "Man, can I have a word with you." When Man didn't acknowledge his words, the man went on, "Wouldn't you like to come to my office so we can talk?"*

*Man wasn't there, he had taken his mind to another place.*

*After a moment, the chaplain looked at the guards, unsure of what to do. Finally, he said "I'm sorry to have to tell you that your friend, Ms. Rita Collins, is dead. I'm really sorry. "*

*Man never said a word. His heart had ripped open and if he had spoken he'd have drowned in his own blood.*

*The next day his mother came to see him and told him that Rita had committed suicide. Rita had cut her wrists and bled to death in the bathtub. She'd left a note saying that she couldn't live without Man. While his mother cried throughout the one-hour visit, Man did his best to comfort her. Once the visit was over, he went back to his cell and stared at the floor some more. Rita was gone – Why?*

Man had asked himself that question for almost a decade and a half, and still had no answer. Neither Rita, his mother, or his daughter had done anything to deserve what happened. Yet, it happened. And who was to blame? Was it his fault, Man wondered?
Though he didn't want to believe that it was, the thought clung to him like a rap sheet to an ex-con. Could Rita have lived with what happened if he had done nothing? Would she, his mother, and Utopia be alive if he hadn't gone in that basement?

Did he do it to protect them, or was it his pride that led him to kill? Was revenge more important to him than loving Rita? These were the questions he avoided. Still, they lingered just below the surface of everything he did–threatening his sanity.

The sound of the buzzer brought Man out of his flight of misery. He checked the monitor. Pete and Kid stood outside the door. He buzzed them in. It was time to get everything ready for the job, and then, grab a couple hours of sleep.

The job would keep his mind busy–just what he needed. He wanted to deal with the present and let the past rest, although it refused to do so in peace.

## CHAPTER TEN

Black June sat in his favorite chair — a blood red, high-back Louis Treize worth $36,000. The old, elegant brownstone was furnished more like a museum than a residence. Brass and oak beds, along with ivory vanities adorned the bedrooms. The living room and study had natural wood floors that were selectively covered with Oriental rugs, and decorated with crystal chandeliers and glassware. The house was a testament to June's exceptional taste. He enjoyed the finer things in life, and had spent his life hustling to acquire them.

Seated before the small fireplace, June sipped on a glass of Talisker. He was barely aware of his surroundings. He stared into the jumping flames as the shimmering warmth triggered his recollection of days gone. He'd bought the brownstone in October of 1943, on the heels of Harlem's first modern riot—one of the first urban disturbances where Blacks reacted violently to police brutality.

The disturbance had cause Mayor La Guardia to reopen the Savoy Ballroom on Lenox Avenue and 140th Street, which the city had closed for no reason in the first place. The mayor also convened the Emergency Conference for Interracial Unity, which was charged with creating ways to reduce racial tensions in the city. In turn, the housing market was opened to Black folks. Well, those with money, anyway. Even a couple of young hustlers like Black June and Shine got the chance to get in on it and were able to prosper. But not at the expense of the community, like today's hustler did.

When June brought the brownstone on Striver's Row, as 139th Street between Eighth and Seventh Avenues was known, Harlem was flourishing from the political cohesion and literary expression of its Black occupants. Despite the racism of the overall city, in 1944 Adam Clayton Powell Jr. was elected to Congress and Benjamin Davis took the seat Clayton left on the City Council. Then, in 1953 Hulan Jack was elected as Manhattan's first Black Borough President. During this time Harlem was home to writers such as Ralph Ellison, James Baldwin and Maya Angelou, as well as a host of other artists and entertainers. It was the place to be. And coming up under Bumpy Johnson had prepared June and Shine to take full advantage of the opportunities. Although neither June or Shine had had any formal education, Bumpy had stressed the importance of book learning.

After all, Bumpy was college educated and prided himself on having not only knowledge, but wisdom as well. He believed in spreading joy throughout the community and did so every chance he got. Make no mistake, Bumpy was a gangster through-andthrough and perhaps the most dangerous man June had ever known. Even so, to his death Bumpy had remained a champion of the people. He had schooled many up and coming hoods, June and Shine among them, on the code of the life and taught them to treat the community with respect.

Before Bumpy's death, June and Shine had steered clear of the skyrocketing drug trade. But the great man's death was the start of many changes in Harlem's underworld. Drugs ravaged the whole community, and white mobsters, along with their Black counterparts, hastened its demise with their greed and lack of respect for its inhabitants. Then, the middle-class flight out of Harlem in the early sixties turned it into ghetto. Infants were dying at the rate of a Third-World country. Housing was poor and unemployment high. Worst of all, heroin was king and with its rule a new era had dawned.

Junkies lined the same streets that had borne the Black Renaissance, and they would do anything, from selling themselves, to committing murder, to satisfy their habit. The promise of riches beyond imagination eventually lured Shine and June into the drug business. By the mid-sixties they had become major players in the heroin trade.

Although both of them had done short stints in prison prior to their foray into the heroin trade, June was forced to endure a ten-year stretch from 1969 to 1979. This precipitated their exit from the drug business. June sought out young men of character–during his time in prison–just as Bumpy had sought him and Shine out decades earlier. Men that were strong and hungry, but trustworthy.

June was wise to the ways of men, their strengths and weaknesses. He'd seen the best and worst in his long life, from Bumpy Johnson to the dope fiend that would kill his own mother for a fix. He witnessed the transformation of Nicki Barnes–ex–dope fiend, turned drug kingpin, turned snitch. So he chose the men he mentored judiciously.

June saw the rise and fall of many of the new breed of hustlers, and was unimpressed. Where Harlem once produced notorious gunmen, dapper gamblers and slick con men, it now claimed a legion of low-level drug dealers.

In the sixties, the country-boys –a group of rough and crafty men from the south –headed by Frank Matthews, who disappeared into thin air after posting $1,000,000 bail – had been a force in Harlem. The community had been through many changes. And June had seen them all. Shine had kept him posted throughout his bid. So he got all the news and all of it was bad for his beloved Harlem. He also saw the effects firsthand, in prison. The new breed of hood was fair game for the police and the courts. They were filling up the joint, and for the most part, they couldn't be trusted. He'd kept his distance from them.

That's why Man, Eddie and Born stood out. They were strong and unafraid. He knew the story about the youngster, Man, as soon as he'd touched down in the joint. The prison grapevine was better than the 6:00 edition of Eyewitness News.

Michael Ray had let it be known that the kid was his. He bragged about how he'd rape the boy after he beat him half to death, then kill him slowly. Only, he hadn't expected anybody to get involved. And why should he? Mike was on his third state bid, and feared for good reason. He was a mean, sadistic animal who was battle tested. But he wasn't the only one who'd seen battle. Born and Eddie had been down long enough to have made names for themselves. No one knew why they had helped Man. They didn't know him. It was just one of those things. Or was it?

Maybe it was destiny –the destinies of the three young convicts and Mike Ray. Perhaps, it was June's destiny as well, because the incident brought the three young men to his attention. June cultivated his relationship with all three of them. He and his partner, in prison, Sonny Red, had taken the time to school them. And he continued to do so after his release. Although he trusted the three of them, it was Man who June dealt with most often. He had taken to Man, and admired how the younger hood handled his business. Although June and Shine profited off their relationship with Man, it was more than just business, to June.

Even with his distance—a reserve that bordered on coldness–, Man had touched the old gangster's heart. June had fathered five sons and four daughters, and had a bunch of grandchildren. Still, his ties to Man were strong.

He realized the danger in those feelings. The stickup and extortion game was a suicidal one. Each time the gun was put in play somebody could die. But none of that seemed to matter to Man. It seemed as if he didn't consider the risks. June knew that wasn't the case, however, Man took every possible precaution in everything he did. He knew his business and was good at it, even if it was suicidal.

Although the upcoming job was risky, and the payoff huge, June knew that him and Shine wouldn't be in any danger. If something went wrong, it would never come back to them– Man would die before he betrayed them. The nagging fear he had wasn't for himself, but for Man. No matter how hard he tried to picture it, he just couldn't see Man growing old. Man seemed to be living out his life's clock as if he knew how and when it would wind down. The aging gangster stared ruefully at the fire, and said a silent prayer for his young protégé as his mind wandered back to the good old days.

\*\*\*

After Pete and Kid's arrived, Man went over the plan with them. They studied the layout of the house and went over everyone's job. Man was as serious as an undertaker at a paid funeral. Every move, every detail was double-checked before Man was satisfied.
Man laid-out the three sets of forged identifications. Each set had a driver's license, social security card, and job I.D. They were perfect, each of the names belonged to an actual person and the heights and weights matched the three gunmen.
Man had a hookup with a rogue city worker, who had access to a variety of personal records. A set of I.D.'s cost between $400 and $600. It was money well spent; just another cost of doing business.
The pickup truck and van they were using were outfitted with the logo of legitimate businesses. The van bore the logo of a florist in Long Island City, and the truck carried the name of a landscaping company from Hempstead. The decals were plastic and could be peeled off as easily as they'd been put on – like masking tape. The vehicles were checked and ready.
The cache of weapons was removed from the base of one of the many heavy generators stored in the warehouse. Some of the generators were hooked up to other machinery and turned on from time to time, to give the desired appearance of a functional machine shop.
The men picked out their weapons. Pete and Kid each chose sixteen shot 9mm, equipped with silencers. Man grabbed two 10mm pistols, with infrared sights and silencers. They all had small communication devices with clip-on earplugs and mouthpieces attached to their collars. Their outfits were laid out and ready. Pete and Kid's green jackets had the name of the florist across the back, while Man's baggy dark blue jumper had the landscaping company's logo across the front and back. Everything was ready. They took their time preparing, setting the mood.
"Who the Giants playin' Sunday?" Kid asked.
Without looking up, Man answered, "The Redskins."
"That's gonna be a tough one," Pete said as he tried on his jacket — checking the fit with his holster on.
"I'm'a put two gees on them Giants," Kid said with his trademark smile.
"Put ten on 'em," Man said easily. "Unless you scared? 'Cause then you could save yo' money and buy you a dog."
Pete laughed at the way Man always seemed to be ahead ofKid's bullshit.
"I thought you said they wasn't gonna win the Super Bowl this year," Kid asked, smiling.
"That's right. But this ain't the Super Bowl," Man responded. The three of them talked and joked for a while, with Kid doing the bulk of both. In time, each went off to gather his thoughts and relax. It would be time to roll in a few hours. The waiting was almost over.
Kid put on his WalkMan, nodded his head to the beat and started to dance. Pete watched him for a few minutes. *It was strange how Kid just danced through life,* Pete thought with a

shake of his

head. Man, on the other hand, watched Kid and knew that he was getting rid of nervous energy. Kid just had his own method to deal with nerves–jokes, stories and dancing. Kid was who he was, Man thought. Man knew there was more to him than he let people see.

Pete lay on the cot and closed his eyes. Sleep dodged him like a thief slipping by the cops and thoughts attacked his mind like kids rushing an ice cream truck in the middle of August. He was always restless before a job.Pete would do what he had to. He would never let Kid or Man down. He had always handled his end. With Kid and Man holding him down, he knew he didn't have anything to worry about.  He let his thoughts drift to his family—first, his mother and sister, then his two daughters and wifey. Because of moves like this,

he was able to take care of them the way a man should. Pete was nothing like the father he despised–he was there for his family. Making moves like this proved to him that Kid and Man were his family too. What they had would last a lifetime; just like family was meant to, Pete thought.

Man threw a blanket on the floor and sat down in the lotus position. He rotated two small metal balls in the palms of each hand. The balls moved in an easy and disciplined rhythm. Man used them to relieve tension and clear his mind.But as he attempted to let go of all thoughts, his mind was flooded with images of Nicki with her hair thrown back, laughing in that sweet, sexy way she did when they were together. He saw her cross her shapely dancer's legs. She excited and calmed him, all at the same time. He studied the rhythmical sway of her hips as she moved toward… He pushed the images out and sought, once more, to clear his mind.

He couldn't get his mind clear—it snatched images like Black June collected vintage furnishing from around the world. Now, he thought about the two old gangsters, June and Shine. He had to respect how they'd lived their lives–true to the game. He'd heard the stories about Bumpy and Harlem from back then. June and Shine was the truth. Though he had love for them, he would never say it. That's just the way all of them lived: hard. Finally, his mind let go of the thoughts and he began to drift free and easy. There was no space or time and no chance to die, because no gun had been put in play.

## CHAPTER ELEVEN

Mr. Sam and the Fillmore twins sat in Bob's barbershop, ready to discuss any and every subject. After all, it was a neighborhood barbershop. For thirty-six years, Mr. Bob's shop had been the stage for debates on sports, women, religion and politics. Tom and Tim Fillmore had been part of the scene for the last twenty-five years.

The Fillmores had controlled the numbers game in the neighborhood before the state-run lottery put too much strain on their illegal operation in the early 80's. When they'd first gotten into the policy racket in the 40's, it had still been a source of hope and economic activity in Black communities throughout the city.

Once the numbers game was taken over, or co-opted by white organized criminals, the money made from it was taken out of the communities that produced it. Bumpy Johnson refused to back down from the white mobsters, and the battles that followed were the beginning of a legend. Nevertheless, the white mob finally gained control of the game.

Still, the Fillmore twins had done well for themselves. They retired from the business with several properties, including a couple of Laundromats and half-a-dozen parking garages in Midtown. Now, they lived lives of leisure and started most days off at Mr. Bob's shop.

Today was no different. Along with Mr. Bob and Sam, the twins were discussing the state of the world– shooting the breeze, as they called their barbershop pow-wows. Each of them felt their advanced years gave them a broader view of the world. Mr. Bob often said: "You don't meet too many old fools."

While Tom and Tim Fillmore were small at 5' 5" and 130 lbs., they never let their lack of size stand in the way of making their point. Their arguments always carried weight– a point, Mr. Sam and Bob, both large men at slightly over six feet tall and about 225 lbs., could attest to. Mr. Bob was slightly smaller than Mr. Sam, but of a much different temperament; strong willed but with an open mind, while Mr. Sam believed that his way was the only way. The different personalities made for many a lively conversation in the barbershop. They could go back and forth for hours.

The Fillmores appearance, in fact, made a point; they were always perfectly groomed. Each wore a thin mustache and goatee. And with their tailored suits, handmade shoes, and slick fedoras they looked like old time actors. At seventy years of age, they were versed in a myriad of subjects and enjoyed discoursing on all of them. The topic could jump from one thing to another. For example: Who was better, Jackie Robinson or Willie Mays? Who was prettier: Lena Home or Dorothy Dandridge? It went on and on.

Mr. Tim started it off, "I'm telling you, Jim Brown was the greatest running back ever. The only question is who was second?"

"Gotta be Gail Sayers," his brother answered.

"No, he ain't play long enough. Mind you, he was good but he got hurt," Mr. Sam offered.

Mr. Bob shook his head and said, "I'll take O.J. for my money. He was big, fast and had some sweet moves."

"Speaking of sweet. How 'bout 'Sweetness,' Walter Payton? You know he carried the Bears for years," Mr. Tim added.

"That's a fact," Mr. Bob agreed, "I thought that boy, Billy Sims, was gonna really do somethin', till he blew out his knee."

Everyone nodded in agreement.

"Who was the best high school running back in the city?" Mr. Tom asked.

"Man! Without a doubt. He still hold records for most yards and touchdowns in a game and season!" Mr. Bob exclaimed.

Tim and Torn nodded in agreement, while Mr. Sam gave a sour grunt.

Mr. Tim ignored him and said, "The boy was somethin' special with that pigskin wrapped in his arms."

"Lordy, you ain't never lied. Back in seventy-two or three – older I get less I 'member – against DeWitt Clinton, he broke four runs for sixty yards or more," Mr. Tom said excitedly.

"That's right. I was at that game," Mr. Bob stated with pride. "Man had it all: speed, power, and could cut sharper than a razor. He'd have made the pros for sure."

Mr. Tim nodded. "You right about that Bob. But don't forget how he played third base. Boy had a cannon for a arm and could hit the ball a mile."

"You ain't never lied," Mr. Bob said.

Finally, Mr. Sam said evenly, "Yeah, Man was good at everything, but what good did it do him? Look how he turned out. He's good for nothing now."

The Fillmores exchanged knowing glances. They knew that Bob and Sam argued about Man's lifestyle. The subject of Man had become a source of contention between the two old friends.

Mr. Bob stared at Mr. Sam for a moment. "Sam, you might not admit it, but Man does a lot of good around here. He sho' looks out for these kids—"

"How he do that?" Mr. Sam cut in. "By letting them drug dealers have the neighborhood?"

"Like I was saying, Man looks out for these kids and for a lot more folks around here," Mr. Bob finished up.

"Well, there's some truth to what you say. But he still part of the problem. Any fool can see that he's in bed with the drug dealers." Mr. Tim smiled. "For a minute, Sam, I wasn't sure how you knew so much 'bout Man's business. But like you said, 'Any fool can see it,'" he said mildly. "Sam, old as you is, you oughta know the day ain't never plain as it looks."

"Man could run the dealers outta here if he wanted to, and that's a fact," Mr. Sam replied. Mr. Tim looked from his brother to Mr. Bob before he settled his eyes on Mr. Sam. "You say that Man could get rid of the dealers. Well, it seems to me that's what we pay the police for. Hell, what we payin' taxes for?"

"All I'm saying is, Man should care more about the neighborhood. People gotta stop things they know is wrong," Mr. Sam stated emphatically.

"I guess you right about folks stopping what they know is wrong. 'Cause somebody shoulda' put a stop to them Ray boys long before it got outta hand. When they mama moved here with 'em, they was bad children and grew to be worst men. I thought about having them taken care of but never got around to it," Mr. Tim said somberly. "So I know what you mean when you say people oughta do somethin'."

No one spoke–the silence was heavier than *a* swollen raincloud in the small shop. Each man was lost in his own thoughts, or perhaps in his failure to take action against the Rays so long ago. Why had the job been left to a 17 year-old? That was the question none of them dared to ask out loud.

Mr. Sam shook his head, then ran his fingers through his thinning, gray hair. "Man can still do somethin' bout the drugs. He lives here too, and if—"

Mr. Bob cut him off. "You expect too much from Man. He got a life of his own. Well, what's left of it anyway."

Mr. Sam insisted, "Man can still take care of this."

Mr. Tom, who had been quiet for the most part, got up and walked to the window and with his back to the room said, "Like he had to take care of the Ray brothers. Is that what you mean, Sam?"

\*\*\*

Ms. Nez moved nervously around her small kitchen; she had tossed and turned and awakened in the middle of the night. She didn't know if it was a dream or a feeling of dread that had interrupted her sleep. But whatever it was, it had something to do with Man.

The one thing she was sure of, from the minute she woke up, was that he was in some sort of danger. She'd tried to convince herself it was nothing, but being aware of signs and omens, Ms. Nez knew better than to disregard them.

Ms. Nez was a "Yoruba" priestess, and believed there were forces of nature, or extensions of God — spirits that dealt with the affairs of men on earth. So, she didn't discount any message she received–dreams, symbols or signs. She didn't know what was going on with Man, but she trusted her intuition. So, she had lit a candle for him and asked one of the "Orishas" to watch over him. She'd also prepared an offering of food and drink for the "Orisha" to whom she made her request. It was all she could do for Man, because she knew he wouldn't tell her if he was in trouble. Although prison–and everything else– had changed Man, he'd always kept things bottled up inside.

Ms. Nez had known Man since he was a baby. His mother, Willona, had moved in the neighborhood when he was only eight months old. He'd been the cutest, fat little thing, Ms. Nez thought–a baby that was slow to cry, but quick to smile. Willona was little more than a child herself. Nevertheless, the young girl had been an excellent mother and was determined to make a good life for herself and her son. She had worked and put herself through nursing school, while raising Man.

Ms. Nez and a few other older women had helped out as much as they could – everybody wanted to baby-sit. Willona had become like a little sister or daughter to them. They were all proud of her. Little Man was an extension of the joy his mother brought them. He was definitely his mother's son.

Although his skin was a little darker, it had the same reddish hue, and his features, though sharper, were definitely hers. There wasn't any doubt that the handsome, cheerful, little boy belonged to the gorgeous young woman. As he grew over the years it became easy to think of them as brother and sister. It was a shame she died so young.

Though Man had grown into a strong person, his sorrows seemed to create emptiness in him. It settled around him in the guise of serenity. Man appeared to be bothered by nothing, but when the three people you loved most in the world were unexpectedly and violently snatched away there had to be pain. Ms. Nez shook her head. Maybe in order to turn off the pain, Man thought he had to turn his life off. Just as her eyes began to mist, there was a soft knock at the door. "Thank God, Mary's here," she said aloud.

"You looked worried, Nez," Ms. Mary said as she entered the small, neat apartment.

"It's nothing. I just had a restless night is all," Ms. Nez said hurriedly.

Ms. Mary looked down at her friend, and let it go. She knew if her friend needed to talk, she would.

Ms. Nez brought out tea and pastries. As they fell into an easy conversation, discussing topics of interest, a pleasant calm descended on the room. Ms. Nez put on a Nancy Wilson album. The song, *Guess Who I Saw Today,* enhanced the mood as both women drifted on Nancy's sweet, hypnotic voice.

Finally, Ms. Nez said, "Mary, I'm worried about Man. You know all the rumors and..." Ms. Mary waited for her to go on, but when Ms. Nez remained quiet, she said, "I know what you mean; he always looks so sad. Even when he's smiling." She got quiet for a minute then looked Ms. Nez straight in the eye. "And them rumors is just that, rumors. I get to hear about every last one from Sam. The fool thinks Man's responsible for everything that's wrong with this place."

"Why do you think Sam's so hard on Man?"

"Girl, I wish I knew. I can remember when you couldn't pay him to say a bad word about Man."

"Ain't that the truth. When Man was growing up, it was Man this, and Man that. Only then, it was all about how good he was," Ms. Nez said. "You know I remember he had Man working in the shop, and he and Bob used to argue about who Man liked working for best. Sometime, I wonder if he blames himself for what the Rays did? He always said those boys were no good. Maybe he feels he shoulda' done something about them?" Ms. Mary finished.

"Hindsight is always 20/20. But he shouldn't take it out on Man," Ms. Nez replied.

"I know you're right, Nez. And I bet that fool of a husband of mines know it too. But, you and I both know he won't admit it."

"I guess you're right. I'm just worried about Man."

"I know, but all we can do is pray for him," Ms. Mary said.

"Pray? Well, you know I done that. I wish he'd talk about what bothers him. He holds everything in."

"Uh-huh, I watch him sometime and just wanna cry. You can see it plain as day."

"Mary! Please don't use Sam's pet saying, 'plain as day.' You know everything is plain as day to that man of yours," Ms. Nez said laughing.

"Girl, I been married to the fool so long I'm starting to sound like him. Anyhow, his bark is a whole lot worse than his bite. He's just a big, old Teddy bear," Ms. Mary replied with a soft chuckle.

"I always said you was a saint to put up with 'im. But he is a good man," Ms. Nez said, offering her friend a smile.

"You know that's right or I wouldn't have been there these forty-three years. But he needs to understand that there's more than one way to be a good man."

"Ain't that the truth," Ms. Nez said, with a nod. "And whatever Man is involved with, I know he's a good man too." After a short pause, Ms. Nez added in a playful tone, "Oh, have you noticed that our sweet li'l Nicki is in love with Man. Now, wouldn't they make the perfect couple? And the babies those two would make, umh, umh."

Ms. Mary smothered a giggle. "Nez, you too much. But you sho' right. Them'd be some pretty babies. Besides, love can heal what ails a body and heart."
Both women smiled and nodded their agreement. Then they fell silent, once again caught in the pleasant grip of Nancy Wilson's voice.

After a while, each one said a silent prayer for Man, and Nicki. Being the wise women they were — from the tears and years they'd seen — they believed in both the power of prayer and the power of love.

## CHAPTER TWELVE

Tyrone sat behind his desk, staring out the window at the early morning traffic, buried in introspection. The passing cars had become the years and events of his life – memories – some good, some bad, but all gone.

He'd done well for himself, especially for a kid outta Brooklyn – straight off Blake and Stone Avenues. First Howard, then Harvard, and finally Wall Street. Actually, Water Street, he thought with a mischievous smile. Although just a short ride on the subway, Brownsville was worlds away from his lower Manhattan office.

Sometimes, he couldn't believe he had actually made it. But made it, he had. His annual salary easily exceeded $2,000,000 with bonuses. He shared a beautiful home with his beautiful wife and three wonderful kids. He had made the most of every opportunity and done it against great odds.

Many of his childhood friends had fallen victim to the street, prison or drugs. Sometimes a combination of the three had brought them an early death. Thinking about where he'd come from gave Tyrone cause to look deeper at his life. At 35, he was a rich man with a wonderful family and everything to look forward to; he shouldn't have had a care in the world. Yet, he was troubled by the plight of young Black people in America. Why were so many young Black men trapped in the justice system? Why were drugs thriving in Black communities throughout the country? He had some of the answers: lack of opportunities and hope, a system that was harder on darker skin, a well-devised plan by the powers-that-be and the desperation of the inhabitants. Ty knew that few brothers from the hood had the wherewithal to transport large quantities of cocaine and heroin into the country.

Yet, these, mostly young, brothers were the ones being sentenced to long prison terms. Clearly, the discrepancy in the sentencing guidelines between crack and powder cocaine was designed to punish those with the least, the most. Another thing, little of the profits from the drug trade stayed in the communities that generated it. Those who entered the drug trade with dreams of making it big usually made it dead or received big time in prison. The dream of being a successful drug dealer was a pipe dream–fool's gold.

However, the second rate education of the public school system made such a foolish dream seem like a good bet. The communities with the greatest need received the least amount of assistance: Brownsville, Harlem and the South Bronx were last in line when it came to effective teachers, quality job training and decent housing. These same neighborhoods were over represented in the prisons, a byproduct of their abundance of hopelessness. Without hope, life was bleak at best – and unbearable at worst.

Growing up in the 60's and 70's, Ty knew the importance of hope and, at least, the possibility of change. He'd witnessed his people striving for a better life despite the heroin that flooded their neighborhoods. Black folks had owned and operated the Mom-N-Pop corner stores now called bodegas. They were the gypsy cabdrivers that worked long hours and went places the yellow cabs refused to go. And they were the superintendents of the tenements that were kept spotless. They had believed in the American dream and a system that was supposed to reward hard work.

But over time the dream had become a nightmare. People were disillusioned and cynical to the point where they'd rather drown their sorrows and disappointments in a vial of crack, a bag of dope, or a cheap bottle of wine. A 40-ounce and a blunt had become the medicine to get through the day. Young men and women strived for little else. It was what they hoped for.

Yet, he had made it out. He had acquired degrees, wealth and social status. But what did it matter if he couldn't, or wouldn't reach back and lift up those left behind? The politicians and community leaders were useless. Although they were realizing the American dream, the people they represented faced an increasingly frightening reality. But what could he do? He was only one man.

He did, however, know of one man who'd done something. Man. Man had sent kids, who otherwise never would have made it, to college and donated money to a number of charities through the *We Raise Up Foundation*. Ty was perplexed by the things Man did. Though Man's income was legally accounted for, Ty had doubts about its true source.

He'd discounted drugs — Man definitely wasn't a dealer — but had a hard time believing the "gambling winnings" Man claimed on his tax returns every year. Man wasn't someone who gambled–at least not on games of chance. Man was too selfcontained, too well organized to place his destiny in the hands of fate.

His investments were always well thought out and profitable. Even the ones Ty thought to be risky had proved to be wise. Man had a feel for what would and wouldn't work. In fact, Ty thought, Man could manage his own money. He'd have done well at Howard and Harvard, too. Ty's smile grew sad as it dawned on him that Man had spent those years in prison. The reason why made it worst and reinforced Ty's belief that Man wouldn't trust his future to fate. Maybe he should ask Man about setting up a foundation of his own to help inner city kids. Man seemed to know where the assistance was needed the most. Ty guessed that was because, unlike him, Man had stayed in the hood—even as his bank account grew. Ty had the feeling that Man was someone he could trust, someone who would do what was right. He'd have a talk with Man about doing some good. The decision made him smile.

***

Kid stood off to the side watching Man's graceful movements. All the moves were slow, deliberate, and fluid. Although he'd seen Man perform them many times over the years, Kid still marveled at Man's early morning *Tai chi* exercise. Man had explained and worked with him on the exercises a few times. Though he enjoyed it, Kid wasn't really sold on the idea of a martial art that didn't involve self-defense. What Kid didn't understand was that Tai chi's primary purpose was to serve as a defense against disease and degeneration of the body.
Kid preferred speed and force in his workouts. He'd take the bar (chin-ups and dips), pushups and weights. Although Man did those exercises, as well as the heavy-bag, he swore by his Tai chi routine.

Kid smiled as Man finished what Kid jokingly called his *Jane Fonda Workout*. While Man was in the bathroom, Pete got up from the cot. He called out to Kid, "Yo, what's up?"

"Yeah, what's up with a li'l *Close-Up* on that dragon, homey?" Kid said with a serious face, before breaking out in laughter. He stopped laughing long enough to yell to Man that Pete needed to use the bathroom to slay his dragon. Pete threw the blanket at him, which only made Kid laugh harder.

Once they were all dressed, they got down to business. They applied clear nail polish to their fingers and palms – eliminating the chance of leaving prints if their gloves ripped or came off. They wiped down all their equipment, guns and all. The joking, as well as the waiting was over.

A rough drawing of the street and layout of the house in Jamaica Estates lay on the table. "Pete, you're driving and I want you to park the van right in front of the door. That way, it'll be harder for anybody to see what's happening."

"Right," Pete responded.

"Kid gets out first and opens the back of the van. By then you're back there too, and make a show of checking your clipboard and the house number in case anybody's watching." Kid and Pete nodded. They'd already gone over it, but knew Man liked to go through everything one last time. Plus, it eased their minds.

"You each take an end of the basket, and keep your joints underneath it from the start. That way you won't have to reach for your joints and nobody'll be able to see them. Pete you ring the bell and do the talking."

The younger men gave Man their undivided attention. Every word was absorbed. After checking the large 4X2-foot basket of roses and the rest of their props, they went to different corners of the warehouse and tried out the communication units.

With the earpiece plugged into one ear, and the tiny microphone clipped on a shirt collar, the system worked perfectly, they heard each other clearly.

"It's on," Man said, holding both of them in his gaze. "Let's make sure we all got the same time," he said as he looked at his watch. "I got 8:30."

Kid and Pete checked their watches, they knew timing was important on this one; it could be the difference between success and failure and, possibly, between life and death. Man looked at Pete. "Tell me the route you're taking?"

"Throng Neck Bridge to Clearview Expressway, exit at Hillside and 212th Street, come down hit Hillside, then cross Sutphin Boulevard," Pete answered with confidence. Man nodded, and turned to Kid. "Kid once you in...?"

"I go to the right, check the den, then hit the stairs and check the three bedrooms," Kid responded, without a hint of his usually playfulness.

"Okay, good. Now once you ring the doorbell you gotta keep them busy while I come through the backdoor. Whether they open the door or not — and they probably won't — you gotta keep them talking."

Kid and Pete nodded their understanding; neither of them would let Man down, not even if it cost them their lives. They both knew he'd die twice for them if he could.

To say that they loved Man barely touched the depths of their feelings. He was their hero, and not out of no goddamned book. Man was real and had put them down, and made them the real deal in the game and they'd live it until it killed them. This was their thing and the best life they could have, and they owed it all to Man.

Man broke the silence with a smile and said, "We leave in ten minutes. Although we'll be able to, we won't speak directly. Y'all just carry on a conversation, giving me a play by play of what's happening."

Seizing his chance for a joke, Kid smiled and said, "I'll do most of the talking, so you'll see the world like I do."

Pete and Man smiled. Man held out a fist, as the two younger men touched theirs to it, he said, "Lets rock and roll."

## CHAPTER THIRTEEN

Bigum swept the sidewalk in front of the game room as he did every morning. However, on this morning his usual vigor was absent. He knew that Man and the two young bandits, as he affectionately called Kid and Pete, were on the move.

He felt that he should be with them, and make sure they were okay. But Man hadn't even considered it. He had insisted Bigum's job was making sure the game room was safe. Still, Bigum felt he should've gone with Man and the others, just in case. He knew Man could take care of himself, but... He continued to sweep, although the sidewalk had been spotless for the last forty minutes. He was too jumpy to sit still.

He spotted Nicki corning out of the center with a mob of youngsters. She waved him over, and greeted him with a big smile. They had always gotten along well. After all, they had common ground–they both loved children and they both loved Man.

"Bigum, how you doing this morning?" Nicki asked, still smiling.

"Oh, I guess I'm doin' pretty good. And you?"

"I'm fine, and busy," she responded, gesturing toward the children who crowded around the giant from the game room. Nicki liked the effect the huge, gentle man had on the children. It was one of the reasons she liked him so much—that and his obvious concern for Man.

Returning her smile, Bigum thought, *she sure is fine, and busy loving Man.* Maybe Nicki's love would save Man from himself. That is, if Man would let her get close enough.

"I can't think of a better way to be busy," Bigum said, looking down at her and the tiny pre-schoolers. Three or four little ones began to climb on him before the words were out of his mouth; he laughed and reached down for them.

"Jason, Mark, all of y'all get off Mr. Bigum," Nicki said sternly.

"Don't you worry none. I'm just happy to be able to give 'em somethin' to do," Bigum said as two more children joined in the fun. They grabbed legs, sat on feet and jumped up and down. He laughed some more, and the deep rolling sound that came out of him was contagious.

Nicki and the kids laughed along with him. "Bigum, you just as bad as the kids," Nicki said after she caught her breath.

Bigum stopped laughing long enough to say, "I know. Ain't it great?" Twenty minutes later the two other teachers led the children back inside.

"How's Man?" Nicki asked casually.

"Oh, he's fine. You know how Man is," Bigum replied, uneasily. Still, it was good to have something else to think about.

Nicki smiled ruefully. "I wonder if anyone really knows how Man is?"

"I know what you mean. But he's okay. Man is strong," Bigum said thoughtfully.

"Sometime, I think he's too strong."

Bigum looked down at her. "I don't know if anybody can be too strong for what the world gives us to bear. Either it makes you strong or breaks you. And there ain't always a choice in the matter."

"There's always a choice, we just have to make the right one. Man doesn't have to push the whole world away," Nicki said in a forlorn voice.

Bigum felt for her. Though she mentioned Man pushing the world away, she could just have easily been speaking of him pushing her away. "Well, in life we find ourselves traveling roads we never meant to be on. But more times than not, even those roads takes us right where we was meant to be. Man'll find his way," the big man said sagely. Holding her with his eyes, he added, "It might help if somebody drew him a map."

Nicki laughed softly and said, "A map, huh? Well, that shouldn't be too difficult."

"Not for somebody who really cares, and I bet it'll be worth the effort too."

Nicki stared up at Bigum. She didn't know what to say. That was okay — he'd said it all. "Oh, look at the time. It's 9:40. I have to get back inside. See you later, Bigum." She started toward the steps of the center.

"I'll let Man know you was looking for him, okay?" Bigum said quickly.

Nicki turned and faced him. For a minute she wasn't sure if that was what she wanted, then she nodded and ran up the steps before Bigum could see the tears welling up in her eyes.

\*\*\*

The house was back off the street, in an exclusive section of Queens–Jamaica Estates. It was chosen as a stash house for just those reasons. Who would expect enormous amounts of drug money to be stored in such an upscale place? The owners had finally rented the house, through a broker, after it was on the market for over a year. It just wasn't a good time to be selling a house, especially one so expensive. So, when the broker said he had a couple looking to rent and willing to pay $8,000 a month, few questions were asked.

The couple was chosen for the same reason as the house; they were beyond suspicion. They were from a prominent family in Tumaco, Columbia. Though the Valencia family was prestigious, it was in name only. The family fortune had been squandered years ago. The Valencias, brother and sister, were posing as husband and wife and their aristocratic bearing placed them beyond suspicion. They were paid handsomely to live in a beautiful house, complete with two late model, luxury automobiles. The only catch was that two to three times a month, they had to baby-sit millions of dollars for a day or so. The setup was one of many operated by the people the Valencias worked for.

The money wasn't guarded by armed men. The security was in the secrecy of the operation, as well as in the influential standing of the neighborhood. The irony that their drug money was actually, though unknowingly, protected by the police was not lost on the people who rented the house.

It wasn't unusual, however, for someone to check on things. Mainly to keep people like the Valencias honest. When dealing with such large sums of money, even the most trustworthy employees were capable of greed.

Man walked through the grounds of the estate directly behind the one occupied by the Valencias. This house was also up for sale, but the owner hadn't been able to sell or rent, so it sat empty. The fall and approaching winter weather had created a need for some minor landscaping on the property. So, it wasn't unusual to see the black pickup truck with *Tree Top Landscaping* on its door, pull up.

Man parked in front of the house and did some work on the lawn, before moving to the back. He carried two large burlap bags tied together across his left shoulder. He wore a dark blue knit cap that matched his jumper.

His work boots were soft-sole *Rockports* that allowed him to move without making a sound. Although his eyesight was perfect, he wore a large pair of glasses on his face. To the few people who noticed, he looked just like any other hard working sap as he inspected the lawn, hedges, and small tress on the property. So no one paid him the least bit of attention when he crossed over into the adjoining yard.

At exactly 9:40, a white delivery van from the *Best Roses Flower Shop* of Long Island City turned into the small circular driveway of the house on Bally Road. Two young men, wearing green windbreaker-type jackets with the company's name on them, exited the van. The shorter of the two men double-checked the house address with the one on his clipboard. The men removed a large basket of flowers from the rear of the van.

As they approached the front door with the basket between them, they carried on a light conversation, with the taller one doing most of the talking.

At 9:43, Pete rang the doorbell and Kid said in a clear, steady voice, "I hope they hear the bell. I want to get this delivery over with."

Man stepped onto the back porch as Kid spoke. He moved silently toward the door. Pete rang the bell again – two short urgent bursts – calling for immediate attention. Kid gave a play-by-play of what was happening.

A small voice that could barely be heard, asked, "Yes, what is it?"

"Flowers for a Ms. Valencia," Pete said in a hurried tone.

"No, I no buy anything," the voice was a little stronger now.

They're for you, lady. Somebody sent 'em for you."

"No, I no buy."

Pete shook his head and said in the same hurried tone, "Look, lady. I mean Ms. Valencia, the flowers were sent to you by somebody..." Pete made a show of looking down at his clipboard.

"They're from somebody – wait a minute – from Tumaco, Colombia. I ain't got all day, now if you don't want 'em or—"

"Tumaco?" The voice cut Pete off, and was much stronger this time.

Pete went on, "You want them or not. I would leave 'em out here but you gotta sign for 'em."

Man stealthily slipped a key in the lock of the back door, then silently pushed it open and stepped into a spacious kitchen. A large gun in his gloved right hand.

The voice on the inside of the front door asked, "Tumaco? I no understand. Who?" The woman was puzzled, but curious.

Man walked through the kitchen, straight down the short hallway, his eyes scanning everything. His senses alert for any sounds or movements. He could hear the woman and Pete, but he had no idea where the man was. He didn't like that.

"Listen, lady. I can't stay here all day," Pete said as if he didn't care one way or the other.

Man stepped into the large living room and saw the man standing just behind the woman who was listening intently to Pete's every word. Now Man had a gun in each hand — a red dot from the scopes trained on both, the man and woman. He was only two feet from them when he said, in broken Spanish, "Open the door. Fast."

The woman let out a little yelp. Whereas the guy, who was tall but slight, like the shorter woman, looked as if he was about to faint. Instead, he just crossed himself and mouthed a silent prayer.

Pete was still speaking when the door opened; he and Kid stepped in as if they were in no hurry. But as soon as the door closed behind them, Kid raced off to secure the other rooms and Pete was busy using plastic wraps to subdue the Valencias, who offered no resistance. First, he bound their hands behind their backs, then their feet. Once they were both restrained, he placed small black cloth bags over their heads.

Having checked the den, Kid went upstairs. Man was checking the other two rooms downstairs, a study and small sitting room.

They'd been in the house for less than four minutes, and everything was going as planned. As Kid came down the stairs, speaking into the mic on his shirt, he caught a glimpse of someone stepping out of a small alcove down the far wall. The man, a short, stocky Spanish-looking guy, held a gun in his hand that he was aiming at something beyond Kid's view.

Kid spoke urgently, "Red Dog. Red Dog." Their code for trouble.

Man sensed the movement behind him at the same instant he heard Kid's signal. He spun around – saw a gun pointed at him. In less than a second, Man's red dot found its target–the gunman's chest.

Reacting like the professionals they were, Man and the Spanish gunman, squeezed the triggers of their weapons instinctively. The only sound was the soft, muffled noise from Man's silenced weapon.

The guy staggered back, causing Man's second shot to miss its mark. But the left side of the guy's head exploded – Kid had turned the corner shooting. Blood splattered the wall and the lush white carpet, as the body fell with a thump.

Man quickly stepped to the body. He snatched the gun off the floor – a small 9mm. – and checked it. There was a bullet in the chamber and the safety was off. But the gun hadn't fired.

Man was sure the guy had pulled the trigger. He didn't understand it, but there was no time to consider it. They'd been in the house close to five minutes now, and were falling behind schedule.

He went directly to the terrified couple. "One dead, don't make it three," he said in a voice as frightening as the death scene they'd just heard. "Where's the money?"

The Valencias told Man what he wanted to know — they couldn't get it out fast enough. Pete retrieved the three large suitcases that contained close to $4,000,000, from beneath a concealed trapdoor in the floor of the pantry.

The money, all hundred and fifties, was quickly transferred from the suitcases into the basket that had held the roses and the two burlap sacks Man carried. They barely spoke a word as they went about their business.

Nine minutes after they'd entered the house Kid and Pete left through the front door, just as they'd come: two delivery men from *Best Roses,* carrying the large basked minus the beautiful flowers they'd arrived with They placed the basket in the back of the van, and drove away slowly.

Thirty seconds later, Man exited through the back door and stepped into the yard where he expertly pulled up a small, dying shrub. He thought he might be able to save it by replanting it in better soil. He placed the shrub into one of the heavy burlap sacks, the roots hanging out gave the impression the sack was full of shrubs.

Man's gait was purposeful, but unhurried. He was just another laborer doing his job. And from the dirt and leaves that covered him, and the two bags of heavy debris he carried, it was obviously a *hard job.*

## CHAPTER FOURTEEN

José stood beside his red Pathfinder and watched Bigum and Nicki, with all the children running wild around them. The scene disgusted him. *Why the fuck were they so happy?* All he could do was watch and wait, while good money making hours were wasted because of Man's bullshit-ass rule. He hated everything about Man.

Anybody down with Man was on his fuck'em list. He'd like to walk down the street and beat that big Moreno with a baseball bat. First, he'd shoot him in both knees, though. José smiled; he wouldn't take any chances with somebody as big as Bigum. After he took care of Bigum, he'd beat Nicki with some hard dick, he thought with a smile. One thing José knew was that bitches loved a pretty muthafucker, and she was no different. She tried to act like she didn't notice him, but he knew better–of course, she wanted him.

Disgusted, he climbed into his jeep. Other crews were stacking dollars, but his couldn't work while the kids went to school. José fumed. He had to do something. And since Peto had proved to be a bitch, he couldn't count on him. He'd put his trust in that *mamabicho* and look what it got him. And he still had to worry about the shit getting back to Man. Blood didn't mean shit anymore, he thought, as Carlos approached the jeep.

Carlos opened the passenger's door and climbed in. "Damn, it's cold as a bitch out there."

Looking over at him, José said, "No shit. You must be that new weatherman they putting on channel seven."

Carlos didn't respond. Although his expressionless, deep-set eyes remained straight ahead, the wrinkles in his large forehead announced his building anger.

José realized his mistake; he needed Carlos more than ever, and didn't want to upset him. Carlos was big and rugged, with arms like tree limbs and a barrel-chest. Because of his rough look, people often thought he wasn't sharp. But José knew better. Carlos wasn't a genius, but he knew the streets and how to survive them. He wasn't somebody you wanted to fuck with–unless, you were Man, José thought, as the start of a plan took shape in his head.

"Damn, homey, you know I'm just fuckin' with you. It's all this waiting around every morning, and counting money we ain't making." José stalled, then added, "We gotta do somethin' 'bout that faggot Man."

Carlos didn't say a word. The silence made José uncomfortable. He didn't like Carlos' mood. "I shoulda' let you tear his ass up that night he fronted on you."

"Check it, Ze. You know I ain't scared of nothin' or nobody, but the more I hear about Man the less I wanna get at him," Carlos replied in a low but steady voice.

"I don't believe this shit," José exclaimed. "The muthafucker chumps you and you talkin' about you ain't tryin' to get at his ass," his voice laced with contempt.

Carlos exploded, "Fuck you! That bullshit ain't cost me nothin'. Everybody in that room know how I get down, and I ain't never been nobody's chump."

José backed off. He needed a plan, and he needed Carlos.

"Listen, I know you down for yours. That's why I got you down with me. And I hear what you sayin', that shit wasn't 'bout nothin'. But we still gotta do something about Man," José said and thought for a minute. As he thought about it, José nodded his head. The plan was coming together. "We ain't gotta step to Man, we can go after somebody close to him. And maybe we could use Ricky's punk ass. He can't really like paying his punk dues every week. That way we could get rid of both of them."

Carlos grunted, he wasn't in the mood for Jose's scheming. Sometimes Carlos wondered why he put up with Jose's soft, plotting ass. But he knew why–money. People would do just about anything to get paid he thought and wondered if he was a grimy as José, by running with him.

José turned on the radio, the sounds of Guy's *"Crazy"* blasted from the speakers. He closed his eyes and thought about fucking Nicki, and killing Man. A snarl of hatred crossed his delicate features.

Carlos watched as José bopped his head to the song. He tried to imagine what type of sick shit was going through Jose's mind to match the twisted expression on his face, and was glad when he couldn't. Carlos knew the lithe and girlish looking hood was crazy, and couldn't be trusted. Carlos reached for the door. "It's time to get the crew ready," he said, as the cold air rushed to greet him.

Out in the cold, Carlos thought the harsh weather was an upgrade over Jose's company. In fact, a case of V.D. was an upgrade from that psycho.

***

Man arrived at the warehouse a few minutes after Pete and Kid. Their respective trips went smoothly. Nothing about the robbery had come over the police scanners. The people involved didn't want that kind of attention, so the robbery went unreported.
Man got out of the pickup and began removing the license plates and the logo from the truck. Pete and Kid had already taken care of the van.

Man nodded his approval, and touched fists with them. He took the plates, Kid and Pete's jackets, the basket and burlap sacks, once the money had been dumped out, and slipped out of his jumper. He put all the items in the furnace downstairs. He fired it up and smiled, the intense heat turned the evidence into ashes.

Back in the office, Man brought out three money-counting machines from under a floorboard. The three men set about separating and counting the stacks of money.

"Damn, this is what I call a payday," Kid said, with a huge smile on his face.
Man studied the younger men, before he replied, "Yeah, all in all, things went well. You both did good. And Kid you was on point with dude."

"I was a li'l late, but we both was quicker than him."

Pete nodded. "Word. When I heard Kid's Red Dog, I knew the shit was on, and that we was 'bout to get busy."

While Man counted the bills, he wondered why the guy's gun hadn't fired. With time to think about it, he knew he'd been a second late. How had they missed the guy in the first place?

"Like I said, we did good. But the best surprise is the one that don't happen," Man said.

Kid stopped working stacks into the machine. "You know how me and my boy, Peter-Gun, get down. We the shit, but then we learned from the best," he said, with a fanatical gleam in his brown eyes.

"That's right," Pete added, with an identical look. "We the truth and we owe it all to you, Man."

Man had a strange feeling. He didn't deserve their gratitude or admiration. After all, what had he really done for them? Besides teach them how to get out of dangerous situations that he put them in, in the first place? He wondered if the money was worth their lives, or his, or the gunman who died trying to protect it. He also wondered if Kid or Pete cared that someone had died? But why should they? He didn't. Which was why he understood the gleam in their eyes.

"Kid, you changed the barrel on your joint, right?" Man asked, attempting to focus on something other than the questions that were trying to lay siege to his conscience. The moral questions beat against his brain like raindrops on a tin roof. So, he was relieved when Kid responded.

"Yeah, I dumped it along the Grand Central and put the new one in. My nine is ready to rock again."

"Good," Man said. He'd thrown the used barrel of his own gun out the window while crossing the Tri-Borough Bridge. Instead of throwing a gun away after it was used, they would change the barrel of automatics and file down the barrel of the revolvers.

Man turned the counting machine off and stood up. "I'm going downstairs to the range. I want to check out the joint I took off dude," he said palming the pearl-handle, black .9mm.

Kid and Pete nodded, but didn't look up from what they were doing. They were floating-the robbery and money had them pumped, the thrill of the adventure created a feeling of euphoria. They both felt that it was a defining moment in their lives. The game had been raised and they would do whatever it took to maintain the level of accomplishment they felt. And they knew Man was the key.

Man sat at the workbench examining the weapon. He had disassembled it after firing the entire eight-shot clip. The gun worked perfectly. Man didn't understand it. The guy was a professional and his gun worked. *So why didn't he get a shot off?* Man sighed. None of it made sense.

Man slowly began to reassemble the gun. His mind was still trying to come up with an answer that made sense. He couldn't, and that bothered him. However, it didn't bother him that he had killed a man. After all, it was a man with a gun in his hand. The man was a gunman, and the same life he lived got him killed, Man thought. That was just the way life played out,
Man smiled as he made his way up the stairs. He felt good. Before he reached Kid and Pete, the smile was gone. The job wasn't finished yet; the money had to be counted and Shine and June's share delivered to them.

"Where we at?" Man asked, as he walked into the office.
Both Kid and Pete reached for pieces of paper and began calling out numbers.

## CHAPTER FIFTEEN

"What time is Man supposed to call," Eddie asked.

Born rolled his massive shoulders, trying to loosen them up after the 7-mile run and hour of calisthenics they had finished less than an hour ago. "Nine tonight, over on Fourth Street, right by Howard's radio station."

"That's what I'm talkn' 'bout," Eddie said, as he ran the brush across his fade, making sure his waves was laid down.

Born shook his head. "What's that?"

"You said he was gonna call the pay-phone over by Howard University radio station, right?" Without giving Born a chance to respond, Eddie went on, "It ain't that hard to figure out. All them young, tender college girls hanging around."

"If they smart enough to go to college maybe they smart enough to escape yo' hard living ass," Born said with a laugh.

"Ain't no doubt, I live and play hard. But that's just what they young ass needs. A worldly fellow, like myself, to show 'em the ropes," Eddie responded with a smirk, as he checked his hair in the mirror on the living-room wall.

"Damn, ropes? Eddie, they too young for your crazy ass to tie 'em up. Next you gonna pull out whips and shit." Both men laughed.

Born got up from the couch. As much as he enjoyed his time with Eddie, he was restless. And it wasn't the city that bored him; he loved D.C. Even the rough slums of the South East and North West held a certain appeal for him. Born was glad that Eddie had set up his base in the nation's capital, just as he was glad Man worked out of New York. He went back and forth–he'd spend a few days at Eddie's place near Rock Creek Park, then a few days at Man's condo on Riverside Drive, and wherever his spirit moved him in between.

As well as they got along, the three of them didn't spend a lot of time together. Prison had made them appreciate space and solitude. Plus, the fact that they were alpha-males meant they had to have room to spread out. In any event, Born thought that hey had finally figured out how to live in a world that didn't understand or want them.

"God, what you thinking so hard on?" Eddie asked.

Born focused his eyes on Eddie, grunted and said, "We come a long way. From nothing kids that ain't nobody want to cons walking the yard and all that shit, to men who live life the way they want. Like they say in the Dirty South, we come from shit to sugar."

"And we ain't finish yet, God. We still got moves to make, and I bet Man got somethin' lined up for us."

Born gave up a gapped-tooth smile. "I know that's right."

Eddie nodded, then changed the subject, "C'mon, let's go to Curtchfield's. I feel like some fresh seafood."

"Word, and it's on me," Born said, as they went for their jackets and weapons. Staying armed meant staying alive.

Born said, "Maybe we'll run into Sugar Ray punk-ass again. You know he always up in the spot," as he climbed into the passenger's side of Eddie's green Jaguar.

"We going there to eat, not so you can dis Ray again," Eddie replied, as he started the car and pulled out of the driveway.

After finding a radio station, Born settled back. "You know I ain't dis the li'l fellow. I just told 'im that Marvelous Marvin whupped his ass. We was at that fight, and you and Man agreed with me that Hagler put it on him."

"Yeah, I thought Ray got beat. But why you had to keep telling him that shit and calling him 'li'l fellow'?"

"You see how his li'l ass was trying to stare me down. I thought his ass was gonna call me out, but the boy ain't just a warrior, he smart as shit too. 'Cause if he had to run from Marvin, what he gonna do with the God," Born said, throwing his head back in laughter.

As Eddie crossed over into Silver Springs, he shook his head and thought: *Not many men could stand toe-to-toe with the God.* Damn, he hoped that Man had something big enough for the three of them. It would be nice if they could work together, Eddie thought, as he pulled into the restaurant's parking lot. Man could even bring his cubs, Kid and Pete.

***

The bitter, winter winds cleared the Harlem streets as effectively as a patrol car full of racist cops. Although it was only 7:00, few people were out battling the cold night. So the old bum pushing the shopping cart full of cardboard boxes, rags and a shoe shine box, attracted little attention as he made his way down Edgecombe Avenue. The fierce winds threatened to snatch the homemade sign from the front of the cart: *Shoeshine — $1.50 — Best In Town.*

The man's labored gait was slow but determined, as he battled forward through the wind. He pushed his cart with gnarled fingers, covered by numerous pairs of old socks. He wore two overcoats, one of them an old and worn Chesterfield with a black velvet collar. Beneath the coats, a cheap suit jacket attempted to hold in the old man's body heat. Around his neck a bunch of tattered, ugly, multi-colored scarves fought against the biting cold.

Two middle-aged men sharing a bottle of *Wild Irish Rose* wine in front of the Buy Rite Liquor Store, on 139th Street, stopped arguing long enough to yell something at the old shoeshine man. The man paused and pointed at the sign on the front of his cart. The men laughed and waved him off. The old man nodded and turned down 139th Street, where a stylishly dressed couple quickly crossed the street to avoid him.

Though his clothes were old and worn, they were clean. The colors didn't match, but with the newspaper sticking out of his battered boots, he had chosen warmth over fashion.
He stopped in front of the last brownstone on the block, his beat-up, old watch cap pulled down on his head, covering his ears. After quickly straightening his outfit, he rang the bell on the wrought iron gate.
After a moment, Black June opened the handsomely finished oak door. Dressed in a midnight blue set of satin pajamas, with a lush bathrobe of the same color, he stared out at the shoeshine man.
The old man pointed at the sign on his cart and waited.

June stood in the doorway for a moment before he nodded and said, "Okay, I guess I could use your services tonight. C'mon round to the side door, that way you won't hav'ta' carry your stuff up the steps."

Once around the side of the house, the old man waited patiently. He was a man familiar with waiting. Finally, Black June opened the door, and the shoeshine man brought in the two large boxes, as well as his wooden shoeshine box. Once he sat the boxes down, the old man straightened up and was a full 3-inches taller than he previously appeared.

June embraced him, then stepped back and looked into his eyes. "I swear, each time I see you in this getup, the less I see you. I mean, I see an old man, and gotta remind myself that its you, Man," June said with a shake of his head.

Man smiled at his mentor. "That's the point, Mr. J. Anyway, I've been told I have an old soul, so maybe that's why it works so well."

Shine stepped into the room and grabbed hold of Man. "Boy, you look older than me and June." He stepped back and added, "It's good to see you."

"You gonna really think so once you see what's in those boxes," Man said, pointing at the cardboard boxes by the door.

Looking over at June, Shine replied, "The money is a bonus. Ain't too many bonds in this-here game that's worth a shit, and me and June been in it forever. So we know the value of real friendship and loyalty."

Man nodded, but said nothing, as he watched Shine and June nod in agreement. He hadn't expected such a show of emotion from the two aged gangsters.

"How did the key work?" Shine asked.

"Right as rain," Man answered.

Black June grunted, "For half of what's in them boxes, it shoulda' been."

Shine and Man laughed, then Man said, "June, you know that's just part of the price of doing business."

June smiled. "I see you learned well. As long as everybody's happy, business gets done. And how was business?" he asked, as he took a seat at the old wooden poker table.

Shine sat down, also. Man slipped off the overcoats before he joined them. He pulled off the cap, revealing a head full of what appeared to be gray hair.

June got up close and scrutinized Man for a minute. "Damn, I can't tell if it's a wig or not. Can you Shine?"

Shine examined Man's face and head from his seat before moving directly in front of him. "Only when I'm right up on him, and looking for it," he said nodding. "That's damn good, Man. And that gray stubble on your face looks real too."

Man removed the socks from his hands, the clay that gave them that gnarled look visible. He smiled at the interest and excitement of the normally smooth old-timers. They were both like teenagers about to get head for the first time. Man suddenly realized that June and Shine lived vicariously through him. Though too old to follow the scent of big paydays, June and Shine still yearned for the adventure and danger of the game.

"I don't know if you heard, but we had a little trouble," Man said without emotion.

"Yeah, we got the word from the same people we got the key from," June responded.

Shine stood up.

"The information we got beforehand didn't say nothing about the lame y'all had to put down either."

"You know how that shit goes. Shit happens. By the way, it was $3.8 million altogether. So, its $1.9 million in the boxes... half, like we said."

June's smile was brighter than a July sun at noon. Shine jumped up and threw a quick combination – two short jabs and a short right cross. They slapped palms and smiled their approval.

"Let me get that bottle of Chivas Regal," June said, and took off for the stairs.

Shine studied Man, he wondered about his lack of emotion. Nothing seemed to make him happy. Shine knew the story, and it was a sad one for sure. But it was over and Man needed to let it go and learn to live his life—the one he had now.

Shine also knew if you walked with death it would only lead to more of the same–a man that turned away from life was turning towards death.

Man slowly raised his eyes from the cigarette burns on the table and settled them on Shine. He shrugged his shoulders, as if answering an unspoken question. It was as if he knew exactly what the older man was thinking.

"I don't want to stay too long, just in case somebody was watching when I came in. It wouldn't look right, the shoeshine man hanging around."

June walked in on the last of Man's words. "Well, I know you got time for at least one drink with two old men."

Man accepted the glass from June and said, "Fo' sho', even the old shoeshine man need a li'l taste to keep the hawk from biting."

They touched glasses, turned them up and emptied them; smiles and nods all around. As June refilled the glasses, Man was slipping on his overcoat and rearranging the two .45's in their holsters.

## CHAPTER SIXTEEN

"Yo, Pete, what you gonna do with your half-a-mil'," Kid asked, as he flipped through the pages of the *Amsterdam News*.

"It ain't a half-a-mil'. Remember, we both told Man to take $75-gees out for Born, Eddie, and Bigum," Pete replied, as he snatched the paper from Kid.

"C'mon, I ain't finish yet," Kid said, trying to get the paper back, as Pete avoided his efforts and returned to the couch.

Kid waved his hand at him. "So what you gonna do with your loot?'

"I'm'a check out that guy Man told us about. The one from Wall Street. Its time to step the game up."

"Word. You ain't never lied about that shit. I'm thinking about letting homey invest $400,000."

Pete looked at Kid. "You serious?"

Kid smiled and said, "Yeah, I don't need nothin' and I'm tired of fucking my money up."

Pete returned the smile. "I see all that shit Man be talkin' done rubbed off on yo' ass, huh?"

"Nah, homey. You know me and Man can't see eye to eye," Kid said with a laugh. "But even I gotta admit, all that shit about investing makes sense. I already got close to 200-gees in the stash, and my car is paid for, and I got this co-op. All of this shit I got and the house I bought Ma-duke before she died is because I listened to Man.

"So, why not keep listenin'. I ain't fuckin' this four-and-change up," Kid said seriously. Then he laughed and added, "Well, I might fuck up the change. I could use a new Rolex and a li'l vacation."

"Damn, Kid you almost sounded smart for a minute," Pete said, laughing at the look Kid gave him.

"Boy, you know I'm smart as shit. How much you gonna invest?"

"I dunno' but I'm thinking about buyin' a house down south. Man said he'd help me clean up my dough."

"Yeah, I can see yo' ass down south on a farm and shit. "Heehaw, buddy," Kid said, exploding with laughter.

Pete shook his head and joined him. Kid was a fool, but Pete knew that they were partners for life. They would always have each other's back. But Pete knew it would be smart to get out of the game now, while his pockets were fat and shit was good. Even if he could talk Kid into getting out, which he knew he couldn't, how could they walk away from Man? They were tied to Man until the end. And in truth, that's just how it should be. Man had started them out.

Turning back to the paper, and away from his thoughts, Pete asked, "You read this shit Les Matthews wrote?"

"I saw that bullshit. Old Les still snitching with his punkass."

"Punks who ain't never been in the game always wanna talk about it. If he know so much 'bout the life, why his bitch-ass ain't living it?" Pete wondered out loud.

Kid nodded in agreement "You know how that shit is. Everybody wanna be down, but ain't too many muthafuckers willing to pay the cost." Kid knew the cost. He didn't expect to have a long life, but he intended to make sure it was full of fun and big paydays. The way he saw it, he and Pete had arrived.

Although he knew he'd ride with Man until the end, Kid wondered if Pete felt the same way. He knew Pete was down, but he also knew how he felt about wifey and his little girls. In time, Kid knew, Pete would want to get out. And he'd do everything in his power to help him. Man was another story, Kid thought. Man'd stay in until the end, and Kid had already decided he'd go along for the ride. They'd have the life for as long as they had life. But why shouldn't Pete live the family life he really wanted?

"Yo, on the real side, that down south shit is a good idea,' Kid said seriously. Pete stared at his friend, waiting for the joke. When it didn't come he asked, "You think so?"

"Hell yeah. It's cool, and it's what you want. And you know, we always get what we want."

Pete was quiet for a minute, then he smiled. "That'a right, we make shit happen."

Kid jumped up and stuck out his fist, "That's 'cause we the truth," he said, as Pete's fist met his.

***

"Come here, Terry," Ramsey shouted as he stood in front of 442, the building Blue Seal operated out of.

"Boy, what' cha want," Terry, yelled at him, as she made her way across the street.

"Why you always fronting me?" Ramsey asked with a smirk.

"You wanna smoke a blunt of chronic?" he asked, pulling a dime bag of weed from his pocket.

Terry flashed a smile worthy of a Mid-Town billboard. "I hope that shit ain't home-grown."

"See, that's what I'm talkin' about. You always tryin' to dis' me."

Terry placed her hands on her shapely hips, pushed out her firm breast, and said, "Boy, you know I just be playin' with you."

"Why I gotta be a boy?"

Terry ran her tongue slowly across her full lips, as she smiled sweetly. "Well, I guess when you grow up you won't be a boy no more, but until then..."

"Fuck you," Ramsey said with a frown.

"Maybe when you grow-up, but right now you too young for me," Terry said as she patted Ramsey's cheek.

"I got somethin' you can pat," Ramsey said, as he pushed her hand away.

"I know you ain't getting on no sucker shit 'cause I'm teasing yo' ass," Terry said, as she reached up and took the cigar out of Ramsey's hand.

"Girl, just roll the blunt."

She unwrapped the cigar, split it open and dumped the tobacco out. Once she finished, she licked the inside of the leaf and held it out so Ramsey could spread the weed in it. She rolled it, stuck it in her mouth and slowly pulled it out, with her eyes on Ramsey the whole time. When she saw that she had him stuck, Terry lit the blunt, took a deep pull and blew the smoke in his face. "Damn, this that shit."

"I told you. I only smoke the best."

"At least you can do somethin' right," Terry said with a giggle.

"I'll show you what else I can do right if you bring yo' hot-ass over my house."

"Oh, I know you didn't call me hot. But since you did, that's right, I'm hot, but for a grown man."

"Girl, you need to quit frontin', 'cause we the same age."

"Boy, everybody know that women mature quicker."

"Yeah, right," Ramsey said and laughed.

Terry put her hand on her hip. "For real." As they passed the blunt back and forth, they talked about the neighborhood they'd grown up in. They talked about who was getting paid and who was perpetrating the fraud – pretending shit was good, while their ass was broke.

They were so caught up in their conversation that they didn't notice José until he was right on top of them. "Y'all smoked the whole blunt without me, huh?"

Terry ignored José, while Ramsey smiled nervously. She always felt uncomfortable around him, his smile, and eyes were mean.

Ramsey just wanted José to go away; he was used to the "Big Willies" – dudes getting drug money – throwing their weight around.

José offered a sardonic smile. "I didn't want none of that chuck weed anyway," he said. Then, he looked Terry up and down and added, "But I can sure go for a piece of that."

Terry turned to Ramsey. "I'm out. I'll see you later."

As she passed José, he reached out and grabbed her by the arm. "Bitch, I ain't say you could leave yet."

Ramsey stepped forward, "Damn, Ze, why you gotta come over here fuckin' with us." Without releasing his grip on Terry, José looked at Ramsey. "First things first, only my peoples call me Ze. And I know your punk-ass ain't tryin' to get in my business."

Ramsey backed off. Though he was a couple of inches shorter, he outweighed José by at least 20 pounds. But he knew he wouldn't get a fair one, and there was no guarantee Ricky would back him either.

Terry, however, had none of Ramsey's reservations. She snatched her arm from Jose's grip. "Get the fuck off me, and yo' mama is a bitch."

Jose's eyes narrowed, his face twisted up with anger. "You black bitch." He drew his hand back to slap her. "I'll beat the shit outta your freak ass."

Although his hand started forward, it never reached Terry. Suddenly, José was lifted off his feet, and where once his face showed contempt, it became a mask of pure fear as Man spoke in his ear, "You wanna hit somebody, hit me." With each word, Man's grip tightened on Jose's neck.

José struggled to get free; his toes barely touched the ground. Man pulled him closer. "Don't ever put your fucking hands on her again, and that goes for Ramsey too. If I even think you wanna do somethin' to either one of them, I'ma lose yo' ass."

José gagged as he tried to fill his lungs with air. Man smiled at the boy's troubles, and effortlessly tossed him against the building. "Now get yo' bitch-ass outta here,"

José scrambled to his feet. He started to speak, but Man turned his back on him and asked Terry if she was okay. She ran to Man and wrapped her arms around him. "Thanks, Man."

As Man comforted her, José slunk down the street with an enraged look in his eyes. But instead of stepping to Man, he chose to keep going.

Bigum, who'd watched the whole thing from outside the game room, came up the block and stood beside Man. Although Bigum didn't say anything, his presence spoke loudly.

Man gently stepped out of Terry's embrace and turned to Bigum. "Take Terry down to the game room."

Before she left, Terry stared adoringly at Man. "Thanks for saving me."

Man nodded, but said nothing. As Bigum and Terry walked off, he turned to Ramsey. "What was you thinking?"

"C'mon, Man. It wasn't my fault."

"Who fault was it then?"

"Me and Terry was just chillin'. You know how José think he can fuck with people 'cause he gettin' paid and got a crew. That red-top shit got him frontin'."

Man ran his hand across his head, like he was mixed up about something. "So you telling me that just because that chump is putting crack in little capsules and got a crew, you'd let him hurt Terry?"

"I tried to stop him. It wasn't like I didn't do nothin'. You know if I hada' stepped to him, they woulda jumped me, and maybe even gunned me down," Ramsey said in his defense.

A vein stood out along the left side of Man's temple, as he stared at Ramsey. Folding under Man's unyielding gaze, Ramsey looked away. Man stepped around him, forcing Ramsey to meet his eyes. "I don't know but one way to tell you this; I don't give a fuck what it cost you, if you got shortie with you, it's on you to make sure she safe." Man leaned in closer, and added in a voice only Ramsey could hear, "If you had to kill that piece of shit, so what? Life ain't always fair, but you still gotta live it."

Ramsey dropped his eyes. He wasn't sure he could do what Man said. It just wasn't as simple as Man made it sound. There were times when you couldn't stand up, even when you knew you should.

As if reading his mind, Man said, "It ain't always easy to do what gotta be done, but it's the only way a man oughta live. Or die, if he gotta."

"Damn, I really did try to stop..."

"You ain't try hard enough. You was a coward today, what about tomorrow?" Ramsey hung his head. Man's last words hit him hard. He had to fight back the tears that welled up in his eyes.

Man turned away from the boy, he had nothing else to say. He was full of smoldering emotions, and none of them offered solace to Ramsey. After all, he'd been about Ramsey's age when he chose to do what was right by taking a life for the first time. He had no use for weakness. Man knew from experience that only the strong survived–whether right or wrong.

## CHAPTER SEVENTEEN

Terry stood in the middle of the game room, giving a play-by-play of her run-in with José. Man watched, as the kids hung on her every word. She gave the story her own spin, changing what she didn't like. It reminded Man of the stories about him and the Ray brothers-told and retold until they'd grown into something that never happened.

Man thought Terry was enjoying the attention too much. It was if she didn't realize it was negative. She expected men to abuse her. In her mind it was normal for a woman to be manhandled, especially if the man had some type of power. She'd come to not only expect it, but also to accept it. What wasn't normal was that someone would save her.

Man felt a growing fury as images of black women being captured, beaten and sold into slavery, pimps preying on poverty stricken school girls, and fathers, husbands, and sons disrespecting wives, mothers, and daughters played out in his mind. Although he closed his eyes, the images remained. When he opened them, he realized he'd broken out in a sweat.

Bigum watched Man from behind the counter, and from the hard set of Man's jaw, he wondered how long José had to live. José had awoken a sleeping dog and found a bloodthirsty wolf. Maybe it was for the best. José was mean, and dangerous.

The sight of Jamel making his way over to Man interrupted Bigum's thoughts. At five-years old, Jamel was usually the youngest child in the game room and was treated as the baby by everyone. The game room provided the family setting missing from most of the kids' lives.

"Man, you sweating. You want some of my carrot juice?"

Man looked down at Jamel and the cup he held out in his tiny hand. He cleared the unpleasant images from his mind, took the cup from Jamel, then scooped the child up with his other hand and carried him over to Bigum. "No, thank you. You drink it. It's good for you," Man said as he sat the boy on the counter and handed him the cup.

Jamel giggled, "I know it's good for me, that's why I want you to drink some. You sweating and it's good for you too."

Bigum and Man looked at each other, then laughed. Jamel stared at them momentarily, and joined in the laughter.

After a few seconds, Jamel's laughter stopped and his face became serious. "It is good. And Mr. Bigum said, 'It'll make you big and strong like him,'" the child said with a huge smile. "That's why I always drink my juice. Don't I, Mr. Bigum?"

Man and Bigum laughed some more, and once again Jamel joined them. But after a moment he stopped, his little face serious again. "For real. Right, Mr. Bigum?"

"That's right Jamel," Bigum said.

Pleased with himself, Jamel smiled. "See, I told you, Man."

Man rubbed the child's head. "You're right as rain."

"How come rain is right?" Jamel asked.

Man and Bigum laughed until Jamel repeated his question. His eyes widened as he waited. "Huh, Man?"

"Check it out li'l man, the rain comes and wash everything clean and makes it right again," Man said.

Jamel thought about it for a second, decided that it didn't matter, and said, "I like the rain, but I'm gonna drink all my carrot juice so I can grow up to be just like you, Man. Uh-huh, I'ma be just like you and ain't gonna let nobody bother nobody either." He grabbed Man's hand and put it back on his head.

Bigum saw the anguish wash over Man's face. Man tried to smile, but his eyes wouldn't tell the lie.

"You have to be better than me, Jamel. You grow up and be a good person, okay?" Jamel looked from Man to Bigum, then back at Man. "But Man, you good. You always good to us, and we love you real hard."

Man was left speechless by the innocence of the child. Jamel smiled up at him, still holding on to his hand. Bigum gracefully saved Man from having to say anything more, as he lifted the child in one huge hand. "C'mon, li'l man."

Jamel laughed as he went airborne and began to scream with joy. Man sighed and thought how lucky the child was to not know the difference between good and bad, yet. "I'ma take Terry home."

Bigum nodded as some of the other children came to get in on the fun.

Man crossed the street with Terry and entered the small lobby of her building, a five-story, pre-war tenement. The whole building needed a good cleaning and paint job. The lobby and staircase were littered with trash; empty 40-ounce beer bottles, plastic quarter-water juice containers turned into crack pipes (a hole punched in the side, with the lid still intact), and a brown paper-bag full of garbage.

The building's poor condition was the rule rather than the exception throughout the neighborhood. Man understood that most of the landlords lived outside the community and didn't care. But what he couldn't understand was, why the people allowed them to get away with it? Why did people accept the substandard living conditions their landlords put on them, and why did they seem to fit right in with them? No one should relinquish control of his or her life and go along just to get along.

People had the right to create and control their own lives. Yet, in hundreds of neighborhoods throughout the country, a cloud of despair and desperation had settled and left the land barren and without hope. Man knew that the police and courts had turned their backs on these neighborhoods, and wondered if God had abandoned them also.

"What's wrong, Man?" Terry asked, noticing the sour look on Man's face.

Submerged in his thoughts, it took Man a moment to get back to reality. In that flash Terry became his daughter, Utopia. Though the feeling was fleeting, it was strong. He realized that had she lived, Utopia would be about Terry's age, and just as pretty.

Terry stared at him. "Man..." she said questioningly, concern evident in her voice. Experiencing a stab of loss and longing for the daughter he never had the chance to see grow up, Man's voice was strained, "Yeah, I'm alright."

"You sure? You don't look alright."

Man shrugged, sighed. "Of course I'm a'ight," he said, using the slang to lighten the mood. "But what about you? You a'ight?" He looked in Terry's face and smiled. He wanted her to know that she should always feel safe, to know that she was worthy of the best in life. He wished that he could make her and every other kid that came in the game room safe, but he was only a hood, nothing more.

Terry smiled up at Man. "I'm a'ight, especially when I'm with you."

Man missed the true meaning behind her words. "You gotta make sure that you're always alright. You can't let..."

Terry threw her arms around Man, cutting his words off. "Oh, Man, I love you."

Once more, the daughter he'd lost came into his mind and his heart. "Don't worry, I got you."

***

After dropping the money back into the red Fila gym-bag, Ricky leaned back in his chair, and smiled. The $27,000 was the day's take from his new spot.

The fact that he was getting paid without Man knowing about it made him smile. He enjoyed outsmarting Man. Ricky had learned to put up with Man's rules— drugs could only be sold from a couple of spots and only during certain hours, the street and building had to be kept clean, and the days of *BeatDowns* were over. With Man around, even the crack heads had rights. Man had changed everything, Ricky thought with a sneer. But when he remembered that he'd found a way to stay one step ahead of Man, the sneer was replaced with a smile.
Short-Dog watched Ricky put the money back in the bag. The $27,000 was the lowest take of the last ten days. The spot was blowing up— $33,000 a day was the average–however, ShortDog had little to show for the additional loot.

It was the same old story; Ricky got the cake while he got a few crumbs. Although he was the major reason for the success of the spot, his weekly salary had only increased to $2,200 from $1,500. A lousy $700 for helping to bring in all them gees. Unaware that Ricky was watching him, Short-Dog shook his head in disgust.

"What's wrong with you?"
Afraid of Ricky's temper, Short-Dog kept his thoughts to himself. "Ain't nothin'. I was just thinkin' about all this hustling shit."

"Dog, you know you ain't got no business thinkin'," Ricky said with an evil laugh. Short-Dog didn't answer. He could tell that Ricky was in one of his moods. Ricky threw the Fila bag to Short-Dog. "Put that in the safe."

As he put the money away, Short-Dog couldn't help but wonder why Ricky trusted him with so much, while treating him so bad? But Short-Dog knew the answer–Ricky had beaten him into submission.

Sitting in the living room, Ricky's thoughts mirrored those of Short-Dog. He knew he had instilled fear in the smaller man–a fear that would ensure everlasting loyalty. Ricky would send the little bastard straight to the everlasting, if he even thought about crossing him. As Short-Dog came back into the spacious living room, Ricky was laughing at his own joke. The East Seventy-third Street condo was Ricky's safe house for the cash from the new spot. Every ten days or so, he transferred the money to a stash only he knew about. He was blowing up, and Man's smart-ass ain't know shit about it.

He knew he was smarter than Man. The money that he gave Man each week was just part of how he made his money. If Man was so smart, he'd have a lot more going for him than that piece of shit game room. Ricky laughed again. Everybody thought Man was the shit, but the truth was–he was just shit.
Short-Dog cut into Ricky's thoughts, "You gonna tell Man about the new spot?"

It was like a trapdoor opened in the pit of Ricky's stomach. While fear bit him square on the ass, Ricky's ego forced him to ignore it. "Fuck Man. He don't know shit and don't need to. Shit, he's lucky to get what he gets from me, the dumb muthafucker."

Although Short-Dog nodded, he didn't share Ricky's feelings about Man's intelligence or luck. For once, he was glad he wasn't in Ricky's shoes.

"You hear 'bout Jose's run-in with Man?"

"Yeah, I heard about the fool. José thought he could challenge Man, but when he did his heart got weak." Ricky swelled up with self-importance. "See, Dog, you gotta play Man. He likes to read all them fucking books, and talk like he educated and shit. But he ain't nothing but a thug and if you remember that you can control him.

"Don't get me wrong. I know the muthafucker's dangerous, but so is those pits we keep in the basement of 442. Yeah, Man is like a pit-bull. He's a prize fighting dog," Ricky said, laughing at the thought.

Although Short-Dog remained quiet, his face became a mask of doubt. "What? You that scared of Man?" Ricky asked, as the laughter died in his throat.

"It ain't that. But just like them pits we fight, some of 'em is meaner and smarter than others, and even when they dying all they wanna do is kill something. It ain't that I'm scared of those dogs, I just stay the fuck out they way. Same with Man."

"Fuck Man," Ricky said, again. The last thing he wanted to think about was getting in Man's way. "Go down to the Yorktown Deli and get me two corn beef on rye, with mayo. And get yourself somethin'," he told Short-Dog, attempting to put Man out of his mind.

As he exited the building, Short-Dog was so deep in thought he didn't notice Pete watching him from the old white van parked on the corner. Pete smiled as he also made a mental note of the doorman's movements.

## CHAPTER EIGHTEEN

"Nez, I heard your boy beat up one of them drug dealers 'round the corner," Mr. Sam said with a judicial expression, as Nez stepped through the door.

Ms. Nez looked around the cleaners. The pictures on the walls showed the neighborhood in various stages over the last 35 years. However, missing, were the pictures of Man's sport achievements that had once hung proudly on the walls of Sam's Cleaners. "Sam, you liable to hear just about anything."

"So, you saying it didn't happen?"

"What I'm saying is that what you hear and what actually happened ain't always the same thing."

Mr. Sam snorted and shook his head in disgust. "I see you still defending that gangster. You, Mary, and li'l Nicki refuse to see the truth about Man."

"No, Sam, you see what you want to see. Especially when it comes to Man."

A wave of sadness washed over Mr. Sam's face, he grudgingly recalled the easygoing kid who'd been so helpful and considerate. Once, he'd thought that any man would be proud to call Man his son. The boy was a shining light—gentle, and intelligent, and as tough as any boy in the neighborhood. He'd been a source of pride for the whole community, a young man of character.

Pushing the memories aside, Sam said, "The boy went bad, that's all I need to know."

"I don't believe even you can think its that simple, "Ms. Nez said, rolling her eyes. Before Mr. Sam could respond, his wife, Ms. Mary, came through the door. "Hey, Nez. How you doin' girl?"

Noticing the strained expression on her friend's face, Mary knew something was wrong. Her eyes went from Ms. Nez to her husband. "Sam, I hope you ain't in here acting a fool? But for you it might not be much acting involved," she said, turning up her lips. When the silence grew, she asked, "Sam, please tell me you ain't going on about Man again?"

The continued silence answered her question. "I just mentioned that he beat up one of them dealers."

Ms. Mary regarded him skeptically. "Did you bother to mention the part about the li'l hoodlum attacking Terry?"

A haunted look came into Mr. Sam's eyes as his wife added, "That's right. Man was protecting another young girl. God knows the child is too grown, but God also knows she shouldn't be abused."

Ms. Nez nodded. "I'm just glad Man was there."

Ms. Nez waited for Mr. Sam to respond, but Ms. Mary saved him, "Sam, why don't you go down to the barbershop and spend some time with your cronies. Nez and I can watch the place for a while."

Mr. Sam nodded his agreement but reflectively said, "Now, you know I don't like leaving you alone..."

Ms. Mary quieted him with a waved of her hand. "First, I ain't alone, and second, we all know the stores around here are safer than those on Fifth Avenue—and we all know who we have to thank for that."

Mr. Sam started to say something, but again, his wife saved him. "You could use a break, and me and Nez could use the time to gossip."

"You know that's right, girl," Ms. Nez said, quickly. She placed her hands on her hips and added, "And tell them old fools, the Fillmore twins, to keep my name out of their mouths 'cause they too old for me."

The tension finally drained from Mr. Sam. "Nez, you know can't nobody tell them two what to do but you. You're the only one they listen to," he said with a smile.

"You know that's right," Ms. Nez replied. They all laughed as Mr. Sam left the cleaners. Ms. Mary asked, once the two women settled in behind the counter, "Ain't it nice to feel safe in your own store?" She sucked her teeth, "Now, you know how bad it was around here before Man came home."

"I know what you mean, but maybe you shouldn't have brought that up with that husband of yours'?"

"Sam is a fool sometime, Nez. I don't know what done got up his ass 'bout Man. And no, Man ain't perfect but the good sho' outweigh the bad. And just because he ain't the boy we watched grow up, it ain't necessarily bad."

"Ain't that the truth," Ms. Nez answered with a nod. A look of anguish crossed her face. "That boy's been through so much. I just don't know if he'll ever be right again?"

"Now, don't you worry? Remember, there's still Nicki," Ms. Mary reassured her friend.

***

Kid smiled as Pete made a rough sketch of Ricky's stash crib. Pete spoke with the confidence of someone who knew what he was talking about. He had done his homework. Over the past three weeks he'd spent hours casing the building on East Seventythird Street—the coming and goings of Short-Dog and Ricky, what doorman worked when, and how each handled their duties. Pete laid it all out.

The attention that Man, Eddie, and Born gave to Pete, as he spoke, confirmed Kid's belief that they had become major players. The three older men were top gunmen. Shit, Kid thought to himself, *Man's history alone was a muthafuckin' gangster movie.* Kid's smile grew as Pete finished up.

"Like I said, Short-Dog drops off the loot every day. What I don't know is how Ricky moves it to the next spot, but I think he lets the shit pile up first."

"How you know he moves it at all then?" Born asked.

Pete considered the question, before answering, "I know how Ricky thinks. Me and Kid used to work for his punk-ass. He don't trust nobody, and with the money rolling like it is, he ain't gonna let it just sit there."

Eddie glanced at Man. "What you think?"

Man looked straight at Eddie. "If Pete says it's ready... It's ready."

"What we looking at, paper wise?" Born asked, his tone all business.

Although Pete smiled, his tone matched Born's. "The key is catching them right before they move the loot, and if we do, $200,000 to $400,000, easy.

"Maybe we can find out where the mother lode is," Eddie said.

Kid spoke for the first time, "I don't know. I tried to get a handle on that, but couldn't. I watched his dope spot on 111th Street, right of a' Second Avenue, but all I came up with was the condo."

Eddie turned to Pete. "What you think?"

"I ain't get nothing else either. So, I don't know."

"Shit, I can work with the numbers Pete just threw out," Born said with a shrug. "If we can get at his other stash, good. But I'm ready for this now."

The plan came together quickly, with Born and Eddie taking the lead roles. Kid and Pete would provide support for them from a distance. This way, Ricky and Dog wouldn't see them, otherwise, Ricky and Short-Dog would have to be killed, and no one wanted that. Especially when the prospect of bagging them again in the future was so good. Why kill a good thing?

## CHAPTER NINETEEN

José sat in the dark room, licking wounds only he knew were there. He was afraid and ashamed. Although every light in the apartment was off, his mood was much darker. Too embarrassed to venture out, he'd been hiding out at his mother's since his encounter with Man. He knew Carlos could handle the workers and the block.

Surrounded with the dark and his hate, José needed to figure out a way to get Carlos to handle his troubles with Man. And if not Man directly, then somebody Man cared about. Somebody had to pay. José swore under his breath. And if he couldn't find anybody willing to do the job, he'd do it himself.

***

Short-Dog was late. He rushed around the corner, nearly knocking the older man off his feet.

His first instinct was to tighten his grip on the $32,000 in the Adidas bag. But once he saw that the man was blind, he became concerned with retrieving the man's cane and briefcase. Although the dark wrap-around glasses had remained securely in place, the man's cane and briefcase laid at Short-Dog's feet. He snatched them up. "Damn, I'm sorry. I ain't see you."

The blind man flailed around helplessly. Short-Dog almost laughed, but caught himself, and simply smiled. "Here you go."

The man reached out awkwardly, missing the cane and briefcase Short-Dog held out to him. Embarrassed, Short-Dog guided them into the guy's outstretched hands. The blind man gripped each item tightly, tilted his head, and used his hearing to get his bearing. "Thank you. I apologize for any trouble I've caused you."

Now, Dog really felt bad. The man actually thought it was his fault. "No! I wasn't looking where I..." Short-Dog swallowed the rest of his words, embarrassed, again.

"Well, that makes two of us," the man said with a laugh. "I'm late for a doctor's appointment so I was rushing."

"Nah, man, I shoulda! been watchin'..." Short-Dog closed his mouth and shook his head. The guy laughed at Short-Dog's self-consciousness. His conservative gray two-piece business suit, and heavy wool overcoat, hinted at reasons for his confidence–blind or not, he appeared to be a successful businessman. "It's okay. I just need to make it to my doctor's office." Short-Dog glanced at the bag of money in his hand, then let his eyes roam both ends of the street.

"How far you gotta go?"

The man hesitated. "I'm fine. I don't want to bother you."

Short-Dog realized that the guy was one of those disabled people who tried to do everything for themselves. He felt bad about bumping into the blind man, however. "It ain't no trouble, especially if the office is close by."

After another moment hesitation, the man said, "Well, it's just down the street...I think? Dr. Mackin's, at 532 Seventy-Third Street." Short-Dog smiled. "Word. I'm going to that same building."

The blind man smiled also. "Great! It'll really make things a lot easier for me."

***

Ricky glanced at his gold Rolex and shook his head. Where was the little punk? He'd told Short-Dog a hundred times about taking care of business the right way. Ricky snatched the remote off the couch and changed the channel to the music videos. Keith Sweat moved across the screen. Ricky smiled at Keith's begging-ass. He started to change the channel again, but the dancer caught his eye. "Damn, look at that fine ass video-ho," he said aloud. He might do a little begging himself for that, he thought with a smile. No – his smile turned predatory – he'd just hit her off with some money, and then dog her ass out.

Ricky knew all about women, and their shortcomings. His mother? What else was there to say–she was the perfect example of a useless life. And his wife, Pat … greedy and manipulative. Marrying her was the worst move he'd ever made. But now she knew too much about his business, so he couldn't get rid of her. Unless, that is, he really got rid of her.

His anger building, Ricky paced the large living room, pounding his fist into the palm of his other hand. He'd made up his mind–he was going to pimp-slap Short-Dog as soon as he walked through the door. Hell, maybe he'd do more than just slap the little punk, he thought.

When Short-Dog entered the lobby with the blind guy in tow, he didn't see the doorman anywhere. Just as he started toward the office, – he'd drop the blind guy off there and be on his way – a muscular man in blue workman's overalls with a canvas tool-bag over his shoulder came out and closed the door behind him.

The man's eyes locked on Short-Dog. With a sense of dread, Short-Dog instinctively backed up, bumping into the blind man. With nowhere to go, the guy in the overalls was on top of him before he knew what was happening. He couldn't believe how fast the guy had moved, nor did he know where the gun in his hand had come from–it hadn't been there when he first saw the man.

Before any answers could come, the blind guy was duct taping Short-Dog's hands behind his back. Short-Dog knew the guy's vision had to be 20-20 because of the speed and dexterity he was using.

Short-Dog was led into the elevator between Eddie, whose cane had been folded and slipped in his jacket's pocket, and Born. Once the elevator doors closed, Kid stepped out of the office wearing a jacket exactly like the building's doormen and sat behind the desk.

Ricky jumped up when he heard Short-Dog's key in the door. Ricky reached for the doorknob just as the door flew open and Short-Dog, wearing some type of black hood, crashed into his chest, knocking them both to the floor

With Short-Dog firmly on top of him, Ricky screamed, "What the fuck is..." The rest of his words died in his throat as the slim deadly looking black, Luger 9mm. pistol was shoved in his face.

Born Equality stared at him from the other end of the gun. "Don't move. Don't even breathe too hard."

Eddie locked the door, stepped around Born, and placed a black cloth bag over Ricky's head.

Ricky and Short-Dog was face down on the floor with their hands taped behind their backs. While Born searched the rest of the apartment, Eddie turned up the volume on the television. Squatting down between the two men, he said, "I'ma ask you some questions and if I get the right answers we'll be outta here in a few minutes." Eddie paused as Born came back into the room.

"But if I don't, we'll still be leaving, but y'all won't–not alive, anyway."

Ricky couldn't wait for Eddie to finish, it seemed, as he whimpered, "Please don't hurt me. I...I...I'll do whatever you want. Please..."

Born cut him off, "Shut the fuck up." It was always the ones who did all the tough talking that folded the quickest, he thought. Like the cell-gangsters in prison–tough as long as they were locked behind bars and you couldn't get at them. His voice filled with the promise of violence, Born went on, "Give me them scalpels. Ain't no need to waste bullets or words on this punk."

Eddie smiled at his partner's mood as he passed him the box of scalpels. The faint sound of steel against steel reached Ricky's ears over the noise of the TV.

As Short-Dog was about to yell that the safe was in the bedroom, Ricky moaned, "Oh my God. You don't have to..."

"Shut yo' bitch-ass up."

"Lets all chill," Eddie said as if they were all old friends discussing dinner plans.

Ricky couldn't help himself "Please don't hurt me. I got money and..."

"Didn't I tell you to shut the fuck up?"

"Let the boy talk. I mean, he is talkin' money," Eddie said pleasantly. "Okay, don't fuck this up. 'Cause if you do, I'm gonna give li'l man here a chance to outlive you. Now, where's the money?"

Short-Dog lay there wondering what Ricky would do, though deep in his heart he already knew. Ricky wasn't anyone's fool... he'd give up the cash and be glad to be rid of these crazy muthafuckers. After all, it's exactly what Short-Dog was gonna do if his turn came.

Born led Ricky into the bedroom. He had to hold him upright because with his legs weak, Ricky could barely move one foot in front of the other. In the bedroom, Born pushed Ricky in front of the safe and used one of the scalpels to cut his hands free, before pushing him to his knees. He removed the bag from Ricky's head. "Open the lock, but not the door."

Ricky fumbled with the dial, unable to get the sequence of the numbers right, and in a fear driven panic he lost control of his bladder. A dark, wet stain showed at his crotch and spread down his left pant leg.

Born shook his head in disgust. "Start over, and this time say the numbers out loud."

"Eighteen," Ricky recited in a shaky voice as he spun the dial. "Thirty-six." He exhaled. "Fifteen." With the smell of his own piss a far second to the smell of his fear, Ricky began to tremble as tears rolled down his cheeks. "I swear that's the right..."

"Push the handle up, fool."

As soon as Ricky pulled on the safe's handle they heard the lock disengage. Born pulled Ricky away roughly, re-taped his hands, put the bag back over his head and shoved him in a corner. Born opened the safe and smiled at the neat stacks of cash. The sight of the two handguns among the cash wasn't much of a surprise either.

Once the money was placed in the briefcase, and canvas tool-bag, they questioned Ricky about other stashes. After a few minutes Eddie and Born realized it was one lie after another, and the only way to check the lies was to take Ricky with them. They let it go–maybe another time.

Eddie made his exit first. A minute later, Born followed, and gave Kid a slight nod on his way out of the building. Seconds later, Kid slipped the doorman's jacket off and walked calmly away from the building.

Eddie hailed a cab on the near corner looking like just another businessman headed home. Born walked to the far corner and got in the van as Pete started the engine, then slowly drove off. Kid sung Prince's *Thieves in the Temple* as he went down the steps of the subway station, token in hand.

## CHAPTER TWENTY

Nicki beamed with pleasure as she introduced Ms. Nez and Ms. Mary to the room full of children. "Girls and boys, Ms. Mary and Ms. Nez have volunteered to spend the afternoon with us, and tell us about the history of Kwanzaa."

The two older women smiled. They often stopped by the center to drop off homemade treats for the children– at least that was the excuse they used, but the visits usually lasted hours. Nicki was thrilled whenever they showed up. She wanted the children to get some idea of the compassion and wisdom that she'd known as a child. Evidently the children recognized the sincere love coming from both women as they clapped and cheered.

Ms. Mary spoke first, "Who can tell us what Kwanzaa means?"
Little Jamel jumped up and said, "I can, Ms. Mary."

"Okay baby," she encouraged sweetly.

"It means first fruits, in Ze…hilly," Jamel said proudly.

"That's right." Ms. Nez responded, laughing softly. "Kwanzaa does mean first fruits in Swahili," she said, correctly pronouncing the African term. "It was first introduced in 1966, by Maulana Karenga."

"Shoot, that's old stuff. I thought it was new," exclaimed Kamira, a pretty, little, dark brown girl.

All five adults in the room laughed, soon it became contagious. The children joined in. Once the laughter died down, Ms. Mary continued, "Who knows the first principle of Kwanzaa?"
Five-year-old Mark stood up. "It's Umoja, and it means unity."

"That's right. And who knows the second?"

"I know, I know," six year-old Raheem shouted.
Ms. Mary smiled at the handsome, jet-black boy. "Okay, baby."

"I can't say the word, but Man said it means... Yeah, self-deter-mi-nation, and Nia, means purpose," the child beamed.

Ms. Mary glanced at Ms. Nez, who smiled. Raheem's responses set the room off–the seven principles were belted out and explained from every corner.

"We learned about Kwanzaa at the game room. Man and Mr. Bigum taught us," Jamel said with a huge smile, then his face became serious. "Man taught us about Nat Turner and Malcolm X too."

"Good Lord," Ms. Mary whispered, "Man is gonna have these children ready for anything."

"It's what we all need," Ms. Nez said.

Once the discussion was over, the cupcakes and fruit juices took center stage. While the children busied themselves with the treats, Nicki seized the opportunity to spend time with Ms. Nez and Ms. Mary. "I'm sorry there wasn't much for y'all to tell the children today."

"Nicki, you know Nez and me just like being around these babies."

"That's right," Ms. Nez said with a smile. "And between you and Man, they sho' don't need two old women teaching them nothing."

"You two are exactly what they need. It's important that the children connect with the past," Nicki replied vehemently.

"Oh, Nicki, will you relax." Ms Nez said lightly.

"Uh-huh, you know we here for these babies. But Nez is right. With you and Man on the job, these kids are in good hands."

"It's just that the odds are against them," Nicki said sadly.

"You right, but I feel better knowin' you and Man are around," Ms. Mary said.

"Ain't that the truth," Ms. Nez said. "Nicki, you doing a wonderful job, and with Man's help y'all just made the odds a lot better."

"I can't thank Man enough for all his help," Nicki said, her eyes full of emotion.

"Oh, I think you can figure out a way to thank him," Ms. Nez replied.

"Ms. Nez! Please don't start," Nicki said, unable to hide the smile in her voice. Ms. Nez's teasing was a game they both enjoyed.

"Nez, leave that child alone."

"Mary, you know as well as I do that our li'l Nicki is a full-grown woman, and Man's been mannish before he could walk." The older women giggled like teenagers while Nicki blushed some more. She didn't mind that she and Man were the source of their fun. "I guess I could cook him dinner one night," Nicki said in a sweet voice.

Ms. Nez sent a hand to her hip. "Well, it's okay to start in the kitchen with dinner, as long as desert is served in the bedroom."

Ms. Mary laughed as Nicki gasped. "Nez, you too much."

"Mary, long as you been married, I know you know just what I'm talking about. And if this chile don't, we sho' better teach her in a hurry," Ms. Nez said–her neck moving to emphasize her words.

"I think you're right, Nez."

Nicki looked from one women to the other, but before she could get a word in Ms. Nez continued, "We have to figure a way to get the two of them beyond their own foolishness, because the only thing in the way is them."

"You sho' right, 'cause any fool can see they love each other,"Ms. Mary replied with a nod.

Nicki opened her mouth to speak but nothing came out. When she finally got herself together she mumbled, "I can't believe you two. You're both—"

Jamel ran over and grabbed Nicki's leg. "Ms. Porter, can you call Man and tell him to come over? We miss him," the little boy said with a bright smile.

The women looked at one another, then back at Jamel. "Outta' the mouths of babes," said Ms. Nez.

## CHAPTER TWENTY-ONE

Eddie chose the Dupont Plaza because of its proximity to Ricky's stash crib. He liked the idea of celebrating so close to the scene of the job.

The suite, on the 24th floor, with its lush brown leather furniture in the front room and king-sized beds in both bedrooms, overlooked the F.D.R. Drive and the East River. Eddie turned his gaze from the view, and admired the thick carpet, small, well stocked bar, and 42-inch TV. He was glad he had decided to do the split at the suite. It added class to the whole thing. And having everybody together was good. The $382,000 was reason enough to celebrate, but just living through another job was the ultimate reason.

Every gunman knew the two constant threats that chased him – prison and death. To pick up the gun was to tempt both. The old-timers in the joint called sticking-up the *suicide hustle*. Each job could be your last; you could catch a body or become one. Kill or be killed. Eddie didn't waste time worrying, though. He was a proud member of what he knew was a dying breed– stickup kids, jack-boys, heist-men. It was his thing and he had love for anybody worthy of the profession.

"Man, your boys did good."

Man nodded at Eddie. "They get down," he said, simply.

"I know they was on time," Born said, with a nod of his own.

Kid laughed. "I know you muthafuckers laid that shit down with the quickness."

Born stood and took a slight bow. "That's how me and my man, Eddie King, get down. Bag 'em, quick, fast, and in a hurry." He laughed and winked at Eddie. "And we got some major shit in the works. Ain't that right, Eddie?"

Eddie nodded, reached into one of the plastic, drawstring, sneaker bags, and came out with bundles of cash. He hit Kid and Pete off, first. "That's 10% apiece." Then he sat a bundle in front of Bigum. "It ain't no fun if you don't get none, big man." He closed the bag and tossed it to Man.

Pete smiled, "Good lookin 'cause I ain't do much."

"You did your job," Eddie said.

Bigum was uneasy. Whenever Man, Born, and Eddie got together it unsettled him. They fed off each other's heart and strength, and might attempt something as crazy as jacking the Federal Reserve. "Thanks, but I don't need it," Bigum said, as he pushed the money back across the table.

"That's you," Eddie said, his eyes leaving no room for debate. "You know how we do. You down by law."

Born stood up, ending the issue. "It's just about party time."

"Word, where the party at?" Kid asked, as he jumped up and did a quick dance step.

"In twenty minutes, six fat-to-death strippers gonna walk through that door and the party'll be right here," Eddie said with a chuckle.

Bigum looked at Man and stood up. "Well, I got an early morning."

"It's just a li'l fun," Eddie said quickly. "You know, wine, women and whatever you might need to let the good times roll."

Man stood up also. "Y'all go head. Me and Bigum, we outta here."

Kid looked at Pete. "I'm hanging. What about you?"

"Y'all go head," Man repeated before Pete could answer.

"Hold up, I know y'all gonna bust one of these bottles of Don down with us before you roll out," Eddie said.

"Hell yeah, we'll have a drink, but you better bust two of them pieces 'cause me and Bigum can drink one by ourselves."

The room erupted in laughter–palms were slapped; fists touched, and quick embraces were exchanged. Since they shared the risks, it was only right that they shared the rewards.

Once Man and Bigum left, Eddie came out with a plastic baggie full of fish-scale. "Look-a-here," Eddie sang as he held the bag up. "Cocaine and freaks go together like stickup kids and somebody else's money."

"You ain't never lied 'bout that shit," Kid boomed, ready for whatever came his way.

"You a fool." Pete laughed.

"You ain't seen nothing yet," Kid replied, as he pulled out a handful of blunts along with a $50 sack of Tai-stick and another sack of Skunk. "This that exotic shit."

After he rolled a blunt from each bag, lit and passed them around, Kid took a one-and-one of coke. "Damn!" he said, as the cocaine seemed to travel straight up his nose to his brain. In minutes, the heavy aroma of marijuana added to the festive mood. The interruption of the phone only promised more good times.

Eddie hung the phone up. "The ladies are on their way up. Let the games begin, and remember, I got the hottest two shorties," Eddie said with a laugh, as he hung up the phone.

***

Bigum guided the big car onto the northbound lane of F.D.R. Drive. The Cadillac handled like a magic carpet. Bigum loved driving the vintage 1973 Sedan Deville–another joy he owed to Man.

Man had found the car sitting in the front yard of an elderly widow in Greensboro, North Carolina. He bought it, had it restored and transported to New York on a flatbed, with a cover on it, so that the 500-plus mile trip wouldn't blemish the precise restoration. The colors were the original dusk-blue and cloud-white. The leather interior had its original style and color, white. The car looked just as it did when it was rolled off the assembly line sixteen years before.
It had been a birthday gift for his first birthday outside the walls of prison in twenty-seven years. After just four months, he was riding in style. But, as much as Bigum appreciated the car, it was the least of all the things Man had given him.

For two years after Man was released, Bigum received a card with a $500 money order every six months. Inside each card were words of hope that meant more than the money. Each message told him that, just maybe, he could have a life after prison.

Along with the words, each card contained the same phone number. Night after night, Bigum stood in his cell, looking through the bars, wondering if he'd make it out, and what he'd say if he called the number. He had no doubt that the number would lead him to Man; unless Man was dead–then it would lead him to Man's grave.

Even in death, Bigum knew Man would keep his word. That was just the way he was. He said what he meant and meant what he said. But Bigum had often wondered if Man would make it out there or if he even wanted to. It seemed as if he was in a rush to submerge himself in death's current just to be carried away. Nevertheless, he continued to surface.

Two days after his release, Bigum made the call. And, as they say, *the rest is history.* Man gave him a job at the game room, a chance for a new life and family–Man, Kid, Pete, and the children.

Today, he was part owner of the game room, surrounded by the laughter of kids who needed and loved him, people who respected him, and had more money than he could use. It was all because of Man too. The car paled in comparison.

Bigum thought about the bond Man had with Eddie and Born, along with the one he shared with June and Shine; Man would kill, and die for each of them. Bigum knew that Man felt the same way about him also. Even so, it was all on Man's terms– killing and dying were things Man felt comfortable giving. But other things, like himself, he just couldn't give. The only exception was with the kids –Man couldn't deny them anything. His love for them was without restraint and full of hope. Still, Man's terms came into effect–the hope was for them and not him.

"What, pray tell, has you in such a pensive mood big fellow?" Man asked, shaking Bigum from his thoughts.

Bigum laughed, he wasn't sure Man would want to hear what he was thinking. He gave Man a quick glance. "Pensive? Now, that's a word you wouldn't have used fifteen minutes ago. And your proper grammar wouldn't have come up either."

Man laughed and shook his head. "True. But that's only because I adapt to the milieu I find myself in. And since I'm self-educated I don't need to pretend – I just like to talk slick sometime."

They both laughed, then Bigum got serious. "It's funny, as well-read and sharp as Eddie and Born are, you'd think they'd have more on their minds than women and drugs. All three of y'all can hang with Harvard grads and hold your own in any boardroom. But, all y'all wanna do is live on the edge and push as hard as you can. Cain't nobody keep taking risks like y'all do and not get caught out there sooner or later."

Bigum paused, and sighed, "I know you love 'em and I respect the bond y'all got. But y'all cain't live the way you always did just because you always did. See, sometime, in order to keep on living we gotta let go of what helped us survive."

Man remained silent, his eyes on the murky waters of the passing river. He reached for the cassette adaptor and put Johnny Hartman's *Lush Life* in, and slid it in the caddie's eight-track. The sound was sweet and pure. The JVC sound-system was the car's only concession to modern technology.

Man let the title cut soothe him for a minute. "Eddie and the God know what they doing," he said, his eyes roaming the darkness outside. Hartman's rich voice and Coltrane's tenor sax, filled in the silence following Man's words.

Man pulled his mind from the music, his eyes from the dark, and settled them on Bigum. "Life is a contradiction; we live just so we can die. Yeah, we can kick it with Harvard grads and run a boardroom, but don't none of that mean shit. We from the street, straight hood and ain't nothing gonna changed that. It ain't about living on the edge. It's about living our way. We can't go along just to get along."

The silence between them settled in the car again like misty rain – remarkably subtle, yet undeniably there. After a while, the tape stopped. Man took his time picking out another cassette. He finally settled on Curtis Mayfield's *Super Fly* and let the words of the title track tell the story: *Super Fly, you gonna make your fortune by and by, but if you lose don't ask- no questions why; the only game you know is do or die...gambling with the odds of fate.* The lyrics grabbed Man while they spoke of hopelessness.

Bigum spoke, "Man, it don't have to be that-a-way no mo'. You got money now. You can start your life over and—"

"Start my life over?" Man jumped in. "What would I wanna do some shit like that for? It's been hard enough already. I ain't ask for none of this shit, but since it's the hand I was dealt I'm gonna play it out."

"You ain't gotta play nothing out," Biguin shouted, then caught himself– it hurt him to hear Man resigned to a life without hope – and continued in a pleading tone, "You can decide to live your life anyway you want. You and Nicki could start—"

Man cut him off again, his voice tight, "I'm living my life my way. And Nicki? She ain't got nothin' to do with none of this. Everybody gotta do they own thing."

Bigum kept his eyes on the road. He wondered if he'd said too much, but he couldn't stop himself. "What about Kid and Pete, who life they living? They caught up in this thing with you. It seems to me they living the life you, Born and Eddie chose."

Man grunted out a mirthless laugh. "On the real side – we ain't chose nothing. It's just what we got, so we decided to be damn good at it." Man paused, rubbed a hand across his face and added, "Kid and Pete? They wasn't no choirboys when they got with me. They was already slinging steel. I just gave 'em the game raw and uncut."

Bigum shook his huge head. "So you think it's okay them boys up there doing drugs and Lord knows what else?"

Man laughed softly. For a man who had killed two men with his bare hands, Bigum's virtuous notions were as good as any Sunday-going-to-meeting-person Man knew. "That what else, is called fucking. Something both of them do a lot of– at least, I hope they do. And the drugs – ain't neither one of them gonna do nothing they don't wanna do."

"You coulda told 'em to leave. They would'a listen to you."

"Yeah, they probably would'a. But if what they wanted was back there they'd have found it someplace else. I know when I was doing that shit I always found it without looking too hard. "I told you about my first couple of years home–coke and freaks was my cure for this fucked-up life you say I can start over. Like I said, everybody gotta do they own thing, and bet Kid and Pete are safer with Eddie and the God than they'd be with their own fathers."

Bigum remembered the stories of all the women and drugs. Man hadn't tried to justify it, just told it like it happened. But Bigum knew that while Eddie did it for fun and Born to unwind, Man had needed to dull the pain of his very existence. It hadn't worked so he had backed away from the women, drugs and partying. Now, a few women could expect nothing more than the occasional late night booty-call from Man. He didn't believe he had anything more to offer them.

Bigum got off at the 135th Street exit. He didn't know what else to say. He didn't have the answers, and wasn't even sure there were any.

Man leaned his head back. He inhaled deeply, then exhaled. In a voice that said he'd heard and seen it all, and was only waiting for the ending, he said, "I'm a back-alley man, somebody who moves good in the dark–the kinda guy you don't want your daughter around or your mama to meet. But the kind you want around when you got trouble.

"I'm good for taking care of trouble, but I ain't gonna get no invite come Christmas. But I ain't mad or even disappointed about none of that. It's okay. I ain't ask for this life but I'm living it, and with as little regret as possible. Although I'd like to understand what all this shit means, I don't expect to. So, I just live. And in the end, just die. But even that'll be my way– probably with my boots on and with some muthafuckers to keep me company."

Bigum looked over at Man and had to fight back the tears. He wished that he could change Man's outlook, but didn't know where to start. He thought about Nicki, but said, "Two days after you got out, your man, Sonny Red, walks up to me in the yard and says, 'Don't worry,

Bigum, Man gonna live forever. The righteous ones never die.' All us old timers was thinkin' about you. So, back-alleys, dark moves or whatever, you ain't never been nothin' but the pure truth, and bet a few old cons knew that from day one."

Man smiled as he thought of Sonny and the others. He'd picked their brains for every nuance of the game. They'd given him insight and direction, and he'd studied as if he was acquiring a Master's Degree. And, in fact, he was–Master of the game. He felt that much of his success was owed to them –men with bloody histories and bleak, ominous futures. They were his mentors. He'd paid them with regular money orders since he got out, and he'd have something for them if they ever made it home. Men that stood strong should be remembered, Man thought. So Bigum's last words meant something.

Bigum interrupted his thoughts. "Man, you wanna stop by Reliable's and get somethin' to eat?" he asked as he turned up 145th Street.

"I guess I better eat if I'm gonna live forever," Man said easily. Their laughter lightened the mood, as the big car crossed Lenox Avenue.

# CHAPTER TWENTY-TWO

"Well, that about wraps it up for today, Mr. Jenkins," Mr. Hines said as cordial as possible, considering the circumstances. His office, the Securities and Exchange Commission, was conducting interviews with employees of Tyrone's firm. Ty had been with Whitman, Brown and Pauls – one of the country's largest trading, investment banking and brokerage firms – for the last eleven years.

After graduating from Harvard, Tyrone had spent three years at a small investment firm in mid-town. It was there that he'd made a name for himself in the financial district. Tyrone Jenkins was famous for his aggressive trading style and acute knowledge of the market. His success attracted quite a few of the larger firms; Lehman Brothers, American Express and Morgan Stanley. Whitman, Brown and Pauls had offered the best opportunity and greatest challenge.

When he came aboard, Ty was the third ranking minority employee. That distinction, however, only placed him in the middle of the pack of the firm's 300 employees. But that would change in only three years. His fast deals and growing client-roster propelled his ascent through the firm at a record pace. Now, as a valued and respected member of the company, and with only the President and two managing partners holding more clout, Tyrone Jenkins had arrived. He'd gotten there with hard work. He was known as much for his business acumen, as the long hours he put in. Which is why he couldn't understand what was happening. Why did it seem like Mr. Hines' investigation was focusing on him? Maybe I'm being paranoid, he thought. No. After three meetings with Hines, Tyrone knew something was very wrong. Also, he detected subtle changes in the attitude of the firm's hierarchy–the higher-ups seemed to be distancing themselves from him.

Tyrone sat at his desk, trying to make sense of it all. Although Hines had left ten minutes ago, the man's patronizing and accusatory manner still lingered. The office seemed smaller, confining. Ty felt like the walls were closing in on him. He stared at the picture of his family on his desk. Just looking at their happy smiles usually relaxed him, but not today.

He needed to get out of the office. Maybe a walk would clear his mind. "Ms. Minns, I'm going out for a while," Tyrone said as he stepped into the outer office.

"What about your two-o'clock, with Mr. Booth?"

"Oh, I completely forgot about it," Tyrone said embarrassed that he'd forgotten the appointment. "Call and cancel it, but set up another date."

"Okay," the secretary replied giving Tyrone a look of concern. She admired her young boss; his confidence and good manners were refreshing.

The annual bonuses and birthdays off were impressive, but not as much as the man himself, she thought. His work ethic and commitment to his family and community were traits she wanted her own sons to have. So, even though she'd been with the firm for 14 years before becoming Tyrone's personal secretary, her loyalty was to the man, not the firm.

As an African-American woman, Ms. Minns knew the struggles that Black men faced on a daily basis. Fortunately, she had raised two sons who had managed to avoid the drugs, gangs, and prison sentences that snared so many young Black men. With the way the media portrayed Black men, you'd think they were the second coming of Genghis Khan. However, Ms. Minns knew better and wanted to see the best in Black men–something that Tyrone Jenkins personified. Tyrone was honest, strong and compassionate. He mentored both of her boys, giving friendship and guidance.

In Ms. Minns' eyes, Tyrone was as close to a saint as humanly possible, and beyond the petty water cooler gossip that he'd become the subject of lately. Her first encounter with the scandalous whispers happened to be her only encounter. She had unleashed the fury of a mama-bear on every loose tongue in earshot.

Though Ms. Minns was determined to put a stop to the rumors, Ty had ignored them and went about his job as if nothing was wrong. But today he seemed preoccupied. "Everything all right?" She asked timidly. She didn't want to upset him anymore, but she was concerned and couldn't help asking.

"Yes, everything's fine," Tyrone said, matter-of-factly.

Ms. Minns' voice became stronger, "Fine?"

Tyrone stopped, his head dropped, but he couldn't think of what to say. Ms. Minns went on, "You know, we can't plan the weather. It doesn't matter where we live or even how we live, stormy weather finds us. No, we can't control storms, but we can control how we weather them." As his head came up, she busied herself with papers on her desk.

Tyrone sighed. "How come you're so smart?" he asked, forcing out a smile. "I'm sorry for being..."

"You don't need to apologize. You just need to get back to being yourself."

"I'm going to disagree and agree, respectively," Tyrone said with a smile that was no longer forced. "I do need to apologize and I am. I'm sorry for brushing you off. And, I do agree, I need to get back in step."

They both laughed as the tension disappeared like steam out an open window. "Would you please call Mr. Booth and reschedule him at his convenience. And no, everything isn't fine. As you probably heard, there's an ongoing SEC investigation." He inhaled deeply, took a moment to let it out, then continued, "But whatever the problem is, I had nothing to do with it. I've done nothing wrong, and I refuse to be anyone's whipping boy."

"Now that's the attitude I'm used to in this office!" Ms. Minns said. "And whatever it is, we're going to beat it."

Ty nodded. "Thanks. I may be gone the rest of the day, but don't worry. I'm going to see about some raingear and storm windows," he said, leaving the older woman smiling.

## CHAPTER TWENTY-THREE

The sweat dripped off Eddie's body. Kid circled him, feinted left, and then quickly came in from the right. Eddie smiled as Kid hit the mat for the fourth time during their workout at the Capoeira Academy.

It was their fifth practice of the Afro-Brazilian martial art Capoeria since their arrival in Miami seven days ago. Eddie was enjoying himself, thinking about how much better he liked the warm, sunny, weather when he landed on his back. He smiled up at Kid, then sprang up without using his hands — Capoeira concentrated on the use of the legs and feet.

"Now that was good. I guess I gotta keep my eye on you, huh?"
Kid only nodded. He didn't want to take a chance with a slick reply and end up on his back again. He feinted one way, then the other, coming back with a leg-whip. But for all his effort he connected with empty space as Eddie flipped over him, landed behind him, and expertly dropped him to the mat again.

"Shit!" Kid exclaimed as he struggled to his feet. "I had yo' ass,".

"Yeah, you did, but you got had in the end," Eddie said with a smile. "But you getting the hang of it."

"Yeah, I'm gettin' the hang of busting my ass on this fuckin' mat."

"Nah, Joe. You gettin' it. You a soldier, and in no time yo' shit gonna be bumping."
Kid laughed at Eddie's D.C. slang. Eddie reminded him of Man—one minute he was talking like a professor, and the next he'd kick it straight from the hood. And with Eddie, it might be any hood. Eddie played the whole east coast and even hit Detroit and Chicago from time to time. *Eddie was Man, that is, if Man ever decided to have some fun,* Kid thought to himself, laughing.

"What's so funny, young'en?"

"Ain't nothin', I was just thinking about Man."

"Yeah, that's my boy. I wish he was in on this. But you, me and the God'll be enough to loose these chumps from that paper."

"When is Born getting here?"
Eddie shrugged. "Probably in three days or so. We got time before the move."

"I'm ready," Kid said, as he tried a quick thigh-kick that Eddie effortlessly sidestepped.

"Damn, I forgot that Man had you read *The Art of War*. But I read that shit too," Eddie said with a chuckle.

Both men focused on their workout for the next hour–Eddie teaching, Kid learning, but neither giving much ground.

Back at the hotel in Palm Beach County, Kid took a quick shower, but had to wait while Eddie soaked in the large tub.

Kid was anxious to get out and take in the sights. He'd been cooped-up, working out, or checking out the job. He was ready for some fun and games. He'd heard all about the hot strip joints in Miami and wanted to see those rump-shakers for himself

Eddie came out of the bathroom wearing baggy shorts, a ripped-up muscle shirt, brushing the waves into his freshly cut fade. Kid looked down at Eddie's outfit, then at his own. Something was wrong.

While he was dressed to party — casual, gray blue herringbone silk slacks, a blue-heather silk tee shirt and Polo loafers of the same color, Eddie was dressed to chill inside the suite for the seventh straight night.

Eddie stopped in mid-stroke, held the brush above his head and gave Kid an incredulous look. "I know you ain't plan on going out," he said as he resumed brushing. "This is business, we here to set this shit up. We can workout, do a li'l swimming and shopping, but the main thing is to set this shit up right. That's why we staying way out here in Palm Beach County with white folks. So when the God show, we can rock and roll and be out."

Kid nodded. "I know. I was just tryin' on my gear."

"Okay," Eddie said with a smile. He knew he had rained on Kid's parade. "Put a towel against the door so we can spark up a blunt."

Kid smiled at that. "Word. I wanna check out that Hawaiian bud we coped."
They passed the blunt back and forth—talking shit and making plans for money that still belonged to someone else.

Eddie was cool with Kid's playful ways because he knew it was possible to joke without being a joke. He knew the younger man got down for his.

"Yo, Eddie, Man know that Capoeira shit?"
"Hell yeah. Man learns shit just so he'll know it. Now, me? I learn shit just so I can use it."

"What about the God?"

"Yeah, his big ass learned it too; just to prove he could. He damn sure don't need to know the shit. The God is stronger than the average three men and meaner than the average four," Eddie replied with a laugh.

Kid joined in, he appreciated any reason to laugh. "Word! So you sayin' Born is stronger than you and Man put together?"

"Hell no! I said he was stronger than average fools. You know ain't nothing average 'bout me and Man."
Kid laughed again. "True."

"But on the real – Born can bench-press close to 400 lbs., and squat 600 lbs."

"Word?"

"That's word."

"Damn, I can see why he don't need to know nothin' but how to break a muthafucker in half."

"Yeah. When we was up north in white-folks prisons, Born snapped some fuckin' handcuffs."

"Get the fuck outta' here," Kid said with raised eyebrows.

"Word up. Check it out; he was cuffed behind his back too. Them cracker-ass guards thought because the God was cuffed they could beat on 'im, but when he snapped the fuckin' cuffs they looked at them punk-ass sticks they had and got the fuck outta there."

"Damn!" Kid said, his eyes begging for more.
Eddie looked at him and smiled. "Yeah, the God the real deal. You see how the muthafucker built, and all that shit is rock hard. Word, back in the days we used to call his ass Rock."

"Rock?" Kid asked with a laugh. "Yeah, that shit fit like a hot ho on some hard pipe."
Eddie shook his head at Kid's wit and laughter. The boy was all right.

Kid stopped laughing and asked, "Why he got down with the Five Percent thing?"
"Check it out. Back in '72, when we first came through the 'El'— it was our first time in a state prison, and Elmira had a rough rep back then — we had to get busy and put steel in a few chumps. So, after we got outta' the box we ended up in Comstock — that joint was called gladiator school — and ran into Born Allah, one of the 9 First-born, and—"

"The First-born 9?" Kid cut in. "What's that?"

"Alright, when the Father, Clarence 13X, left the Nation of Islam and started the Five Percent Nation, Born Allah., Uhara and seven other brothers were the first Gods. So they was the first-born...I guess, to the nation of Gods."

"That's some deep shit. But how come they was—"

"Nah, man. We ain't gonna do this all night and I ain't even sure about all this. You gonna have to save all that shit for the God, or even Man. He know all that shit too."

Kid was puzzled. "How come Man know 'bout the Gods?"

"Man know every fuckin' thing 'cause he read every fuckin' thing and ask a million questions like somebody else I know," Eddie answered with a sideward glance.

They both laughed, then Eddie said, "Kid, if you roll another blunt I'll tell you the story of the Riverridge."

"The what?" Kid asked, as he reached for the box of cigars.

Eddie stood up and spread his arms out. "The muthafuckin' Riverridge—the nastiest, freakiest strip joint ever." Eddie smiled and rubbed his hand together. "Listen, this spot was the shit. I mean the kinda spot where anything goes. It was uptown, behind some old warehouses over on…"

## CHAPTER TWENTY-FOUR

Thump, thump, whang! Man's punches echoed through the basement. He worked the heavy-bag with a vengeance as he slid from side to side, punches landing with each move. He tried to chase his past sorrows away with the force of his blows. He punished the bag; every blow for the hard blows life had hit him with. Each punch was a savage response to his suffering. Sweat glistened on his bare torso, his muscles flexed. *Thump, thump* – double left jab. *Whang* – straight right. *Thump* – jab. *Whang! Whang!* – double hook! Man was in a rhythm, his footwork and punches created a symphony of controlled violence.

His two-hour workout was coming to an end (sit-ups and crunches followed by forty-minutes of jumping rope, with a short stint on the speed-bag). This was his tenth and final 3-minute round on the heavy-bag. Man shifted to his right, circled the bag and flicked out a left jab. His punches were still sharp, crisp, and powerful.

He shot a left hook off a jab, followed it with a straight right cross. The sand-filled bag and thick chain danced to Man's hardtime boggie. He began to set up another combination, but one of the red warning lights flashed.

He moved quickly and silently to the table, ripping the baggloves off. He reached under the towel. Once the comfortable weight of the blue-black Colt .45 was in his hand, he exhaled and wiped the sweat from his face.

He stepped into the dimly lit passageway, checked the second warning light. It was also lit. Whoever had entered the basement had continued on to the small apartment down there. Man relaxed. He moved stealthy down the narrow corridor– his bare back nearly touching the rough concrete wall. As he neared the apartment's front door, he heard furtive movements inside. Whoever was there wanted to go undetected, but their unfamiliarity with the layout of the place betrayed them.

Man reached the door, steadied himself and dropped into a crouch. He slid to the side, his back against the wall, turned the doorknob, pushed the door open and slipped inside. He closed the door behind him; shut his eyes for a moment – enabling them to adjust to the dark quicker. He opened his eyes and scanned the room–a small study with shelves of books lining two walls and a large ornate wall-cabinet on another. The cabinet was made of African mahogany, with rainbow-colored stained glass, and delicate pieces of crystal and jade figurines on its shelves. In the middle of the room sat a small escritoire. On it was a hand-carved, ivory, African chess set, with red and green pieces in the shape of huts, masks and weapons. On the back wall, overlooking the writing desk and chess set, hung Romare Bearden's painting: *Serenade.* The room was masculine with brown and beige, straight-backed leather chairs.

Man quickly searched every inch of the room before he settled his hard gaze on the kitchen. After making sure no one was hiding there, he moved on to the bathroom. With its door to the right of the bedroom, the two doors formed an L-shape.

He had left both doors open. Now they were closed. Although he moved toward the bathroom, he remained conscious of both doors. He pushed the bathroom door open–nothing. That left the bedroom. Man quickly turned the doorknob and slid in with gun in his right hand, and murder at the tip of his trigger-finger. In a second – maybe less – he sighted his target! The low glow from the brass lamp on the nightstand made it easy.

He had already started to apply the pressure that would add another kill to his name. The gun aimed at the shape on the king-sized bed. It took enormous strength to stop the pressure in time. In a sense, it was easier for Man to kill than it was for him to care enough to spare a life.

With gun aimed, finger on the trigger, and his face set as tight as a junkie's who'd just watched his last fix spill to the floor, Man beat down the instinct to kill and sighed.

Laying naked in the middle of the huge bed, Terry gasped– fear and confusion ran across her pretty face. Instinctively, she tried to cover herself with her arms. "Man, I was..." Her words, along with her eyes, were lost in the depths of the gun's barrel. But worst than that black hole at the end of the barrel, was the unrelenting look in Man's eyes.

Man checked the room, then lowered the gun. "Terry, what the hell you doing?"

Still unsettled and unsure, Terry said, "Man, I... I came to spend the night with you." Man's expression went from anger, to confusion, to sadness. Man, his eyes hooded, looked at Terry's naked body, leaned back against the Sheraton armoire. He let the adrenaline drain away. He'd been ready for a battle, but not the one laid out in front of him.

His silence restored the girl's confidence. Terry stretched her body out and put her hands behind her head. A sultry smile danced on her face. Her young, firm 36-C's with their large, brown areola, and raspberry-shaped nipples screamed for attention.

Man stayed where he was. Not speaking, and the expression on his face giving away nothing. His eyes were distant. But Terry's eyes were a wanton invitation. The smile slipped off her face as she ran her tongue over her lips. She bent one slender, shapely leg at the knee. Her foot flat on the bed, she swayed the leg from side to side.

Each time her leg moved away from her body it gave Man a view of her sex. She lazily swayed her leg farther out, closed her eyes and let one hand drift across her flat stomach. With the heat mounting between her legs, she glided her fingers through her fine pubic hair. In seconds, she was dripping. She raised her fingers and sucked hungrily, then returned them. Her eyes closed in rapture.

Terry parted the lips of her womanhood and slowly began to rotate her hips. She wanted Man. She'd dreamt of this moment for so long, and it was finally about to happen. She heard Man move toward her, she waited, bit down on her bottom lip and opened her legs wider.

The weight of the sheet hit her like a brick dropped from a skyscraper. Her eyes flew open. The sheet lay across her body; the fantasy gone.

"Get dressed. I'll take you home," Man said roughly.

Still, she tried him. "But... I just..."

"Get dressed," he said, cutting her off and closing the door behind him.

Although she dressed quickly, Terry took her time leaving the room. As she entered the study timidly her eyes avoided Man. She looked everywhere but at him.

Man motioned for her to take a seat across from him as he continued to study the chessboard, contemplating how best to protect his king without exposing his queen. The dilemma had him stuck. Finally, he decided the only thing to do was to give up a piece for a positional advantage.

He finally looked up from the board and studied Terry with the same intensity. "You shouldn't have come down here," he said, in a low but hard voice.

She still couldn't meet his eyes. She didn't know what to say. Her head hung; there was no eye rolling, no teeth sucking, no smart remarks with neck movement. Man had made her feel like a child.

"You can't just run and sleep with any man, it's not..."

"You ain't just any man. I love you, and you take care of me. So why can't I take care of you?" Terry asked, her eyes settling on the chessboard.

Man stood, ran his right hand over his jaw and shook his head. How could he tell her that love and sex didn't necessarily go handin-hand? He wanted to tell her that love was something special. Instead, he barked, "Fuckin' ain't love; you too young to know that though. And you need to stop actin' so damn grown."

Emotion played across her face like a prediction of bad weather on the six o'clock news. Terry's face went from hangdog, to pouting, to indignation. "Man, you ain't gotta be no certain age to know about love. And I ain't acting grown — this is who I am. What? You want me to be something I ain't just because you don't want me?" she said, finally meeting his eyes.

Man held her stare. She was young, but on the verge of womanhood. Man tried to look behind her eyes. What was there? He couldn't tell. He had been about her age when he'd become a father. But that was different—he had loved Rita and they had planned a life toget …

What did it matter? In a blink of an eye it was all gone; love or not, special or not. It didn't matter. Maybe Terry was right, he thought. She just wasn't right for him. All he would do was corrupt her young-ass.

He watched the tears well up in her eyes. But he didn't try to ease her pain. His gift wasn't in giving comfort or preserving dreams. He dealt in paybacks and payoffs. "No, I don't want you to be somethin' you ain't. But you oughta wanna be everything you can and fuckin' grown men ain't gonna help with that."

"Man, I can't help being young. But being young don't stop me from being a woman either, do it?"

Man considered what she said, then replied in a gentle voice, "No, it don't. But fuckin' won't make you a woman. Only time and the way you carry yourself will do that."

The tears came. She'd fought them as long as she could. Man watched them fall, and was glad that she, at least, could still cry. "Go wash your face so I can take you home."

*** 

Short-Dog sat in his red, kitted out Honda Accord, listening to Keith Sweat's *"You May Be Young, but You're Ready.* He worked the gooseneck, blasting the system. The low-riding skirt made the car look like a spaceship. The dark tinted-windows added to the effect, as did the shiny $3,000 rims.

He had made the late night trip back to the block in search of some action. He'd brought five blue-caps and wanted some head. Short-Dog laughed—fair exchange ain't no robbery, he thought. Shit, $25 for a little head was more than fair.

He looked up at Vicky's building and laughed again. He wondered if her freak-ass mama was on the loose. Vicky had always thought she was too good for him. She only messed with Big Willies. But now that her mom's was smoking on the low, he'd show her who was too good for who. The fact that he'd grown up with the girl or that she'd never actually done anything to him never entered his mind.

Just as he reached for the door, he saw Terry coming out of the basement with Man. "Damn?" He nodded his head. "No wonder Man stay lookin' out for shorty," he announced to the empty car, as he watched them cross the street and head for Terry's building. He smiled.

"Now, that's how you do it. All the young, hot, pussy you can get at. Ain't nobody playin' like Man. Ze and Ricky don't know shit. When I step out, I'ma do it like Man. Nah, fuck that. Bigger and better, that's how I'ma go."

He turned the radio down and scooted lower in his seat. But as he watched Man walk behind Terry's swaying hips and fat ass, he knew Man wouldn't notice a 747 trying to land on the sidewalk right now.

Throughout his life, Short-Dog had learned to use his lack of size to his advantage. His greatest strength was that people saw him as harmless and disregarded him. His eyes narrowed with contempt. Soon all the jokes and disrespect would stop. He could feel it in his heart–he was destined for the power of a top player.

Watching Man leave Terry's building, he wondered if Man had got a little quick head in the hallway. He giggled at the thought. Some goodnight head beat a kiss anytime. Once Man disappeared into the basement Short-Dog straightened up and pumped up the music.

## CHAPTER TWENTY-FIVE

Bigum sipped from the large mug of coffee as he stared at the headline of the morning paper: Whiz Kid Investment Manager Arrested. While the photo of Tyrone Jenkins being led out of his office in handcuffs disgusted Bigum, it didn't disturb him as much as the smug look on the faces of the two agents flanking Ty.

He became more disgusted as he read the article. True to form, the Post already had Tyrone tried and convicted. The word *allegedly,* was only there for legal window dressing. The more he read, the tighter his jaw muscles got. "Aw bullshit," his voice boomed around the small office. The article angered him so much, he was glad it was too early for any of the kids to be in the game room–he didn't want them to see him in such a foul mood.

The paper claimed Tyrone had cheated clients out of millions of dollars in a kickback scheme. The article accused him of cherry-picking–picking trades that were winners for himself while steering his clients to losers.

The accusations riled Bigum. Here was a man who had worked his way through school and graduated with honors. He was a success, and a credit to the community. He gave something back–donations to charities, assisting and mentoring youngsters. But none of that mattered. As a Black man he was guilty until proven innocent.

Bigum relaxed his grip on the mug and put it down "Ain't this some bullshit!" his voice boomed once more. He'd known Tyrone for years. The man was honest. From the start he had explained that any business he handled had to be legit. The man wasn't just honest; he was a man with convictions and the strength to stand by them. Hell, next to Man, Tyrone was the best man he knew, Bigum thought, as the office door opened.

As Man entered the room, Bigum pulled his attention from the paper. He smiled for a moment. Man had somehow raised the gate and opened the door to the game room without making a sound. Remembering the paper, Bigum's smile disappeared. "Did you see the paper yet?"

Man studied Bigum for a few seconds before replying. "No. But I know about Ty's troubles."

Bigum waited, but Man just sat down and started to inspect his hands. He looked closely at each of his fingers. Bigum couldn't take it any longer. "Okay?"

Man pulled his eyes away from his hands as if he wasn't finished there, yet. "Oh, yeah. I got a call from his secretary yesterday. When they arrested Ty they snatched up his files and computer, and locked her outta the office." Man paused and went back to studying his hands for a fast minute. "Anyway, she didn't trust nobody at the firm, so she called me," he added casually as if commenting on the latest street gossip.

Anger sang out from Bigum as he studied Man. "You don't seem too upset 'bout none of this." Bigum waited for a response but when Man turned his hands over and started examining them like he wasn't sure they belonged to him, he added, "I mean, don't you care that they tryin' to hang another brother?"

Man finally grew bored with his hands and dropped them in his lap. "It's always another brother. Tyrone ain't the first and he won't be the last Black man to be blamed for some shit he ain't do, or discredited just 'cause he's Black. Just look at history. It's just another lynching.

"Malcolm and Martin got murdered. Adam Clayton Powell got discredited and run out of office. And look at how they hounded Professor Jefferies over at CUNY. America ain't tryin' to let no Black man be no man...Not unless he gonna be their man." Man stopped, rubbed his hands together, then added, "Plus, you and Ms. Minns mad enough for all of us right now."

Bigum huffed, "So that's it. You ain't gonna do nothin'."

Man did something few people would feel safe doing–smile at the big man's anger. His smile grew as he responded, "I don't need to do anything." Before Bigum could get out his retort Man went on, "It's been taken care of already."

Bigum's face let the tension go, his expression turned from anger to interest. "Okay, don't keep me waiting. What's the deal?"

"Well, since all of Ty's assets have been frozen, the Fillmore twins gonna handle his bail. They hooking up with Reverend Barnes over at the African Methodist Episcopal Church on 137th Street, between Seventh and Lenox."

"That's what I'm talking 'bout. I'ma go with y'all."

"I ain't going, and before you leave I need to cue you in about Terry, and Short-Dog." Confusion painted Bigum's face, so Man continued, "Last night, Terry snuck her grown-ass downstairs, got naked and jumped in my bed."

"You bullshitting, right?"

Man shook his head. "I wish I was, but shortie was tryin' to fuck harder than an undercover fag in the joint."

Bigum forgot Tyrone for a minute. "What you do?"

Man stood up. "A couple years back, I'd have hit her young ass and thought nothing of it. But once I realized all I was doin' was busting a nut and passin' a li'l time..." Man sighed, before continuing, "Anyway, I told her to get dressed, and tried to talk some sense into her. But you know I ain't good at explainin' shit. Well, not shit like that anyway. Now, if it's getting a muthafucker to put the money in the bag or tell where it's at, then I'm your man."

Neither man spoke for a moment. The silence was as heavy as the burdens they each carried. Both men had blood on their hands, though only one wanted it washed off. Bigum finally broke the spell. "I can see why she feel the way she do. It's because..."

"What the..."

"Wait a minute before you go off." Bigum insisted on being heard, "Think about it. You look out for her and she coming into womanhood, so in her mind she oughta be with you. And you just saved her from that punk, José."

"But—"

Bigum waved him off. "Let me finish. You do things for all these kids that don't nobody else even think about doin'. Hell, you they hero. Why wouldn't she fall in love with you? And ain't she about the same age you and Rita was?" Bigum concluded wisely.

Man shook his head as if trying to clear it. "What me and Rita had was..." He couldn't go on. He looked off in space–his eyes distant for a moment. "And whatever these kids see in me, it ain't 'cause of what I do, it's because of what the rest of the world don't do. Shit, none of them should have to live the way they do, but this fucked up world don't give a shit about them.

"All Terry tryin' to do is find a way out. And even if she do find an older dude to sponsor her, dress her, and put money in her pocket, don't mean he gonna love her. No, what he gonna do is turn her young-ass out. It's an old story–wolves preying on sheep. And what difference does it make anyway? Look at how shit turned out with me and Rita," Man finished with his head down.

Bigum watched him then changed the subject. "What ShortDog got to do with all this?"

"When I took Terry home, I saw his li'l ass creeping."

"So?" This his hood, and—"

Man cut in, "Yeah, but he ain't want me to see 'im, and that put me on point. It might not be nothin'. But?" Man finished with a shrug.

"I got you, but shouldn't you be the one to handle this?"

"I ain't gonna be around for a few days. I'm hooking up with the God in Atlanta. We gonna head down to Miami. But I'll get with Pete and put 'im on point before I break out."

Although Bigum wanted to say more, he held his tongue. He kept his eyes on Man, who'd gone back to his space-staring. Bigum wondered where Man went when he got that far away look, but then admitted that he didn't really want to know. Some things were better left alone.

***

Ricky jumped out of his red Toyota 4-Runner and checked out the block. Even at 10 o'clock in the morning, his crew was getting paid. The crackheads were snatching up the caps quicker than the runners could keep the twenty-packs supplied. The action brought a smile to Ricky's dark face.

It was one of the few times he had smiled in the weeks since the robbery. Getting robbed had been bad enough, but it had become the least of his worries after Man's visit a couple of days later.

Man had applied the pressure like a booty-bandit on a new jack in a prison's bathhouse. Long story short, he was giving Man an additional $20,000 a week now. He wondered how long it would be before the $45,000 wasn't enough.

Shit, it might be cheaper to just kill the muthafucker, Ricky thought. The problem was doing it and not getting his self bodied, because if Man got wind of some shit like that, Ricky knew that his body would never be found.

He had to figure out a way to get out of Man's death grip. Paying the money was bad enough, but the humiliation of it made it worst. He was still making more money than he'd ever made and things were running smooth. But he was powerless against Man. And power was the reason he'd gotten into the drug game in the first place. Growing up, there had always been somebody stronger, somebody tougher to push him around. So, he had used his brains to change that. With drugs, money, and a crew, he had become the man.

But Man had him under pressure and his crew was useless. Short-Dog was a punk, and Bo and the others idolized Man. The same was true of Mack and Sammy–they would never cross Man. So there was no one he could trust to move with him against Man. Well, maybe he could play José into doing something. But he knew he couldn't trust him either. He had to think of something, though.

"Ricky? Ricky..."

"Huh? What's up," Ricky finally answered Bo.

"Damn. I called yo' ass five times. What the fuck you thinkin' so hard about?" "I'm just tryin' to figure some shit out." "Like what?" Bo asked, checking Ricky out as if he doubted his sanity.

Ricky shook the stare off. "Like how to get paid some more."

"Shit! We stacking dollars like a muthafucker since we got down with Man's program," Bo said with confidence. Ricky gave a quick smirk and headed for his truck, leaving Bo with a confused look.

# CHAPTER TWENTY-SIX

Man hung up the pay phone and headed back toward the game room. With time to kill before getting with Pete, he decided to stop by the daycare center. Although he told himself he wanted to discuss some things with Nicki, he knew he just wanted to see her. As soon as he walked through the door, children rushed him like a blitzing defense after an unprotected quarterback. They shouted and jumped around excitedly.

Jamel was in the front. "Man, where you been?" He asked, with wide eyes. Before Man could answer, Lucita, a cute, five year old, Puerto Rican girl, asked in a tiny voice, "Man, can you please tell Jamel that I'm not Spanish?"

Man laughed, it seemed that every child had something to say. He didn't have a chance to answer any of them; however, as Nicki smiled she moved in to rescue him.

"Okay, okay. That's enough. Y'all leave him alone." Nicki waited until she had most of their attention and added, "Plus, he came to see me this time. Right?" She settled one hand on her hip and her eyes on Man, daring him to deny it.

A surge of heat hit him as he met Nicki's stare. He forgot about the kids. "Uh-huh," was all Man could manage to say. Nicki quickly shooed the youngsters off and led Man to her office.

"My, my, you sure do stir things up around here," she said, pointing Man to the chair in front of her desk as she slipped into hers. They saw the children watching them through the glass wall of office, until a couple of Nicki's assistants chased them off.

Man was glowing, relaxed, and obviously feeling good. Children always brought out the best in him. "Yeah, you know how easy it is to fool kids," he said with a sly smile.

"You need to stop it. You ain't foolin nobody but yo'self 'Cause you ain't nothin' but a big kid," Nicki said suggestively, as she got up and stood in front of him.

Man let his eyes travel the length of her petite, but shapely body. "Li'l Nicki, I know you ain't being fresh, and talkin' like you from the hood," Man said, as he stood up.

With both hands on her hips, Nicki looked up from under lowered eyelids and said, "I can be fresh if I wanna be. I learned it from this mannish boy I grew up with in the hood."

"I don't know why I try to out talk yo' li'l butt. Ever since you was a li'l girl, you had an answer for everything," Man said, slipping his arms around her waist.

Nicki fell into his embrace, memories of their childhood fueled images of something more. The spell was broken by the sudden outbreak of cheers. Man and Nicki disengaged, turned and laughed at all the little faces whooping and hollering on the other side of the glass. Nicki's assistants shooed the kids away again, but were unable to hide their own smiles.

"Look at all the excitement you caused," Nicki said smiling. "You the one started actin' up. Just like when you was a li'l girl."

"Man, you need to stop it. We was kids at the same time. You ain't but a couple of years older than me."

"Yeah, but I was born a man."

"No, you was born with the name, Man, that your mama gave you," Nicki replied. She regretted the words as soon as she heard them. Man's face darkened like a spring day with a rainstorm approaching. Nicki reached out, touched his arm. "I'm sorry. I didn't—"

Man interrupted her, "You didn't do anything." He shrugged, then added, "I just remembered what I wanted to ask you. I need a couple of favors."

She resisted the urge to wrap her arms around him. She wanted to comfort him, tell him that everything would be okay. Instead, she simply asked, "What?"

"It's Terry and Ramsey." Man put his hand up to stop her from asking questions. "You know that Ramsey caught up with the hustling bullshit. I was thinking, maybe you could offer him a job here. I'd pay his salary, but he don't need to know it, though. I think the boy wanna do something more than sell crack. What you think?"

Nicki bit down on her lip as she thought about it. "He definitely needs an option, but the only real way he'll get one is if he finishes school. So, if he'll go back to school, I'll hire him. And we'll split his salary."

Man smiled and nodded his agreement. "Now, Terry..." Man stopped, not sure of how to continue.

"What?" Nicki asked again.

He sighed and shook his head. "The girl needs somebody to show her what being a woman means."

"Well, Man, you could—"

"No." He said through clenched teeth, as he inhaled deeply and started over. "I can't do nothin'. She needs a woman's touch, some womanly guidance."

"They all need that, as well as a man's influence. And she is almost grown—"

Man cut her off again, "Almost ain't grown. I found her waiting in my bed, naked. Shit, my daughter woulda been about her age."

Nicki almost laughed, but the look on Man's face and a touch of jealously stopped it cold. Looking into his eyes, she wondered how he could care so much about people while not allowing anyone to care about him. "I don't know what I can do. But I'll try. I could try to get her back in the dance class. I guess I could set some things up outside the center too."

Man smiled. "I knew you'd know what to do."

"Oh, don't think that's all to it. These young girls don't always have a choice when it comes to growing up. Sometimes the street is safer than being at home. Then, you got these no-good-ass men taking advantage of them." Nicki sighed and shook her head. She'd seen it too many times– a young girl being misused because she wanted to be loved.

"Maybe I can get Ms. Nez and Ms. Mary involved," Nicki said, as she thought for a moment. "Yeah, I'll make some plans. But it's gonna cost you."

"Huh?"

"If you can huh, you can hear," Nicki said laughing and rolling of her eyes. "You'll have to let me cook dinner for you this weekend."

Man smiled, nodded, then snapped his fingers. "I'm leaving in the morning, but when I get..."

"No problem. I can fit you in tonight."

Man laughed. "Well, since we got that settled, what time should I be there?" "Since it's an early night here, make it 8:00." They both laughed—pretending to ignore the obvious.

***

"Wanna go to the game room?" Lisa asked Terry.

"Girl, I ain't got time to be hangin' around a bunch of kids."

"EX–cusee me?"

Terry rolled her eyes but otherwise ignored the remark. "I need my own room. Shit, I need my own apartment," Terry said, looking around the small, cramped bedroom they shared.

"You better not let mama hear you cussin' cause she—"

"Girl, please. I'm grown."

"Grown, my ass," Lisa shot back, as she slipped out the room.

"See ya," Terry taunted. She felt worse now–she couldn't face Man and now Lisa was mad at her.

She jumped up off the narrow twin bed and examined herself in the full-length mirror. Anyone could see that she was a grown woman, she thought. It just didn't make any sense. Men older than Man were constantly trying to get with her. Didn't the money and gifts prove how much they wanted her? Guys, five, ten, fifteen years older than her had been sweating her since she was fourteen. But Man had been angry, even hurt, that she wanted to be with him. It just didn't make sense.

"What you looking in the mirror all dumb for," Lisa asked, as she stuck her head in the room.

Eying Lisa through the mirror Terry placed her hands on her hips, and said, "Children should be seen and not heard."

Lisa laughed. "That's just what I been tryin' to tell you."

Despite her mood, Terry laughed with her sister. Lisa always had that affect on her, but she still wasn't going to the game room.

***

The gray skies and the dull gray color of Yankee Stadium seemed to sing backup to the prediction of rain. Pete and Man walked along the oval track across the street from the stadium. With their hats pulled low and collars up, they watched a group of boys playing a rough game of two-hand touch football.

The boys on the field ran wild; their reckless abandon shouted that they would live forever. As Man watched one boy do a full somersault just to gain an extra yard, he knew better.

"Oh, shit! You see that shit?"

Man looked at Pete, who was more excited than the kids playing the game. Though he could understand Pete's excitement at the game – running wild just for the fun of it – he couldn't imagine running up and down the field without his gun. "Yeah, them boys playin' like it's the Superbowl."

They watched the game in silence for a while. "I'm rolling out in the morning," Man said as he looked away from the game. "I'm hooking up with the God in Atlanta and going—"

Pete interrupted, "Hold up. I'm down too."

Man put up his hand. "Chill. You know Kid already with Eddie, and with me and Born, that's it." Plus, somebody gotta hold Bigum down."

Pete's chest heaved and he turned back to the game.

"I know you wanna be down with this, but we got some shit here that we gotta stay on point with."

Pete's eyes locked on Man's face. He wasn't sure if Man was serious or just trying to make him feel better about being left out. "What's up?"

"First, we gotta keep an eye on Ricky. I caught Short-Dog sneaking around and it's hard to believe his li'l ass is doing anything without Ricky's okay."

Pete waited. He knew there had to be more, and his patience proved him right. "You know 'bout how I had to hem José ass up, and bet he gonna try something."

"Pete exploded, "Punk muthafucker. I'ma—"

"Pete, chill," Man said, cutting him off with a wave of his hand. "Once I get back..."

"I can take care of that while y'all gone," Pete said, before Man could finish.

"I know you can, but right now you gotta hold Bigum down and stay on top of everything."

Pete hesitated and chewed on his bottom lip. "You got my word. Whatever gotta be done."

Man nodded at the sincerity in Pete's voice. "I know how you go, homey. But don't forget to spend time with them pretty little girls of yours."

Pete stared into Man's eyes. He wondered where him and Kid would be if it wasn't for Man. "You know we all family. I got mad love for the crew." Pete stuck his chin out, his hazel eyes full of loyalty. "I'ma take care of my girls. But I gotta ride with y'all too."

"Ain't no doubt. We down by law. That's why I need you here." Man reached out and dropped his hand on Pete's shoulder. "We got some shit to take care of, but soon everything it'll be right as rain."

They walked off as the laughter and free-and-easy feelings on the football field seemed as far off as peace was in the Middle East.

## CHAPTER TWENTY-SEVEN

José slid into the last booth at the back of the crowded restaurant; his eyes darted around like those of a snake being stalked by a mongoose. After his meeting with Peto, he'd been afraid of somebody finding out he'd tried to have Man hit. He had no idea who had called him. But since he was still alive, he was sure Man wasn't behind it

His cousin hadn't betrayed him completely, he thought, as he jumped at the sound of loud voices and laughter from a table off to his right. Fuck! Why had he agreed to meet at Jimmy's? The seafood spot was too popular and it was only a few blocks from Man's spot.

The reason he had agreed was simple –he didn't have a choice– meet or word would get back to Man. Although the caller hadn't identified himself, he left no doubt as to who was in charge. He had laughed at Jose's denials and hung up on him, sure he'd show up. The prison-yard voice had been scary, but not as scary as having to deal with Man.

Fear danced in Jose's eyes as he watched the door. His pulse raced as the wide-bodied man in the undertaker's suit edged through the door on a tilt. He checked the fat man out – baldhead, cheap suit hanging awkwardly on his frame – and dismissed him.
José strained his neck to see around the fat guy, as he waddled down the aisle. He wanted to shout: *Hey, fatso, yeah you, the one taking up all the space, get the fuck outta the way.* The thought made him chuckle, then the fat man stopped directly in front of him.

Before José could speak, he was being crowded into the corner of the booth. "I'll have the seafood platter," the raspy voice said.

José looked around, fear flowing through his veins like KoolAid at a back yard fish fry. "Yo, I'on't know what the fuck—"

The fat man's laugh sounded like gravel being crushed. "Ain't no need for foul talk. I don't go for all that cussin' and carryin' on."

José could barely move, he decided to play along. "Look, man, you got me mixed up with somebody else. I'm gonna—"

The raspy voice shut him down. "What you gonna do is order my platter so I can eat. Then we can get down to the business of killin'."

José felt like a trapdoor had been opened in his chest and swallowed his heart. He tried to speak but couldn't with 300-plus pounds pressed up against him. "Order the food 'fore I git' up and go on over to Man's place."

Cornered like a rat, but without its instinct to fight, José signaled for the waitress.
The fat man ate like a starving Rottweiler; face buried in the plate, and barely coming up for air. He didn't bother speaking until a second platter was history. "Okay, let's get down to business," he said, pushing away his empty plate.

"I'on't know you from a can of paint," José said, trying to hide his fear. "You lucky I got yo' fat ass them platters."

The fat man gave José a stare that caused him to slide his eyes away. "Aww, sorry. I ain't mean to curse. But I ain't tryin' to be caught up in no bull—"

The large man's gravel-being-crushed laugh was released with additional volume as José stopped short. A few people turned to stare. Attention was the last thing José wanted. He peeked around, his fear acting as radar.

Before he could speak, the fat man leaned in close and whispered, "I'm the Deacon and I comes to save you from the evil of *Man.*" Another burst of the ugly raspy sound made José cringe. "That's kinda funny, ain't it?" José looked as if he was sick. "You ain't got no sense of humor, but I won't hold that against you."

His eyes darting around the restaurant, José wanted desperately to escape. "I gotta..." "I know you gotta go," the fat man said, cutting José off "So, pay the lady and lets get on with our business. The business of killin'."

***

Man grabbed the bottle of Hennessey Paradis off the shelf in his office. He turned and frowned at the conspiratorial grin plastered across Bigum's face, but decided to ignore it. That is, until Bigum started singing Barry White's, *Stone Gon'*.

Man's frown grew as he explained that it was *just dinner*. Bigum smiled, sniffed the air, and remarked on how good Man smelled. Man's frown ran out of space on his face as he shook his head. Before Bigum could think up anything else, Man made a quick exit.

On his way to Nicki's, Man laughed at Bigum's antics. Once the older man had found out about their dinner date, you'd have thought he had hit the number for twenty dollars, straight. Bigum's dirty mind and unconcealed joy made Man laugh as he passed the Redtop crew. Business was better than usual; maybe it was the Christmas spirit. Crackheads might not have money for gifts, or time to eat or wash, but they had money, time, and whatever it took to chase their pipe-dreams.

"Hey, Man! Damn, you sho' looking good."

Man stopped and stared at his admirer. Although Billy-boy was about Kid and Pete's age, he looked twenty years older. His undernourished body had a ten-car-freeway-pileup look to it. He looked half-dead. His skin, dull and gray, looked worse than his dirty Lee jeans. And the orange, small hoody was so tight on his head it resembled a comical space suit.

Though he'd offered no reply to Billy's greeting, Man's eyes stayed on him. The silence threw Billy off for a minute, but his mission – getting high – forced him on.

"How you doin', Man?" he asked, as he blinked repeatedly. "Shit! I know you doin' good," Billy exclaimed as he danced from one foot to the other. "Lookatya', in black and shit. You the grim reaper, huh?"

Man pulled up the collar of his black lambskin coat. He wondered if it was the brisk December wind, or Billy's words that chilled him. Although he'd chosen his matching black Italian wool slacks, mock-neck, and black Allen Edmonds chukkas for style, the choice gnawed at him now. Maybe his outfit matched his mood, he thought.

He shook it off and looked at Billy's dirty, red sneakers –a pair of Pony's, three sizes too big. "That's a hell of a fashion statement you makin'," Man said with a smile.

"Huh," Billy grunted, still doing his dance.

"Ain't nothin'. What's up?"

Billy chewed on the inside of his mouth. "I'm cool. You know how I do." His dance sped up. "I just need a few dollars to get me a 'li'l somethin' to eat."

"So you just wanna get soomethin' to eat?"

Billy's eyes dropped to the ground. "Uh-," he replied, still unable to meet Man's eyes. "And... You know, get... Get me a hit."

Though it was only four years since Billy had attended Fordham University, majoring in computer science, even he couldn't remember what that person had been like. He'd given up his dream of designing software for a pipe dream that was sucking the life out of him. Now instead of the binary system and random access memory, the going rate for stolen hubcaps and car batteries filled Billy's mind.

"Billy, how long you gonna give yo' life to the pipe?" Man asked, in a quiet voice.

Billy opened and closed his mouth. He peeked up at Man and shrugged his shoulders. Man recalled Billy's fall; he had started out buying $5 vials to freak off with crack-hookers, but ended up doing more smoking than fucking.

Man knew it was impossible to fight the pipe—only the addict could beat such high odds, and even that wasn't a sure bet. So he saved his breath and reached in his pocket. "Billy, get somethin' to eat before you get high," he said, holding out a $10 bill.

Billy's dance went into overdrive. "Damn, Man, you a good muthafucker. That's my word," he said, as he reached for the bill.

Man pulled it back. "Just make sure you get you a $3-special from the Chinese joint," he said as he dropped the bill into Billy's discolored, crusty fingers.

"I'ma do that right off', Billy sang, in time to match his dancing feet. "You know how I love them wings and fries. And I'on't care 'bout 'em cookin' they shit in pork grease either."

Man smiled as he watched Billy-boy run off, Billy moved as if he was answering the bell for the last round of a championship fight—one he'd probably lose.

Man wondered what had happened to the place he'd grown up in? *Crack* had happened. It was an epidemic in Black and Hispanic communities, just as heroin had been in the sixties and early seventies. Crack was now doing what heroin had failed to do to the Billy-boys and their female counterparts back then, and the onslaught would continue into the coming decade that was only weeks away. He knew it wasn't by chance either. The drugs, guns, second-rate education, and under-employment were part of a plan designed to capture and crush the next Malcolm—by *any means necessary.*

Man pushed the thoughts away as he reached Nicki's building. As he raised his hand to knock, the door opened.

"Hey," Nicki said, pulling him inside and taking the bottle he held out. "What's this?"

"Just a li'l after-dinner drink."

"Hennessey!" She said after she slipped the bag of "This is too strong for me."
Man laughed. "Yeah, sometime I forget just how young and tender you are. But this here is Henny Paradis. It's pretty smooth, so even a Tender-roni like you can handle it."

"Anything you can handle, I can handle," Nicki said, with her hands on hips, lips twisted to the side, and her head rocking with every word.

"I hear you talkin'," Man said as he looked her up and down, and took in her attitude as well as her outfit. She wore an old-style oriental dress, made of green silk. The dress was high collared, with a long split in back. It clung to her body like a horny lover, and showed off her dancer's figure, as it demanded attention. "By the way, you look better than any meal you could have made."

"Thank you. I think?" The compliment threw her off, her usual sass gone—she was blushing.
As his eyes traveled slowly over her body, Man opened his mouth but forgot what he'd intended
to say. Finally, he pulled his eyes up to her face and smiled foolishly.

Nicki also smiled; however, hers was one of knowing. She liked the affect she was having on him. "You're late," she said.

"I thought you said, 'around eight,' Man replied looking at his watch as his smile grew. "It's seven after."

"Oh, so now we playing word games?" Nicki asked, with a hint of provocation in her voice.

They laughed as she stepped into his arms. He inhaled her scent and felt his body respond. He suddenly broke the embrace and held her at arm's length.

"Damn, you look good. And I love the dress. The color goes with your complexion, but how the hell you walk in that thing?"

She spun around. "The split lets me walk. See?" She took a few small steps, turned around and came back.

"I see alright. It must be a house-dress."

"Man, I'm a grown woman," she said with a mischievous smile. "And I have my own business to prove that I'm taking care of business."

"All little girls are grown. And everybody's business ain't nobody's, and that's definitely a house-dress," Man said, returning her smile.

They both laughed as Nicki took his hand and led him into the living room. The memories rushed him—when he was a kid it had always been open house at the Porters'. Nicki's parents had treated all the kids like family, and took a special interest in Man. Back then, he thought, neighbors were family and neighborhoods were close-knit places where concern and love were shared.

But all that concern and love hadn't been enough to keep him from the fate that hounded him. Images of death strolled through his mind, changing his mood as quick as a moist wind on a sunny June day. He shuddered from the chill brought on by memories that ate at his heart like maggots devouring a week-old corpse.

Nicki reached out and ran her hand along his face. "Man?" You okay?"

Man snapped out of it and smiled—a smile so sad that Nicki wanted to hold him and take away the pain in his eyes. She caressed his face and pulled him close, he was rigid at first, but she refused to give up, and slowly his body relaxed until they meshed together. Nicki forgot the dinner she'd spent hours preparing. The nourishment she wanted to give him wasn't in the kitchen, although it was reaching a boiling point.

She buried her face in his hard-muscled chest. As she reached beneath his jacket and massaged his upper-back, she ignored the huge gun under his arm. It didn't matter that Man carried a gun. She just wanted to take his pain away. Her desire to comfort him was mixed with her passion for him. She realized that she wanted the comfort of him, his love, lust and strength. She wanted him in every way. Right then Nicki decided she wanted to belong to Man.
She tugged at his jacket until it fell to the floor. His hands explored her body, lingering in certain places–the small of her back, along the dimples of her butt, then up her back to the nape of her slender neck. She guided his mouth to hers. Their lips touched fleetingly before their tongues met and unleashed a frenzy of lust, as she sucked on his lips and tongue.

Man forgot his vow of no attachments. He continued to caress her ripe, perfect body, squeezing her heart-shaped ass. He pushed his tongue deep into her mouth–the force of his kiss fueled by his desire for her.

She lifted his shirt and kissed his stomach and chest. His hands found her breast: his thumbs stroked her nipples until they were erect. A small moan escaped her mouth as she felt his hard manhood pressed against her leg. Her hand brushed across the gun in his shoulder holster, the cold steel heightened her excitement. The thought shocked her, but didn't stop the building heat she felt.

They undressed with a sense of urgency. Man needed to see her, to admired her body. With her spread out before him on the thick rose-colored carpet he said, "Damn! You're gorgeous." He let his eyes and hands explore her. He turned her on her stomach kissed her calves, the back of her knees and glided his mouth up and down her body. "You're pretty all over."

Soft cries escaped her lips. Her body trembled as she turned over and whispered, "I want to feel you inside of me."

He lowered his body on her. Though much of his weight rested on his elbows, he let her feel him as his hardness discovered her soft wet center.

She cried out as she pushed up to meet him. Though it was brand new, their love was as natural and ancient as Isis and Osiris's. As perfect as Yin and Yang. It started out slow and built to a feverish pitch. It went back and forth, from a raging inferno to a smoldering heat. They lost themselves in the release of their long pent-up lust. While she went wherever he took her, she was also an adventurous and creative guide.

Nicki was lifted up, bent over, turned upside-down and inside out. But she gave as much as she got. Her low moans were matched by low, growling sounds from deep in Man's chest. And when he talked dirty to her, she asked for more. It was nasty, yet sweet—exactly what they both needed.

Hours later, Nicki awoke in Man's arms. Her head rested on his chest. They were right where it had started, on the living room floor. The smell of their sex was strong. *Damn*, she *thought with a smile, this is what every woman should have.* Then, she laughed softly as she thought about all the work she'd put into last night's uneaten dinner.

"What's so funny?"
Slightly startled, she said, "I thought you was asleep."

"I was just thinkin'," Man said in a heavy voice.

"Well, you just better be thinking about me. Better yet, about us." Nicki said with a smile.

"Yeah, I was. I mean... you know I care about you. And you know how I live. So—"

She stopped him, rose up on his chest and stared in his face. "Man, Puh-leeze. You don't just care about me, and you know it," she said, daring him to dispute what she'd said and felt. When he didn't, she went on "And yeah. I know how you live. Well, as much as you let me know, anyway. But none of that matters. It's all about us being together."

Man exhaled. "You don't understand..."
"I understand that I love the shit outta you. And I know you love me too." She paused, taking his silence as confirmation and added, with her usual sass, "Plus, you ain't gonna be just hittin' this and runnin' off."

"What's wrong with yo' mouth?"

"Man. Puh-leeze! You wasn't complaining about nothing my mouth was doin' last night."

"You gonna make me spank that li'l ass." Man said, playfully.

Nicki giggled. She wanted him to know how happy she was. "You promise. You know I love your hands on my butt."

He laughed with her but grew pensive after a moment. "Nicki, we gotta talk before—"

"We are talking, and see how easy it is for us. Just like last night, it's supposed to be like this." She climbed up on his body and looked down at him. "I'm not saying it's gonna always be easy, but I know you can feel how right this is." She became quiet, surprising even herself with that simple logic.

Man tried to get up but she wouldn't move. "Man, I'm a big girl. I can handle mine. And I ain't just talking about last night either. I know what you've been through. I've had my share of pain too," she said with feeling. She leaned down and touched her nose to his. "I wanna be your woman."

Man locked his eyes on hers. Looking... for something he could not describe. She slid her legs up, on either side of him. "You know it's right and you know that you can trust me. And I'll do what you say, so you won't have to worry about me." She bit his lip and smiled. "Now, kiss me."

Although he could talk as slick as any high-priced attorney, Man was stuck on stupid. The emotions he felt left him speechless, so he kissed her. Somewhere in the back of his mind, he still knew that they needed to talk but he couldn't put the words together as he watched her raise up and guide him inside of her.

# CHAPTER TWENTY-EIGHT

As his eyes locked on Man, Short-Dog smiled. He slid down in the driver's seat as Man stood in front of Nicki's and glanced up and down the street before moving off. The long hours Short-Dog had spent in the cold, beat-up hooptie turned out to be worth every minute.

When he'd seen Man pass by the spot last night, Short-Dog decided to follow him. So he had slipped around the corner and jumped in the old Ford. The half-blue and primed Escort was the crew's incognito transportation for guns and drugs. Old and run down, it blended well with the neighborhood. The car had a hidden compartment that could hold three kilos and two handguns.

Although it had taken a couple of minutes to get to the car, Short-Dog easily caught up with Man as he walked up the path to Nicki's door. Short-Dog smiled as Nicki opened it before Man could knock. *Damn! Man was getting all the choice ass in the hood,* Short-Dog thought to himself. First Terry, now Nicki. "Shit., its good to be the *Man*," he said to the empty car.

Caught up in his thoughts, Short-Dog jumped at the face, scarred, with a mouth full of broken, rotten teeth – pressed up against the driver's side window. He almost pissed on himself. Fear forever stalked Short-Dog.

"What you doin', li'l dog?" Billy-boy cackled.

Short-Dog, fighting back the fear, shouted, "Fuckin' crackhead. I oughta kick yo' ass."

"Aw, what's wrong li'l dog? I scared the shit outta yo' ass, huh?"

Short-Dog stared at Billy, who continued to laugh. "Who the fuck you callin' li'l dog'? You fuckin' crackhead, faggot."

Billy laughed louder. His brain scrambled by drugs, he was happy as a faggot in Boy's Town. "Want me to call you Mad Dawg? Cause you sho' is mad," Billy said as he did a slow spin, dancing to music only he could hear.

Short-Dog was heated, and his temper gave him courage he didn't normally have. He reached for the door-handle and pushed as hard as he could. The door slammed into the back of Billy's legs, almost knocking him down.

Billy danced away, laughing even harder. Just as he spun around, he saw the baseball bat coming at him. Short-Dog swung like the clean-up hitter for the Bronx Bombers.

His high leaving him like the traitor it was, Billy's eyes got bigger than a fat man's stomach at an all-you-can-eat buffet. His laughter died in his throat. He threw his arm up just in time to stop the bat from crushing his skull. He screamed as the blow shattered his right arm–the right side of his head was still intact, though.

He jumped out of the way as the second blow barely missed, and took off running, holding his arm. Pain played across his face.

Short-Dog looked around wildly. The violence was like a drug. "Who the fuck scared now?" he shouted with his lips curled as he felt larger than ever. "Yeah, I guess I'm a mad dog now, muthafucker, huh?" He started after Billy, but lost his heart after a few steps. He hurried back to the car and drove off. The fear he lived with returned like a dope-fiend's $200-a-day habit.

Billy hit the corner and headed for the first alley he saw. He had to get off the street before Short-Dog got his crew after him. His arm hurt like hell. It throbbed as he crawled under a large, green dumpster.

Billy whimpered as he cursed his life, or what he'd made of it. He blamed it all on Short-Dog. He couldn't believe that ShortDog had batted him down just for playing with him. Shit, he thought, even smoked-out, I could probably beat that li'l faggot.

But a crackhead could expect beatings from the young dealers, even if the crackhead had watched the drug dealer grow up. The young dealers would sic pit-bulls on crackheads for fun. If they could get away with it, that is. But with Man around, they couldn't. "Shit!" Billy exclaimed, as he thought, I shoulda' stopped Man when I saw him leaving the lady from the daycare center's house. But he'd been too ashamed. He'd spent all the money Man gave him getting high. He'd fucked up, when Man told him to get something to eat.

If he wasn't such a strung-out fiend, he thought, he would have been able to tell Man about Short-Dog spying on him. Billy rocked and gritted his teeth against the cold and pain of his broken arm, and from the life he had chose to live.

For about the millionth time, he wondered, he swore he'd quit getting high?

***

Tyrone listened intently, as his lawyer explained the situation – his assets were frozen, including the joint accounts he shared with his wife, and a lien had been placed on their home. He couldn't believe what was going on. It had broken his heart when his parents and in-laws offered to put up their modest homes and life saving to bail him out of jail.

He had refused. He just couldn't put them through that. But, after much thought, he'd reluctantly accepted the offer of bail from Tim and Tom Fillmore. Though uncomfortable with them risking such an enormous amount — a cashier's check for $100,000 and two commercial properties — he knew their net worth far exceeded it. And, as his lawyer had pointed out, the fact that two of Ty's current clients were standing by him was a positive statement in itself. The lawyer went on to say that Reverend Barnes' presence was another plus.

Leaving the Park Avenue law office with Reverend Barnes and the Fillmores, Tyrone saw Bigum standing on the sidewalk, next to his Caddie. Although no one had mentioned Man's name, Bigum's presence confirmed his involvement. Before Ty could bring it up, Tim Filmore said, "Hey, Bigum. I didn't know you was coming down. Why don't you give Tyrone a ride to our place?"

The twins and Reverend Barnes left to retrieve their car from the parking lot.
Bigum stuck his hand out, gave Ty's a firm shake, then pulled the smaller man close for a quick embrace–his bulk dwarfed Ty's 5'10" medium frame. "I tried to make it down to the court on Centre Street, but couldn't get away in time." Shaking his head, he went on, "With Man outta town, I hadda wait on Pete to show up."

After they climbed in the car, Ty settled into the comfortable seat, and suddenly wished that his life was as comfortable. "Thanks," he said, solemnly. Once Bigum pulled out into traffic Ty added, "I appreciate this, but I need to know how much Man had to do with all of it."

Bigum fiddled with the car's sound system—finally, settling on Louis Armstong's *What a Wonderful World*. The distinctive voice of Satchmo filled the car before Bigum answered.

"You know Man ain't got nothing but love for you, but he knows y'all live in different worlds. So, all he did was let the Filmores and Rev. Barnes know 'bout yo' troubles." Bigum fiddled with the radio until he got the sound just right and smiled as Louie sang on. "Tim and Tom was the ones introduced Man to you in the first place. You done business with them for years."

After a moment's reflection, he added, "Sometimes you gotta let somebody else handle things."

Ty nodded, and both men relaxed with each passing mile. Bigum drove cross-town, then took the Westside Highway to the Cross Bronx Expressway as Louie gave way to the extraordinary voice of Joe Williams, who gave the blues an infusion of color even a blind man could see.

Bigum got off the expressway at Jerome Avenue and took the side streets to the Filmore's house. He parked behind Tom's mint-green, Mercedes. The street was as empty as Madison Square Garden after another Knick loss.

Once inside, the five men gathered in the parlor. Tim Fillmore brought out a bottle of Chivas Regal and a deep, rich lacquer finished box of cigars. As Tom poured the drinks, Tim offered cigars.

Tyrone took his drink with reservations and looked questioningly at the offered cigar. "This seems like a celebration. And I can't see any reason to celebrate."

Tim in one of his dapper, gabardine, wool suits, smiled and looked down at the cigars. "These here is Honduras smokes, they got a rustic and rough sorta taste to 'em. Pretty much a straightforward cigar." Pausing for effect, he added, "It comes at you head on. No bullshit in these. So what we doing is celebrating our chance to step up and do what's right."

Before Ty could respond, Tom added, "Ty, when you've lived a while longer you'll celebrate being able to fight, too. The Black man gotta live to fight or he won't live long. We know you had doubts about letting us help you, but we ain't had none." Tom said, pausing and nodding in his brother's direction. "You been handling our money for years. We trust you!"

"Tom, I don't mean to sound ungrateful. I just wasn't sure about y'all risking so much money," Ty finished, in a strained voice.

Tim jumped back in, as usual the Filmores answered for each other and carried the conversation as one person, "We ain't risking nothing. You plan on runnin' off?" Tim asked shaking his head as if the thought was crazy. "Not only do we know you ain't going nowhere, we know you innocent of this here bullshit they done cooked up. And we with you."

Confusion, followed by appreciation slid across Ty's face. "I don't know what to say." After all of his accomplishments and success, Tyrone was shaken by everything–his situation and the support he was getting.

Reverend Barnes stood up and cleared his throat, making sure his preacher's voice was ready. "Tyrone, when the church needed help, Man gave us your number and you was there fo' us. Whether you know it or not, you helped a lotta folks. Folks that really need it–senior trips, summer camps and all.

"Now them same folks wanna help you. We ain't gonna stand by and let an innocent man be persecuted. We all know that more times than not, in this country, a Black man is guilty until proven innocent. And it's time for us to make some noise about any and every miscarriage of justice," the Rev. finished vehemently, wiping his brow with a white handkerchief

Nods and "Amens" followed the Reverend's speech. The room became all business. The twins had dabbled in local politics since the late 60's and knew just what favors to call in. The names of media personalities like John Johnson, Gil Noble and Les Matthews were mentioned. Ideas and suggestions flew around the room like bids at an auction.

## CHAPTER TWENTY-NINE

Twenty minutes after his flight landed at Atlanta's Executive Airport. Man hooked-up with Born Equality at the *Underground*. He wanted to pick up a couple of outfits for the warmer weather in Miami, while Born just wanted to take advantage of his last chance to sample the tasty southern treats. B.E. enjoyed the outgoing, down to earth, beautiful women of Atlanta, as well as the candy shops that were common throughout the *Underground*.

With almost three hours to kill before their flight to Miami, the *Underground* had more than enough shops and boutiques to keep them busy, plus, it was close to the airport. While Man stopped in Banana Republic and Benetton, Born reminisced about his previous night of "southern female comfort," as he called it, and seemed to stop in every candy shop that they passed.

Man was preoccupied with his shopping, and the memories of his own female comfort of the previous night. Nicki kept invading his thoughts, which is why he allowed Born Equality to carry the conversation. This was fine with the God because he had a story to tell–the honey he'd spent the night with had been the adventurous kind, and the play-by-play of their encounter kept Man mildly amused. B.E. wasn't much of a pussy-hound, but running around with Eddie might've changed that, Man thought to himself as a smile crept across his face.

"What you smiling about? I ain't bullshiting you. Shortie was *baaad,*" B.E. said emphasizing.

"I know the God don't lie," Man responded, smiling, as he examined a Willie Smith shirt.

"C'mon, Man. I'm for real. Shorty was bad. Shit, even you and Eddie woulda been happy to bag her."

I'm sho' you right," Man said, putting the shirt down.

"See, that's that bullshit," B.E. responded.

"Nah, I know you did yo' thang, homie. After all, you learned from the best, Eddie King."

Born Equality laughed. "Yeah, not to mention the one and only Man. I 'member how you was slaying hos up and down the east coast a few years ago, boy," the God said, nodding his head.

The reference to Man's dog-days reminded him that he hadn't used condoms last night with Nicki, something he'd made a habit of doing since the days he'd tried to lose himself in sex and drugs.

The God went on, "Man, I know you ain't forgot how you was freaking every shortie and they mama. You and Eddie was muthafucking porno stars."

"That shit been over for me, though," Man said. "I left all that shit to Eddie, and it looks like to Kid too, huh?"

B.E. laughed again. "Yeah, that li'l muthafucker always talkin' bout how he be slaying some pussy."

"Yeah, the boy sho' talk that shit. But fuckin' with Eddie he gonna have to back that shit up, we both know Eddie King is gonna make it happen with the honeies."

Nodding agreement, the God added, "I hope them fools is using rubbers. You know that monster is killing black muthafuckers like the L.A. Police Department."

The God was right; AIDS was definitely taking a toll on the black community. Brothers and sisters from all walks of life were turning up HIV positive, and no one seemed to care. The disease wasn't receiving the attention it deserved and would soon grow out of control.

Man was pretty sure that Eddie and the God used rubbers as a rule because during their time in prison all three of them had become aware of the threat of AIDS. Prisoners and homosexuals were the first to be hit by the disease. Two groups that society considered undesirable and expendable.

His first couple of years home, Man had played a kind of sexual Russian roulette with his life–using condoms if he felt like it and not using them if he didn't. Although he'd had more one night stands than a struggling *R&B* group, and had picked up more dancers at strip joints than a talent scout at amateur night at the Apollo, Man had gone raw-dog–without a condom–more often than not back then.

While he rarely thought about those days anymore, Born Equality's words, along with his own night of unprotected sex with Nicki, had forced them to resurface. It wasn't that he thought Nicki was out there like that, but he knew that HIV didn't announce itself and say watch out. All it took was one time and the monster had you.

It wasn't that he didn't trust Nicki, but he felt that she shouldn't have trusted him. Normally, he would use condoms, but he'd never expected to go there with Nicki–or did he? He sure hadn't done anything to stop it. And what if she got pregnant? How could he bring a child into this world? That was the last thing he wanted to think of. So, he pushed the thoughts away and in a rush to escape them, he turned to Born. "God, ain't it about time we headed over to the airport."

"Yeah, but we got time to grab some real food though. I'm starving like Marvin punk-ass," B.E. answered, after checking his watch.

Man laughed at the God's remark. "Now, why Marvin gotta be a punk?"

"Man, you know only a punk gonna let himself starve. Even a broke-dick dog gonna eat when it's hungry," B.E. said with sincerity.

"Yeah, that's right God. Let's find us somethin' to eat and get outta here."

\*\*\*

Nicki gazed at Ms. Nez, with a look that said—I'm too through with this child. Ms. Nez smiled and turned her attention to Terry. "I think it's a good idea, Terry. You should really think about it before you turn it down."

"I 'on't wanna work with them bad-ass kids." Terry said, as she picked at her food. Ms. Nez took a fork full of candied yams from the plate of delicious soul food in front of her, smiling at Nicki's reaction–a look of frustration. Since it had been her idea that she and Nicki take Terry to lunch, she was determined to enjoy her meal. The restaurant was famous for its home-cooking. Ms. Johnson, the owner and cook, did to soul food what B.B. King did to the blues; she forced people to take notice. Ms. Johnson's sweet potato pies and peach cobbler were legendary. People came from all over the city to purchase them, especially during the holiday season.

Carolina Kitchen, one of Man's favorite restaurants, was only a few blocks from the Village Day Care Center and Badlands game room. It had been a mainstay in the neighborhood for the last three decades. And the fact that Terry was sitting there with an attitude was getting the best of Nicki. She was fed up with the teenager's childish behavior. Nicki took a deep breath and thought; *soon it'll be an all out foot stomping tantrum.*

Nicki calmed herself and tried again. "Terry, you wouldn't have to work with the younger children. Actually, you could learn the business side of things and—"

"What you mean? Like runnin' the center?" Terry asked, cutting Nicki off in mid-sentence.

Nicki took a minute to collect herself. "Well, like balancing the books and making orders. It's a lot more to running a daycare center than just taking care of children. Though that's definitely the most important and difficult part of it," Nicki answered, patiently.

Sensing the girl's interest, Ms. Nez added, "You'll have to learn to work the phones like an executive though. You know, a Black businesswoman gotta be sharp. Being a woman is hard, but being a Black woman is ten times harder."

Aware of Terry's building interest, Ms. Nez continued in a quiet but firm voice, "Black women have to demand respect by the way they carry themselves. It's up to us to decide how we're going to be treated. It's a shame that we rarely get any thanks for being the backbone of our families and our race. White women scorn us but want our full lips and hips. Then, their men want to bed us as if we were just exotic sex-slaves. But worst of all, our own men don't respect or honor us like they should."

For the first time Terry felt connected to the older women. The feeling brought a smile to her face. When her eyes sparkled, as they did now, Terry was an exceptionally beautiful young woman.

Nicki looked from Terry to Ms. Nez, and realized that she had a smile on her own face, to match theirs.

"Ms. Nicki. I've been thinkin' 'bout getting a job," Terry said, scooping up a spoon full of peach cobbler. She seemed to be enjoying the desert, and the company of the older women. "I just don't wanna be flipping no damn burgers."

Realizing that she had cursed, Terry looked at Ms. Nez and covered her mouth. "I'm sorry," she said, with her eyes wide.

Ms. Nez smiled. "That's all right, but let me do the cursing. I've earned the right by getting old."

Nicki and Terry giggled together for a moment, until Terry caught herself. It seemed as if she didn't want to like Nicki too much. As Ms. Nez watched the two younger women, she realized that Terry was a woman-child interacting with a certain amount of restraint. The two younger women were kind of dancing around each other, never truly dropping their guards.

"Terry, if you don't want to flip burgers, you're going to need skills and the best way to acquire them is by going to school," Nicki said, seriously.

Terry's lips turned up at the mention of school. "They don't hardly teach nothin' at Taft. I might as well hang out on the corner. Shoot, that's where the rest of the students hang out anyway."

Ms. Nez chuckled. At least the girl said 'shoot,' instead of shit, she thought. "Well, then we gonna just have to find another high school for you. One that will teach you something," Ms. Nez said, nodding her head, which was covered in a beautiful blue and gold headdress. "What do you really want to do, Terry?"

With enthusiasm, and no hesitation, Terry answered, "I wanna be a dancer." She quickly averted her eyes. "No. I'on't really know what I wanna do."

Ms. Nez smiled. Things were working out just right.

# CHAPTER THIRTY

As Bigum and Pete played a friendly game of pool in the game room, it quickly turned into a heated competition as the audience of young onlookers cheered every shot. The video games went quiet as the shots became more skillful. Every time they missed a shot, Bigum and Pete had to endure catcalls from the kids. Lisa led the cheering; though it was really more like good-natured heckling. She had a witty remark for every shot, missed or made.

Lisa's good mood was a product of her sister's presence in the game room. She'd finally convinced Terry to come to Badlands with her. Terry had avoided the game room since Man's rejection. But now, even she was enjoying the lighthearted atmosphere and Lisa's playful mood. Terry egged her younger sister on at every opportunity. The laughter seemed to push aside the everyday struggles of the ghetto. The entire group was having fun. Crime, poverty and police brutality, all staples of ghetto life, were forgotten for the time being. The game room was filled with a jovial energy that offered hope, even if it was fleeting.

"Lisa, you better stop messin' with Mr. Bigum," Little Jamel said with the air of a grownup.

Lisa laughed at the little boy's seriousness. "Oh, I'm sorry," she said playfully.

Jamel pointed at her and nodded his head to emphasize his reply. "I ain't playin' with you, Lisa. You better stop bothering Mr. Bigum, and Pete right now."

Lisa laughed, as Bigum and Pete encouraged Jamel. "That's right, Jamel. You tell her," Pete said, smiling.

With Jamel stealing the spotlight, the pool game was forgotten for the moment. Lisa immediately recognized the fun to be had with the boy. "If I 'on't stop, what you gonna do, Jamel?"

"I'ma get you," Jamel said, smiling, as he took a small step back. He was looking forward to being chased. Having the older kids chase him around the game room was one of his favorite forms of entertainment. As he continued his teasing of Lisa, he didn't notice Terry sneaking up from behind. Lisa ran at him and in his rush to get away from her he ran straight into Terry's arms.

The two girls smothered him with kisses as he struggled to free himself.

"Ugh, get off me," Jamel cried, in between fits of laughter as he tried to wipe away the kisses.

"Aw, c'mon Jamel. You know you want us to kiss you," Terry cooed sweetly.

"Pete, Mr. Bigum, help me. Get 'em off me," Jamel cried out in-between the girls' kisses and his own laughter.

Bigum laughed as he shook his head. Then Pete said, "Jamel, you gotta learn how to treat women, and this looks like the perfect time to start."

The Smith brothers, Kevin and Joe, tried to free the boy but the other nine or ten girls in the game room formed a protective circle around Lisa and Terry and kept the brothers back. The sisters continued to hug and kiss the little boy as he squealed with joy at their attention. Yet, he couldn't wipe the kisses off quick enough. He finally struggled free and ran, laughing to Bigum.

"Save me, Mr. Bigum. They tryin' to get me."

As Bigum and Pete laughed, amused by the little boy's woman troubles, Bigum grabbed Jamel with one huge hand and lifted him up out of the reach of the two pursuing teenagers.

Jamel screamed with glee at Terry and Lisa's futile attempts to recapture him. All of a sudden the rest of the kids started chanting Jamel's name. The child clapped his tiny hands as he settled on Bigum's shoulders. He loved the attention and played to it, to the delight of the other children.

Bigum's wore a smile as bright as those on the children's face.

This was what Bigum loved about Badlands and what Man had created there–it was one big family. Although it wasn't always happy, it was real. Family had to endure the bad with the good and stand together through it all. He looked at Terry and thought about how mixed up the woman-child was, as she made the transition from girl to woman. He had just watched her behave like a girl but knew that womanhood was only a small step away for her. He prayed that Nicki would be able to assist the girl, because he knew that Man really didn't have a clue.

Once they closed up and had sent everyone home, Bigum and Pete moved to the office. Bigum offered Pete a drink, which he declined. Pete wanted to roll a blunt from the $20 bag of Buddha in his pocket, but put it on hold out of respect for Bigum and the game room. Drugs weren't allowed in the place, not even weed. So the $20-sack and blunt remained out of sight in Pete's inside jacket pocket.

"Now, what's this 'bout Billy-boy?" Bigum asked.

"Yeah, like I was saying, I saw Billy-boy yesterday, hustling change at the carwash on 169th Street. His arm was broke and—"

Bigum interrupted, "How the hell did the boy break his arm?"

"He said that Short-Dog hit him with a bat cause—"

"What?" Bigum said with obvious anger.

"Wait, that ain't all of it. Billy said Short-Dog hit him because he caught Dog spyin' on Man down the street from Nicki's."

"Let me get this right. You sayin' Short-Dog was watching Man the other night?" Bigum asked with interest, as he recalled Man's suspicions.

"Yeah, from what Billy said, the little punk sat out there for hours in an old hooptie. I'on't know if it means anything but..."

Bigum locked his eyes on Pete's. "It means somethin' all right. Man thought that boy might be on some sneaky mess. Where's Billy at now?"

Holding the big man's steady gaze, Pete replied, "I took him over to Lincoln hospital, then got him a room for two weeks at the old hotel on the Grand Concourse by 184th Street. He was scared and wanted to see Man. I figure Man'd wanna' talk to him anyway. So, I stashed him over there."

"That's good. Maybe we can save Billy and get him to leave that damn crack alone. You done right."

Pete smiled at the older Man. "I know. I was trained right. That's why I'ma be paying close attention to that punk, ShortDog. But, Bigum, can't nobody fight the pipe. Billy-boy gotta save his own self."

"I guess you right. Be glad when Man get back."

"They oughta be 'bout through, but ain't no tellin'. Every move gotta go the way it goes," Pete said, with the confidence of a veteran gunman.

Bigum just nodded. Pete's nonchalant attitude about armed robbery unsettled him. The gunmen's code was beyond him. He couldn't understand why all of them were so drawn to it.

Pete checked his inside pocket, as he stood. "I'm out Bigum. I gotta make a quick stop, then get home to my li'l girls."

Bigum walked Pete out and locked up for the night. Once back in the office, he sat behind his desk in deep thought. He wondered what Short-Dog was up to, and where it would all lead. He was troubled by everything that was going on. Man and 'em down in Miami, Tyrone's legal problems, and now the mess with Short-Dog. *What was next?* he thought.

***

The room was clean, but like the sagging private house, its best days were long gone. As Deacon moved his bulk around the sparsely furnished room with difficulty, the sounds of traffic drifted up from the street below, occasionally overshadowed by a nearby subway. Even though he'd turned sideways to navigate his way between the old plywood dresser and sturdy, but worn, iron frame bed, it was a struggle. The 10' x 20' foot room was made smaller by his ample dimensions. However, Deacon was used to the difficulty of carrying 330 pounds on his 5'6" frame, and was oblivious to the obstructions the task presented.

He'd been obese from childhood, and had endured the cruelty of both children and adults during the first eight years of his life. But after the death of his mother, he'd started to repay each word and act of cruelty with a brutality and ruthlessness that frightened anyone who witnessed it, and had served notice that the funny looking, little fat-boy was anything but jolly. Over the years, his well-earned reputation for viciousness had grown. He had punished those who'd committed sinful acts, and as he was apt to say, they'd reaped exactly what they'd sowed. Because of his propensity to dish out violent retribution, Deacon's services were in demand.

With the lone dresser, full-sized metal bed, and dim, hanging light bulb, the room was comparable to one in a monastery or prison. Deacon believed that the less comforts one sought in this world, the more he'd have in the next. He lived a frugal and somber life. His three suits were exactly the same–single breasted, black and cheap. These he wore with plain white shirts and thin black ties, which always sported a perfect Windsor knot.

His one vice was food. Deacon was an un-repentant glutton. As a child, he ate to escape the hell that was his life. But that was all in the past, he was at peace with who and what he was now. He reached for his Gideon Bible and kneeled in the corner to pray. He opened the Bible and began to read devoutly from the book of Lamentations: *"For men are not cast off by the Lord forever. Though he brings grid; he will show compassion, so great is his unfailing love.'*

***

After his meeting with Deacon, José wanted even less to do with the block. Although he knew the amount of money each kilo of crack should generate, the only way to be sure his money'd be correct was to stay on top of his crew–so, he made a rare appearance.

Ricky had watched José exit his Jeep. He'd wondered where he'd been hiding out and why. Ricky went over to him and started up a conversation. While they stood on the block overseeing their respective crews, Ricky continued to pay close attention to José. Although both crews were making plenty of money, José was uneasy. Maybe it was because of what Man had done to him?

Ricky wanted to know exactly what was making José so nervous. He was sure that whatever it was held a hint of something to come, a plot of some kind, and knew that finding out would give him the upper hand. Maybe he'd be able to benefit from it? Although he didn't trust José, Ricky secretly hoped that whatever he was up to would rid him of Man as well as José. *Wouldn't it be sweet if Man killed José and ended up back in prison,* Ricky thought as a calculating smile crossed his face.

"Ze, you got that joint hooked up," Ricky said admiring Jose's Jeep. "What's those?" Although he seemed preoccupied, José muttered, "Twenty-six's."

"They look better than the 24 inch rims," Ricky said, nodding his head. "It's always better to get Hammers in twenty-six's, anyway. Yeah, you got that ride looking right," he added with an ingratiating tone.

Looking at his jeep, José nodded his agreement.

"Water, coming up." one of the lookouts yelled from the roof of the building. This meant that police were coming from the south end of the block.

Ricky and José continued a casual conversation about cars, rims and auto sound systems, as the patrol car crawled along the street, stopping every few feet to stare people down. The white faces of the policemen's carried scowls of hostility and superiority–directed at all those who happened to come under their hard stares, law-abiding citizens as well as criminals. Many of the residents were just as frightened of the police as they were of the drug dealers. The police were seen more as an occupying, oppressive force than as any kind of protector to the average person in the ghetto.

Ricky laughed as the patrol car stopped twenty yards up the block from him and José, and one of the officers called Joe Smith over to the car and gave him the third degree. Joe had squared up and was as straight as a barber's razor, yet he was being treated as if he was still a street hood. He'd also taken a lame-ass job at the daycare center across from the game room.

Ricky had had big plans for Joe. Though he was a little wild, he had heart, and Ricky always had a use for the ones with heart. He let them see the jewelry, cars and total ghetto-fabulous lifestyle he lived. He had hooked Joe with promises of the American dream, ghetto style.

It wasn't true that every Black man could sing, dance and play basketball. And there were only so many NBA teams. Therefore, selling drugs had become a way of escaping poverty. So what if it was more glitter than actual gold, and usually led to prison or death. When the deck was stacked against you and you had no hope, you'd eagerly trade away a future you didn't believe existed. Any hope was better than none. Ricky didn't waste time thinking about such things; all he could think about was that Man continued to stand in his way of gaining the power he craved.

Ricky chuckled, as Joe walked away from the police cruiser, "Look at that shit. Joe dumb ass stopped gettin' paid and ain't shit change for the fool. He shoulda' stayed down with Blue seal."

José seemed to be miles away, as he nodded absently to Ricky's words.
Intrigued by the other man's mood, Ricky continued, "But, nah. He had to listen to that crazy ass, Man."

Jose's anxiety increased at the mention of Man's name. He fumbled with his car keys and began to look around furtively.

Ricky pinned José with his beady eyes, and felt in his gut that he was up to something. "Damn, Ze, you a'ight?"

"What?"

"Yo, what's up? You okay, man?"

I gotta go," José responded abruptly, and headed for his Jeep.

Ricky watched José make his departure, and was so caught up in figuring out what was going on with him that he never noticed Short-Dog watching them from behind the curtain of the second floor window.

# CHAPTER THIRTY-ONE

After checking into the South Beach Marriot, Man and Born Equality hooked up with Kid and Eddie, and got down to business. They spent the next week preparing for the coming job. Eddie purchased guns from a source in Liberty City—one Makarov .9mm, two .40 caliber Glock handguns, and a Heckler and Koch MPS submachine gun.

Once they settled on their plan, Man got four white jumpers, with the logo of a local window washing company, and a United States Postal worker's uniform–window washers and mailmen usually went unnoticed. Things were falling into place, and everyone knew exactly what was at stake. Whenever large sums of money were involved, people were prepared to do just about anything for it. The four gunmen understood that and their weapons and detailed plans testified to the fact. They'd make their move in two days.

"So, it's all set," Man said. "Everybody know what they gotta do, right?"
The men nodded, Kid with a sly smile, and Eddie and Born with grave expressions. Kid took center stage, as the mood in the room lightened. "Yo, E.K., tell 'em 'bout them white girls by the pool."

Eddie smiled at Kid's rhapsodic nature, but before he could respond, Kid continued, "Man, them white girls was on me like I was Wesley Snipes, but handsome," he finished with a burst of laughter.

Born looked at the young gunman and shook his head. The boy could sure act a fool.

Man also scrutinized Kid, wondering when he'd lose the act and face life for what it was. Then, he thought, that maybe Kid was better off as he was.

"Check it out. I coulda' hit all four of them white bitches, too."
"Yeah, you probably coulda', but them "*Miss Anns*" might'a killed yo young ass." Eddie said with a serious face.

"What? I'll slay a white bitch. It'll be like that muthafucker in that slave movie. The one Ali used to dis' all the time. Damn. What's the name of that shit?"

"You talkin' bout Ken Norton, punk-ass, in "Mandingo," Born said with a laugh. "And you see how his ass ended up in that pot of boiling water. That's just why Ali dissed that fool."

"Well, you know the Kid ain't no slave. Not while he be 'bout slingin' steel and takin' money," Kid responded, with his trademark smile, as he slipped on his gloves and began to handle the 9mm with professional care.

Looking straight at Man, Born asked, "Why you ain't school this boy?" He didn't wait for Man to respond before turning his gaze on Kid. "Guns, don't make you a man, or free. Money either. Look at all the black folks killin' one another for a few dollars, or cause somebody looked at them wrong."

Eddie glanced over at Man and smiled. He knew that the God was about to go into his teaching mode. Man remained silent.

"I ain't no petty stick-up kid. I'm 'bout taking real paper and if I lay a chump down its cause he had to go," Kid replied with pride, looking at Man for reassurance. From his seat by the window, Man pushed the curtain slightly aside and took in the view of the hotel's pool.

Born Equality got up from the twin bed he was sitting on and positioned himself so that he faced the other three men. "That's just how we live but it ain't real living."
Although Eddie was stretched out on the other bed, with his eyes half-dosed, he followed the conversation with interest. Man had given up the poolside sights and sat with his chair tilted back against the wall, precariously balanced on the two hind legs. He observed the discussion without any intention of getting involved.

The God continued, "You think because we take money and stay strapped that we free? Shit, we just playin' our roles. It don't matter that we good at what we do, cause what we do ain't nothing but what white folks want us to do."

Kid shook his head. "You telling me they want to see us strapped with automatic weapons and taking ours? I'on't believe that shit, B.E. White folks fear the Black man that'll go out for his," Kid stated with passion.

"What? I know you don't believe that bullshit. Long as we doin' crime they ain't gotta worry 'bout us becoming the next Malcom. All we doin' is playin' a losing game. A game that we don't make none of the rules to. Every time we pick a gun up, we put our life on the line. We ain't makin' no real—"

"Nah, Born. We free 'cause we call our own shots," Kid interjected.

"Kid, all we doin' is living the life that's been forced on us."

"So, B.E., what we suppose to do? Just work at some bullshit ass nine to five, or sell drugs?

"Ain't none of us no drug dealers but ain't nothin' wrong with working. The key is working for self, though. Just like the key to freedom is self-knowledge. If a man don't know his self, he 'on't know nothin'. It's like Malcom X said, 'we been bamboozled. Look at us, our claim to fame is being gunmen, not fathers or husbands, not even sons. Just gunmen," Born Equality said in a quiet voice.

"B.E., I ain't sweating all that family shit."

"I guess not," Born responded lightly. "Especially when you can party with Eddie King, the king of strip joints and one night stands."

"Hey, I ain't got nothin' to do with this," Eddie said, smiling.

"We all got somethin' to do with it," B.E. answered seriously. "Even with the lessons of the Father, I still find time to party with you every now and then."
"Damn, homey, I—"

Born interrupted Eddie. "It ain't yo fault that I get caught up with that shit. Man was running neck and neck with you and he cut it loose. So..."

"It ain't like you hang all that much, anyway," Eddie added with a chuckle.

"What's wrong with a partyin', and who's the Father?" Kid asked.

"The Black man is being exterminated so we ain't got time to party. And the Father was Clarence 13X, who came to free the 85%, the so-called American Negro. Clarence 13X was his Muslim name before he left the Nation of Islam in 1963 and..."

As the God laid out the history of the Five Percent Nation, Man sought refuge from memories awakened by the mention of family. The memories cornered him like a heavyweight slugger adept at cutting off the ring. There was no escape to be had–the memories were too vivid.

*"Man, you happy?*
*Man looked at Rita and knew that he'd always love her. "Of course I'm happy."*

*"But, what if you can't go to college because of the baby?"*

*"Girl, stop yo' worrin'. Everything gonna be fine. I 'ma make sure of it. I'ma take care of my family."*
*Rita smiled up at Man. "We gonna take care of each other, and our baby. But promise. you'll never leave me.*

"Man? Yo. Man?"
Man shook himself free of the past and focused his eyes on Kid. "Yeah, what's up?"

"We gonna run through the plan again tonight?" Kid asked, reaching for the submachine gun.

"That's cool," Man replied; glad to have something to occupy his mind. "Let's start from the top."

The four men gathered around the table and began to review their plans. Although Man busied himself by going over the robbery, the memories lingered.

*** 

Tyrone Jenkins sat in his study and each time he considered the situation, he couldn't believe it. He'd spent his life on the right side of the law, yet he'd been indicted by the grand jury. He shook his head in disgust. The whole thing was nothing more than a lynching. He'd gone over his accounts with a fine-tooth comb and there were no signs of malfeasance. How could this be happening? He'd worked hard and played by the rules. Rules that sometimes seemed to be in place just to hold him down. The same rules he was fighting now.

"Honey, come to bed."

Ty looked up from the papers on his desk into the calm face of his wife, and thought, as he often did, *How did I get this beautiful woman?* – "I'll be up in a few minutes."

"Oh, I think you better come up now. I have something for you that can't wait," Doris said, smiling coyly.

He was so disturbed by the situation that he didn't notice the beautiful negligee she was wearing. For the first time in their life together, her presence failed to arouse him. Instead, it filled him with sadness. It was a struggle just to look her in the face. He felt that he'd let her down.

Ty avoided her eyes, fumbling with the papers in front of him. "I'm just about finished here."

Walking directly to her husband, Doris took the papers from his hands and placed them aside in a neat pile. "Mr. Jenkins, I have some work that really needs your personal attention," she said, forcing him to look at her.

When he didn't respond, she took his hands in hers. "Ty, baby, we're going to get through this. It's not the end of the world."

"That's just it. It is the end of the world I worked so hard to build for us. I let you and the kids down. And what about my parents, and yours too? They expected me to provide for their daughter but now I..."

"Ty, you haven't let me down. We have two beautiful children, who love and admire their father. And both of our parents know that you're a good man. And sometimes I think if I hadn't married you, my parents would have," Doris finished, with a smile.

When he didn't return her smile, Doris came around the desk and kneeled beside him. "Baby, I'm happy with my husband and I know—"

"Doris, that's just it, the happy days might be over. I know I haven't done anything wrong, but the fact is I've still been indicted and I'm being treated like a damn criminal. We can't even spend our own money. I worked hard and followed the rules. This isn't the way it's supposed to be for us. You gave up your own dreams of being a doctor to raise our children and..."

"Is that what you think? Being a doctor was important to me but it was always second to being a mother and a wife. The only way it's supposed to be, is that there's always an us. When I was a little girl I wanted a house like the one I grew up in. A family with a man like my father, who was there showing love and making everybody feel safe.

"My dad would come home from a double shift, tired and beat down, but he'd make me and my sister feel as if we were the most important kids in the world and he treated mom the same way. He wasn't perfect but he was damn close. And though I never thought I'd say this, I may have done even better than mom. I married the man of my dreams and wherever that dream takes me I'm happy it's real. I meant every word of the vows we took eleven years ago. Now, c'mon. It's time for you to perform some husbandly duties," she said, climbing in his lap.

Tyrone finally smiled, and after the first kiss the passion was back. *How did I get this beautiful woman*, he thought, once again.

***

Tim Filmore walked into Bob's barbershop dressed as if he had a date with Diahann Carroll, who starred in *Julia,* the first television series with a Black woman, as its' main character. Mr. Tim claimed that he'd been romantically involved with Ms. Carroll some thirty-five years ago. With his expertly tailored, light brown, woven-herringbone suit, Egyptian cotton dress shirt, dark brown crocodile shoes, and brown fedora, anyone was likely to believe him.

However, this was part of his everyday wardrobe. The Fillmore twins' reputation for fashionable elegance was well earned, and Mr. Tim was determined to keep the tradition alive. Today, his stylish ensemble was complemented with a red oak, ivory-topped walking-cane. Business was slow in the middle of the week, especially near noon. Only one of the four barbers had a customer and Mr. Bob sat by the window reading the sports section of the daily paper. The mood in the shop was mellow.

"Hey, Tim," Mr. Bob said folding his paper.

"Hey, yo'self, young man," Mr. Tim responded.

"C'mon, take a seat and let me whup you at a game right quick."

"I'll take the seat but since the only way you can beat me at checkers is if I let you, I'll pass on the game today," Mr. Tim said with an easy smile, as he pulled up a chair.

The older men settled into a friendly conversation that eventually moved to the subject of Tyrone Jenkins.

"That was a good turnout at the church the other night. It was good that folks came out to support Tyrone. We gotta let them courts know they just cain't railroad an innocent man." Mr. Bob said.

"Yeah, it was a good turn out and it's important that Ty has a show of support from the community. We both been around long enough to know that he's gonna need it. A Black man is always guilty until proven innocent. So the more people we get to pay attention to this whole mess the better chance the boy got."

"You ain't never lied 'bout that, Tim. It's just like Judge Bruce Wright said, '*Black robes and white justice.*' That's why I been working the phones. I'm calling every member of the Small Black Business and Black Barbers Association, and tellin' 'em to call a friend. We gotta keep the heat on this thing."

"Now, that's what I'm talkin 'bout. We gonna come out in force for Tyrone Jenkins and let the so-called powers that be know he ain't standin' alone."

"Good, good. But why wasn't Man there. I thought for sho' he'd be there showing his support,"Bob said.

"Man set the whole thing in motion, but ain't been around since. And you know how he feels about churches and religion in general. He thinks that as long as people patiently await rewards in the next world, they accept whatever this one brings 'em. Sermons don't mean much to him, he's 'bout action and we know how longwinded preachers can be," Mr. Tim said, as he finished with his head slightly cocked to one side.Mr. Bob's face took on an amused expression.

"Now, Tim, just because I had to go to the bathroom in the middle of Reverend Barnes' speech don't mean I wasn't interested in what he had to say."
"No, but the fact that it took you almost twenty minutes to get back means you was either constipated or thought that the Rev. was full of—"

"Oh, no. Don't you put yo' stuff on me. If you wanna do Reverend Barnes like that don't go using me to get it off," Mr. Bob said with a chuckle.

"Bob, you know I don't mind good preaching. And Barnes is good, even if he is a might longwinded. But if he can keep people riled up 'bout Ty's situation, I ain't got no complaints." "I second that. Old Barnes done grabbed hold of this like a hungry bulldog on a butcher's garbage can."

Mr. Tim nodded his head. "Now we just gotta hope his lawyer is as good as Ty thinks he is."

"Well, what does Man say about it?" Mr. Bob asked, as the door opened.

"Who cares what Man has to say about anything," Mr. Sam said, closing the door behind him.

Mr. Bob and Mr. Tim exchanged looks that said neither one of them wanted to hear another one of Sam's diatribes about Man.

## CHAPTER THIRTY-TWO

The late-afternoon sun beamed down on the crowded Miami street as traffic moved at a steady pace up and down Brickell Avenue. The people on the sidewalks were as rushed as the cars in the street. It seemed that everyone was in a rush to get home or finish off their Christmas shopping. After a long workday, and with just two days left before Christmas, no one gave the two window washers a second glance as they exited their van carrying large white buckets, with long handled squeegees sticking out of them. Spray bottles and hand towels dangled from their belts.

As the first window washer reached the door of Stein's Mortgage Company, he allowed a mailman, who had suddenly appeared, to go in ahead of him. With his head down, the mailman dug in the huge leather mailbag on his shoulder, and went directly to Mr. Stein's office. Both window washers went to the full plate glass window, and before anyone questioned them, applied the cleaning solution from their spray bottles, effectively blocking the view from the street.

"Mr. Stein, I need your full attention, sir."
Mr. Stein looked up from his cluttered desk, puzzled by the mailman standing in his office. His befuddlement was replaced by fear as his eyes settled on the large, chrome, .40 caliber Glock in the mailman's hand.

Man wasted no time. "Sir, keep your hands where I can see them," he said coming around the desk and helping Mr. Stein to his feet. "I want you to take me to the vault room down the hall, and please don't do anything that'll force me to hurt you," Man added in a firm voice.

As they made their way to the vault room, Mr. Stein saw that his entire staff was herded together in the reception area, and that the windows had some type of substance covering them.

With his window washer's outfit on, Eddie King walked up as Man and Mr. Stein reached the vault room. "Everything's cool. Let get this shit over with."

Once inside the room, Man ordered Mr. Stein to open the safe. "Don't play games with us. We know you can open it."

Mr. Stein returned Man's stare, and said, "Since you know so much about my company, you should know whose money is in that safe."

Smiling, Man answered, "Sir, shouldn't you be more concerned with your wife, Elizabeth, and your son, Frederic?"

"Wha... what are you talking—"

"Just open the safe and your family won't be hurt," Eddie said, cutting the man off.
Man nodded, "The sooner we're finished here, the sooner we can make the call that'll get your family back to you."

Sweating profusely, Mr. Stein protested, "You don't know the people I work for. They'll—"
"You don't know us," Eddie said. "Now open the safe so that your wife'll be able to pick li'l Freddy up from St. Marks like she does every day."

The fact that men with guns knew his wife's daily routine, and his son's school, was all the incentive Mr. Stein needed to do as he was told.

The huge vault door swung open, revealing more than forty large canvas bags, stacked neatly against the back wall. Man stepped in, and quickly checked each bag as he started tossing them out to Eddie.

As he secured the bags, Eddie also made sure of their contents–cash money.
Exactly two minutes after Man, Eddie and Born entered Stein's Mortgage Company, Kid stood

on the sidewalk, with the sliding door of the van pulled back. He moved the folded drop cloths and cardboard boxes around. His every move, kept him within reach of the 30-shot machinegun that was in one of the boxes.

As he worked at looking busy, the seconds stretched out into mind-trips. Kid hoped that the information they'd uncovered from watching the Steins and collecting a week's worth of their garbage would provide the leverage needed to make the job go smoothly. Kid knew that if Stein believed that his family was in danger the chances of him going along were much better.

Born's quiet strength and confidence kept the six employees calm, although very frightened. No one wanted to arouse violence from the broadly built man with the gun. Born remained silent as he guarded the employees and the door. He paced the small area like a bull in a pen with an open gate, but with no inclination to run wild, yet.

After bringing out fourteen bags, Man and Eddie moved the employees into the vault with Mr. Stein. Exactly four minutes after they'd entered the office, Born was on his way out the door with six bags. Eddie and Man, now wearing white overalls, with four bags each, followed him. Born and Eddie climbed in the back of the van and once Man tossed his bags behind them Kid slammed the door and got behind the wheel. He looked over and smiled at Man. If anyone looked, it would appear as if two window washers were finishing their last job of the day.

***

Pete parked down the block from Badlands and tried to get a feel for his old hood. Since they'd stepped their game up, he and Kid didn't hang around the old neighborhood the way they had back in the days. Once major crime became a part of their lives, it made sense to avoid the streets and all the chance encounters with the police.

The City's history of justice for young men of color was anything but fair. It was full of young black, brown, and yellow men who had fallen victim to being in the wrong place at the wrong time when the police happened to be on the prowl.

Death or prison was usually the result when the full force of NYPD confronted poor people of color. It could be something as innocent as a football inadvertently hitting a blue and white patrol car, or something as criminal as jumping the turnstile in the subway–either one was enough of an offense to end in justifiable homicide.

The Yusef Hawkins and Michael Griffiths of the city could tell you that it wasn't only the City's police force that would end a Black life without a second thought–get caught in a neighborhood of angry whites and see what happen. But dead men tell no tales. Eleanor Bumpers would tell you that it wasn't only young men of color being murdered, that is, if a crew of the City's Finest hadn't gun down the emotionally disturbed grandmother in her apartment.

Pete knew the history, more importantly he respected it. Man had taught him to learn from history and to turn those lessons to his advantage. Also, the last thing any professional gunman wanted was confrontations with the police because, in all probability, it would be the last one he had. Because, in the end, the police could muster more forces than the best armed gunman could ever imagine. From S.W.A.T. teams to firebombs dropped from the sky, the police would fire hundreds of rounds in the street to bring down a lone gunman, bystanders be damned. The MOVE Organization in Philadelphia, where over sixty homes were destroyed and eleven MOVE members were killed, including five children, was a perfect example.

Pete considered all of these things as he waved Joe over to the car. Joe strained to see into the car's interior. "Damn, Pete, I ain't recognize you. This ain't your regular joint. but the way you and Kid puttin' in work y'all might be driving anything, huh?"

Pete laughed and said, "Hop in, homey. I wanna kick it with you."

As Joe climbed into the passenger's seat, he slapped palms with Pete. "What's up?" "I'm tryin' to find out what's up around here," Pete said as he turned his gaze toward Blue Seal's spot.

Joe followed Pete's gaze. "You know I'on't fuck with these lames no more. Ricky always tryin' to play a muthafucker."

"Word," Pete replied.

For a couple of minutes, both men were off into their own thoughts. Though both young men had Man to thank for the direction of their respective lives, the roads they were traveling couldn't be more different. Joe worked at the daycare center and was on his way to Howard University next fall, and Pete would go as far as his gun took him. Yet, neither man had any complaints.

"Joe, do me a favor and keep an eye on them chumps up the block. I wanna know what's happenin' with 'em."

Joe smiled, "No doubt, homey. You know I ain't got no love for Ricky and 'em." Pete nodded and turned to face Joe. "Shit, welcome to the club, but you gotta wait your turn. Me and Kid been waiting for a while to break Ricky off a li'l somethin'," he said in a menacing tone. Slowly, Pete let the anger drift away and smiled. "What's up with school? You ready for them fly D.C. honies?"

"Shit, I ain't had time to think about nothin' but studying. Ms. Nicki got me taking some remedial courses at Bronx Community to get me ready for Howard."

"So you'll be ahead of the game and have some time to get to know the city. D.C. is hot and it's black. Black folks everywhere."

"Damn, you sound like you rocked that spot. It's all that, huh?" "Sho' is and since yo' name is Joe you won't have to get used to hearing cats call you Joe."

"What?" Joe asked, puzzled.

"They use Joe the way we use Yo. It's their slang. They got they own style, slang, clothes and everything else. See, when somebody say you lunching they mean you bugging out, and if they call you a Bama, it's a dis."

"Damn, I'm a need a class just on the city. But I can't wait." Pete laughed at Joe's eagerness. "Soon come, homey. And you better represent the hood."

"Ain't no doubt," Joe answered with a nervous chuckle. It was important for him to do well. He'd be the first one in his family to go to college and as Man and Mr. Jenkins had explained–younger family members would follow his lead, especially his younger brother.

"You gonna do good. Plus, we got yo back, young'en. That's some more D.C. slang," Pete said, easing Joe's concern.

Joe leaned over and clasped Pete's extended hand and thought: *Damn, it's good to have people holding you down.* Though the world was cold, it was a lot warmer when someone had your back. Damn right, he'd keep his eye on Ricky's spot and if needed, he'd do whatever it took to hold his people down. It worked both ways. Just like Man, Bigum and Pete and Kid had his back he had theirs.

*\*\*\**

Despite the cold weather, Deacon sat on the bench, enjoying the sun. This section of Central Park was pretty quiet during the winter months. The ice skating rink was on the other side of the lake, and when he listened, Deacon could hear playful shrieks and laughter. But he chose not to listen. He'd selected the spot for its solitude.

The lake was partially frozen and the cold winds battled the sun for control of the temperature, and was easily winning. The chill in the air didn't bother Deacon; it actually matched his mood as he planned his next move. He realized that he had to move cautiously, but in the end vengeance would be his. He began to recite, over and over, from the book of Isaiah, in a singsong voice, "For the Lord has a day of vengeance."

"Hey, Kool Aid. How you doin', fat boy?"

Deacon came out of his trancelike state and stared into the faces of the two young men. Barely out of their teens, the men mistook Deacon's huge bulk for softness, but that wasn't their worst mistake. The larger of the two men smiled at his partner and stepped closer to Deacon, that and thinking that the serene look on the fat Man's face was either stupidity or fear were both worse mistakes.

"Fat boy, me and my road-dog need a li'l loan. C'mon, man, help a brother out," the first man said, with a mocking laugh.

"Word, big-man. I know yo' greedy ass holdin' some ends. Hit us off so we can be gone and you can go back to dreaming 'bout all them Big Macs and shit," the smaller man added, as he stepped closer to Deacon in a show of bravado.

Deacons smiled as the two men positioned themselves to keep him from getting away. Deacon outweighed the two of them by at least 50 pounds. So, he had no intention of trying to escape, at least not yet. He just needed them a little closer.

"C'mon, fat-boy. It's up to you. It can be easy or hard, but you coming up off that cash," the larger man said as a large hunting knife appeared in his hand.

"That's about it. You heard my man–easy or hard. We getting' paid today."
Deacon sighed and shifted his body on the bench. He reached towards his back pocket.
The smaller man shook a short piece of iron pipe out of his coat sleeve. Black tape covered the upper half of it as he muttered between clenched teeth. "Hold the fuck up, fat boy. Don't make me put this pipe to yo' fat ass."

"Well, my money's in my wallet," Deacon responded, as if he hadn't quite realized the threat.

Both men laughed as the wallet came into view, but Deacon couldn't decide which one to give it to and dropped it on the ground between them.

Following the wallet with their eyes wasn't only their worst mistake... it was also their last. In one motion, Deacon stood and slammed their heads together with all the force of his 330 pounds. The sound of their skulls colliding was sickening. Well, it would've been, had anyone other than Deacon been able to hear it. While both men writhed on the ground, groaning in pain, Deacon placed his massive, callus, meaty hands on their necks and crushed their windpipes.

Only minutes after Deacon's wallet hit the ground both men laid dead. Deacon retrieved his wallet, stood and brushed his suit off. After a quick glance around the park, he walked away, unconcerned.

## CHAPTER THIRTY-THREE

Eddie rounded the corner like a homerun hitter cruising into home with the game-winning run. As he stepped into the shadows of the tree-lined street, his smile said it all–a difficult job well done, as expected. Hey, he was *Eddie King*.

As he scanned the cathedral's entrance, his smile matched his gait, confident and deliberate. Before he could decide whether to remain in the shadows of Pirate Alley, or cross the street, Man suddenly appeared on the steps of the St. Louis Cathedral. Though he'd been watching for him, Eddie couldn't swear exactly where Man had come from. It was as if he'd materialized out of thin air. Then, they were in the Big Easy, New Orleans–a city known for its magic.

Eddie stood and studied his friend for a moment–silently wishing that everything was like it was when Man first got out of prison. Back then, every job was a cause for celebration. They would party until the damned band couldn't play another song and the hottest good-time girls had had enough. Man and him had toasted more good times than Marie Antoinette and everybody had ate cake, Eddie thought ruefully. He shook his head at his retrospection and stepped forward. Both men surveyed the area as they approached one another. They fell in step together and headed toward Pere Antoine's Alley, on the other side of the cathedral.

"How did it go?" Man asked, casually.

"Like home cooking: good. But when you're bringing good news things usually do."

" Man smiled at Eddie's confidence. "Maybe it wasn't enough good news for her?"

"Eight-hundred Gees oughta be enough," Eddie responded as they crossed the street again. If anyone were following them, the crossing of the street and unpredictable stops would flush them out.

After taking a minute to face Man, giving them both a chance to check their surroundings, Eddie continued with an easy chuckle, "Shorty got damn near a million. Ain't much can go wrong with that."

"Well, she could've wanted more. After all, it was her info' about Stein that got us over $5,000,000. After expenses, and $250,000 apiece for Pete and Bigum, we still end up with $900,000 and change each," Man pointed out.

"And, she got her $800,000 without putting a gun in her hand or putting her life on the line. No matter what, she was safe. Nothing woulda made me give her up. Shorty ain't got no beef. Stein's dick got him bagged for that South Beach drug money."

Man nodded, "Yeah, that was some expensive pussy there. I hope it was worth it."

"Yo, you think they bodied him 'bout that money? Eddie asked, smiling.

Man shrugged, "It depends on how crazy that drug money done made his business associates. Having the power of all those millions and the guns behind them can make some fools lose they minds. You know Stein gotta be worth a lot more than $5-million. He's been laundering money for a long time. And how long would it take him to work the five-mil off ?"

"Yeah, he gotta be getting twenty cents on the dollar, and with drops of at least $3,000,000 a week from three different crews, he's doin' pretty damn good for himself," Eddie said, as the numbers ran through his head.

Man laughed, "Yeah, I guess he can afford to party a little, huh?"

"Speaking of partying, let's do New Year's in New Orleans. It'll be like old times. We can close down a couple of cathouses and help a few lucky hos earn money for college," Eddie said with a mischievous grin.

When Man hesitated, Eddie attempted to persuade him. "You know that Born and Kid made it home with the loot, and it's been a while since you and me painted a muthafuckin' town. Shit, I remember when we tore some down, put 'em back up and tore 'em down again." Eddie finished with a flourish.

"Yeah, its been a while since I acted the fool with you, and I do miss the shit sometime. But I can't go back to doing it. Eddie, I just got tired of all of the bullshit. Don't get me wrong, it was fun but after awhile fun ain't enough" Man answered, seriously.

"Man, we live hard, so we play hard. It's why we live like we do. Why we walk in a strip joint and shout: Let the games begin, wine and women for all. Fun, that's it. Ain't nothing else."

Though his pace remained steady, Man's sense of direction was off. He truly felt lost. Living as he had in the past, for the excitement of the moment, had been easy. Yet, it had done nothing to ease his pain. So, instead of sophomoric adventures or real happiness, he reluctantly sought answers to life's mysteries

"Eddie, I did all the drugs and women, the high risk jobs and hard living to take away the pain, but all that shit did was dull it for a minute. The shit always came back. I can't be like you, without a fucking care in the world. I found out that fun and excitement couldn't make the shit better. And, neither could revenge. But, don't worry, just because I can't do the partying thing no more don't mean I'm gonna stop making muthafuckers pay," Man said in a solemn voice.

Eddie stifled an angry reply. After all, Man was his brother and if you said blood brother, it couldn't have been truer–they had shed blood together, their own as well as others'. Yet, he was being forced to consider things he wanted no part of. Eddie King had decided, as a child, a nothing child that nobody wanted, to live everyday as if it was his last. Damn right, he'd have fun; his life would be a fool's paradise.

Sensing the tension and turmoil his words had caused, Man stopped and looked into Eddie's eyes. The eyes of both men held things that few others had looked upon–destruction, death and despair, but most of all, the will to survive. Their bond had been forged in death as well as life. Man knew that he'd have probably died in prison if Eddie and Born hadn't stepped up when they did. He extended a clenched fist toward Eddie. "Eddie King, you the best who ever did it. Ain't no doubt about that and I love you, my brother. I just can't chase the good times with you no more," he said with sincerity.

His eyes locked with Man's, Eddie slowly smiled and touched his fist to Man's. "You ain't never lied when you say I'm the best that ever did it. That's just what I been tryin' to tell that big, old, cornbread, collard-greens eating B.E. for years."

Both men laughed as they locked forearms and quickly embraced each other with their free arm. Though people often mentioned how much alike he and Man was, Edidde knew how different they really were. After all, they'd come from totally different worlds. Man had had a mother who loved and cherished him, while Eddie's had abandoned him in a bathroom on a D.C. to New York Greyhound bus. Even Born Equality had had a brighter beginning, he'd known his heroin-addicted mother for the first nine years of his life before she'd died of an overdose, and there was Born's younger brother. Although he was a grimy crackhead, Born treated him like family and took care of him.

Although Eddie wouldn't admit it, he'd settle for a dead, dope-fiend mother and a trifling crackhead brother. If a dopefiend could keep her child, what kind of woman had given birth to him, Eddie wondered. While Born had the Nation of Gods and Earths, along with a family history, sordid as it might be, and Man had his memories, painful or not, he, Eddie, had nothing.

Shit, he didn't even know what state he was born in. Less than a day old, he'd been left on a bus in a goddamn King Edward cigar box.

A cloud came over Eddie's handsome face, but unlike Man, he needed no answers, so he shook it off. Life was what it was, leave the troubles behind and let the good times roll or as they say in the Big Easy: *Laissez les bons temps rouler.* New Orleands was Eddie's kind of town, a place where you could surely lose yourself in the moment.

As Man observed the changes on Eddie's face, he wondered if he should hang around and keep an eye on his partner.

As if he'd felt Man's eyes on him, and read his thoughts, Eddie snapped out of his musing. "Look-a-hea', let's go on over to Faulkner's bookshop. I think you need something to quell your profound intellect," Eddie said with his mischievous smile back in place.

With their troubles forgotten, both men laughed and headed down Pirate's Alley to the house where William Faulkner lived when he wrote his first novel, *Soldier's Pay*. The title was fitting, after all, *they were two soldiers of fortune, or was it misfortune?*

## CHAPTER THIRTY-FOUR

Deacon lumbered down 125th Street, while all the stores displayed holiday decorations, he paid little attention to them. He was oblivious to the pseudo-gaiety. The merchants and shoppers, alike, were all fools and apostates. To celebrate the birth of Christ, they drunk and fornicated, and thought that the exchanging of gifts was the high point of the whole thing. More importantly, they didn't even know the true day or meaning of Jesus' birth. He wondered if they read their Bibles, or even owned any. No wonder Hell had few vacancies. Still, he'd soon be sending a few new residents, he thought, as he smiled. He just had to be patient, and continue to collect information. The more he knew about Man and his people, the better he'd be able to do his work.

As he passed the Apollo Theater, Deacon failed to register the historical significance of the place. He had more important things on his mind as he crossed the street and entered the 125th Street Mart. Although he stopped at a few of the stalls where the vendors hawked their wares, he had no intention of buying anything. He cared nothing about the vendors trying to make an honest living. Their Blackness and honesty meant nothing to him.

He exited the Mart by using the 124th Street exit and stood in the shadows as he waited for the man he was supposed to meet. He had spread around a few hundred dollars of the $20,000 José had given him up front, and was due to receive another $20,000 once he finished the job. He knew that in order to get to Man he needed as much information about him and his people as possible. With his back to the wall, Deacon relaxed as thoughts of murder danced across his mind.

The brisk winter night brought a clean, pure smell to the run down neighborhood. Even with the constant hustle and bustle, and nefarious nature of Harlem there was a pristine and noble quality to the night. Although it was drug infested and crime riddled and its glory was long gone, Harlem's artistic accomplishments and edification rode on the night's air like a tribal warrior on a proud black stallion.

However, Deacon had no time for such nostalgia as he watched the young slender black man get out of his late model, money-green Mercedes. He wanted the information he'd paid for and nothing else. Actually, he despised the man who approached him. Although he drove a $40,000 dollar car, he probably lived in the projects with his mama, Deacon thought.

"What's up, Heavy," the man asked with a smirk, as he examined Deacon's suit. "Damn, you looking sharp, big fellow."

Deacon stared at the man until the smirk disappeared from his face. His eyes stole the courage of the man who'd thought the fat man with the hundred dollar bills and cheap suit was a joke.

"You got something for me," Deacon asked in a conspiratorial voice when he finally spoke.

"I got good news and bad news," the man with the designer clothes and gaudy jewelry said, regaining his confidence. When Deacon didn't respond, other than to continue his death stare, the man looked around nervously and took a step back. "Okay, chill. I got somethin'. But it ain't about that dude, Man. It's about some of his business uptown and one of his partners."

Deacon said two words. "Go on."

"I found out that those young cats down with him pick up strong-arm money from a spot up in the Bronx every week." The young man puffed out his small chest before he continued, "And, I know the address and date of the pick-ups."

Again, Deacon said only two words. "What else?"

"I also got somethin' on the God-body dude, Born Equality, one of the cats your boy, Man, was up north with," the slim man said, building up his heart. Now it was his turn to stare, his smirk back in place, he added, "Here's the bad news. With all the shit I came up with that li'l $500 you hit me with was just a down payment. I had to dig and put myself out there askin"bout these cats."

Seconds ticked by as neither man spoke; finally the man turned to leave with a shrewd shrug that said their business was finish unless...

Deacon smiled at the young hustler's back, and thought about cutting his throat as he reached in his pocket and fingered the straight razor he carried. After a minute that stretched beyond mere time his smile dissolved. "Hold on," he said, as the young hustler turned around.

Deacon brought his hand out, a large roll of bills in plain view, and counted off ten, one hundred dollar bills. "If it's good, you'll get ten more of these," he continued as he extended his hand just enough to make the other man step forward.

With a savvy nod the man greedily grabbed the money. Confident, he told Deacon about Born Equality's crack-addicted brother, who lived just a couple of blocks away in the St. Nicholas projects, and the location of the drug-crew Kid and Pete made their weekly collection from. He gave directions and descriptions, never once questioning Deacon's motives.

Though Deacon listened intently, he continued to caress his ivory-handled straight-razor, all the while thinking about slicing the con man's throat, jugular and vocal cords. Shutting him up, and watching him die a silent but painfully death. The man would sell his own mother out for the right price without ever realizing how cheap his own life was. After finally deciding that the man's lack of principles actually made him an excellent source of information and more useful, for now, Deacon released his grip on the razor.

As he took in the information, Deacon felt a surge of satisfaction, deadly satisfaction. Though Deacon had taken Jose's money, Man's death and the deaths of those close to him was the only thing that could truly satisfy him. The Bible said that a murderer must be put to death, and without question, Deacon knew that Man was a murderer, at least three times over. God only knew all the murders Man was responsible for.

As he pulled away from the curb, in the comforts of his new car, the young man wondered what the fuck this day of reckoning was the crazy fat, muthafucker was mumbling about. He was as crazy as a crackhead with a bag of rocks but without a lighter or matches, thought the young hustler as he glanced through his tinted window at the fat man talking to himself. But as he drove off, his last thought was of the fresh $1000 dollars he'd just made.

Deacon stood on the dark, cold, street and recited from Isaiah 10:3: *What will you do when disaster comes from afar?* To whom will you run for help? Deacon knew what Man'd do. Die like the coward he was.

# CHAPTER THIRTY-FIVE

Seated at his desk, in the office behind the game room, Man thought about Nicki–she seemed to be occupying his thoughts more and more. Although he knew it was against everything he believed in, he was becoming attached to her. What the hell was he doing? If asked, he'd say his life was a tragic comedy filled with adventure–not any damn romance. Yet, if he were honest, he'd have to admit that he had enjoyed spending the last couple of months with Nicki. They'd become almost inseparable after bringing in the New Year together. It wasn't just being around the kids that kept him close to Badlands now.

However, not even honesty could get him to admit that he was in love with Nicki. He didn't want that responsibility. In Man's mind, and maybe in his heart, love only brought pain. He knew firsthand of the pain and suffering that came with it. He'd rather not feel at all, than to endure the hurt again. So Man looked past the joy and happiness that Nicki's presence delivered, gift wrapped especially for him. Nor would he say if asked, that he'd been following his heart since he'd returned from the Miami job.

Nevertheless, thoughts of Nicki continued to stalk him, surround and engulf him. The memories of last night played across his mind like a feature film, staring Ms. Nicole Porter. The images of her toned and shapely body, laid out on yellow silk sheets, danced in his head and stirred his emotions. He'd bathe her from head to toe, slowly running his soapy hands along the curves of her body, gently exploring every contour. Then, after he rinsed her off he dried her with his mouth. Some drops of water were licked off and others were dried with his lips and breath.

As he carried her into the candlelit bedroom, the flickering flames and burning incense gave the night a surreal quality–a quality that was matched only by Nicki's sheer beauty. He massaged warm, jasmine scented oil into her body, spending extra time on her perfect, heart-shaped derriere. When every inch of her exquisite body was covered with oil, he stepped back and admired his work. Well, actually, he admired God's work.

The thought of a God snapped him out of his reverie. His life was proof that any such belief was a fallacy at best and a cruel joke at worst. Man saved his faith for the .45 he carried and the preparations he put into his actions. If a God could allow women and children to suffer day in and day out, he wanted no part of its power. His idea of a higher power was to withstand the pain and make whoever brought it beg for a quick death.

Just when he felt his defenses were in place, Nicki forced her way back into his mind. She had danced for him, teasing then pleasing him until the early hours of the morning. Uh-huh, she sure was something special, he thought. He enjoyed her company, her sassy remarks, the faces she made and the way she carried herself. She had discovered ways to touch him with something as simple as a smile or gesture. She could make him laugh and excite him at the same time. She gave herself to him with a force that wouldn't let him deny her gift of love.

*Damn that woman,* Man thought, as he abruptly stood up. His life wasn't no damn romance. He would probably die with his shoes on in a street, just like the one where Badlands was located. Though he'd stayed close to Badlands lately, he knew the neighborhood was just another violent ghetto and death was always near. That was what he should be thinking about. In the ghettos of America, violence was constant and often as bad in the homes as it was on the streets. So with violence as the main cause of death for Black men, it wasn't much of a stretch for Man to assume that he'd meet his death in the streets– especially with his chosen lifestyle. Nicki was a luxury he couldn't or wouldn't afford himself.

A walk would clear his mind, he thought, as he started for the door. The game room wasn't due to open for hours, anyway.

Once on the sidewalk, he breathed in the cool March air. So far, March was holding true to form, coming in like a lamb with mild temperatures, and he figured he would enjoy it before the lion showed up and the temperature dropped. It felt good to be outside; it was just what he needed to get his mind off of Nicki. As he considered giving Eddie and Born a call at their hotel in Mexico, where they'd been for the last three weeks, his eyes drifted across the street and landed on Nicki. She stood on the steps of the daycare center, watching him as if she'd been waiting for him.

Once their eyes met, they held the gaze for a moment that seemed like it could go on forever. They communicated silently. No words were necessary, because their connection transcended the necessity of spoken words. Finally, Nicki broke the spell by placing her hands on her hips and tilting her head to one side. When Man didn't speak, or move toward her, she gave him a bug-eyed look that said: *Well?* Though the word hadn't been spoken, Nicki's sassy attitude made it clear what she meant. As she made her way down the few steps, Man turned back toward the game room door.

"Man, don't play with me," Nicki called from across the street.
Man cocked his head as if he wasn't sure he'd heard her. He turned around slowly, studying her with an innocent expression on his face.

Nicki stomped her right foot and gave Man a look that could kill. Man laughed at the sight of her stomping her little foot on the pavement.

"Man, don't play with me," she repeated, her neck moving with each word. When he continued to laugh, she sucked her teeth. "See, you been playing with them kids too long, but I ain't playing with your butt."

Man stopped laughing long enough to reply, as he crossed the street, "Well, since you ain't much bigger than most of the kids, I figured you wanna play too." Once he stood in front of her, his laughter started again.

"Oh, so you showing off, huh?

"Now, showing off is definitely something you'd know about," Man said, slipping his arms around her waist.

"I didn't hear you complaining last night," she whispered, as she melted into his embrace. With their bodies swaying together, Man worked his fingers along the small of her back, innocently brushing them over the rise of her buttocks.

"Oh, on the contrary My Lady. When I mention your showing off, it's a complement of the highest regard. I enjoyed your performance last night and eagerly await the next time you grace me with one," Man said, as he pulled her closer.

"My Sir, I don't think you'll have long to wait, especially if you keep massaging my back like that and talking all sweet," Nicki purred with passion. With their eyes and bodies locked no one else existed.

Something about defenses nagged at the back of his mind, but with the feel of Nicki in his arms and her scent exciting him, the thought was chased away.

Terry stood at the window in the little office she used at the center watching Man and Nicki. She had noticed Man and Nicki spending a lot of time together the last few months, but this was too damn much. Nicki was all over him and Man was just as bad. She shook her head. Man should be hers. *If only he didn't think of her as a child.*

Terry fumed as she watched their bodies moving in rhythm to music only the two of them could hear. She should be the one Man was holding. Although she was sure he loved her, she knew that he loved her like a daughter and not as a woman.

All of a sudden she pictured Man and Nicki doing the nasty, and began to laugh. The laughter kept coming, and it felt good. Hell, if she was Ms. Nicki, she wouldn't be ashamed of doing anything with Man. "That's right Ms. Nicki, handle your business," Terry said, with another burst of laughter.

Terry had to admit that Nicki was cool. She'd been true to her word–Terry was learning how to run the center and in a few weeks she would take her G.E.D., which she fully expected to pass because of Nicki's help. And more importantly, she was dancing again. It was the only thing she knew that she was good at. But was she really good enough to dance professionally, like Ms. Nicki said?

Though she wanted him for herself, Man did seem happy and that was good because he was usually so sad. Well, she thought, with another laugh, doing the nasty could make anybody happy. The thought of Ms. Nicki doing the nasty with her prim and proper acting self was really funny. Terry just bet that Man wouldn't be using all them big words he liked so much either. Tears welled up in her eyes as she went into another fit of laughter. As she watched Man and Nicki head toward the park, she whispered. "Oh-oh," Ms. Nicki don't come back here with your hair all messed up," as she laughed heartily.

"Terry, what in the world is so funny?"

Startled, Terry spun around and stared at Ms. Sara, Nicki's top assistant at the center. "Oh, I was..." Before she could finish she lost control of herself and erupted into another fit of laughter.

"Girl, what is wrong with you?" the attractive, forty-ish woman with the voluptuous figure, and pretty dark skin, asked with a big smile.

All of a sudden, Terry wondered if Ms. Sara was getting any, and laughed even harder. Then she thought of Ms. Nez and her hot self. It was *so funny.* Maybe getting old wasn't so bad after all?

"Please let me in on the joke, Girl. You know I like a good laugh," Ms. Sarah said, shaking her head.

Terry finally regained control and answered, with a smile, "I was just thinking about Ms. Nicki's hair getting sweated out."

Sara gave Terry a puzzled look, and said, "I don't get it, but as long as you're happy, I'm happy," adding a few giggles of her own. They both continued to laugh as Terry thought: *Yes, I am happy for the first time since I was a little girl.*

***

"Ze, I see you been playing the block lately. What, you put a hit out on that midget that was after yo' ass?" Short-Dog asked, with a chuckle.

When José nervously looked in the direction of the game room without offering a response, Short-Dog continued in a sardonic tone, "I see you peeping around and shit, ain't nobody watching you is they?"

Short-Dog was in a good mood and felt like having some fun at Jose's expense. His mood would've changed considerably, had he known that because of Billy-boy's warning, it was him and not José that Man was concerned with. Fear would've colored his mood, if he'd known that, thanks to Pete and Joe Smith's vigilance, Man knew enough about him to wake him up every morning.

Although José felt more secure since learning that his cousin's partner, Ice, had been shot and arrested by the D.E.A. shortly after his meeting with Peto, he still wasn't sure if Man knew that he'd tried to have him killed. Since Man hadn't moved against him, he figured he was safe for the time being. That left the fat man, Deacon, to worry about. After he'd given him $20,000, Deacon demanded another $20,000 and when he had refused, Deacon had slapped José like he was some punk and threatened to expose him to Man. Of course, he'd given Deacon the money. What choice did he have? José didn't know who he wanted dead more, Deacon or Man, but if Deacon got rid of Man, he'd figure out a way to get rid of Deacon. Damn, he thought, *caught in the middle of two crazy muthafuckers.*

Short-Dog watched José. He knew that the pretty muthafucker was scared and thought it was funny that Man had the boy so fucked up. "Ze, what you thinkin' so hard about? I mean, yo' crew clocking dollars, you iced out and yo' ride is fresh. Shit, you shouldn't have a care in the world," Short-Dog said, with confidence that José wouldn't step to one of Ricky's lieutenants.

Finally, José spoke, "You right. Shit is good, and you know what, its only gonna get better."

Caught off guard by the strength of Jose's words, Short-Dog said, "I hear that."
As he and Short-Dog stood watching the crackheads bringing money to their respective crews, José decided that once Man and Deacon were out of the way, he'd killed Ricky and Short-Dog too.

At the same time, Short-Dog was thinking of how he could play José into crossing Lo or even fuckin' with Man, so that Man would kill the fool.

"Yo, its good to have you on the block, homey. I missed yo' fly ass and all them fly hos that come checkin' fo' you," ShortDog said, with all the false sincerity he could muster, adding his best smile for good measure.

"Word. You know how we go, Dog," José responded in kind.
As the two drug dealers clasped hands, in a show of camaraderie, they were thinking of how nice it would be to attend the other's funeral.

Lo's primitive face – his forehead hung over, while his jaw jutted out – had a fierce look even when he was happy. Nevertheless, watching José and Short-Dog turned his stomach, and it showed on his face. He knew that neither one of them meant whatever bullshit they were saying. *Two fake-ass muthafuckers playing like they was cool.* Shit, from their four years together, Lo knew that José was only cool when it helped him get whatever he wanted.

Nevertheless, he still ran with José because....Money. It wasn't hard to figure out. Where else could a 26-year-old, uneducated, Puerto Rican make four or five grand a week? Nowhere! Maybe he'd become a movie star with his good looks. Hollywood needed somebody to play the roles of monster and villain and he definitely had the look for that, he thought, somberly.

As he observed the crackheads and pitchers going through the ritual of *cop-n-go,* Lo felt the weight of poisoning his own community. Although he hadn't grown up around Badlands, he'd always called a neighborhood just like it home. In his thirteen years in the drug game, he'd worked on more than a dozen drug-blocks in Manhattan, the Bronx, and Queens. He'd gone wherever the money was, and of course that had sometimes led to gunplay. He had always stood up when pressed. That, along with his size and rough look, made him stand out and had put him in demand.

From the start, in the street, he'd had work. *Ain't life a bitch?* he thought, shaking his huge head, *a muthafucker gets put on for being big and ugly, as much as for having the heart to hold down a block.* But watching the crackheads beg and do just about anything for a hit, while punks like Josê and Short-Dog got off on the shit it broke his heart.

He'd grown up with a heroin-addicted mother, and watched as she paraded men in and out of her bedroom to support her habit. As a child, he'd seen his mother degraded and humiliated by men just like Short-Dag and José and he had to admit, like himself. When she'd finally died of AIDS five years ago, he secretly rejoiced because nobody could hurt her anymore. At least, he hoped.

Through the years, he had used his lack of opportunities to justify his actions and blamed the system for his choices. But he knew that they were his choices. Even with the lack of opportunities and the second-rate education offered him, no one had forced him to sell drugs. He'd even pushed the memory of his mother aside, so as not to let it interfere with what he had to do to survive. Just remembering what she'd gone through said it all... it was wrong to bring pain to people who were too weak to help themselves and benefit from their suffering.
Lo fought off his blues and went to check on the workers. After all, his job was to make sure the money kept coming in.

Lo smiled, ruefully, as Ricky turned the corner in his Beamer, the car gleaming as if it just came out of the showroom, the system was pumping BBD's *Poison.* The drug transactions continued uninterrupted, the police were paid off and the block was under Man's protection, safe from the stick-up kids. It was business as usual and business was good. But it was more than just about the business of making money. Yes, Lo, Ricky and all the rest of the young men chasing a fast dollar had made their choices, but it had been a setup from the start. They'd been shown a dream, the American dream without any concept of how to acquire it. *Freewill be damned when you were broke and without hope.*

***

With her blue and yellow traditional outfit and head covering. Ms. Nez burst into Sam's Cleaners like a strong African wind. "Mary, girl, c'mon now, let's go. You know we due at the center, all them babies waitin' on us. Now c'mon and let's go, girl," Ms. Nez shouted, without stopping to breathe. Her voice, like her outfit, was full of life.

Mr. Sam, who was behind the counter, twisted up his face. "Hmph! Nez, we don't need all that racket in a place of business."

"Now, Sam, ain't no sense you getting any uglier than you already is, so go on and straighten out yo' face. And it don't look like you doing much business," Ms. Nez said, looking around for any sign of customers.

"Good God, fo' a li'l woman you sho' talk a lot and..."
"Well, Sam, that cause I knows a lot" Ms. Nez cut in, looking around him as Ms. Mary came from the back.

"Hey Nez, you looking good."

"Thank you Mary. You looking good too, and you a saint too," Ms. Nez said, shooting a narrow-eyed look at Mr. Sam.

Ms. Mary covered her mouth to push the laughter down. "C'mon then girl. you know we running late."

"That's what I been sayin', but yo' husband cain't seem to understand me to save his poor soul. But girl, you a saint." Both women giggled as they started for the door.
"I know y'all ain't walking to the center with them boys out there selling more drugs than the A&P sells groceries?" Mr. Sam said with a sanctimonious air.

The two women looked at each other for a moment then turned their eyes on him. "Sam, how else we suppose to get to the center if we don't walk the three blocks?" his wife asked calmly.

"Hmph, first of all, y'all ain't gotta go; ain't nair one of y'all getting paid for going, and another thing, it—"

Ms. Mary said, "Sam, you the biggest fool the lord done made," stopping him cold.

Ms. Nez shook her head. "Ain't you the one that always talking 'bout how these kids ain't got no respect or direction. Well, we tryin' to give the young ones some of both, so they won't end up out there selling drugs."

Mr. Sam's brow furrowed as he stepped in front of his wife and gave her a look of disapproval. "Well, it ain't safe for y'all to walk down that street. So the least y'all can do is go 'round the park or just don't go."

Before his wife could respond with what was sure to be a strong telling-off, Ms. Nez moved besides her and said, "We'll be just fine. Man is already out there sweeping the sidewalk in front of the game room. And even if he wasn't, them fools know Man won't allow 'em to mess with the folks 'round here."

At the mention of Man's name Mr. Sam became icy, his eyes narrowed with contempt. "Man is what's wrong around here and if—"

"Sam, not today. We ain't got the time or patience to listen to yo' foolishness 'bout Man. And what you need to do is stop puttin' blame everywhere and help fix things," Ms. Mary said in a strained voice.

When her husband opened his mouth to speak, Ms. Mary turned her back on him. "C'mon Nez, let's go."

Mr. Sam stood alone in the middle of the cleaners, his face hot and pinched with his resentment for Man. He wondered why people couldn't see that Man was no good. It didn't matter to him that Man had put a stop to drugs being sold any and everywhere in the neighborhood and had run off the majority of the dealers. He'd rather put up with drug dealing all over the neighborhood than have Man around. Anything associated with Man left a bad taste in Mr. Sam's's mouth and Man's total disdain for him only made it that much more difficult to take. *Who the hell was Man to judge people?*

# CHAPTER THIRTY-SIX

"Your Honor, in light of this new evidence, the defense moves for a dismissal of all charges against Mr. Jenkins."

The judge examined the documents before him, studying each one as if it was the Holy Grail. After perusing the papers, he trained his eyes on the prosecutor with a disgusted look on his face. "Mr. Wheeler, what is the government's position at this time?"

Mr. Wheeler, the lead prosecutor on the case, nervously shuffled his folders around in front of him. He glanced quickly at one of his assistants, seeking help, then cleared his throat as he continued going through the files on the table.

"Mr. Wheeler, is there a problem?" the judge asked, sternly. "Ah, ah... Well, your honor, I seem to have misplaced my copies of the Whitman, Brown and Pauls financial statements and the purchasing orders Mr. Karp is referring to."

"Does that mean you are challenging the validity of these documents," the judge asked impatiently.

"Your Honor. What Mr. Wheeler is—"

"Mr.?" The judge interrupted the assistant, and added in an unsympathetic tone, "If you have something pertinent to offer this court, I advise you to do so in the proper fashion."

"Pardon me, your honor. Mr. Milken, for the prosecution. What Mr. Wheeler means is that the documents haven't been authenticated—"

A brusque wave of the judge's hand silenced Mr. Milken in mid-sentence. "That's enough. Now, as to my question, is the evidence being challenged?"

"Umm ahh... Well, your honor, as Mr. Milken was saying, we haven't at this time, had a chance to—"

"Hold it." The judge said firmly as he shook his head. "It's my understanding that these papers came directly from the Securities and Exchange Commission's investigators, and that they've been in your possession for five months."

Tyrone could barely control himself; he desperately wanted to speak in his own defense but he sagaciously remained silent and allowed the proceedings to continue.

The judge pushed his glasses up on his beak of a nose, and gave the prosecution's table a long stern look. Mr. Wheeler and his three assistants avoided the accusatory stare that came from the judge. "This is not a moot court, gentlemen. We do not practice at being lawyers here, we practice the law."

Turning his attention to the defense, "Mr. Karp, I'll entertain your motion, nonetheless, the court will have a rejoinder from the prosecution at this time. Mr. Wheeler?"

After exhausting a futile search for his pen, or perhaps his dignity, Mr. Wheeler answered, without looking up, "Your honor, the government has no objection to the defense's motion."

Before the judge could rule, Mr. Karp spoke, "Also, your honor, I'd like the record to reflect that we expect a statement from both the prosecution and the SEC, vindicating Mr. Jenkins of all charges. And, that on Mr. Jenkins' behalf I will begin a civil action..."

"Fine, Mr. Karp," the judge said with an amused look on his hawkish face. "Now, to the business of this court–charges are herein dismissed. Mr. Jenkins, you are free to go just as soon as the formalities are handled properly. And I assure you, Sir, they will be expedited. Isn't that right, Mr. Wheeler?"

"Yes, Your Honor," the prosecutor mumbled in a defeated voice.

Bob's Barber Shop was humming with news of the dismissal of the charges against Ty. The Filmores, dapper as usual, Reverend Barnes, Mr. Bob and a few other regulars enjoyed the June evening by discussing the matter thoroughly. Although Reverend Barnes was an orator by profession, a down-home Baptist preacher, none of the others were easily outdone. Each man took this turn as keynote speaker. Anyone keeping count of their respective two cents would've needed a calculator.

Mr. Bob, who had been shooting the breeze and one-upping all comers in his shop for almost four decades, had the floor, "See, I knew that it was all a goddamn witch-hunt from the start. The boy was doing too good, and too much good for too many people, so they thought they'd knock 'im off his high horse. But what they ain't know, couldn't know, was that old Tyrone Jenkins' horse had wings and could fly."

"Uh huh, you ain't never lied, Bob," Tim Filmore threw in from his seat across the checker table from Mr. Bob. "But its yo' move right now and it don't much matter what you do cause that king is mine's."

"Now, any other time I'll be mighty upset 'bout losing a king. But today, we all kings cause justice was done."

"That may be true, but it riles the hell outta me that when they arrested him it was front page news in all the daily papers. But the dismissal is only in one paper, and little more than a paragraph, buried on page eight," Mr. Tom said indignantly.

Nods and words of agreement came from around the room. "The Lord was on this one though, brothers. Evil may be alive and well, but it was still defeated. And you read what that lawyers said 'bout a civil suit. So they can write about that when that old devil gotta pay the righteous man since they don't wanna write about the man being righteous," Reverend Barnes said with his preachers' cadence.

"Though, most of the time I find yo' sermons a li'l longwinded, I like the sound of that," Mr. Tom said with a smile.

"Maybe cause it was short," someone called out, as the shop burst into laughter.

"Well, I'm glad everybody so happy 'round here," Bigum said, as he came through the door.

"Bigum, please tell me you ain't walk by this big ole window without me seeing you cause if I can't see you I'm completely blind," Mr. Bob said with a slow shake of his head.

Bigum smiled and replied, "Now Bob, you know I'm too big to sneak up on you in plain day light. And you know I came from the other way."

Mr. Bob and Bigum shook hands, then Bigum greeted the other men with handshakes as well.

"Bigum, you heard from Ty since we left him at the courthouse last Tuesday?" Reverend Barnes asked, as he stood to greet the big man.

"Sho' did. He came by to see Man early Wednesday morning. He did say that he wanted to discuss some business with you, though. Somethin' 'bout grants and proposals for a summer camp and some training classes. Him and Man kinda loss an ole country boy like me with that talk of this and that," Bigum said, with a self-depreciating smile.

Reverend Barnes and everyone else who knew the big man, knew he was far from the big, simple, country boy he often portrayed himself as.

"I knew Tyrone wouldn't forget us, and I knew he'd hook up with Man just as soon as he could," the Reverend said.

"Yeah, he said that he wanted to thank Man right off: but Man changed the subject before Ty could get the words out," Bigum said.

"Man ain't much for words." Mr. Tom said, with a knowing nod.

"Speaking of Man, where is he?" Mr. Bob asked.

"Oh, him and Nicki, took Terry, Lisa, the Smith brothers and a bunch of the younger kids fishing early this morning," Bigum said.

"Fishing?" The Fillmore twins asked at the same time.

"I remember when Man was a young'un, the boy'll walk to City Island and back to catch fish for his mama. He'd come home with all these fish, and be just as proud. But Willie got tired of all the extra work the boy was bringing her, so she taught him how to clean and fry 'em," Mr. Bob said with a chuckle.

Suddenly, everyone became quiet. Memories no one wanted to recall had crept into the shop. It was if the Ray brothers were once again terrorizing the neighborhood. And all these years later, what it cost to stop the brothers haunted every man in the shop, just as it did Man.

Mr. Tom broke the feeling of dread. "It seems that Man and Nicki is doing a lot of things with the kids, huh?"

Bigum returned the knowing smiles from around the room, "Well, seeing how the daycare center and the game room is across the street from each other, it's only natural."

"That's right. Some things is just as natural as man and woman," Mr. Bob said easily.

"As Tim likes to say, 'You ain't never lied there,'" Reverend Barnes added, as the room full of older men laughed like teenage boys at their first dance.

*** 

With the kids gone and the game room closed for the night, the meeting in the office moved along undisturbed. Kid and Pete were basically observers, while Man discussed a business proposition with Sammy and Mack, the bosses of Green Top. Man explained that he'd come into six-dozen "Joker-Poker" slot machines, and had close to thirty bodegas, mom and pop restaurants, and afterhours spots willing to take one to three of the machines for twenty percent of the revenue generated. Although profitable, it was a venture too time consuming for him to get into, he explained.

"Man, we don't know shit 'bout no slot machines. I mean, other than how to put quarters in, pull the arm and hope it's the jackpot, we 'on't know jack 'bout slots," Sammy said with a smile.

"Yeah, we damn sure know about losing money on them muthafuckers. Shit, we better off tryin' to start a C-lo or craps spot," Mack added.

Before Man could reply, Sammy went on, "We don't know nothin' 'bout no slot machines. We wouldn't even know where to start with no gamblin' shit. Especially when all we ever did was lose money fuckin' with dice or them machines."

Man leaned forward, resting his forearms on the desk as he looked intently at the two young hustlers and said, "That's my point. You and just about everybody with a spare quarter will play 'em. And all you really need to know is that the house never loses. Why do you think they call 'em one-arm-bandits, huh? And I know a cat, Misdemeanor Bill, who'd school y'all on the gambling hustle. Bill is the real deal and you can learn the game from him and you can wait until you kick it with him before you decide on this thing.

"And make no mistake. You're definitely gamblers. Every time you cop a key, or hit yo' workers or collect the loot you gambling with yo' freedom and life. And another thing, just cause drugs'll probably always be around don't mean that they gonna always be around here."

Kid and Pete exchanged looks. Although hoods, Kid and Pete were grateful to Man for steering them away from the drug game and realized that in his own way, he was attempting to do the same with Mack and Sammy, who both knew that Man looked down on the drug game and cut their eyes at each other in a silent message. Though he'd always been fair with them, they understood that Man was dangerous and that there was more to the discussion than appeared on the surface. Life in the ghetto, as well as hustling, had given them a *sixth/street* sense about such things.

"Okay, how much can we make off each machine and how much you want for all of 'em?" Mack asked, letting his street sense take over.

While Pete and Kid chuckled. Man smiled at Mack's direct approach. "Here's the deal, it's all about location. The better the spot, the more people will play. Now, as to the price. I guess they gotta go for at least $500 each, that's $6000 for a dozen."

"Damn, Man, that's a li'l steep for..."

"Wait. That's just the lowest price you'll find 'em on the market for, but it ain't the price I'm giving y'all." With that, Man had everyone's attention. Sammy and Mack were on the edge of their seats and Pete and Kid was eager to see what was coming next. "At $500 apiece, that's $36,000 for all of 'em–seventy-two machines, but what I'm a do is give 'em to you for the price you payin' for a key right now. A key is what? Twenty-two, twenty-four thousand? So, twenty-three for the whole setup."

Sammy looked at Mack. Neither one spoke, but it was obvious that the wheels were turning in their heads as they added it up.

"The price is cool, but ain't them machines controlled by the mob, with Po-Po backin' 'em?" Sammy asked.

"I was hoping you'd be up on that. 'Cause the only way to make it in the life is to be up on every angle," Man answered, and then nodded at Kid and Pete. "That's why I asked them to join us. While I hook it up with my people to take care of Po-Po, I'll handle the fat, white men with cigars stuck in their mouths. Pete and Kid'll hold y'all down.

"And the same way some of your drug money end up in the police's pocket, some of that loot from the machines will too. But I'm not going to leave y'all fucked up," Man finished with sincerity.

That was good enough for both Sammy and Mack. They knew that Man's word was like gold – even better – it never varied in worth. And they hadn't missed the nods of agreement from Kid and Pete that followed Man's words.

"Shit, we down, right? Mack asked, looking at his partner.

Before Sammy could respond, Man stood up and said, "There is one more thing, and I want to be clear about it before we finalize our agreement, gentlemen. I want you to come to your decision based on the facts, as well as your faith and understanding of my position."

Another silent message passed between Sammy and Mack, each man knew that whatever was in store could be a turning point in their young lives – one that might not include the possibility of a u-turn later. Though two of the younger men in the room trusted Man with their lives and would kill for him, all four knew that a deal with him might as well be written in blood. He'd hold you to your end and honor his. Although Man often switched back and forth from the neighborhood vernacular to a more proper pattern of speech, his word was always good.

Mack held his breath, steadied his nerves and in an even voice, just above a whisper, asked, "What's up Man?"

"No need to be so grave, my young outlaw associate. It's not the end of the world, though as all things must come to an end, so too must all things begin. I'll give you the machines: all of them, for half now and the rest six months from the day the last machine is installed. But y'all gotta let the drug shit go and start claiming gambling winnings each year," Man said, as he resumed his seat and looked over at Pete and Kid.

"They can tell you how to handle your money by paying taxes on gambling proceeds." After a quick look at Pete and Kid, Sammy said. "We don't know shit 'bout all this gambling shit. It ain't like—"

"Yo, Sam, if me and Kid could learn the shit, I know you 'n Mack can too. Shit, once you get yo' paper in order you can do what the fuck you want. The government don't care who get rich as long as they get to tax it," Pete said, with the confidence of an up and coming executive of a Fortune 500 company.

"Word!" Kid exclaimed flashing his trademark smile.

"Damn, I 'on't know..."

"Just like you didn't know shit about selling crack, but learned where to cop from, how to cook and bottle it. It's like anything else, you gotta go for yours. See, crack is on its way outta this hood, but I recognize hustlers and know they gotta hustle. Ain't no long bids for gambling and Po-Po don't sweat it like they do drugs. Sammy, Mack, sometime we all have to leave shit behind and try something new." Man stated earnestly.

"But Man, we still got work we just copped and we can't—"

"Sammy, I don't expect y'all to do a Richard Pryor and flush yo' shit down no toilet," Man threw at them, drawing laughter from around the room.

Sammy turned to Mack and nodded with the confidence youth gives. Mack returned the nod as both men laughed and faced Man. "We down," they said as one. Man clasped each of their hands and it was a done deal.

*** 

Ricky waited in the dark shadows, by the Pelham Parkway entrance to the Bronx Zoo. The animal sounds and darkness unnerved him as much as the prospect of his impending meeting. Though he'd gone through great pains to set it up, he had the sensation of falling into a black hole without any chance of making it out.

His eyes widened in alarm at every sound and approaching headlights. Although traffic along the parkway was light at two in the morning, Ricky was terrified of being seen. Nevertheless, he waited and prayed that he wasn't trading one hell for another. But, with Man constantly cutting back on the work-hours and taxing his new spot, he needed to make a power move.

He'd grown tired of waiting for José to do something. So, he'd decided to get rid of Man another way. In the beginning, Man's way had worked better for everybody, but he had continued to expand his control and limit Ricky's ability to make money. It didn't occur to Ricky that with a couple of million dollars stashed away he could walk away from the drug game and never look back. Nor did it matter that he was still making over $100,000 a week. All that mattered was that it was time to be free of Man.

Ricky stood paralyzed as the dusty, brown, four-door Plymouth Fury eased to a stop in front of him. He swallowed dryly and worked at being calm. After all, he had a plan, one that guaranteed huge sums of money for the man in the car. It was a plan that would put him in a position of power. If things went as he planned he couldn't lose.

As Ricky started to move out of the shadows, the white man in the front passenger's seat shouted, "Nobody told you to move. Stay your ass right there."

Ricky froze and started to speak, but thought better of it. Damn, he wished that he'd brought a joint with him– at least a small .380.

As the two men in the front of the car continued smoking their cigarettes, like they had all the time in the world, Ricky strained to make out the lone figure in the back seat.

Finally, the front passenger-door opened and a man stepped out and stretched his big, blubbery body. "Keep your hands where I can see 'em."

Fear coursed through Ricky's veins. He didn't know what to expect. He felt like a cheating husband caught on camera as he stared wide-eyed into the pig-eyes of the chalky-skinned white man standing before him. After Pig-Eyes pushed Ricky up against the fence, his partner joined him. Ricky let out a sigh of relief when he saw the well dressed; lean, delicate looking black man.

"What the fuck you looking at? No, I'm not one of your homeys and I ain't your brother. I'm the fucking man," the Black cop said venomously.

Once he was frisked and relieved of his possessions, Ricky was led to the zoo's entrance, which to his surprise; the men had the key to. Once inside, Ricky was pushed face first into the wrought iron fence surrounding the polar bear exhibit and told not to move or speak. After what seemed like all night, but probably was only a few seconds, he heard a new voice, "Ricky Parker, drug dealer."

Ricky flinched at the sound of his name; he hadn't used his last name to set up the meeting. The voice of the pig-eyed man cut in with a gruff order, "Turn around, prick."

Ricky turned around and came face to face with an albino looking white man, his skin pinkish and lacking pigmentation. While the first two men looked to be in their late-thirties, the albino was a fifty-ish looking slim man with a slight paunch, and dove gray eyes and a sneer on his face.

"What did he have on him," asked the albino.

"House and car keys, a beeper and this, Sarge," the black man answered, holding a thick wad of cash.

"A couple of grand, huh Ricky?" the sergeant asked.

"A li'l over three," Ricky mumbled.

Ignoring Ricky, the Sergeant addressed his two detectives, "Split it between the two of you and give him back the rest of his stuff. "

The Black detective examined the bills, mostly fifties and twenties, then divided them as equally as possible without counting them and passed half over to his partner. The doughy detective with the sloppy Wal-Mart sport coat and slacks, greedily stuffed the bills in the inside pocket of his cheap jacket.

As the sergeant watched Ricky's facial muscles twitch nervously, he smiled, but even that didn't remove the sneer etched on his thin, bloodless lips. "Now, Ricky, what can I do for you?"

"I wa-wa-wanted to ta-ta-talk to the man tha-that run thinthin-things in the 44th precinct"

"What do you want?" the man interrupted.

With sweat running down the back of his thighs, bringing up an odor of fear, Ricky said, "I know y' all gettin' paid from my spot and ..."

Before he could finish, the big, blubbery detective kidney punched him. Ricky doubled over and fell to his knees. He felt the bile rising up as his dinner threatened to soil his Gucci loafers.

"Watch your mouth, punk," Black cop said the as he snatched Ricky up from the ground. Ricky gagged as he choked down his vomit and couldn't get a word out, but it was just as well since he was too scared to speak anyway.

"Now, I'll ask you one more time, just one, what can we do for you, Ricky?" Through teary eyes, Ricky looked at the sergeant and answered meekly, "I just wanna b-b-buy some p-p-protection, Sir." Ricky had never stuttered in his life.

His back pressed into the fence behind him when the cop with the pig-eyes reached in his pocket, but the cop came out with nothing more dangerous than a pack of cigarettes, lit one for himself, then offered the pack to Ricky. Ricky tried to say no but couldn't get it out and settled for a shake of his head, and waited.

The sergeant turned his back on Ricky, looked at his watch, then inspected the creases of his pants, before turning back to face Ricky. While Pig-Eyes wore Wal-Mart, and the black cop looked like he shopped at Barney's Fifth Avenue, the sergeant was Brook's Brothers all the way.

"We don't sell protection." His cold eyes silenced Ricky's plead before he could get it out. "But, we do protect our interests."

The Black detective smiled and Pig-Eyes snorted, which Ricky realized was a laugh. The sergeant continued, "And, now that you're one of our interests, we'll take care of you. First thing you need to know is that you work for us, not the other way around. We get $20,000 a week, and from time to time we'll supply you at a better price."

Scared to death, Ricky could only nod.

"And secondly, we need information about other dealers. After all we are the police," said the albino sergeant with a mocking laugh. Abruptly he started back toward the Zoo's entrance.

Although fear made it difficult for Ricky to put one foot in front of the other, he was led out of the zoo with a detective on each side. The sergeant was already seated in the backseat, with the window down, a cigarette burning in his bloodless lips. As the Black cop went around to the driver's side, Pig-eyes guided Ricky to the open window.

"We'll be in touch, and don't worry, we won't let your criminal friends in on our agreement. Well, not unless you make us," the albino said in a bored voice.

Pig-eyes pushed Ricky away from the car, then sprawled into the front-seat. As the engine came to life, Ricky said, "I already got some information 'bout one of the biggest dealers in the city, guy named Man."

When the car continued to move off, Ricky wasn't sure if he had been heard. Then he remembered that he didn't have any money and he'd left his car in a garage all the way over on Jerome Avenue.

As the unmarked police car turned off Pelham Parkway onto White Plains Road, the driver glanced in the rearview mirror and said. "So, this doesn't make it to the captain, huh?"

"I think we'll handle this ourselves. The captain is losing his touch for the dirty work. Look at the way he handles the two old coons who own Shine's. It's a goddamn disgrace to the department. Yeah, we'll handle this alone, and we'll find out who the little snitch was talking about," the sergeant said no longer bored.

*∗∗*

Eddie King glanced around his den—he had decorated the room himself and often thought of it as his sanctuary. The paintings and sculptures purchased personally from galleries around the country were mostly from African American artists. Normally, his pieces from the Harlem Renaissance, including works by Laura Wheeler Waring and Palmer C. Hayden enabled him to escape life's day-to-day trials. But not today, no matter how hard he tried to escape, he couldn't.

He had been restless since returning from Mexico, although, in truth; the restlessness had started in New Orleans after Man had left. In New Orleans he'd entertained himself with three of the most exotic and erotic women any man could dream of–three different sizes and shapes of beautiful women. One, was tall and stacked like an African Queen, another an exquisite beauty, of Japanese and African ancestry, barely five-feet tall, the third a hometown shapely Creole beauty. The stamina he displayed had amazed all three of them and was the start of the restlessness that threatened to drive him crazy.

Eddie had spent over $8000 partying with the three women. Although their usual fee was $1000 for a night, they'd accepted $1500 apiece for the three nights and two days they'd spent with him. The other $4000 had been spent on the hotel suite, cocaine and shopping. Though it was normal for him to celebrate after a job, Eddie'd attacked his latest celebration with a vengeance.

His partying had always helped him escape thoughts of his birth and cured his loneliness. But, now, Man's foolish search for something more in life was affecting him and he wanted no part of it.

As he rose, Eddie exclaimed, "Damn Man and all that bullshit." He needed to get out of the house. He wished that Born hadn't stayed in New York once they'd arrived there from Mexico, but the God wanted to check on his brother. *Crackhead or not, at least the God had somebody,* Eddie thought, against his will.

Eddie locked his front door and headed toward the garage, then stopped–he'd walk, it would do him good. But that was also what he'd thought about his 8-mile run through Rock Creek Park and his 90-minute workout at the Washington's Health and Racquetball Club, earlier in the day. Well, he figured, at least a walk couldn't hurt, after trying to work through his mood in New Orleans and Mexico; he really didn't know what else to do.

His walk led him to the Sunshine Art Gallery. It was nice and cool inside and after the mile and half walk in the D.C. heat, the air-conditioned gallery was a welcome change. After exchanging pleasantries with the couple that owned and operated the gallery, Eddie was left alone to browse. Over the years, he'd become a regular at the gallery. He had even brought his young protégé, Mark-O, to the gallery and exposed the kid from Southeast to artistic beauty. Man wasn't alone in the belief that gunmen were trained and should be cultured and taught to appreciate the beauty in life. Hence, Eddie took pride in schooling young Mark-O on things besides gunplay.

Thinking of the kid's amazement at his first trip to the gallery, Eddie finally began to relax. The memory of Mark-O playing roughly with a Yoruba drum and Eddie laughing, until told that the drum cost $18,000, and how he'd snatched it from the kid's hands made him laugh. It felt good to laugh, so he didn't hold back. He laughed like a fat girl surrounded by a bunch of cute skinny guys.

"'Girrl, look at him. He just laughing."

"He must have had some of that love-boat D.C. is famous for."

The two young, pretty women giggled as they watched Eddie. As they continued to observe him, Eddie picked up a Native peace pipe, adorned with feathers of an eagle and symbols expertly carved into the long stem and bowl. He pretended to take a toke– his cheeks puffed out as he affected a strained cough... and burst out laughing again.

"See, I told you. That's that love-boat," the tall, slender, café au lait colored woman affirmed to her companion.

"Ali, you're too much. Just because the man is having a little fun you think he's on drugs," the shorter woman with the shapely figure and rich brown complexion said.

"Yeah, fun all by his self, huh?"

"Well, as a modern woman of the new decade, I'd think you'd know all about having fun all by yourself, Ms. Ali."

"Oh, no you didn't. Kia, just 'cause you ain't getting none don't mean I'm not."

*"Girrrl, pul-eeze,* if your batteries are dead so is your sex life," Kia said smartly.

Both women laughed and squared off as if ready for a battle. What followed was a battle of the dozens, funny and friendly. "Now, I know your li'l butt ain't talkin' 'bout somebody not getting' some when the last date you had was when yo' li'l brother drove down and helped you move yo' stuff off campus," Ali said, as her neck moved to accentuate her point.

"Would that be the same li'l brother's bones yo' hot ass so desperately wanted to jump." Kia responded, barely holding back the laughter.

As the two young women went back and forth with their good-natured insults, their college decorum was forgotten for the moment and replaced by the attitudes shaped by their respective neighborhoods. They could have just as easily been two homegirls from Southeast, playing the dozen, as two law students from Howard University. They were so caught up in their fun that neither one realized that the man they'd been observing was now observing them. And as strange as they'd thought his behavior was, one could only imagine what he thought as he watched them with a puzzled smile on his face.

Ali noticed him watching them first and tried to relay to Kia that they had an audience, albeit of one. But Kia was on a roll and missed the signal.

"Girl, wasn't you the one dating that midget? I know they say size don't matter, but that's taking it to a new level. Well, for yo' sake I hope God blessed him with some inches somewhere else," Kia said, placing her hands on her hips.

Kia' eyes widened in embarrassment as Eddie's laughter reached her. She covered her mouth with her hand as she turned around and then whispered, "Why didn't you say something?"

"I tried to warn you, but no, you just... Oh-oh, here he comes."

The young women held Eddie's attention with their style, especially the short, brown skinned one. As he watched them whispering back and forth, he wondered why he hadn't noticed them earlier. Nevertheless, he was glad that their playfulness had attracted his attention and he was sure they got attention wherever they went.

As he made his way over to them, Eddie thought it was just the type of distraction he needed. "Hello, I couldn't help catching your little show. What was it? The home-girls' production of 'We be buyin Art'," Eddie said with glee. He was clearly pleased with himself.

Although Kia thought his line was cute, she wasn't about to fall for it. She smiled sweetly. "No, it's our *Let's act a fool and see how many strange men will approach us',* production."

Ali giggled and shook her head, her golden locks swinging loosely. "I apologize for my friend. She's always like this when she's attracted to a man."

Kia stared at her friend in disbelief. "You was the one who said he was on Love-boat," she said looking from Ali to Eddie.

Now it was Eddie's turn to divide his gaze. Though both women were attractive, it was difficult for him not to stare at the almond-eyed, chestnut colored one. *Damn, shortie is holding,* he thought as he took a quick look at her shape.

"Y'all are good. But you won't know how good until you let me escort you to *Mr. Henry's* for open-mic night," Eddie said with poise.

Despite her intention to be difficult, Kia found herself smiling into the face of the handsome stranger. He was definitely cute, and the loose silk shirt was doing little to hide his well-muscled body. *But,* if he thought his line was going to get him anywhere, he had another thing coming. She knew all about smooth talking men–after all, her father was the smoothest of the smooth.

Still, she couldn't stop smiling at him and she had to admit that he had a beautiful smile. As they stood there smiling at each other, Ali cleared her throat and said, "Hi, I'm Alicia and this is Kia."

"I'm Eddie. Hello Alicia," Eddie said in a gregarious manner, before turning his attention back to Kia. "Hi, Kia. Kia. That's a beautiful name. Who named you?"

"Thank you. My father," she answered returning his candid gaze.

"Oh I'm sorry, Alicia is a pretty name too," Eddie said, forcing his eyes away from Kia for a brief moment.

Alicia laughed at his attempt to be polite, but it was obvious that sparks were flying between her friend and the good-looking man. "Thanks, but don't worry about me, because you got your work cut out for you with Ms. Kia, here."

"Alicia!" Kia exclaimed, not knowing what else to say she just shook her head. "Girl, you know how picky you are, so if he—"

"Alicia, I'm not playing with you..."

"No, Kia, that's cool with me. I'm used to hard work, and you definitely look like you're worth it," Eddie said smoothly.

Checking out Eddie's Ralph Lauren khaki slacks, beige, short sleeve, Perry Ellis silk shirt, and brown suede Penny loafers, Kia said, "It must be difficult working hard, dressed like that?"

"It all depends on the job," Eddie answered easily, as he openly admired Kia's pink and white, strapless sundress and white, Huarache sandals. His smile grew as his eyes lingered on her pretty little feet.

Alicia watched with amusement–Kia was always complaining that men were so shallow that a woman could spend an hour doing her toes and getting her feet pretty and a man wouldn't even notice. Now that she had one who'd made it clear that he noticed and was extremely interested, Alicia couldn't wait for Kia's response. Kia was notoriously hard on men.

"Well, it was nice meeting you, but we have to get back," Kia said, as she tore her eyes away from Eddie's and gave Alicia a pointed look.

As Alicia stared blankly at her, refusing to help, Kia shrugged helplessly. "We really do have to go."

Eddie couldn't help but notice how pretty her shoulders were as he realized she was scared of him, or maybe it was her own reaction that scared her. He wanted to know more about her. "Okay. I'm sorry if I bothered y'all. It's just that this was such a fortuitous meeting; I didn't want it to end. I didn't mean to scare you by—"

"Who's scared?" Kia asked, as she cut him off and placed her hands on her shapely hips. "Cause it sure ain't me."

Alicia had to control the urge to scream. *'You go girl,*" at her friend–instead she simply turned to examine one of the paintings hanging on the wall.

Eddie chuckled and let his eyes roam over her body, before locking them on her face. "Since neither one of us is scared can we *at least* exchange numbers? I say at least because my invitation for *Mr. Henry's* is still open, to both of you."

"Oh don't mind me. Y'all work it out", Ali remarked over her shoulder.

Kia and Eddie laughed. The conversation flowed from there and after exchanging numbers they agreed to discuss a date for *Mr. Henry's* open-mic night.

"Well?" Alicia asked, as they left the gallery, and when Kia didn't answer she continued, "Girl, you know you hear me."

"Well, what?"

"Oh now it's well what, huh?" Alicia said, smiling. "You know damn well that man was fine and he couldn't take his eyes off you."

"Okay, he was cute. But you know all the bullshit the cute ones put you through and..."

"Shit! I don't believe you complaining because he's cute. And, I bet he's educated–fortuitous, no less," Alicia said, giggling.

"Girl, just cause he's smooth don't mean he went to school. Look at my father, talking to him, if you didn't know any better, you'd think that he was a college professor."

Alicia nodded in agreement, laughed, and said, "Yeah, but your pops is fine too. Damn, if you wasn't my girl I'll have to give him some."

"You're crazy. You done went from my little brother to my pops. You're shameless."

"Shameless my ass. I just settled for li'l bro 'cause daddy ain't here," Alicia said, as she walked ahead of Kia and threw an extra switch in her hips. They laughed and continued on.

Though she wasn't sure what she was going to do, Kia couldn't get Eddie out of her thoughts.

After Kia and Alicia left, Eddie talked with the owners of the art gallery for a while, but was thinking about seeing Kia again. When he finally left, he decided to stop at the Caribbean restaurant, Montego Bay. He was in the mood for a fruit salad and some ice cream. It was a dish that reminded him of Kia. Eddie smiled, his troubles forgotten.

## CHAPTER THIRTY-SEVEN

"Man, I know that li'l workout ain't got you wore out like that," Born Equality said with a smirk on his face.

"You know better than that," Man answered, as he pulled himself out of the hammock that sat on a stand in the middle of the room. He rolled his shoulders and rotated his head in circles to loosen his tight muscles.

"I don't know? You look kinda beat homey," Born said.

Man laughed, then said, "I hear ya' talkin', but wasn't you the one having trouble finishin' those twenty sets."

Born flexed his massive biceps, and puffed out his chest, emphasizing his huge pecs to hide his chagrin at the memory of his struggles completing the twenty sets of push-ups, chin-ups and dips. "Yeah, but I did 'em, right?"

"That's right. Just like I did your crazy-ass arm routine," Man "That's right. Just like I did your crazy-ass arm routine," Man replied, remembering his struggles curling 60 and 70 pound dumbbells, which Born seem to accomplish with little effort. "I ain't no weightlifter, God," Man added.

"And calisthenics ain't my thang, but I got that money. Shit, we both got money in that stank-ass gym you like so much," Born replied.

"Yeah, we put some work in this morning, and unlike Eddie, I like a real gym, not no spa with steam-rooms and Jacuzzis," Man said as he paced the spacious living room of his Riverside Drive condominium, and placed the palms of his hands in the small of his back, stretching.

Though sore, Man felt good. And it was good having the God around. Born had spent the last couple of weeks in town and as usual, when in New York he stayed at Man's condo. Although they hadn't spent much time together during his stay–the God was busy checking on his brother and Man had Nicki and the game room to keep him busy–the bond between the two men was as strong as ever, which made Man think of Eddie.

"B.E., what's up with Eddie'', he asked, as he stopped in front of the large bay window and looked down on the Hudson River.

"Well, he probably making his regular visits to the health club, and it ain't just to work out or because of any steam-room, Eddie gotta chase the ladies."

Except for a couple of minutes over the phone Man hadn't spoken to Eddie since New Orleans. It was almost as if Eddie was avoiding him.

Born sprawled across the green, leather, Chesterfield sofa, settled his gaze on Man and noticed that he had one of his pensive expression on his face. "What's up? You all right?"

"Yeah, why?" Man asked, attempting to make light of Born's concern.

"C'mon, Man. You got that look...you know, like you got some heavy shit on your mind," Born said, refusing to let it go.

"I'm cool. I was just thinking 'bout Eddie. Since the Big Easy, I ain't been able to get at him for more than a minute here and there on the phone."

"You know Eddie gonna be Eddie, or whoever Eddie wanna be at the time," Born said with a dopey smile as he thought of his long time partner. "All the way to Mexico he just had to give me his play-by-play of his three nights in New Orleans. After you left, he did what he do, party like the world is gonna end.

"And, I guess, in the first week in Mexico, he ran through nine, ten different women. Then, for the next few days he got on some gambling shit and almost got us into a couple of brawls because he kept beating chumps at arm wrestling and downing shots of tequila," Born said with a shake of his head and a big smile.

As the smile disappeared, he went on. "After all that though, he just kinda seemed outta it. I mean, he ran on the beach just about every morning, then he'd swim so far out you couldn't even see him. But he didn't want to be bothered. He had some shit on his mind, too."

Man didn't miss the emphasis Born placed on his last word, but chose to let it pass, turning his attention back to the Hudson.

Though silent, Born thought of his two partners: Eddie and Man, different in so many ways, were alike in so many others. Both men embraced the troubles of their lives, keeping them close, though Eddie never admitted it and Man only because it satisfied his need to punish himself, Eddie hid behind an urbane and affable façade, savoir-faire to the max. But as hard as he chased women and good times the loneliness and desolation chased after him. And the same was true of Man, who strived to apply a stoic logic to life, which did little to erase his passion and even less to fill the void in him.

Though they didn't actually look alike, one reminded you of the other with their similar features and athletic builds. While he didn't have Eddie or Man's good looks, Born didn't need them. He had never needed women for a distraction. And, in fact, he'd often thought neither one of them was pleased with the attention they received from the opposite sex. It seemed to confuse them even more–was the interest real? Eddie and Man's troubles made Born consider his rough, block of a face that sat on his larger block of a body, a blessing. His appearance also served as a deterrent, few people would think of the God as a victim. Now, Man and Eddie, they were another story, he thought with silent amusement, if they wasn't tough guys, they'd be pretty boys. A fool who couldn't perceive danger might make the mistake of taking their looks and mannerisms for something it wasn't and end up dead.

Born looked around the interior of the living room, the high ceiling made the room appear even larger than it was, especially with the smooth parquet floor. With its wood molding and arched doorway, the room spoke of an era when workmen took pride in their craft. Examination of each of the six rooms in the condo would tell you of the work and craftsmanship that went into making each room what it was, but a look at Man, or Eddie would reveal little. One would need to know their respective histories, the tragedies, and their reactions to them, and even then, comprehension might prove elusive.

It was the height of irony that two lives that started out so differently had ended up so similar. One had been abandoned at birth, never knowing his mother's love, and the other had known that love to such a degree that he'd started his own family at seventeen, only to have it all snatched violently away. Circumstances beyond their control had put them on the same path–the path of lost souls–a path the God walked with them by choice because of his bond to both men. Though he knew that his own life hadn't been ideal, Born didn't waste time rationalizing. He didn't need answers, nor did he care about reasons to justify his actions. Just as he embraced the lessons of the Nation of Gods and Earths, he embraced life, and if it didn't always add up, that was okay with him. He'd decided long ago that living life was the only answer he needed. Nevertheless, the irony of him spending the last few minutes on introspection escaped the God.

"Yo. Man, I'ma jump in the shower and go check on my li'l brother," Born said, as he lifted himself from the sofa.

"You want me to roll with you, God?"

"Nah. I'm just gonna meet some fat preacher dude he's supposed to be working with. I wanna make sure it's on the up and up and ain't no drug shit," Born answered nonchalantly as he headed for one of the bedrooms.

***

Nicki smiled at Ms. Nez. "Ms. Nez, you know that you shouldn't be askin me stuff like that."

"Oh, chile' please! You think you and Man the first one to do it in a park? Well, y'all ain't," Ms. Nez said with a naughty gleam in her eyes.

"Ms. Nez, me and Man ain't hardly do nothing in that park," Nicki said, as modest as she could.

"Oh. I know y'all didn't."

"You do?"

"Girl, it was too cold out there to do the grown-folks' dance." Ms. Nez answered with a sly grin.

"You too much."

Ms. Nez giggled. "Hmph, from the way you and Man carryin' on all of a sudden, you the one that's too much. Y'all make me want to be young again. It's so special being in love and having..."

Nicki's wistful expression brought Ms. Nez up short. Although Nicki sat just across the room from her, it was obvious that, her thoughts were miles away. She sat on the velvet, rose-patterned, love seat thinking about her battle to share her love with Man. Ms. Nez's words brought back the memory of the confrontation they'd had shortly after the New Year: *She had awoken to find Man staring at her from the other side of the bed, and when she raised her brow in question, he answered, "You're beautiful."*

*"Thank you," she replied, pushing through the haze created by their night of lovemaking.*

*"No, I mean it. You're beautiful," he stated as if she'd missed the full meaning of his words.*

*Alarmed by his tone, Nicki moved into his arms. Although he returned her embrace, his was stiff and unnatural. "Man, what's wrong," she asked turning her face up so that she could look into his eyes. The sadness she saw almost brought tears to her own eyes. "Man, what's wrong? What did I do?" She was confused and hurt. After weeks of them sharing, not only passionate nights but hopes and dreams together, it was painful to think that she was the cause of the pained look on his face.*

*The silence stretched and seemed to crush her. The tears came from deep in her soul–the man she loved didn't want her. It had to be that, what else could it be? But wait, their night of lovemaking as freaky as it had been, was filled with love, she'd felt it. Man loved her, but...*

*"Man, you have to talk to me. If you don't tell me what's wrong I can't..."*

*He gently pushed her away from his body and sat up in the bed. He shook his head. "You can't change what is, Nicki. Don't you see, it's no good ... I'm no good," Man said fixing her with a hard gaze, daring her to contradict him.*

*"You just told me that I was beautiful, and that's exactly how you make me feel. I love—"*

*Man's voice remained low, but its intensity was unmistakable as he stopped her in mid-sentence, "Nicki, you don't know what you're doing. Life ain't no fairy tale. I can't keep you safe, and I won't be respon—"*

*She'd jumped out of the bed, naked and unashamed. "Man, I'm a grown woman. I don't need you to protect me... I need you to love me. I mean that is if you do. I told you that I wasn't the little girl from our childhood. And I know what I'm doing. I'm loving you and I'll fight to do it. Don 't push me away.*

*"I know what I want, what I need–You. If you don't love me then just say that, but if you do then give me what's mine–all of you."*

*Nicki crawled on the bed and straddled Man before he could respond. She kissed him deeply—pushing her tongue in his mouth, sucking on his bottom lip. She grabbed one of his hands and put it between her legs.*

*"See what you do to me, baby," she said as her juices covered his fingers in seconds. With her hands behind his head, as she continued to kiss and lick Man's mouth, nose, eyes, and neck, she pushed her forearms down on his shoulders and lifted her body up, rotating her hips until his hardness found her hot, wet center. Then, she pushed down, taking his manhood into her. "See how much I need and want you. I just need you to let me be all the woman I am," Nicki moaned, as she rode him.*

*"Nick, you gotta listen to me," Man growled as she clawed his back and licked his face like a woman welcoming her man home from a trip that lasted too long.*
*Nicki cut his words off by sliding her tongue in his mouth, then said, "No, you gotta listen to our bodies, and our hearts." She increased her pace. "Tell me that you don't love me and I'll stop..."*

*Her words caught in her throat as Man began to pull her forcefully down onto his stiffness, she felt him deep inside of her and cried out; "Aiiee, oh yes. That's it. Right there, baby!"*

"Nicki? Nicki? You okay?" Ms. Nez asked as the younger woman's face became flustered.

Embarrassed, Nicki shook her head as if clearing it and answered, "Yes, I'm fine." After a deep calm breath she added, "I guess I was just thinking."

"I guess you was, huh?"

Nicki glanced at the older woman, afraid to make eye contact as if it would give her away. "Ms. Nez, you need to stop it," she said lightly.

"Well, I just hope Man don't stop whatever he's doing. Cause its good for both of y'all. See, when you get old like me you gotta pay attention to somebody else's love life if you want excitement," Ms. Nez said with a salacious wink.

Nicki gave an exaggerated look of innocence, but before she could speak, Ms. Nez said,

"Oh, chile, save those li'l cute looks for Man. Though I'll bet he knows exactly what's behind every one of 'em already."

"Ms. Nez!"

"Ms. Nez nothing, I've been around and I know how it is when it's good and right. And I can see that's what you and Man got. Somethin' good and right."

Although Nicki's smile was happy, a wistful look followed it. Ms. Nez missed neither one. "If it's that good, that right, it's worth whatever y'all got to go through. Love ain't always no cruise, them waters can be rough sometime, but it's still love," she said, sagely.

"It sure is hard sometime. Man, always trying to tell me that—"

"Nicki," Ms. Nez cut in, "Is he always loving you; I mean, even when he's trying to tell you whatever it is he thinks it is you need to know, can you still feel his love?"

Although she hesitated, Nicki's expression answered better than any words could. Her eyes crinkled with pleasure and with the joy of being in love. She couldn't deny the fact, or force of Man's love, even when he tried to keep it from her.

"You're right, Ms. Nez, Man's just so hard headed sometime."

"Chile, ain't nothing like a hard and difficult man. They the best kind, and it's better that they're hard than soft, especially, in the *right place*, "Ms. Nez said, as she stood up and placed her hands on her hips.

"Ms. Nez, you oughta be ashamed of yourself," Nicki said, laughing.

"I'm a woman, and don't intend to let getting old change that. I wish that I could give some of Man's hardness to these old folks that keep trying to get in my bed."

Nicki was speechless; all she could do was laugh at the older woman's spunk and desire for life.

# CHAPTER THIRTY-EIGHT

Pete's twin daughters clung to his legs. Although they had his wide, expressive eyes, the girls were small replicas of their mother, which was fine with him. In Pete's eyes Pam was as beautifully as any woman. With a leg for each of them to hold on to, the girls were having a ball and effectively kept Pete from leaving the house. At five the girls were old enough to understand that their father had things to do, but still young enough not to care. The girls craved his attention and Pete worked hard at meeting their needs. His family meant the world to him. He often looked at them and their mother and thought how lucky he was. Without a father figure around, he learned the importance of family from his mother.

As the only male in a household that included a younger sister, Pete learned early on to honor and protect the women of his family. Although he understood that the lack of male role models in African-American homes hampered the development of young Black men he couldn't figure out why more women didn't realize that they could raise their sons to be the type of men they themselves longed for just as his own mother had done. She'd refused to allow him to let the influences of the street override her mothering and his good home training. She had supplied the foundation, and reinforced it throughout his life, never letting him forget the lessons she taught.

From early childhood, Pete was charged with the care of his sister, who was now a junior at Brown University. Good home training wasn't gender biased in the Holden household. Ms. Holden — and she was quick to let you know that it was "Miz." and not Mrs. — had taught both of her children by example. Just as Pete learned how to be a man, his sister had learned what it meant to be a woman. Respect and responsibility and accountability were drummed into their heads daily. Pete was raised to be the fence that protected the women in his life and to acknowledge that they were the flowers that sustained him.

Which is why he rarely went along with Kid on his womanizing and partying jaunts. Although there were times he envied Kid's carefree and hedonic pursuits, the thought of having his childhood sweetheart and the twins waiting at home was usually all the motivation he needed to go home. He'd gladly let Kid have the nightlife and the different women that came with it, for the family life and the opportunity to know one woman completely. Most nights Pete got to tuck the girls in bed, which was more joy than any night out on the town with Kid had ever brought him. Nevertheless, he didn't regret his bond to Kid, Man, and Bigum, or even Eddie and Born– they were family too. And, part of his loyalty to them came from his mother's teachings: *You take care of those who take care of you.*

"If y'all let daddy go now, I'll be home in time to tell y'all a bedtime story," Pete offered.

"No, daddy, don't go," the girls, shouted in chorus. "We wanna..."

"Y'all get off your father. Didn't he just tell y'all he'll be back in time to tell y'all a story for bed," their mother cut in, as she came up behind Pete and wrapped her arms around him. Pete leaned into her embrace as his hands rested on top of the girls' heads.

"And I want more than just a bedtime story, Mister," Pam whispered. Pete's hands smoothly left the twins and found their way to their mother's waist. "We gonna make our own story. It's called making a boy-baby, by Pam and Pete" he whispered in her ear. Pam laughed and tried to pull away from him, as the horn sounded for the fifth time. Kid was getting impatient.

"Okay, I gotta go. Your Uncle Kid is out there going crazy."

"Daddy, daddy, let 'im come upstairs and play with us."

"Uh, uh, let your father go," Pam told the twins. "Baby, please go before Kid comes up here and make the girls crazy. He'll have them running all over the house. He's worst than five sets of twins."

"He plays more than the kids. Shoot, sometimes they gotta tell him to stop. He got the right name. Just put "Big" in front of it," Pam finished with a smile.

"He can't help it. That's just Kid," Pete said, as he laughed.

"Okay, kiss your father and let him go. He has stuff to do and we want him back as soon as possible. So, you two—"

Mommy, can we go down—o"

"No, just let your father's legs go. Now!"

Once Pete made it downstairs and climbed into Kid's BMW, Kid forgot that they were running late. "Yo check this out," he said, handing Pete a small Swiss Army knife. As he pulled away from the curb, Kid's face showed his delight over his new toy.

Pete examined the knife for a few seconds and started to pass it back, but Kid waved it off. "Naw, man, that one's yours. Open it. The blade sharp as shit."

Pete looked at his partner and shook his head, thinking about what Pam had just said about Kid. He gave the knife a more enthusiastic look, knowing that if he didn't Kid would go on and on.

"Damn, it is sharp," Pete said, running his finger gently along the small blade. "Yo, I thought these joints was suppose to have all kinda shit on 'em, like can openers and screwdrivers," Pete asked, putting the knife in his pocket.

"Yeah, I thought the same shit. But Bill said it's a florist's knife, use to cut flowers and…"

Pete gave Kid a sideways glance as he cut him off. "Misdemeanor Bill? What the hell he know about flowers?"

"He used to own a flower shop." Kid answered, laughing.

"Get the fuck outta here."

"No shit. See, you thought he just went around committing misdemeanors, huh? Nah, Bill ain't just smart enough to know not to fuck with no felonies," Kid said with a chuckle.

When they'd taken Mack and Sammy to meet with Bill, Bill explained that anything more than a Class E felony was off limits for him. He spent his life doing petty crime and was proud of the fact. In twenty-five years of crime, he'd never done more than 6 months in jail, and had never seen the inside of a prison. As Man put it, Bill knew his limitations and was smart enough to stay within them.

"That's a sweat deal Man gave Mack and Lem," Kid said as he guided the car onto the Major Degan Expressway.

"Yeah, he looked out for them. It's only right though, I mean, since he's about to cut the drugs out," Pete said, shook his head and added, "You know that shit is gonna be a bitch to pull off"

"But, you know if Man says he's gonna do it, it's as good as done," Kid replied, with unwavering confidence in Man.

Pete nodded in agreement. "But what I don't get is why he got us holding down Mack and Sammy when we oughta be watching his back. You know, it ain't like everybody gonna be happy that he's stopping the drugs in the hood."

"Yeah, you right. I can see us going to war 'bout this shit, but fuck it. At least he said he already took care of that shit with Mack and Sammy, they got the green light now. And Man ain't about to leave us outta the game, though I wish he'd come up with another move soon. I'm ready to go back to work."

"I know you ain't beefing. You was down on the last joint in Miami," Pete said with an air of disappointment.

Kid turned up the radio, BBD's *Poison* blasted out of the speakers. "You got your cut. After Eddie and B.E. broke you and Bigum off me and Man put our shares with it and split it four ways, so—"

"It ain't 'bout no cut," Pete interrupted with a defensive tone to his voice.

"Pete, you down by law, and you know that ain't never gonna change, *homey*. It's us, in this thing forever," Kid said, glancing at his partner.

"I shoulda' been in Miami with y'all."

"Yo, somebody had to take care of home base and with the girls it was better that it was you anyway."

Pete was silent, but his mind was racing. Although he wanted in on every move, he cherished his time with his family and hadn't really missed being on the road. But he felt that he had an obligation to Man and Kid. "I just wanna hold up my end."

"Yo, ain't no doubt you do that. I could'a made the pickup by myself, but yo' ass won't go for that. Shit, I know Pam wasn't tryin' to let you out. And, I know the twins had a fit."

"Yeah, everybody loves daddy," Pete said with a smile on his face. After a moment he became serious, "Man wants us to work all the pickups together, and the last couple of times I been gettin' a bad feelin' about that chump Easy. I think somethin's up. So, yeah, I gotta ride with you."

"I wish Easy would try somethin'. I ain't never liked his punk ass anyway," Kid said, with a ruthless look on his face.

"Yeah, I hear that. But, *we* just gotta be ready for whatever these lames come up with." Pete paused for a moment, his expression stony, "We still don't know what Short-Dog was up to either."

"Like I told Man, we shoulda laid his sneaky ass down when we got back from Miami," Kid said, as if killing someone he'd grown up with was the most natural thing in the world.

"I 'on't know, Kid. That's kinda cold. I mean..."

"Fuck that." Kid said, "The muthafucker did it to his self."

The silence was heavy as Kid eased off of the Major Degan onto the Cross Bronx Expressway. "Pete, I know what you sayin' 'bout Dog, but if he scheming on us his ass oughta be laid down, and with the quickness."

Pete nodded in agreement but remained silent. Although he'd been called Peter-Gun since the first time he'd picked up a gun at age 12, he'd never been one to shoot first and ask questions later. Pete was a first rate gunman, but wasn't an out and out killer.

True to form, Kid didn't dwell on the seriousness of their conversation. "Yo, you hear 'bout that new strip joint up on Boston Post Road–*Fool's Paradise?* It's the shit. Damn, it be like twenty-five, thirty strippers up in there." Kid laughed as he recounted his latest adventures. He had no need to be philosophical about loving women or killing.

***

Born stood on Eighth Avenue watching the projects. It was his third attempt to find out what was going on with his brother. Since his brother had told him about the fat preacher he was working with, Born hadn't been able to catch up with him. Born guessed that meant there was money being made, because the only dreams the boy had was pipe dreams. So if he was busy, it was the business of getting high.

Born was tired of getting the run-around from the crackheads who hung around his brother's place. Every time he showed up, they had a story ready and it always ended with a plea for a few dollars.

With knowledge of self, Born Equality couldn't understand how anyone could live the way crackheads did—dirty, smelly, broke, and a slave to drugs, without any hopes or dreams. Their only concern was the next high and doing whatever it took to wrap their lips around a pipe and take a trip to nowhere.

Although he didn't judge them, the God acknowledged the futility of their existence. It was beyond him that anyone would settle for such a life. Life was what you made it, and to make it a crack mission was a waste to the God. Life came complete with enough misery as it was and adding the burden of addiction to it was the ultimate surrender. While the addicts suffered, the dealers were only marginally better off. They chased money like the crackheads chased the next hit. No price was too high– neither prison, death, nor the destruction of their own neighborhoods could deter them from their distorted American dream.

As he moved down 127th Street toward Seventh Avenue, deep in thought, Born still noticed the green Mercedes Benz creeping up the street. He thought that it was the same car he'd seen around before, and recalled that each time he'd seen it he felt the driver watching him. And, what was worst, the man seemed to be working hard to make it appear otherwise. That and the fact that in the twenty minutes he'd been there the car had drifted through the block four times put him on guard. He mentally recorded the license plates and the driver's description, as best as he could through the tinted windows.

He didn't know what was going on. But whatever the chump was up to, Born was ready. He scanned the windows of the projects and the tenements across the streets. Most of the tenements' windows were dark, and a few were covered with plywood. Born checked the parked cars as well as those moving. He started toward the Benz, turned quickly and headed the other way. He stopped and made as if he was checking addresses with a piece of paper in his hand. Then, he turned and stared at the building his brother lived in.

Born's eyes narrowed with suspicion as he made his way into St. Nick, and headed straight to his brother's building but instead of going to the elevator, he went straight out of the back exit and slipped through the projects onto 1 26th Street. Although he gave his surroundings long, searching looks, he didn't notice the fat man watching him from the shadowy doorway of an old tenement, as he watched the Benz.

# CHAPTER THIRTY-NINE

Bigum rushed over to Man, who smiled, amused at the big man's impatience. "You talk to Shine? What he say?"

Man's eyes gave away nothing, as he suspiciously scrutinized everyone within hearing distance. Bigum wasn't as restrained. The detectives' visit to the game room had shaken him up. He wanted to know what a Detective Sergeant, and his two men wanted with Man. Man's silence only added to his anxiety.

He fell in step beside Man, who'd started to move through the busy stalls of the Fulton Fish Market. At six in the morning, the place was an absolute madhouse. Buyers and sellers crowded together, which was why Man had chosen it in the first place. With people going and coming from midnight to nine o'clock in the morning, delivering, selling and buying fish, two men talking and picking out seafood was as common as a hot pants clad hooker in Hunts Point after dark.

No longer able to hold back, Bigum whispered, "Well?"

As Man picked out a half dozen midsize Red Snappers and instructed the worker how he wanted them cleaned, he nodded at Bigum, acknowledging him but not answering. Moving farther down the isle of iced-filled stalls he pointed to the jumbo shrimps. "Gimme three dozen of those," Man said, before shifting his attention to the scallops. "And let me get five pounds of scallops too."

As his order was being filled, Man turned to Bigum and asked, "Did you make it to the Yankee game?"

The big man was exasperated by Man's discursive manner, but answered the question, "I ain't feel like goin'. I gave the tickets to the Fillmores."

"That was magnanimous of you. I'm sure Mr. Tom and Mr. Tim enjoyed the game." Bigum hated it when Man started playing with words, as if nothing else mattered. He couldn't stand it anymore; he stepped in front of Man and open his mouth to speak. But Man gracefully moved around him to pay for his purchases.

Bigum closed his mouth and shook his huge head. Man's devil-may-care attitude was a goddamn pain. He followed Man to another stall where Man brought four lobster tails before heading outside. Bigum could barely contain himself.

As they neared the old docks, Bigum stopped and planted himself as firmly as an old oak tree, refusing to move until he got some answers. "Well?"

"I'm cooking dinner for Nicki tonight," Man said with a smile, as if that explained everything.

"You might think it's a joke when cops come 'round looking for you, but—"
Man interrupted, "Bigum, that's what cops do – come around, mostly looking for money."

"Yeah, but what did Shine say?"

"Oh, he knew 'bout 'em. They stopped at his place too. And he know 'em from his man in the four-four. But they talkin''bout how things is different now cause they takin' over from Shine's man."

Bigum frowned. "Well, why didn't Shine talk to the man he been dealing with?"
Man's eyes danced around, then settled on Bigum. "He tried, but couldn't get 'im. But that don't mean shit, thirty year police veterans who make Captain, and career criminals ain't exactly suppose to have easy access to each other."

"Man, you don't sound too concerned, but I'm telling you this is trouble. If you had'a seen 'em. One looked like a goddamn ghost, white as a sheet and meaner than a mongrel bitch in heat. And the other two–the skinny black one reminded me of a rattlesnake, he'd bite you just 'cause he can, and the fat one looked like a pig with a mean streak."

Man laughed at Bigum's description of the three detectives, then sniffed the air as if a foul odor had floated in off the murky waters of the East River. "I 'on't need to see 'em.

Between you and Shine, I already know they ain't nothing but bad news and I'ma make sure they don't see me. Shit. A ghost, a snake, and pig – sounds like a movie I can do without," he said, as his eyes searched the water like a man waiting for his ship to come in.

Because he was lost in his own thoughts, Bigum didn't noticed Man's weary expression. While Man just seemed tired of life, Bigum was worrying about keeping the life he had. He felt selfish, thinking about what it all meant to him and the game room. It wasn't lost on him that Man had gotten the place by the same kind of drama they now faced.

"You can take care of the game room, and Pete and Kid'll take care of everything else," Man said, as if reading Bigum's mind.

Bigum felt guilty. "You gonna stay at the condo?"

"Nah, Born is there. Ain't no sense us both being there. I put 'im on point. And, I got a spot to lay low in," Man said, without offering any details.

After Bigum drove off in his Caddy, Man walked over to China town where he'd parked the nondescript, gray, five-year old Ford Taurus with the 5.0 engine and quickly left Manhattan. He drove through different sections of Brooklyn, making sure he wasn't followed, before making his way toward Greenpoint. He took Bedford Avenue to Grand Street, then followed Kent to the red-brick warehouse he'd purchased a few years back, in the shadows of the Williamsburg Bridge.

He drove the car into the back alley and onto the ramp of the loading bay. After a couple of minutes of waiting and watching, all the while caressing the .45 in his lap, he got out of the car, key in one hand, gun in the other. He released the dead-bolt lock, then punched a five digit access code into the keypad – the steel garage door lifted.

Once back in the car, Man pointed a remote at the inner metal door, which lifted up like the first one as he drove onto the freight elevator. He parked the Ford next to an 1100cc GXR Suzuki motorcycle and closed both doors. Finally, he used another key to start the elevator. He had turned the empty, two-story building into a secure and comfortable dwelling over the years. He soundproofed the entire place, and while the lower level only had a heavy-bag and free weights scattered around, it too had been cleaned up and renovated. Two of the three entrances had been sealed up, leaving the freight elevator and a roof hatch as the only ways in and out.

He had made good use of the open space on the upper floor; in one corner was a kitchenette, complete with a small dishwasher and stove. The stove was an old, four-eye, gas-range model with an oven. A high wooden counter, with stools served as a dining table and culinary station. The area was small but efficient. Another corner housed a concert grand piano, which Man had discovered at an auction. He had gotten it for a little more than the price of transporting it. The piano was in bad shape, but he refurbished it, replacing the key bed, keys, strings and pedals.

Although he didn't play, he'd done most of the work himself. He spent hours working on it and now the huge, black Grand sat gleaming in its corner like a gem.

In the corner farthest from the piano, was a large porcelain bathtub standing on short feet with a brass frame around it. It was complete with a matching three-step porcelain and brass ladder and jet sprays that created whirlpools when switched on. A matching sink stood to one side and along the same wall was an old fashioned white commode, thick and sturdy. A full-length mirror finished off the area.

In the last corner stood a large Sheraton bookcase, a Windsor chair and a small writing desk, with an L-shaped, brass lamp on it. The books ranged from fiction to history, philosophy to political science, and anything else that might be of interest. Authors included Edgar Allen Poe, Faulkner, Dumas, and Toni Morrison as well as Richard Wright and Chester Hines. A few feet from the bookcase were a vast collection of music LPs, CDs and cassettes, with an expensive sound-system.

In the middle of the 4500 x 7000 square foot floor was a king-sized bed. At the head of the bed was a thirty-gallon fish tank, colorfully designed and ready for the fish that would never come. Though he loved looking at the tank, he'd decided that even fish should be free. As Man had done in the apartment beneath the game room and at his condo, he'd tried to create a safe haven out of empty warehouse space. He had failed with all three. There was no safety anywhere, he thought. And, now the cops were threatening the most important of the three. But what could he expect, he killed to get the game room and it was his violent reputation that made it safe for the kids. However, for them to be safe now, he had to stay away. And in spite of his act of indifference with Bigum he had a bad feeling.

Man looked at his watch. "Damn, Nicki is gonna have a fit," he said, as he headed to the elevator. He was supposed to meet her in front of Junior's. He had chosen the restaurant as much for its famous cheesecake as the constant flow of traffic around it. Nicki had wanted him to come and get her, but he'd explained that it was best that they meet at Junior's. Though the conversation had taken place over the phone, he knew she had rolled her eyes and frowned-up her pretty face. Although the image made him smile, he wondered if Nicki was a complication he could afford right now. Things were getting a little crazy.

He couldn't believe that he'd let her get so close to him, but he had. And, if he had been honest, he'd admit that he hadn't tried all that hard to keep her away. In fact, he had helped it along in his own way – the walks home, the hugs and his constant visits to the daycare center – and had known all along that it was just a matter of time before things heated up between them. If it was only sex, it wouldn't have been a problem. But he cared about Nicki, although he continued to tell himself that that was only because they'd grown up together. After all, he was incapable of being in love. He decided that love wasn't for him. He wasn't even sure if it was love for the kids that drove him to do what he did for them. At times, he thought he was just paying a debt he owed.

Once he exited the alley, he placed the gun in its stash behind the air-conditioner vent. The guns, cops – all reasons why he had to pull back from Nicki – Would it ever end? For years, he'd lived without worrying about the outcome. He'd gotten his by hook or crook and defended it the same way. But, in his mind, no matter what he took or who he made pay, he could never even the score.

He couldn't help what he was, and until Nicki he hadn't cared. Yeah, it was time to pull back from her he decided as he nodded to Lisa Stansfield's, *Been Around the World.* Maybe it was time for him to do some traveling. But he wouldn't have to look for his baby like Lisa Stansfield, he thought, because he knew where the bodies were buried, Thinking of Rita, his daughter, and his mother, made him want the gun in his hand. He fought off the ghosts, put on Tony, Toni, Tone's, *It never rains in Southern California,* and laughed as he spotted Nicki standing in front of Junior's– hands on hips and patting her little foot. Just that quick, he forgot what it was he'd been thinking about.

Eddie smiled — with one hand on Kia's calf, he rotated her foot with his other hand — he was enjoying himself

"I 'on't know what you smiling for."

Eddie raised his head with a look on his face that asked, *Who Me?* "I'm just trying to assist a beautiful woman in distress," he responded.

Kia smirked, but couldn't restrain herself from smiling. "It's your fault I twisted my ankle in the first place."

Eddie was enjoying himself too much to remind her that he had offered to guide her through the trails in Rock Creek Park, not once, but on three different occasions, and once even before she slipped and fell for the first time. He had to give her credit, she was a trooper. She had jumped up and brushed herself off each time, except for the last time when she twisted her ankle. She looked so cute sprawled on the grass, he thought. Good thing she had that soft cushion to land on – and he didn't mean the grass.

"Oh, you really think this is funny, huh," Kia said, snatching her leg from him.

"Aww, don't be like that. I'ma hook you up, shortie. I know just what you need," he said with a huge grin on his face.

Kia stretched her bare leg, flexing her ankle up and down – it was a slight sprain, she thought, as she noticed Eddie admiring her leg. She'd chosen the honey-colored Polo short-set because it showed off her figure and silky dark brown skin.

She hadn't put any weight on her ankle since falling, because Eddie had carried her all the way back to his place, though it didn't hurt all that much. The fool had carried her for what seemed liked miles, stopping to rest on a bench every so often – sitting her in his lap, enjoying himself. It had reminded her of her childhood, when her father used to carry her everywhere never letting her feet touch the ground. But she had to tell the truth, what she was feeling now would probably have her father saying, *"Girl, you better watch yo' self"*. Pops was a trip–with all the women he'd run through he had always treated her like a precious jewel. And, with Eddie treating her the same way, it was too much. *"Girl, get a hold of yo' self.*

However, she smiled and looked into Eddie's handsome face and asked coyly, "And what might that be?"

Eddie was caught off guard. It was their sixth date, and though he could tell she was feeling him, she was so cool he wasn't even sure if he'd ever get her in bed. "Well, you know that old bathtub with the claw-feet you admired your first time here is equipped with a whirlpool system just like the Jacuzzi at the health club," he said, recovering from the effect she was having on him.

"And?" Kia said, easily turning the word into a question with a provocative tilt of her head. She slowly ran her tongue over her full lips and pinned him with her smoldering almond-shaped eyes, enjoying what she was doing to the suave Eddie King and the fact that he was kneeling in front of her, massaging her ankle.

He had reclaimed her leg, gently flexing the ankle and massaging her calf. "I mean, twenty minutes in a hot tub'll loosen your ankle up, and I'll even throw in a full-body massage 'cause I feel so bad 'bout making you sprain your ankle and all."

Kia rested her head on the back of the huge leather club chair. "That's awful nice of you, Mr. King. But, wouldn't that mean I'd end up naked in your bed just because of an ole sprained ankle? I could just sit on the edge of the tub and stick my foot in and then—"

Eddie interrupted her, "Bad as I feel about your ankle, it'd kill me if you slipped off that tub, girl." He gently worked his fingers up over her calf as he extended her leg and placed her foot on his chest. He let his skillful fingers work on the back of her knee, dancing just slightly further up and back down again. "No, I think it's better my way. We can't be too careful. The key is getting just the right treatment from the start," Eddie said, with a serious tone, although his eyes were suggestive and teasing.

Kia thought to herself, *Better for who?* Damn, he was making all the right moves. He raised her foot and placed it on his shoulder, slowly taking his hand from her ankle and gliding it up the inside of her leg, as he began to massage her thigh. She felt the heat radiate from her feminine center and spread to her nipples, which began to ripen and push through her sexy little bra. The heat rose beyond her neck and reached her face. Her whole body was alive and flush. Why had she told him to take his shirt off when he first knelt down and put her foot against his chest? She knew why, the same reason she had dressed with such care this morning.

"You might have to carry me to the bathroom," Kia sighed.
Eddie smiled like a fat man about to enjoy ice cream and cake – the only difference being that he intended to enjoy his treat repeatedly – and gathered her into his arms.

Her arms went around his neck and he kissed the side of her face. She moaned and turned her open mouth to his. He sucked on her bottom lip as he carried her, not to the bathroom, but to his bed.

It was their first kiss and it was long, wet and passionate. It finally ended with him brushing his lips down her chin to her neck. She moaned again and pulled him up for another kiss. As they continued to kiss and explore each other's body, he undressed her, stopping only to pull her top over her head.

He pulled away long enough to slip her shorts down her pretty brown legs. Once she was bare to just her gold-colored Victoria's Secret bra and panties, he stood back and admired her.

"Good God almighty. Umm, Umm, you're somethin'." He couldn't take his eyes off her as he thought: *Shortie is bad.* He wanted the night to last. "I better go run your bath."

Kia stretched her arms above her head and parted her legs just a little as her eyelids lowered. "It's a good thing you have a tub big enough for both of us."

# CHAPTER FORTY

The car sulked down the street like a stray dog in a junkyard, searching out prey. Though it was an old, beat-up car, the men inside wore expensive jewelry, name-brand clothes and were armed.

"See that alley right there," Short-Dog said, pointing with his chin. "Well, that's how you can get in without nobody seein'."

"Dog, you ain't showed me shit. I thought yo' ass had a muthafuckin' key or somethin'," José said.

"Look, I'm tellin' you how to get in the bitch house without nobody seein' yo' ass. And I know she ain't home right now. I been watching since yesterday."

José looked back at the alley. "I don't know 'bout this shit. Anybody could look out..."

"Yo, I'm tellin' you it's cool. You just gotta pick the right time to make yo' move," Short-Dog said, as he turned the corner and drove past the side of Nicki's house.

José glanced up at the darkened windows before dropping his gaze to the backseat. "What you think, Lo?"

Lo twisted up his face, which was never a pretty sight and said, "I think it's some bullshit, just like Short-Dog li'l ass."

"You know what? Fuck both of y'all. I ain't the one Man dissed. If you two muthafuckers scared, go by a muthafuckin dog 'cause I—"

Lo leaned forward and let his left hand rest on Short-Dog's neck. "Dog, I'll slap yo' fuckin' head off you front on me one mo' muthafuckin' time, and if you thinkin' 'bout reachin ' , remember...I'm right handed, punk."

Short-Dog panicked and almost ran the car up on the sidewalk. Since the streets were empty at 3:00 in the morning, he had time to straighten it out and continue down the block. As much as the near accident scared José, he was more worried about Lo letting Short-Dog have a couple in the back.

"Chill, Lo, Dog ain't mean that shit. He just tryin' to help us. We gotta..."

"Fuck Dog and fuck this sucker-shit. If I wanna step to Man I'll step to him. I ain't runnin' up on no broad," Lo said, still holding Short-Dog's neck. "Stop the fuckin' car fo' you get blood all over the muthafucker."

Too scared to pull over to the curb, Short-Dog stopped in the middle of the street. "Put it in park," Lo said, as he released Short-Dog and reached for the door. Once the door was open, a cloud of fear escaped from the front seat into the night.

Still, Short-Dog nor José relaxed until they heard the door slam behind Lo, who backed away from them with his gun in plain view.

In his rush to get away, Short-Dog pushed on the gas with the car still in park. He finally got it in gear and drove off, too fast for a side street.

Lo watched them go. "Fuckin' punks," he said as he slid the .9mm back in his waist. *Buy a dog, huh? No, I'ma' sell two—both bitches.*

* * *

Nicki stood naked in front of the mirror, her legs spread apart, bent at the waist, brushing her hair toward the floor. It hung wildly as she brushed the tangled section out. Man sat on the bed and watched her. She watched him right back from between her legs. Looking back at him, she saw that she had his full attention.

"Nicki, what the hell is you doing?"

Nicki, struggling to keep a straight face, said, "I think it's called brushing your hair, but I could be wrong."

"Oh, you ain't never wrong when you in that position and if yo' li'l ass can take what you startin' you can brush all you want," Man said, absently stroking himself.

"I am not starting anything, Mr. Man, I'm just brushing the tangles out of my hair that you spent the last hour putting in. I told you about pulling on it, too."

"If I knew you was gonna brush it bent over like that I woulda' wrapped it around my fingers some more. And, damn, it was only a hour?"

"It was more than an hour that you was being nasty, but you pulled on my hair for a hour. You need to stop that shit, too."

"Not li'l prim and proper Nicki cussin'. I'm glad your father can't hear you talkin' like that."

"You oughta be glad he can't see you trying to break his little girl in half. First you say I'm all tender, then you wanna be pounding on me."

"Now, you know, Mr. Porter wouldn't believe that I'd hurt a hair on your pretty head. You're tender, all right, but you bring the pounding on yo' self," Man said laughing.

"That's funny?" she answered as she dropped the brush and placed her palms flat on the floor.

Man jumped off the bed and went toward her. She twirled her hips around as he reached for her, then pushed back to meet him. With their bodies pressed together, they moved to a beat all their own.

The moisture she felt building between her legs fueled Nicki's passion. His hardness slid through her slippery center, increasing the passion.

"Baby, I'm sore, so go easy, please?" Nicki cooed.
Man knelt and rubbed his face over her heart-shaped derriere. "Since I made you sore, I'll make it all better," he said, as he planted kisses all over each butt cheek before he found his way to her wet center. He covered her with his mouth tasting her heat.

"Oh, Man, I love you," Nicki cried, as her legs collapsed under his attention.

He held her up, pulling her into his face as he stood up. She was on the edge, and wanted him there with her. She reached for his manhood with both hands like a baby reaching for a bottle of sweet-milk. He had her by the waist and their pleasure was one and the same, as their mouths loved and explored each other's sex. Nicki loved the feeling of the blood rushing to her head as she boiled over with passion. Though she was upside-down, everything was right in her world. As they reached the summit of love and lust together, Man's knees almost gave out but he recovered and lifted her around and shared a long, wet kiss with her.

Back in bed, in Man's arms, Nicki smiled to herself. Man was a freak. But, then, what did that make her, she thought as she snuggled closer to him.

The force of their lovemaking always brought on a peaceful exhaustion that pushed sleep away and replenished them in its afterglow.

It was a glow Nicki never wanted to be without. If only she could get Man to let loose in other ways. She needed him to talk to her, to trust in their love. And it was love: She had no doubts about that. She felt it with his gaze, his touch, and his passion. He had to know it as well. It was a tough situation. She loved Man enough to die for him, and that in its own way was the thing that scared him. Nicki knew he'd never admit such a thing. But Man was scared to love, to hope for anything good, especially anything lasting. She had to find a way to show him that love and hope could last.

As much as he tried to fight her, he needed her. She knew it, but did he? Men are little boys at heart, she thought. So damn tough, but without a clue about what really mattered. Ms. Nez was right, of course, a woman had to point a man in the right direction. And thank God they had the stuff to do it with, she thought as she licked on Man's chest and let her hands roam his hard body.

"Man, why haven't you been to the game room lately?"

Man's body tensed, but he made a show of being half asleep.

"You need to cut it out. Hard as this thing is, you ain't hardly sleep," Nicki said, as she grabbed his manhood with her hand.

Man laughed. "I could be sleep and aroused at the same time."

"Yeah, your horny ass probably could. But you're not."

"One day you wanna brag about how you put me to sleep. Now, you wanna tell me I'm wide awake after everything we did today."

Nicki slipped down and kissed his navel before going farther down and running her tongue up and down the length of him. "Are you wide awake now?"

"See, its stuff like that that gets yo' li'l hot ass in trouble," Man said, as he ran his fingers through her hair.

She laughed huskily. "Trouble Man meet Trouble Woman 'cause she can handle her business," she said, as she dropped her head once more.

Although her mind was on what she was doing, she was also working toward the conversation she'd started. After a few minutes, she came up for air and kissed him deeply.

"Now why haven't you been around the game-room?"

Man smiled and shook his head at either her persistence, or her technique. He had thought that they were past that and onto something else, but should have known better. Nicki didn't give up and had her own way of getting what she wanted. He wasn't complaining, just resisting.

"Just 'cause I ain't been by the daycare center don't mean I ain't been at the game room."

"No, I guess it don't. But all the kids keep asking me where you're at does."

Man laughed, but before he could think of an answer, Nicki raised up on her elbows and gazed into his eyes. "So, you'd rather have me think that you don't have time for me than tell me the truth," she said sadly.

He was stuck. Nothing came to mind, nothing that would make sense. This was the part of being with Nicki that troubled him the most – sharing his thoughts, feelings, and most of all his fears. But, with her pretty eyes haunted by sadness Man had only one choice–to tell the truth.

Man sighed, "Listen, it's not a big deal, but the police came by the game room askin' 'bout me." He looked away for a moment before continuing, "I can't tell you what they want because I don't know yet."

Nicki stared, her eyes searching for hidden truths.

"I really don't know what they want, though I can bet it's about money." He reached up and caught one of her nipples between his thumb and forefinger, smiling easily. "As you may or may not know, our esteemed officers of the law are not beyond common thievery. As a matter of fact, it's more the norm than the exception I dare say."

Nicki rolled her eyes. She knew he was trying to dodge the real subject when he started in with one of his rhetorical speeches. It was getting on her last nerve, too. "Man, puh-leeze. Okay. Let's stay on track about the police coming to the game room."

"You tell yo' stuff yo' way and I'll tell mine my way," Man said with a chuckle. He thought it was amusing. "Don't get yo' panties in a bunch."

"You're not funny, Man," she said, pouting.

She was so damn gorgeous with her lips stuck out like that, he thought. Still, how much could he tell her? How much should he tell her? He needed to protect her.

"Look, no matter how I tell it, it's the same story–cops putting the squeeze on somebody's business. And, no, I ain't no regular businessman. But they ain't got nothing on me." Man pulled her down and wrapped his arms around her. "Now, that's as plain as I can say it."

"Okay," she said, settling herself into his embrace–it felt so safe. She wanted to know that he was safe, too. "So what's the plan," she asked, as she tipped her head up to look at him.

He laughed, and of course, once more her panties were in a bunch.

"Oh, so that's funny, huh? I'm a joke. No, wait, a joke and a fuck," she said, losing her temper.

Before he could go into one of his speeches he caught himself. "Nicki, don't be like that, you know better than that."

"No, Man, I know what you show and tell me," she said quietly as she turned her face away so he wouldn't see the tears.

The communication thing was busting Man's ass. He didn't know what to do. Communicating to him was having the crew ready on a job – getting a move to go just as it was planned. Nicki was driving him crazy.

"Nicki, just because you can make me laugh and I can't keep my hands off you, don't mean I think you're a joke. And I definitely don't think of you as a fuck."

"Then tell me how you think of me."

He felt her warm tears against his skin and thought drops of acid would have been less painful. He took a deep breath, "Nicki, you know how much I care about—"

"No, Man, I don't. Not unless you tell me," she stopped him before he could finish. It was tearing her apart that he hadn't mentioned the word love.

"I just wanna protect—"

"I don't need you to protect me. I need you to love me," she insisted without letting him say anymore. "And if you can't, you need to tell me that," she finished sadly.

Man was hurting as much as she was, maybe more. It was so difficult for him to talk about things like this. He'd spent so much time building a wall to keep people out and protect himself, he couldn't be sure how he really felt.

"Nicki, if you got hurt because of me ..."

He stopped in mid-sentence, at a loss for what to say. He closed his eyes and saw the graves of those he loved. Graves he dared not visit anymore, except in his head.

"I don't know what to say. I'm no good at this," he finally said.

"Say that you need me with you, that you want me," Nicki said, climbing on top of him and taking his face in her hands.

The seconds seem to drag on as he struggled to translate his emotions into words. "I do need you, but I need you safe."

"Is that's why you said you wanted me to stay here with you?" she asked, then added, "It should be because you want me close to you. Otherwise, I think I should go home, Man."

Man held his breath, unable to speak until she started to get up. "I want you with me."

She smiled down at him and pressed her mouth to his. Their tongues danced together as his hands settled on her butt. She sucked on his lips and licked his chin as she lost herself in the love they shared. He soon followed her to their special place.

***

Yeah, I know you worried, Bigum. But we gotta stay cool and play this thing by ear," Shine said.

Bigum paced the small office in back of the bar, eating up space like a flock of hungry vultures on a decaying carcass. Although he didn't know what to do, doing nothing seemed to make the situation worst.

"So, what do we do?" he asked, stopping to lock eyes with Shine.

"All we can do is wait," Shine answered, running his hand over his baldhead.

"Wait for what? I mean, shouldn't we be doing somethin'?"

"Bigum, waiting is doing somethin'. Sometime you gotta lay low."

"Now you sound like Man," Bigum said, as a huge stress line grew on his brow.

"That oughta tell you I'm right. You know Man likes action, and if he thinks it' best to lay low..."

"I 'on't know," the big man said as he dropped his weight into a chair. Shine cringed as the chair protested the sudden load. Bigum, who was usually conscious of his size, was reacting like a trapped animal about to run amok. And if that happened, Shine knew that a lot of things would end up broken.

"Bigum; you gotta calm down. This ain't no time to lose control. I'ma keep tryin' to get to my man inside the precinct, but right now ain't a good time. I told you, that ole' albino sergeant tryin' to make a power move and cut the captain out. So we just gotta lay low and wait until shit get back to normal."

Bigum silently placed his head in his hands and Shine added, "I 'member when me and June first got with Bumpy, he told us, 'To be a Black man in this country is to struggle, but to keep struggling as long as it takes is what makes a man a man'."

Bigum slowly raised his head from his hands and nodded. "All right, we do what we gotta do."

# CHAPTER FORTY-ONE

Ali stared at her friend. Kia sat on the edge of the bed, admiring her legs as she put lotion on them. She sang along with En Vogue's, *However You Want It,* as she stretched and flexed her legs to the beat.

Ali smiled. "Damn, girl, he must be really giving it to you." Kia stood up and began to untie her scarf. She started removing the bobby pins, her hair fall loose and framed her face as she worked the pins loose.

"Yeah, that's the first sign – ignoring your friends. And your best friend at that. It must..."

"Oh, puh-leeze! You know you just want some juicy details with your hot ass," Kia said, rolling her eyes.

"You damn right, I wanna know every freaky detail there is. Each and everyone. Shoot, in a month, y'all went out six times. Now, in the last two weeks you been with him almost every day."

"Damn, you clocking me like that? You better get you a life, girl," Kia said, shaking her head.

"From the way you been acting the last two weeks, hearing about yours'll do just fine. I'll probably need a panty-shield, huh? Oh, don't play that innocent shit with me. I know you, and the way he keep coming back you must'a really put it on him. Shit, you got 'im picking you up and dropping you off. But then, when you wait as long as you do to give up your stuff, it probably just explodes."

Kia snatched a pillow off the bed and threw it at Ali. "I know you ain't talking, with your freaky-self"

"Girl, I know I'm freaky. That's why I kept telling you to hook me up with your fine-ass father. But, right now I'll settle for hearing about you and Eddie."

Kia smiled as her mind raced like a rush-hour express train to the hot, sticky sex she and Eddie had stumbled on – by way of a twisted ankle.

"It's good," Kia said, as she licked her lips and looked upwards, "Damn, it's so good, it's scary."

"Girl, don't you mess this up. Now, I wanna know is his body as hot outta all that Perry Ellis and Polo gear."

Kia bit her bottom lip, "Uh-huh. Even better. Ali, he got damn cables for abs. Girl, an eight-pack, not six. And his chest and arms, damn! My baby even got sexy legs," Kia said, dreamily.

"Your baby? Oh, he done put it on your ass."

Kia blushed, and put her hands on her hips. "Well, he did carry me all the way back to his house from Rockcreek Park after I twisted my ankle and..."

"Wait a damn minute," Ali cut in, as she worked her neck and head in disbelief. "I thought he lived a couple of miles from the park."

"You thought right."

"And he carried you all the way?"

"Every step. My feet never touched the ground."

Ali shook her head. "Damn, he got yo' ass for real."

"And why is that Ms. Know-everythang," Kia said as she went back to the mirror, throwing a little extra switch in her walk.

"Girl, he did you just like your father used to do you. You always talking about how yo' daddy used to take you places and your feet never touched the ground. Damn, the brother's good. Or did you tell him about that."

"No, I didn't. And for your information, he ain't got me."

"Oh, puh-leeze! He got you, and that's good. It's okay to be got when its good, and you just said it was *good,*" Ali said smiling. "But you haven't told him anything about your father have you?"

Kia's face lost its glow for a minute. "You know I can't go more than a few hours without mentioning that man."

"But you didn't tell 'im he was in prison did you?"

"I don't know if we gonna be all that and I don't like talking my business", Kia said seriously.

"Kia, as long as you waited to get with somebody, I think it's a good chance this is something special. And from what you've seen and everything that you told me, I think we can safely say that the brother is from the street. You said that he even reminds you of your dad."

"Ali, that ain't necessarily a plus. Don't get me wrong, you know how I feel about my father, but he was a ladies' man. Shit, even I had to wait sometimes while he did his thang. He was a trip. My mother's still in love with him and they ain't been together since I was a little girl.

"Not that I hold that against him, 'cause my mother is a trip, too. But that's a whole 'nother story," Kia said rolling her eyes. "But anyway, even when he was around, it felt like the streets were calling him. And look where it got him – the last ten years in prison."

Ali walked over to the mirror and put her arm around her friend. Kia's face was a mask of sadness. As the two women stood looking at each other in the mirror, Kia's eyes glistened with tears: she laid her head on Ali's shoulder. "It's always some shit in life, ain't it?" Kia said, fighting back tears.

"Kia, you know, like I know, it's hard being a Black woman. But being women makes us special and being Black women makes us extra special. Some days we're ho's and bitches or some freaks every kind of man wants to bed. But we know that we're Queens every day.

"And when we find a man that knows it and treats us that way, we have to accept and respect their love, even with their shortcomings. Girl, when you talk about your pops I'm always a little jealous 'cause mine never made me feel like that. And Eddie sounds like he's making you feel the same way — special. So, you need to lose the tears and be as happy as he's making you. 'Cause, streets or not, he knows that he got him a beautiful Queen."

Kia turned and offered up a small smile. She knew about the lack of interest Ali's father had displayed throughout her friend's life. In fact, Kia knew, her father had done more for her from prison than Ali's dad had done from across town. "Ali, I love your crazy ass, and your father is a fool — a blind fool — 'cause even a fool'd know a Queen when he sees one," Kia said, hugging her friend.

With her eyes now threatening to overflow Ali, sniffed and said, "Now you got me ready to start crying. We a mess– here it is we got less than a year left in law school, you got a fine ass man whipped, and we up here sniffling 'bout every little thing."

"Queens can do shit like that," Kia said as both women laughed and hugged once more.

\*\*\*

Deacon stood in the dark doorway, waiting. He watched the women; some were little more than girls, in their skimpy outfits – their breasts and ass-cheeks screaming for attention louder than the displays in Macy's windows.

The anger came. He was full of it. They deserved to be scorned and punished. Nothing but loose, sinful women selling their bodies. Suddenly, he cursed himself. His body betrayed him as his erection shamed him. It was their fault, though.

Flashing tits and poking out their asses, they teased in sweet voices, "Baby you wanna date tonight. I got what ya' want," as a steady flow of cars and customers streamed through. He touched their skin with his eyes and smelled their whorish odors in his head. Again, he cursed the desire he felt. He hated them. He wanted to wrap his arms around one and crush the life slowly from her foul body.

With his eyes locked on one woman in particular, it was a moment before Deacon saw the green car sitting at the curb. The car groaned as he settled his bulk in the passenger's seat.

"Yo', man, you fuckin' up my ride with yo' fat ass. Fuck we had'a meet down here fo', anyway. You buyin' pussy."

Deacon looked straight ahead without speaking. When he finally turned his gaze on the young man behind the wheel he made his decision. "You get the information?" he asked.

"You got my money?" the young man asked, putting the Mercedes in motion. At 2:00 in the morning this part of Long Island City was a john's candy shop. Hookers vied for business as if they had a peddler's license – offering bargains that even Delancy Street couldn't match. There were all colors, sizes and types of women– with drag queens thrown in. It was a sex marketplace.

Deacon came out of his pocket with a large roll of bills. He counted off $3000, and turned to his companion, "What you got for me?"

With eyes wide, the driver began scheming– he thought the muscle-bound cat was on to him so he hadn't been able to find out anything else about Man and his people. Nevertheless, he intended to pocket the three grand. "Yo, I know where—o"

"Turn here. Go down near the bridge," Deacon instructed.

"Yeah, yeah. I gotcha'. But like I was sayin', I know where the big dude is stayin'."

"So, you followed 'im, huh?" Deacon asked, although he already knew the answer.

"Of course. I'm the—"

"Pull over behind that pillar. I got too much money on me to be sitting out in the open." Deacon said, nervously, glancing around the deserted area under the Queensboro Bridge.

Deacon wrapped the bills in a thick rubber band and held it out. "This better be good."

The young man smiled as he reached for the money, and thought it had been easier than he expected. It was his last thought.

Deacon dropped the roll of bills, and as the driver eyes followed them, Deacon used his other hand to slam the man's head into the steering wheel. He wrapped his thick hands around the man's neck and pulled him close, his 330-pounds taking another life as easily as it took in food. Deacon didn't think about the man he held. He thought about loose women in skimpy outfits.

Finally, he let the body fall. It lay across his lap. He sat there with death in his nostrils, on his hands and lying across his lap. He yawned. He knew that if he didn't get moving, he'd fall asleep. He ripped the pockets of the man's pants–taking what money he had on him. His watch and gold chain were next, then Deacon pushed the body in the back seat. When he bent over to get the keys out of the ignition, he noticed the roll of bills he'd dropped. The roll went back in the money-belt under his shirt, everything else was stored in the inside breast pocket of his suit jacket.

Deacon tidied up his clothes as best he could, inhaled deeply, and slowly got out of the car. Then he made another decision – he would walk over the bridge and get rid of the jewelry and keys on his way to Manhattan.

\*\*\*

Born Equality walked into Mom's restaurant on Seventh Avenue and took a seat at the old Formica counter. After a couple of minutes one of the two young, pretty brown-skinned girls working behind the counter came over to take his order. "You look like you know what you want, but if you need a menu..." she said, giving him a slow once over.

Born smiled at her act; she couldn't have been more than seventeen. He returned her look and wondered if she knew what she was doing. Her body and eyes told him that she did. Her counter mate slinked over and said in a sex-kitten voice, "Jam, you sho' you can handle his order by yo' self ? He kinda big."

"Butter, you know everybody the same size when they layin' down," Jam said, without taking her eyes off Born.

"I hear that girl," Butter replied, with a smile.

Born looked from one to the other. Both were pretty, young and sexy – coming into womanhood extremely well, he thought. And the fact that they'd decided to have a little fun at his expense was fine with him. Though he figured that the soul food would be good, he decided that the sights were even better.

"I would try a li'l plate of hot jam and butter, but it might be too much for me," Born said with a smile.

The girls laughed and took his order. Since it was in between the lunch and dinner rush, and the place was empty, they chatted back and forth throughout his meal of fried whiting, yams and macaroni and cheese. After Born finished his third glass of half-and-half– lemonade and iced tea combination, Jam sweetly asked him if he was ready for desert.

Born responded, running his eyes over each of their young, firm bodies, "I already had a double helping."

As the girls smiled with him, Born slipped each girl $20, then gave Jam another $20.00 to cover his meal. When she came back with his change, Born told her to split it with Butter, and said, "Oh, I was looking fo' my boy...Dark-skin dude, drive a green 300 Benz, with gold hammers."

"You talkin' bout lyin' ass Money? He skinny and think he all that?" Butter asked, twisting up her face.

"Yeah, that's him. You seen him lately?"

"Uh, uh, he come in every now and then with his cheap, lyin' butt" Jam said. "But he too full of shit to be yo' friend. Anyway, me and Butter the only friends you need when you come in here," Jam finished, folding her arms under her breast. When he failed to notice her little trick, she realized that the man with the serious eyes and wide shoulders was no friend of Money's.

"But since you so nice, Money from 129th Street."
He wanted to keep the mood light. "Well, ladies, as good as the food was, the company was better, and y'all know I'll be back," Born said, with a smile.

Born walked up Seventh Avenue enjoying the sounds of Harlem. A few sidewalk vendors hawked their wares–used books, incenses and Dente-cloth spread out on the sidewalk or on folding-tables. On the corner of 29th Street, Born surveyed the long block before going back toward 30th Street and turning in the block.

He hadn't spotted the Benz from the Seventh Avenue end of the block and wanted a quick look from the Eighth Avenue end. The last thing he wanted to do was wake the fool up to the fact that he was on to him.

After a fast pass through the block didn't produce any results Born decided to go back to the condo. He thought about Jam and Butter and smiled. That's right; Eddie and Man weren't the only ladies men in the crew. Plus, both of them were caught up right now. Each time he'd spoken to Eddie he was either with or about to go get his new lady. Damn, the fact that she'd had his attention for almost two months meant shortie was doing something right. And Man, even though he was ducking the pigs, he was keeping his lady, Nicki, with him as much as possible. The God laughed as he entered Morningside Park, the players had taken themselves out of the game and didn't even know it.

# CHAPTER FORTY-TWO

Kid stood in the corner with an impatient look on his face as he listened to Black June explain the situation. While feeling some of the same things, Pete showed more patience. They had come to June's house at Man's request. He'd given them a quick rundown over the phone – it was hot and they had to pull back for a while – and told them to go by June's for the details. Details that Kid didn't like. It wasn't like Man to back off just because the police had come around a couple of times.

June looked from Pete to Kid and decided that Kid was the one he needed to focus on. Pete sat with his eyes on June's face taking in every word. He would hear the old man out.

"So, what we got is a fight for the payoff money. Fuckin' dirtbags can't even split the take without crossing each other," June said, as he got up from his chair, took a cigar from the rosewood humidor on the coffee table. He took his time cutting and lighting it. Once he had it going to his satisfaction, he returned to his seat and let his eyes linger on the chair Kid had vacated once he heard the news about the pickups. "Yeah, with all the crossin' going on, Man is right. We gotta back off."

Pete nodded. It wasn't like any of them needed the money. But he knew Kid wasn't happy about anything that appeared to be a loss. He could feel his partner's tension and was sure June could too. He wished the fool would sit his ass down and chill. Pete might as well been have wishing the Knicks won the championship; it just wasn't going to happen.

"So, we just gonna let them muthafuckers work without payin'," Kid said with disgust.

June turned his eyes on Kid, who leaned against the wall like a cocky gunfighter looking to add another notch to his belt. "Yeah, that's what we gonna do," June said, with the hard look that had enabled him to grow old in the game.

"Yo, I know we gotta duck Po-Po, but letting them punks work and not pay ain't the move. It's like we gettin' soft. First, we hook Mack and 'em up, now we just gonna let Blue Seal and Red Top do what the fuck they want. Nah, fuck that!" Kid said, folding his arms across his chest.

June rotated his cigar in his fingers, examining it with a connoisseur's eye, as if he hadn't heard Kid's outburst. Pete tipped his head down, signaling Kid to be easy. He knew Kid was itching for some action. But he also knew Kid wouldn't convince the old gangster of anything – especially with that hotheaded shit.

"Yeah, you right, Kid," June said, in a calm voice.

Pete's eyes came up at June's words. June's face was a deep black mask of calmness as he stopped to pull on his cigar before continuing, "Both of them crews is doing what they want– working as usual, and closing up when a raid is coming. Just like when Shine was getting' the lowdown from his man in the four-four. Now what does that tell ya'?"

When neither Pete nor Kid answered. June continued. "It oughta tell ya' that somebody done made a deal, and bet that deal got somethin' to do with the pigs askin' 'bout Man. So, this shit is mo' than just what it looks like on the surface."

Pete nodded again. He knew Man had a reason for pulling back and searching under all the rocks for the snakes. It was good that they didn't need the money from the payoffs, because it had to be worked just like any other move.

Kid was silent while June explained what Man wanted them to do – stay on point, watch Ricky, José, and Short-Dog and take the weekly pickup from Easy's spot.

When June finished, Kid shook his head, "I think me and Pete oughta step to all them chumps and shut they shit down."

June sighed, he'd seen his share of young hotheads –always young because they didn't usually live to get old – and knew that without control they'd cause problems. "Me and Shine agree that Man's way is the best way to go at this," he said.

"I still say we oughta step to 'em. I ain't down with all this waiting shit," Kid said fixing June, and then Pete with a sharp stare.

"Yeah," June said easily. "I know you ain't down with letting chumps get away with shit. But I also know you down with Man," he finished, returning Kid's stare.

The tension left his face and Kid smiled for the first time since they'd started talking.

"Yeah, June. You right, we down with Man," he said as he sat down. "Yo, what about one of 'em smokes? What's that, them Cubans?"

"Boy, you know it's against the law to have Cuban cigars."

Even Pete laughed.

***

Although he had made a few runs through 129th Street in the last couple of days Born hadn't been able to spot the green Benz. His brother was no help. He claimed he didn't know of anyone with that kind of car. All he wanted to do was chase the pipe, anyway. Born had left word with Bigum for Man to get at him. Maybe Man'd be able to get a handle on the car for him. In the meantime, he'd hang around his brother's building and see what happened. He figured that making himself bait was the best way to get things jumping, because whoever it was that had him in their sights was about to discover what it meant to go up against the God.

He went to Man's stash in the doorframe of the bedroom and took out the .40 caliber Glock with the stainless steel slide and slipped it in the waist of his black Guess jeans. Then, he put on a heavy, black tee shirt that hung halfway between his waist and knees, to help conceal the gun. With his black Tims and black, baggy jeans, he was ready for a nocturnal hunt. He grabbed his wallet of the night table and as an afterthought, pocketed the roll of quarters he sometimes carried. He nodded at what he saw in the full-length mirror, in the hallway. He was ready for whatever the night brought, he thought.

Once on the street, he found a pay phone and called the game room and left a message with Bigum – he didn't want to page Man and wait for a return call.

Born took his time once he entered the block. He wanted to make sure he was seen. He walked slowly into the projects and then into the lobby of his brother's building. He stopped at the elevator, though he had no intention of using it or going up to his brother's tenth floor apartment. The longer he lingered, the better chance he had of drawing his prey–or was it his predator– out into the open.

He could feel the rush of excitement, a stirring in the pit of his stomach. From the moment he stepped into the projects, he'd felt someone watching him. All he had to do was wait, he thought, as he went around to the back entrance–it was dark...the bulb was out, and it stunk of fresh piss.

Born went into the dark stairwell then immediately backtracked and waited. With his hand under his shirt, resting on the Glock, he was ready.

When the fat man with the cheap suit suddenly appeared, it took every bit of Born's discipline to bring his hand out empty – which turned out to be a mistake. He'd been expecting the skinny, dark-skinned hustler or someone fitting the street image. So, when the fat man stumbled toward him, Born's hand came up in a halfhearted manner–he had made three costly mistakes in a matter of seconds.

With his right hand out in front of him, Born couldn't stop the fat man from crowding him and grabbing for the gun under his tee shirt. When he slipped sideways, reached down to protect his weapon, a fat hand grabbed his neck.

Born dipped his chin and saved his life by keeping the hand from getting a good grip on his neck.

When he heard the gun fall to the floor Born wasted no time going to work with his hands. With his back against the wall and the fat man leaning his bulk into him, Born sent a short, hard, left hook into the man's right side.

The fat man took the body-shot with a grunt as he was trying to get his other hand on Born's neck.

Born kept his chin down and doubled up with his left hook. The two vicious punches caused the man to stagger slightly and take a step back. As he pulled Born with him, Born head-butted him across the nose.

Deacon was in trouble. Although he had wanted to attack in close quarters, he hadn't known the smaller man would be so strong. Other than knocking away the gun, nothing had gone right. He should have been able to get both his hands around Born's neck and should have been able to slam his head into the wall. Now blood was pouring from his nose and his legs felt weak. With the additional room the head-butt brought him, Born stepped into his next body-shot and heard the fat man groan.

Hurt, Deacon collapsed on Born, using his weight to slow him down. In his struggle to keep the dead weight from taking him down, Born eased up on his attack.

Deacon took advantage and reached for his straight razor.

When the fat man dropped one hand, Born slipped out of his grasp and hit him with a right hand to the side of the head.

Deacon screamed, his head snapped to the side. He was hit again, but he had his razor out and open.

Born couldn't believe the man was still standing. He'd thrown two right hands that would've dropped a coked up madman. Still, he had the edge; the fat man was no fighter. He faked another right but dropped down and landed another left-hook to the body. The man grunted and his lazy, overhand swipe barely grazed Born. Deacon took the punch to his gut; it was the only way to get close enough to use the razor.

Born didn't feel the cut across his shoulder until he drew his arm back and straightened up. The four-inch cut opened up and blood mixed with his sweat. He moved from side-to-side and smiled.

Deacon moved with caution; he knew the other man could hurt him. He needed every ounce of his faith to overcome the evil he faced.

Born threw a slow jab, inviting the steel of the razor. Deacon saw the opening he needed and swung the razor and relaxed as he felt Born's flesh part like a loose woman's legs.

Born put all his weight behind a right cross, ignoring the razor that had sliced opened his forearm. The punch sent the fat man to the wall.

Deacon screamed out. He tried to put his hands up, but couldn't. Born hit him again. Blood flew out of his battered face. Then he was falling.

Born closed the small space. He pulled back and landed a jab to the fat man's broken nose as he fell.

Deacon was chocking on his own blood. His hands searched the floor for his razor. He'd almost lost consciousness and faith when his hand landed on cold steel.

Born looked down at the bloody man and said. "My man, I aint got much time. I wanna know—"

The explosion of the Glock was even louder in the small stairwell. The flash lit up each man's face. Surprise covered both.

Born-a gallant heavyweight who didn't know it was over... tried to take a step forward as the bullet ripped into his chest.

Deacon-a fortuitous survivor–fired two more shots as Born reached for him.
The second shot stopped Born in mid-step and the third one slammed him into the wall. He slid down slowly, and left a trail of blood above him as he ended up in a sitting position against the wall. His eyes settled on Deacon. "Bitch, you thought like Nelly, if you thought yo' bitch-ass could..."

Deacon lay on the steps gasping for breath, his chest heaving, each breath burning as it came. He heard the man call him a foul name, then saw the bubbles of blood follow it. Now, no words came, just the blood dripping from his open mouth. Deacon struggled to his feet. He looked at the gun in his hands. He was dizzy. He had to get away.

He leaned against the wall and tried to think. He had the gun, and he had to get away from the building as fast as possible. He tried to slow his breathing down but it didn't work. He was sucking air like an asthmatic pocketbook snatcher being chased.

He turned to leave but looked over his shoulder at the dead man sitting on the floor and thought he saw a smile on his face. That's when he spotted his razor beside the man's leg. He reached for it, stopped, and reached again, as if he thought it was a setup and the man would grab him. Finally, he snatched the razor and stumbled out the back entrance.

***

Kia and Eddie strolled through the crowd on R Street, checking out the sidewalk booths. The streets of Dupon Circle were packed with artists and collectors. Eddie was showing her how an art dealer did business. He explained to her how he bought art and sold it at a profit. In truth, it was how he paid taxes on some of the money from his robberies.

They turned onto Connecticut Avenue. "Well, you didn't buy any paintings," Kia said, she was skeptical about Eddie's claim, and the fact that he had expensive business cards to back up his story did nothing to persuade her. Smooth or not, he was a hustler.

"I didn't see anything that I could make money off. That's the whole point isn't it?"

Kia shook her head: *He's just too damn cool, but I learned from the best.* "Yeah, that's the point. But, since you ain't tryin' to sell me nothin' you ain't got to talk all proper and businesslike," she said, rolling her eyes.

"Awwh, girl, I know yo' good-proper-college-goin' ass ain't actin' up. Half the time, I gotta get the dictionary just to understand..."

"Why you ly-inng, Eddie?"

"Well, you know how y'all do when y'all get them degrees!"

"Oh, first you said me and Ali was actin' like two southeast girls that—"
Eddied grabbed her around the waist and kissed her on the mouth to shut her up. "That's 'cause you're so beautiful," he said, as he loosened his embrace and looked into her eyes.

"Mmmm, that was nice. But I think you just wanted to shut me up," Kia said, licking her lips and pulling Eddie to her. After sucking on his bottom lip, she slipped her tongue in his mouth. Cutting the kiss short, she said, "We better stop before we need to get a room."

Eddie looked around at the shoppers moving up and down the street. Although a couple took a quick peek at them, most were too busy to care. "You know, I never did show you where that boy shot Regan ass at. Well, don't worry. I got it under control. It's right up the street at the Hilton and I just happen to have a suite reserved. Though it's not the presidential, it's fit for a queen."

Kia smiled. "I have to go home and get a change of clothes."

"I think that with all these stores on Connecticut Avenue we'll be okay. There's even a Victoria's Secrets..."

"Eddie King, I hope you don't think I'm your little plaything..."
Eddied grabbed her and pulled her close. "Girl, you know I ain't hardly playin' with your fine ass."

"Eddie, people are looking."

"All right, then we better hurry up and get to the hotel before you get yo'self in trouble," he said, resting his hands on her butt

"Wait til I get you in that room. You want to show off out here, huh?" Kia said, licking her full lips.

"I like it when you talk like that. Damn, let's hurry up," Eddie said, ushering her into Bally's where he'd seen some five-inch heels he wanted to see her wearing.

# CHAPTER FORTY-THREE

Man stared at Bigum as if the older man was speaking in tongues. Although he understood every word, it was like trying to match red, orange, and purple together—something that assaults your senses while making no sense. It just didn't add up.

Man threw his hands up in a gesture to stop everything – even time– if possible. He paced the large den of Shine's Yorkville condo. He'd been enjoying dinner with Nicki when he got the call that brought him to Shine's. When Bigum couldn't reach Man, he'd gone to the bar and asked Shine to make sure what he'd been told was true. After some checking with the police and people in the street, they'd gotten in touch with June and finally with Man.

"Okay, I need you to start at the beginning," Man said, with his back to them. Bigum looked at Shine, who gave a slight nod from his seat across the room. June brought his palms together and rested his elbows on his thighs before leaning his forehead on his fingertips. Bigum cleared his throat and looked more uncomfortable than usual, sitting in a regular sized chair. "It's like I said, 'bout three hours ago I got a call from somebody claiming to be Born's li'l brother—"

"How-do-ya-know it was him..."

"Man, you gotta let 'im tell it," Shine said, walking over to stand beside him. Man moved away and went to the window. He didn't bother to push the curtain aside he just needed his space.

"I pressed 'im on that. He had the right answers. Said that Born told 'im if somethin' ever happened he was 'pose to call that number. Anyway, once he told me 'bout Born, I beeped you a bunch of times but when I ain't hear back I thought I better tryn' do something'..."

Shine jumped in, "I made some calls and found out 'bout a shootin' in St. Nick late last night. I got a name and it was the one Born been using. After I got hold of June..."

Black June lifted his head and sighed loudly. "I got hold of the brother – what's his name, Robby, and he said he identified the body at the scene. Right there in the lobby. After that I got a neighborhood lawyer to ask about it and got the same answers," June said.

Man turned around. "Okay, somebody caught it in the lobby, but that don't mean it was the God," he said, his eyes moving from one man to the other, almost as if he dared them to contradict him. "I gotta be sure."

June stood and walked over to Man. They stood face to face. "I seen the photos and read the crime-scene report. It's him. He was shot three times and had some razor cuts on him."

"You sure, June?" Man growled. Once June nodded Man asked him, "Tell me 'bout the message he left 'bout that green Benz." There was no time to mourn.

After finding out what Born had wanted, Man said, "Okay, I gotta go meet Eddie, he should hit town in a hour."

He looked at each of them, holding their eyes for a moment. "All I need y'all to do is find somebody to claim the body and setup the funeral arrangements. I got the rest."

"What about his brother?" Bigum asked. Man walked back to the window, this time he moved the curtain and looked out at the calm waters of the East River. "That's somethin' we'll know soon," he said with his back to the room.

Bigum raised his brow questioningly and looked at June. When June reached for the phone, he turned to Shine. Shine nodded and said, "That's right. We got this. You take care of what you gotta do, Man."

At that moment all three men understood that Man meant to add more bodies to the count. But only June, who had killed more people than he could count on his fingers, knew how high the count might go. The police weren't the only ones who went to war over the death of a partner.

***

Deacon lay in his bed with a cold towel over his battered face. The weight of the towel on his broken nose brought tears to his eyes; the pain was more than he could bear. He whimpered like a neglected puppy. His whole body ached and it would be days before his nose healed enough for him to breathe normally.

He couldn't even take pleasure in the kill. It was the first time he had used a gun to kill, and now he realized why–it hadn't satisfied his need. And, the fact that even with his razor, he'd been over-powered shook his confidence. It was another reason to hate Man. Soon he'd make him pay for everything, Deacon thought, as a sob rose from his throat.

When he remembered that he hadn't taken Born's wallet and watch, to make it look like a robbery, he snatched the towel off his face and threw it on the floor–the pain stayed with him, though.

He should've killed that crackhead, Robby, before taking on his brother, he thought. But he had decided to kill Born quickly and quietly, then go upstairs and put Robby out of his misery. Now it was too late, but it didn't matter. With all the drugs in his system, Robby had probably forgotten the little he knew anyway.

***

"What y'all got?" Man asked before Pete and Kid were through the door. For the last thirty-six hours they'd been pressing every crackhead, dope-fiend and hood they knew for information. Pete and Kid had snatched Robby off the street, put him in the trunk and delivered him to Eddie and Man.

"We found out that the cat, Money, got hit it a few days ago. His body was found under the Queensboro Bridge, on the Queens side," Pete said, as he took a seat on the desk. He watched Kid pace the room while Eddie and Man sat on opposite sides of the room with their backs against the wall. Both were dead still. Unlike Kid they didn't need to get pumped-up. No greetings were passed. It was all business. The usual bullshitting was as dead as the mood in the small office.

Since Pete and Kid had been part of Man's crew, it was the first time they'd smelled the scent of death, just for death's sake. This wasn't about money...it was about loyalty. They owed a debt to Born, and Pete had thought that Robby might be the first down payment. But after three hours of questions, pressure, and answers, that Man and Eddie could live with–Robby got to keep his life. June and Shine stashed him in a rehab-center in Wallkill, New York.

While the powerful undercurrent of violence had Pete a little unsettled, he realized that Kid was feeding off of it. He took a deep pull of air into his lungs, exhaled and said, "We also got the word he was doing somethin' with a fat dude called the Preacher man."

"All right!" Man shot Eddie a look. "Shit comin' together. It gotta be the same muthafucker Robby called Deacon."

Eddie nodded, "Yeah, and the same muthafucker that Born wanted to check out. For the God to be on 'im like that he felt somethin' was wrong."

"Shit, how-the-fuck did he catch the God out there like that though?" Man wondered aloud, as he stood, his eyes locked with Eddie's.

"Ain't that some shit, muthafucker got the God. But what he shoulda known was that the God is gonna be the death of him and everything he love," Eddie said, as his teeth flashed in what Pete figured Eddie thought was a smile.

***

Deacon stood in the dingy doorway of an abandoned storefront, his bloodshot eyes missing nothing. The Lower East Side was always a dangerous place and if things didn't go as he hoped, the bodega across the street could become a death trap. Sweat collected around his collar, his shirt stuck to his skin and was soiled and wrinkled.

He was a mess. With his swollen, blackened eyes and smashed nose he looked like a fat, sick raccoon. Each breath took enormous effort–he pulled short gulps of air through his mouth and leaned his head against the dirty doorframe. He thought about leaving but he was desperate, so he stepped out of the doorway and moved slowly across the street.

The man behind the counter continued to clean his glasses as if he hadn't noticed Deacon enter, but Deacon knew that was not the case. Deacon moved toward the door in the back of the store and just before he reached it, a small, Hispanic man blocked his path. Although the little man didn't speak, his eyes and the automatic weapon he carried said it all. Deacon stood still, trying to decide what he should say. He knew the man wouldn't speak English – even if he knew how.

Deacon voice was buried somewhere in his gut as his mouth opened and closed. The door cracked a few inches. "Damn, Gordo, you look fucked up," Peto said with half his face hidden by the door.

With the door blocking his view, Deacon couldn't tell if it was a smile or sneer on Peto's face. Peto stepped back, spoke to the little gunman in Spanish and motioned Deacon in, "Close the door, Gordo," he said, as he turned his back and walked over to the recliner. Feeling Deacon's eyes following him the whole time, he picked up a pack of Newport's and took his time lighting one.

Deacon watched Peto for a second before he turned and locked the heavy-duty steel door. Then he glanced at the beaded curtain hanging from a small doorway in the far corner. He wondered how many guns were pointed at him.

"Gordo, who whupped yo' ass, man? Somebody did you dirty, huh?" Peto asked, as he finally turned to face Deacon.

"Yeah, I had a li'l trouble, but I—"

"Whadda-you-want? I ain't seen you since you beg me to put you on my cousin's punk-ass," Peto said, as he took a seat and stared at Deacon.

Deacon felt the sweat dripping off his brow, blinked his eyes to keep the salty liquid out and started to reach toward the inside pocket of his jacket. The slight noise from the other side of the beads stopped him. "I know it's been awhile, but I got somethin' fo' you," he said as he pulled open his jacket and carefully removed a roll of bills. He held the money out for Peto.

Peto looked at the bills, then brought his eyes back to Deacon's face. He made no move to take the money. "Whadda-you-want?"

Sweat ran into Deacon's eyes, he didn't bother with the dirty handkerchief in his breast pocket; instead he wiped his sleeve across his face. "I...I need a place to stay for a few days until..."

Peto took the roll from his hand and flipped through it. The few thousand dollars weren't as important as what had happened since Deacon had overheard him and José talking and had been so anxious to get involved. He should've questioned the fat man back then, but it hadn't seemed important at the time.

Deacon sneaked a glance at the curtain and wondered if he could kill whoever was back there, but knew he wouldn't make it. He'd seen the layout the night José showed up and Peto had him wait back there. The two henchmen kept their guns in their hands, and even with the gun he'd taken from Born, he knew he didn't have a chance.

What he needed was a place where he could rest up for a week or so. He felt dizzy, and he wanted to lie down. He looked at Peto and remembered the last time he'd been there and heard José talk about having Man killed. He had thought it was a message from God. Now, it seemed more like a message from hell. His body slumped and he shook his head to clear it.

"Peto, I got some more money comin' in a few days and—"

"Hold up, Gordo," Peto said, holding his hand up. "I got you. I know a place you can crash for a minute." He wanted the fat man within reach. He didn't know what was going on but it made sense to figure it out. He tossed the money on the table and wished, for the hundredth time in the last five months, that he had Ice to watch his back. Peto spoke a few words in rapid-fire Spanish. A skinny, dark-brown man, with a big revolver in his hand, instantly stepped from behind the beads and nodded.

"Don't worry, Gordo," Peto said when he saw the panic in Deacon's eyes. "Flaco gonna take you over to a spot on Avenue C."

Deacon didn't like it but he smiled, wiped his face with his handkerchief and said,

"Thanks, Peto. And, that money oughta be here soon."

"Yeah, that's cool, 'cause you owe big-time now, Gordo," Peto said easily, trying to put the fat man at ease.

Once Deacon and Flaco left, Peto stepped through the curtain of beads. "Yo, Blacky, when Myria suppose to visit Ice again?" he asked, making a mental note to let Ice know what was what.

# CHAPTER FORTY-FOUR

The street was dark and almost empty. Two winos argued over whose turn it was to suck on the bottle of *Night Train* sticking out of the paper bag that neither would release–if the wine spilled, so would blood. A few houses down, a worn out crackhead was darting her eyes back and forth, searching for anyone desperate enough to risk disease or death. Sex was cheap in West Farms, but life was cheaper.

Like the winos and crackheads, the row houses were barely standing. The girl's dirty short, knit dress showed off her skinny, scared legs and hinted that she wore nothing beneath it. Although she was probably in her twenties, she looked closer to forty. Her front teeth were a distant memory, and she'd learned to use their loss as an advantage in her sexual sales pitch. Her eyes settled on the brown van for a moment, then moved to the two winos that'd finished their bottle and were singing whatever it was winos sing, as they went dancing off. Their joy probably meant they had enough change for another bottle. Maybe that's why she decided to trail behind them–they might not be as broke as they looked.

Man watched them move off through the nearly black, tinted-window in the back of the van. "All right … everybody know what we doin', right?" he asked, without taking his eyes from the window.

Eddie nodded while he worked the silencer on his gun.

"Yeah, I go in first, but pass the room Robby said the fat dude is in. Then, I wait for Eddie," Kid said, smiling at Pete.

"That's right. You comin' out first too, and going down to the corner and get in the car June left for us. I'll be comin' in the back before Eddie gets to you and Pete'll—"

"Just so everybody know." Eddie cut in, looking from Kid to Pete before his gaze reached Man. "Whoever we find in his spot gets it. Two to the head just for runnin' with 'im," Eddie said, his tone and eyes surpassing his ruthless words.

The look in Man's eyes matched Eddie's, and he tipped his head. As Kid nodded, Pete said, "What if it's women and kids in..."

"Anybody and everybody gets laid down," Eddie answered, while his eyes held Man's. Pete looked at Kid who looked away, then turned to Man with a pleading, questioning look. Man faced Pete, but ignored the unasked question.

"Like I was saying, me and Pete gonna come in the back and while I go up Pete'll watch both doors until he hears us comin' down. Once you hear us, you c'mon back to the van. I'll be right behind you and Eddie'll follow Kid," Man said, without emotion.

Pete's eyes dropped, "Yeah, okay," he said, in a quiet but steady voice, as Man climbed out of the van and headed for the alley.

Kid stood on the stairs between the second and third landing of the three-story house as Man and Eddie stood on either side of the plywood door. Man pointed to Eddie, then at the floor. He put his finger to his own chest, then pointed up– Eddie would go low and he'd go high.

The door flew open from Man's weight and Eddie slid in under him–both had their guns ready. The noise brought a tired looking border out of his room at the far end of the hall. Kid was on him before the man could wipe the sleep from his eyes. Kid used duct tape on the man, quickly shoved him back in his room and under the single bed and was back in the hallway a few seconds before Man and Eddie walked out of Deacon's room.

Kid looked at Eddie. Eddie shook his head, "Nothing but some bloody towels and a tore up bloody shirt. The muthafucker gone already."

Once they were all settled in the warehouse the tension eased, a little. Still, a blind man could see the danger hovering around the small office. Eddie had Anita Baker's, *Sometimes*, playing and the words seemed to haunt him: "Sometime you win and sometime you lose." He sat there as if Anita had a message for him. Eddie looked off into space as Anita sang about holding on a little longer and being a little stronger.

Man, who'd been quiet since they returned, got up and went to the door. "I'm going downstairs," he said over his shoulder. Kid looked at Pete before following Man out.

When the Crusaders', *Streetlife*, came on, Eddie tilted his head and focused his eyes. Randy Crawford's sweet vocals seemed to bring him out of his trance. He stood and swayed to the music. He sang along for a minute, until he noticed Pete watching him. "I know you ain't with all this killin' shit. But you know what? It's the way shit is sometime."

Pete didn't respond, he just looked at Eddie and shook his head.

"I ain't make the rules but bet I'ma live by 'em, and you know what? I'ma die by 'em too. So when a muthafucker lay my man down, I'ma make 'em pay," Eddie said as he nodded his head to Randy Crawford's words. He seemed more interested in the words of the song than those he spoke.

"So it don't matter who we kill, huh?"

"Shit. Pete, I on't even worry 'bout what matters or not. I just do what I gotta do. Let me tell you somethin', y'all run with Man 'cause y'all down with 'im. Well, we all down but me and the God come up together and I mean for muthafuckers to pay for what happen, and as many as I can get at.

"I'll tell you somethin' else: Man, he's a sad man that just happens to be bad. Me, I'm a bad man that ain't never took the time to be sad about shit. Me and Born ain't had what Man had, all we ever had was the streets and one another. That was our life, and some fool took the God from me," Eddie said, as the song ended and the room settled into the quiet of deadly silence.

"I hear you Eddie. But no matter how many people we kill it won't bring the God back. So why not just kill—"

"Fuck bringing the God back. Young'en, me and Born come up hard fo' real– since we was knee-high to dog-shit in the gutter ain't nobody give a fuck about us. We fought for everything we ever got. We learned early 'bout life being a bitch, it was just the dying we got around." Eddie stopped, sighed, then continued, "Until now, anyway. But, I 'on't think I'd bring the God back even if I could, 'cause life is a bitch. So what I'ma do is send some muthafuckers behind 'im."

Pete wasn't sure if there was anything to say to that. But while all Eddie, and sometimes Man, could see was death, he saw life. For a second, he thought about Kid and how easy the whole thing seemed to him. "Eddie, you know that I'm down with laying down whoever killed Born. But why can't you still think about living?" Pete asked, trying to make sense of the way they lived.

"'Cause I ain't got nothin' to live for, young'en. I'm just playin' this shit out" Eddie said, as Curtis Mayfield's, *Little Child Runnin' Wild* drifted through the speakers: *Watch awhile, see he never smiles.* The lyrics carried Eddie back to where he needed to be and helped chase away the images of Kia that came and threatened to contradict his words and his logic.

Lo watched Nicki and Terri cross the street, then he peeped over at José and Short-Dog whispering to each other. Not sure of what he'd do if they tried something, he was saved from making a decision by the sight of Bigum trailing behind the two females. The big man walked slowly, as if all he cared about was letting the tough looking, little, brindled-colored pitbull handle its business in the gutter. But to Lo, it was obvious that he was making sure the women got home safely.

Although he knew that Short-Dog and Ze wouldn't make a move now, he knew that they were still fool enough to do what they had planned. With that in mind, Lo watched Bigum continue up the block. He wondered how long it would be before he made it back to Badlands.

*** 

Kia looked at the silent phone and frowned, she turned her attention back to the book in her lap–Zora Neal Hurston's, *Their Eyes Were Watching God*. After another failed attempt at reading, she tossed the book aside and picked up the phone to make sure it was working. The dial-tone taunted her with its strong, steady, buzz.

She had beeped Eddie twenty minutes ago. Here we go again, she thought – you put your guard down and "bam" you get a shot straight to the heart. She hated to admit it but she had fallen for him. She wouldn't make the jump to love, but what she felt was strong. And now, he wasn't returning her calls. Speaking of calls, everything had changed with the call Eddie received during the middle of their last night together. He rushed her home, told her he had to go to New York and would be in touch.

That was it. Well, except for him saying that one of his partners was in trouble. Kia walked to the mirror, twisted up her pretty face and asked out loud, *"So, I guess his friends are more important than me. Well, his ass could at least return my damn call."*

*** 

Eddie felt the beeper vibrating against his hip but didn't bother to reach for it. He kept his eyes on Man. Union Square Park was crowded with people shopping for fresh produce. It was the last weekend for the Farmer's Market, until next summer. The third weekend in September signified the close of the market's season and people always showed up as if they just had to have what wouldn't be available for another year.

With the crowd of farmers and shoppers Eddie still managed to keep Man and the slick-looking Puerto Rican kid he was talking to in his sights. Peto had set up the meet, said he had some information for Man. He used Ice's name – a name Man and Eddie knew from doing time – as a reference. Eddied remembered Ice as a stand-up brother. Nevertheless, Eddie's hand didn't stray far from the Colt .44 Magnum tucked in his waistband, and the pressure of the .40 caliber in the middle of his back gave him an extra surge of adrenaline.

He scanned the park like a bird of prey searching for dinner. He spied two cats holding Peto down and saw a couple of other possible henchmen lurking in the background. That put it at five or six against two, by his count, which Eddie thought was just about fair – though Peto needed a couple more standup gunmen for it to really be even. He was ready to pile the bodies up.

When Man gripped the hand Peto offered, Eddie's hand slipped under his oversized sweatshirt and rested on the handle of the Magnum. He knew that Man liked to pull them close when he gave it to them, especially if it was personal, and this was personal. However, Man and Peto broke the handshake without the sound of death and parted after a few words were passed between them. As Peto made his way out of the park, four men followed. Man stayed where he was for a minute before heading over to one of the farmers' stands and buying a few plums. While Man looked over his purchase, Peto's last backup gunman eased out of the park. Although they never actually looked at each other, Man and Eddie worked their way toward one another. As he and Man looked over a tray of ripe, red apples, Eddie asked, "So?"

Man bought four apples and passed two to Eddie. "I know you ain't much on plums," he said.

"So?" Eddie repeated, as they walked away from the fruit stand.

"To cut to the chase, I got an address for this Deacon cat, the rest of the shit can wait until..."

"What else?"

"The punk who put the shit in play is a muthafucker I done had dealings with. But, first, I wanna take care of this fat muthafucker 'cause he close by. Then, we can get at the other one."

Eddied stopped and stared at Man, "You believe what Ice's man told you?"

"Yeah, enough to get at it right now and put some heads to bed."

"That's good enough for me. You got anymore toast in the car?" Eddie asked, wishing he had more than just the two guns, and one extra clip.

"Ain't nothin' else in the car. But I got a sixteen shot 'Nine' and a three-pound-seven with a speed-loader. If that ain't enough we need to hang up our guns and retire," Man said, as they reached the car.

They checked their beepers at the same time Eddie had two pages from Kia, and Man had one from Bigum. Neither wasted time looking for a phone. They had something else on their minds.

***

Bigum waited half-an-hour for Man to call, then he called Pete and told him to get a hold of Kid and meet him at Shine's. He didn't know if what Lo told him was true or not, but he had to act as if it was. He couldn't let anything happen to Nicki.

As he stepped out of the office and called a couple of the older kids over, the three detectives appeared in the doorway of the game room. "I hope I didn't catch you at a bad time," the albino-looking sergeant said.

Bigum looked into the man's colorless eyes and felt a chill go through him, "No, I'm just making sure the—"

The sergeant interrupted, "Well, that's good... you doing your job and all. But we need a quick word, you and I." When the two teenagers looked at the three policemen and back at Bigum, and made no attempt to leave, the sergeant added, "Alone, Mr. Casey."

As he told the kids to go back to their game of pool and stepped behind the counter, the sergeant's use of his last name wasn't lost on Bigum. As the sergeant followed Bigum, the other detectives wandered around the game room giving looks of contempt to the few kids that were there. Although the looks were meant to provoke and intimidate, they did neither. It was common practice for the police to be abusive and disrespectful to people of color, especially in the ghetto, and it didn't make a difference if the victims were children.

Bigum settled on a stool, and still towered over the sergeant even though the man remained standing. They stared at each other for a moment. Neither man spoke, as they measured one another. Finally, the albino smiled, displaying small, sharp yellow teeth. "Didn't I ask you to have Mr. Soleil call me?" Before Bigum could respond, he continued, "What? Did you lose my card or maybe you just threw it away? Or maybe, Mr. Soleil just said fuck the law, huh?"

Bigum looked into the man's face, again thinking that he was seeing something rotten– something gone bad without the odor. He steadied himself and said, "No, sir. I ain't throw yo' card away." He paused and sighed slowly, "Man just ain't been around fo' me to give it to him."

"Well, you're in luck. See, that's exactly what I've been informed of. That he hasn't been around much lately. Now, that can't be good for business, can it," the man said showing his little rat-like teeth.

The reference to business and the use of Man's surname made Bigum uneasy, but he knew better than to let it show. "Well, it don't take much to run no game room. All—"

"Cut the crap. I know what's what around here," the sergeant said, as he looked around Badlands and flashed his teeth again. "I did some checking. You boys did a lot of time, huh? Y'all boys is real killers too. Now, I see you did a lot more time than your friend and since you probably want to stay out a lot more, I'm going to work with you, okay?"

"Sure, but..."

"All I want you to do is tell your friend that he needs to call me as soon as possible. That's Sergeant Gledhill," the sergeant said, stepping close to Bigum. He leaned forward and his foul breath floated up into Bigum's face. He reached inside his jacket–Bigum tensed–and came out with another business card. "See, I'm even leaving you another card."

Bigum didn't relax until the cops left the game room. He watched the door for a few minutes before sending one of the kids out to have a look around. Everybody was worried. It was the first time that Badlands had been threatened. In the hood, the police produced more fear than anything else. And that's what every one of the kids in the place felt–fear–they just decided to keep it to themselves.

Once he was satisfied that it was safe to go out, Bigum called two boys over and told them to watch things until he got back, then walked across the street to the daycare center. A few minutes later, he exited the back door, and made his way to Webster Avenue and hailed a cab. He really needed to talk to Man now, but had to settle for Shine and June. He couldn't understand why Man hadn't returned his page.

## CHAPTER FORTY-FIVE

Man entered the small tenement first. A minute later, Eddie stumbled through the entrance. He caromed off the walls as he made his way up the narrow staircase, holding the half-full bottle of cheap wine close to his body. He stopped at the second door on the landing. Man was pressed up against the wall to the left of the door.

Eddie knocked softly, two knocks, then a pause and another three quick taps, just as Peto had instructed.

"Yeah?" a hoarse voice asked, from the other side of the door.

Eddie answered by pushing two dirty, crumpled $10 bills through the small hole in the door. A second later, two small glassine bags of heroin were pushed out and Eddie snatched them. As he examined them, he pushed a dirty $5 bill and four singles through the hole. "Looka-hea' baby-pa, let me get one for nine," he said in a whining voice.

"We don't take no fuckin' shorts. Get yo' ass outta here."

"C'mon baby, don't do a nigga like that," Eddie said, as he pushed the bills back through the hole.

"If you don't get your punk ass..."

The words were cut off by Eddie's outburst and the sound of the wine bottle hitting the floor. "Shit! You done made me drop my fuckin' bottle and you gonna pay for that shit."

"Oh, I'ma pay yo' ass alright!" shouted the voice behind the door. Followed by the sound of locks being opened.

As the door swung open, Man brought his gun up and rushed the man in the doorway, bringing the barrel of the heavy .357 down on his head. As the man fell, Man kneeled over him and Eddie stepped over them – both guns drawn and ready. Eddie rushed into the front room and caught a short, stocky man coming out of a nod.

The man's head snapped up, his eyes grew like the headlights of an eighteen-wheeler coming fast in the rearview mirror of a compact car. He shook the drugs off and reached for the gun on the cigarette-burned coffee table. Eddie shoved the table aside with his foot. "Move and die, muthafucker," Eddie said, as he quickly closed the gap between them and slapped the magnum across the man's jaw.

The sound of bone against steel echoed like a home run off Darryl Strawberry's bat. The man fell sideways and groaned in pain. Eddie leaned over him and brought the butt of the gun down on his forehead. Blood gushed across the man's face as he lost consciousness. Eddie grabbed the gun off the floor and rushed toward the bathroom just off to the left.

Man stepped out of the bedroom. "I got mines taped up. They the only ones here," he said, letting the adrenaline rush pass.

Once they had both men with their hands taped behind their backs, Eddie and Man laid them on the living-room floor and went through the apartment more thoroughly – checking closets and dressers, under the mattress and chair cushions.

The taller man, the one who opened the door, regained consciousness and tried to sit up. But with his hands restrained behind him, he couldn't manage the feat. Exhausted and groggy, he looked from Man to Eddie and said, "The money is in the freezer." When silence met his admission, he twisted around and stared at his partner lying beside him. His partner's face was swollen and beginning to turn black and blue, as he moaned in pain.

The man turned his attention back to Man and Eddie. The fact that they had on gloves and hadn't bothered to hide their faces told him he probably wouldn't live through this. Still, he had to try. "Look, the shit is under the oven and there's a bag of dimes behind the toilet that's—"

"Thank you," Eddie said. They had found everything but the stash under the oven. "Where's Deacon?"

You could almost see the wheels turning in the man's head. He thought that if all they really wanted was the fat man Peto had asked them to put up for a few days, he'd give him up and they could be on their way. Then the reality came, if they killed Deacon, they wouldn't leave any witnesses.

"He left. He said he didn't feel safe here and..."

"So he ain't comin' back then?" Man asked.

"Nah, he—"

Eddie cut him off "Good, ain't no reason to keep y'all alive," and pointed the automatic at the man's head.

"He'll be back," the man screamed. "Wait, wait, he went to the store."

Man looked at Eddie, shrugged his shoulders and asked, "Whadda-you-think?"

"I think he's a lying sack of shit and that we should just put his head to bed and wake his man up and deal with him."

When the man started to speak, Man silenced him by waving the big Magnum back and forth and said, "I 'on't know. He might be tellin' the truth?" Eddie's smirk said otherwise, so Man continued, in a deadly serious voice, "What if he gives us his word?"

"Look at 'im. He smell like a five-pound bag of *used muthafuckers* and you want me to take his word?" Eddie asked, raising his brow. "Nah, I can't buy that shit."

"Look! I swear to—"

The rest of the man's words died between his mind and mouth as Eddie and Man aimed their weapons at him. "Yo, shut the fuck up. Goddamn, you stank and you talk too fuckin' much," Eddie said.

"All right, I'll give you the benefit of the doubt and allow you to relay any pertinent information you may have," Man said. The guy looked at Man, his eyes full of confusion. Man shook his head while Eddie rolled his eyes at him. "Just tell us what you know 'bout dude."

"I don't know that cat. Peto sent the muthafucker over here. He told us to keep an eye on 'im for a few days."

"So, y'all just took 'im in like that?" Eddie asked.

The smell of fear coming off the man mixed with the smell of his unwashed body created an odor filled with misery. With his breath coming in short gasps, the man struggled to get his words out. "No, we owed Peto for a package that was fucked up and had to—"

"Enough of that shit. When is fat-boy coming back?" Eddie barked, his patience growing short.

"He went to get some clothes. He said he needed somethin' different than his suit."

"Suit?"

Instead of looking at Eddie, who'd spoken, the man looked at Man with pleading eyes.

"Yeah, he always wears these cheap-ass black suits. Like a fuckin' preacher or somethin'."

"Man nodded, "How long he been gone?"

"He left 'bout twenty minutes fore y'all showed up. We sent 'im over to Sixth Street to the Army and Navy. He wanted some work clothes and—"

"So, he oughta be back in the next few minutes, right?"

"Yeah. I swear it's the truth. I swear on my..."

Man stopped him by sticking one of the guns in his waist and taking out a small pocketknife. "I believe you, homey. Ain't no reason to bring yo' family in this kinda shit. Turn over so I can cut you loose."

When the fear threatened to panic the man, Man added, "But yo' boy gotta stay tied up for now. We only got paid to grab fatboy and bring 'im—"

"Hold up. They don't need to know all that," Eddie said, looking at Man as if he'd gone crazy.

The man relaxed and attempted to roll over but couldn't. Man gave him a nudge with the toe of his boot. When he was on his stomach, Man picked up a square section of cushion from the worn couch. In one motion, he pressed it around the man's ears and grabbed the guy's forehead and ran the four-inch blade across his throat-severing carotid arteries and the jugular. The cushion kept most of the blood from spreading and after a minute or two the guy's struggles stopped. Before Man got up, Eddie had another cushion in his hands and was leaning over the unconscious man with the broken jaw. His work was done just as fast.

They looked at one another, then settled in to wait. For a moment, neither one of them spoke. Then, Eddie gave Man a slow, appraising look and asked, "Why muthafuckers always believe the bullshit you tell 'em."

"Cause I believe the shit when I say it," Man said, smiling as he went to get the drugs from under the oven.

***

Nicki looked at Bigum as if he'd lost his mind. She pushed away from her desk and abruptly stood up with her hands on her hips. "I don't believe this," she said.

Bigum looked like an oversized kid trying to explain something that couldn't be translated to an unimaginative adult. Along with Shine and June, he had decided that it wasn't safe for Nicki to go home, and that she shouldn't be told exactly why–he wanted to leave that job to Man. He wondered where Man was and why he hadn't gotten back to him. "It's just for today and as soon as Man—"

"Where the hell is Man?" Nicki interrupted, rolling her neck with each word.

"He had to see to somethin'," Bigum said, not knowing what else to say in the face of Nicki's anger. When she rolled her eyes at his answer, he dipped his huge head and added, "You know things are a li'l outta sorts right now."

"Well, the fact that the police are asking questions shouldn't stop Man from working. After all, it's not as if he's done anything illegal and he loves Badlands," she said, with a challenging look.

Bigum looked uncomfortable as he felt the sweat collecting under his arms. "Yeah, that's all true, but there's some more stuff going on right now, and—"

"Bigum, you have to be more specific than that," Nicki said, cutting him off again. "Are you talking about his friend that got killed?"

Bigum couldn't disguise his surprise; he really looked like a big kid to Nicki who smiled for the first time since he'd entered her small office. "Yes, Man told me that somebody tried to rob him and ended up killing him."

Bigum recovered enough to say, "Uh-huh." He understood that although Man had confided in her, he had stopped short of letting her in on the sinister realities of what was happening.

As if picking up on Bigum's thoughts, Nicki said, "I hope Man ain't out there doing none of that street shit?"

Feeling even more uncomfortable and with sweat running down his back, Bigum said, "Man just making funeral arrangements," without realizing the double-entendre.

As Nicki stared up at Bigum, he was reminded of how Man seemed to read his thoughts. "Nicki, Man want you to..."

"Bigum, I know you said he wanted me to stay away from my house until he could talk to me. But if it's so important why isn't his butt here now." Seeing the pained expression on his face Nicki conceded, "But I will check with you before I leave tonight, okay?"

The big man sighed and relaxed a little. Nicki had to check the laughter that threatened to leap from her. Men were like little boys, no matter how big, old or tough they were. Just then, the door to her office flew open and Jamel charged in, stopping only when he had a firm hold on one of Bigum's legs.

"Mr. Bigum, you come to take us to the game room. We ready to go play. Ain't we Ms. Nicki," the child screamed with joy.

Nicki watched as Bigum lifted the boy with one hand, holding him up as she would a loaf of bread. Looking from one to the other, she didn't know whose smile was bigger.

While he played with Jamel, Bigum was glad that Kid and Pete were ready to sneak inside of Nicki's house if necessary. Still, he'd feel better if Man was around. With him and Eddie on the warpath, Bigum didn't know what to expect. Although Kid and Pete knew about the meet with the guy that called for Man yesterday, nobody had heard from them since. They had already broken a long-standing rule: *keep in touch.*

Nicki's voice pulled him away from his thoughts. "Bigum, please put that child down. He's supposed to be taking a nap. Isn't that right, Jamel?"

As he was lowered to the floor, Jamel said, "Awwh, Ms. Nicki, I ain't even sleepy."

"Jamel, haven't we spoken about using ain't. You have to learn to speak correctly, okay?" Nicki said, as she bent down and hugged the boy.

Jamel squirmed out of her embrace, "But you say ain't too, Ms Nicki and Man say it all the time, and Mr. Bigum," he said, innocently.

"All right, Jamel. I understand what you're saying, but we all know the correct way to speak. That's why—"

"I know the correct way too; you taught me," the child cut in, with a huge smile on his cute face.

Bigum tried unsuccessfully to smother the laugh growling in his belly. Once it came out, Jamel joined him. Although he didn't know what was so funny, Bigum's laughter and Nicki's smile told him that something was.

Nicki rose and took his hand. "Come on, Jamel. Maybe if you go right to sleep, I'll take you with me to Badlands, later."

As Jamel argued his point, with the pleasant temperament of a friendly country lawyer, Bigum left and went across the street to the game-room. He hoped that Man would check in, soon.

## CHAPTER FORTY-SIX

Sergeant Gledhill hung up the phone and looked at his two subordinates; the snake and the pig looked bored. The two detectives wanted some action but the sergeant seemed content to work the phones. "Nothing yet on our new boy; his black ass seems to have disappeared, and it seems that the resourceful Ricky isn't so resourceful after all."

"Sarge, if we start crackin' a couple'a heads, I bet he'll turn up then," the snake said. The pig lifted his pig-shaped head off his chest and guffawed. Cracking heads was the best part of detective work, even better than the payoff money, to him. He waited expectedly for orders to spill blood, his weak, runny eyes locked on Gledhill.

"I think we'll give it a few more days," Gledhill said, thinking about the anonymous tip that Internal Affairs had received on their captain. "We're in no hurry. Actually, we have time on our side now that I'm in charge of the unit."

The Snake shrugged and the Pig looked disappointed. Neither one knew about the tip to Internal Affairs. Working for a crooked captain or sergeant was all the same to them — the work was simple and the pay good. So if Gledhill could wait, they could too.

*** 

Pete glanced over at Kid, they'd been in the back of the van for the last hour watching Nicki's house. He didn't have to wonder what Kid was thinking. Kid had made his feelings clear: Snatch José and Short-Dog, and put two in their heads—Fuck the proof.

Kid shifted on the milk-crate and returned Pete's gaze for a second. He lifted his brow questioningly, but Pete just shook his head. He didn't know what to say. For the first time in their lives, he felt–better yet–acknowledged a gap between them. The differences that brought them together in the past were starting to pull them apart.

Killing came as easy to Kid as living did, while Pete took both seriously, giving each a great deal of thought. As kids on the basketball court, Pete had worked hard to set Kid up with the best shot possible, whereas Kid took every shot as if he expected to make them all. It was the same with women, Pete wanted one forever, while Kid wanted as many as he could have, as quick as he could have them.

For a minute, Pete wished that they were kids again, but remembered that childhood hadn't been all that great. His smile was melancholic, as the past and future seemed to meet for a fleeting moment in the back of a dark van on a dark street.

But Pete knew he wasn't wrong, sitting there armed and ready to commit murder– he was protecting a woman he'd known since he was a kid and if he had to kill to do it, that was okay with him. He glanced at Kid again, and remembered that he was holding his partner down, as well as Man.

Kid's voice interrupted his thoughts. "Yo, if we don't hear from Man by the end of the night we grab them lames and that be that," Kid said, with his eyes still on Nicki's.

Pete thought about it, they couldn't sit outside of Nicki's house forever and they couldn't leave her unprotected. "That's cool with me," Pete said as he moved next to Kid and looked in the opposite direction. "What you think goin' on with Man and Eddie'?"

With his eyes still on the street, Kid said, "They probably gettin' some blood on they knifes, since they ain't down with gettin' no shit on they dicks," Kid said, laughing into his chest to smother the sound.

Covering his mouth with his hand, Pete chuckled, "Yo, you a fool. If Man hears you..."

"Well, you know they done all that time and shit. I mean, I know they ain't fuck around but I ain't tryin' share no bed with 'em."

"That's my word, I'm tellin' Man."

"Nah, chill. You know how Man be gettin'. He ain't 'bout all that jokin' shit and Eddie might think the shit is funny and still fuck me up."

"All right. If you take them bad-ass kids in the game-room to Coney Island next weekend with me and Bigum, I'll forget I heard that shit."

"Damn, I don't know. Bigum? Shit, he did way more time than...

Pete elbowed Kid. "Yo, I'm tellin' Bigum what yo ass said."

"Damn, homey. I ain't say nothin'. And you know I'm down for the young'ens. Plus, Terry fine ass probably goin'", Kid said, rubbing his hands together.

## CHAPTER FORTY-SEVEN

Deacon lumbered up the stairs, holding a handkerchief over his damaged nose. His breath came in short, ragged gasps as he muttered to himself. He stopped on the landing between the first and second floor and looked up as he tried to get his breathing under control.

He muttered again, anyone in hearing distance would've thought the fat man, with his disheveled appearance, was crazy. Sweat collected around the collar of his dirty white shirt and he struggled with the shopping bags he carried.

He mumbled to himself, repeating Matthew 7:13, "Wide is the gate, and broad is the way that leadeth to destruction" over and over. He seemed lost in a world all his own as his eyes danced around wildly.

With the effort of climbing the stairs, carrying the bags and just plain living, Deacon didn't notice the broken wine bottle in front of the door until he raised his massive arm to knock. Although his hand never touched the door, it suddenly swung open. Deacon stood there with his hand stuck in mid-air, and a confused look on his sweaty face.

Eddie filled the doorway, the big .40 caliber pistol in his hand. "Easy fat-boy, keep yo' hands where I can see 'em."

Deacon dropped his fat fist, his mouth hung open but no words came out as his shoulders slumped. He dropped the shopping bags to the floor and took a small step back. "Hold up. You goin' the wrong way," Man said, from behind him. He'd been waiting in the staircase above, with his gun held low, beside his hip.

Eddie backed up, moving farther into the apartment. "Bring 'im inside, Man."
At the mention of Man's name, rage spread across the fat man's face, adding to the crazed look in his eyes. Despite the gun pointed at his head, Deacon screamed like a dying animal that refused to die alone, spun around with a speed neither Eddie nor Man expected, and charged. Man hesitated; he didn't want to fire in the hallway. That split second was all Deacon needed. The force of Deacon's mad rush slammed Man into the wall, knocking the wind out of him. Man's gun was pinned between them and he hadn't gotten his other hand up in time to keep Deacon's fingers from fastening around his neck.
Eddie cursed as the two men tumbled to the floor. Even if he hadn't cared about the noise, he couldn't fire. He couldn't take the chance. Man and Deacon was a tangle of arms and legs.

"Shit," he cursed again and rushed forward.

Man felt the force of Deacon's weight smothering him, but brought his knee up into his groin, and heard the big man groan. For a second, Deacon's grip loosened. Man quickly tucked his chin to keep Deacon's hands from crushing his windpipe, but it wasn't enough–he couldn't breathe.

Through the fog that was descending on his mind Man heard the fat man scream, "I'll kill'ya. I'll kill..."

Man tried to maneuver the gun but Deacon's weight stopped him and the big man's hands tighten around his neck. He didn't know how much time he had, but his fingers were still wrapped around the trigger. He forced his wrist up as much as he could.
Eddie was just about on them when the sound of the gunshots brought him to a stop. The two shots echoed in the small hallway, ringing in his ears. He pulled the .44 Magnum from his back and waited. Deacon's body moved slowly. Eddie waited.

Deacon groaned in pain as he desperately struggled to keep his grip on Man's neck. Man's first shot had ripped through the fat man's right side, passing through his ample gut without hitting any vital organs. The second slug had bounced off his ribcage and tore into his lung. Even with the damage of the slugs Deacon continued to struggle, but his strength was slipping away.

Man knocked Deacon's hands from his neck, sucking in air that burned as it went down. Using the floor for leverage Man was able to shift Deacon's body and, finally, throw the fat man off him. As Man struggled to his feet, Eddie stepped over Deacon, who lay there on his back, fighting for each breath and mumbling incoherently. Eddie nudged him with his foot. When Deacon moaned from the contact, Eddie pulled back and kicked him. Deacon screamed, his huge body trembled, then he went back to mumbling.

Eddie tried to make sense of Deacon's words but couldn't. He stepped back and fired two quick shots. The first slug ripped through Deacon's throat while the second one went through his left eye. "Keep it to yo'self then."

Blood gushed out and small bubbles formed at both wounds.

As Eddie put another bullet in Deacon's chest Man staggered forward. "C'mon let's get outta here," he said.

Eddie smiled. You a'ight, homey'?" He asked, as he gave Man a quick once over. Man ran his hand over his throat, "Yeah, right as rain. Let's get the fuck outta here."

Eddie nodded and looked down at Deacon's lifeless right eye. "Who the fuck was..."

"I don't know," Man said, moving towards the stairs.

"He knew you though. Muthafucker went crazy when I fucked up and said yo' name."

"Yeah, I know. But right now we gotta be ghost," Man said, giving Deacon one last look as they headed down the stairs.

No doors opened as they hurried down the narrow stairwell. In the ghetto, the less you saw or heard, the better off you were. Eddie and Man removed their gloves and slipped on baseball caps. Eddie put on a pair of sunglasses, and Man put on wide, black-framed glasses.

Once on the sidewalk, they walked at a normal pace and kept their heads down. They had wanted to spend some time with the man who'd brought death to their private circle. But they'd had less than a minute in the hallway with him. His dying wasn't enough for either of them, but now wasn't the time to consider any of that. Though things hadn't gone the way they'd hoped, getting away was all that mattered now.

***

Short-Dog watched Lo out the corner of his eye. He had kept his distance since Lo flipped out about moving on Nicki. He would have never thought that Lo was one of those soft-ass dudes concerned with right or wrong when it came to revenge. He thought that with the way Man had chumped his punk-ass in front of everybody Lo'd be willing to do anything to get some revenge.

Lo's soft-ass bullshit was slowing his plans down. José was scared to make a move without Lo and the timing was perfect. Man had stopped collecting protection money from the crews. Sammy and Mack had moved on to some other shit. Man was slipping and with the right moves his whole empire could be snatched right from under him.

Short-Dog smiled, then nodded at Lo. He'd give him one more try. If he couldn't convince him to back José, he knew he'd have to do it himself. But if he got down with that, he'd have to make sure José killed Nicki. Maybe he'd kill Ze and make it look like he tried to save Nicki. Now, he thought as he approached Lo, *that would be some high-powered shit.*

"What's up, homey?" When Lo nodded, Short-Dog smiled and went on, "Yo, I know we still cool, right?"

Lo raised his brow and shrugged. "Why not? What you done?" he asked with a smile on his rough face.

Although Short-Dog was surprised by Lo's response, it made him believe that his scheme would work, after all. Short-Dog relaxed, reached in his pocket and came out with a $20 bag of *skunk* and a *Philly Blunt* and said, "Twist this up, Lo."

Short-Dog smiled as Lo split open the Blunt and put the bag of *skunk* to his nose and smiled at the strong aroma.

Lo dumped the whole twenty in the cigar leaf and dropped the empty bag on Short-Dog's foot. Once the Blunt was rolled, La lathered it with his spit. Saliva drenched the Blunt as La passed it to ShortDog. "Spark up, homey," Lo said, smiling at the game he and Short-Dog was playing.

*** 

June snatched the phone up in the middle of the first ring. "Yeah?"

"Damn, you waiting on a woman or somethin'."

June breathed a sigh of relief upon recognizing Man's voice. "Nothing like that. I was just sittin' here waiting fo' two of my favorite people to check in 'cause I need to get at 'em kinda bad."

Man glanced over at Eddie, then turned his attention back to the phone, "I hear that. We been kinda busy. But what's up?"

"Well, I need to get outta the house. I guess I'm gettin' old. I feel like a walk in the park, okay?"

"Okay. In what?" Man asked.

"Half-time should be about 4:00."

"That's cool." Man responded and hung the pay phone up. He looked at Eddie. "We gonna meet 'im in two hours by Central Park's 72nd Street entrance. He sounds like he got somethin' to say, too."

"Ain't no doubt 'bout that. He might be old, but June in this thing fo' real."

Man nodded. "You ain't never lied. June done forgot more shit than most lames ever knew 'bout the game."

After returning to the condo they took care of their weapons; cleaned them and filed down barrels–changing the ballistics. Only then did they take care of themselves.
After they showered and relaxed for a half-an-hour Man and Eddie got dressed and hit the streets again. They hadn't bothered to answer the calls that kept their beepers jumping. They had things that needed taking care of– José was next on their list.

When Man explained what he'd learned from Peto, Eddie nodded his agreement that Jose's time had come–only their meeting with June delayed it. They hardly spoke as they walked along Central Park West, they settled into their own thoughts of making things right for the God. With their conservative Brooks Brothers suits and Johnson and Murphy wing-tips they looked like a couple of Buppies (Black Urban Professionals) that raced to and from appointments throughout the day, along with their white counter parts. With time to spare, they stopped at a newsstand. Man bought copies of *Black Enterprise* and *Essence* magazines while Eddie grabbed the New York Times and smiled as if he'd just heard one of Eddie Murphy's jokes. Man ignored the smile and the smirk that followed for as long as he could.

"Okay. You win. I take the bait," Man said as he cocked his head to one side, with his own smirk in place. "What's so funny?"

"Shit," Eddie said and slowed down a step, letting Man get ahead of him. "You look like somebody damn broker or real estate agent. And with that *Essence* in your hand, a woman would think you were enlightened and sensitive."

When Eddie caught up, Man held out a magazine, "Since you look like my damn partner from the firm, why don't you check out what old rich ass Earl Graves talkin' bout. Or, you can get sensitive with Susan Taylor."

As Eddie pushed the magazines away, they both laughed and continued to stroll along the park.

They arrived twenty minutes early and took one of the benches along the sidewalk outside the park, thirty feet from the 72nd Street entrance. They settled into their respective reading. Although neither man appeared to be paying attention to the comings and goings around them, they both saw June as he entered the park. After a minute or two, Eddie and Man got up and walked over and stood behind the bench where the older man sat peacefully.

Black June's face was turned toward the sun, his eyes closed, and his hand folded across his stomach. He had an easy smile on his chiseled black face. The sun creased his features, highlighting his African heritage. "I guess it's good you boys enjoy reading so much," he said, opening his eyes and turning toward them.

Man looked at Eddie, then back at June. They both laughed. "We ain't surprised you saw us, old man," Man said.

"Shit, we woulda' been surprised if you didn't," Eddie added. "June, they don't make 'em like you no mo'. You and Shine the last of the real gangsters."

June picked up his brown fedora from beside him; he twirled the hat in his hands, and studied the younger men. Though he rarely saw Eddie and didn't see Man nearly as much as he'd like, he liked and respected them as his equals. For that reason, Eddie's tribute touched his heart.

As he stared at them through the narrow slits of his aged eyes, June wondered if they were the last of his kind — a breed of men that was dying off. Now with Born dead, the clock was ticking against them all. It wasn't so bad for him and Shine. After all, they were old men with only so many days left. But Man and Eddie had years before them, years to deal with a game where snitching and weakness were no longer the exceptions but the rule.

June's eyes didn't blink while he studied the two young gunmen as they stood in a sunny park, dressed in business suits —he knew that they were armed and ready to die as well as kill, if it came to that—and he almost felt sorry for them. Suddenly, he was thankful that he was an old man. He set his hat on his head, cocked to the right with a corner of the brim broken down. He rubbed his hands together. "I'm glad y'all finally called. That boy, Deacon y'all lookin' fo', he's Johnny Ray son—"

"Wait," Man said, holding his hand up in a motion to stop. "He was one of the Rays?" As Man and Eddie exchanged stares, June recognized the past tense Man had used when he spoke of Deacon.

Eddie's eyes closed for a brief moment. He inhaled deeply, opened his eyes and asked, "Johnny was the one me and the God done, right?"

Man rubbed his face and head with his hands. As he brought his hands down he looked into Eddie's eyes and nodded. Eddie took a step toward him and said, "Fuck it. The muthafucker needed killin.' He kil't yo' mama and daughter."

When Man didn't respond Eddie looked at June. "Me and the God hunted that low-life muthafucker down and done what we done 'cause it was the right thing to do and I know the God'd do it again. Ain't that right Black June?"

"Sure it's right," June answered, speaking to Man as much as Eddie. "We all know how this thing go. We do what we do until we cain't, then hopefully we die the way we lived," he said with his eyes locked on Man.

He knew Man was blaming himself. The Rays were his problem, or at least that's the way he saw it. But June, and Eddie knew better. They knew, as Man did, that when something foul turned up somebody had to throw it out, and it didn't matter who. Born and Eddie had found something foul – Johnny Ray–and got rid of it.

"There's mo'," June said, as he nodded towards the bench. They took seats on opposite sides of him, each leaned in close as if they was back in the prison yard. Their circle was tight and each set of eyes checked a different direction. With words spoken from lips that barely moved; they had closed ranks. Although their backs weren't against the wall, shadows of the prison wall and gun towers draped over them like desolate, gray rain clouds. Some memories are unshakeable.

June leaned back, tilted his chin down and spoke just loud enough for them to hear his words – if they strained. "Charles Ray is the boy's name. He got tagged with Deacon 'cause he killed a Reverend he caught fuckin' his mama in the church's basement." June stopped, shook his head and grunted before continuing, "Story is that mama was one of them Bible-thumpin' freaks, drop to her knees in a minute, and not just to pray."

"So, the boy seen her gettin' some. I mean that ain't nothin'" Eddie said, with a shrug.

"It's something, if all she did was tell 'im what'a sin it was. Anyway, he see mama takin' it from the back and grabbed a kitchen knife and gave it to the Rev. from behind. I guess he was 'bout eight or nine and since then he been in and out of mental joints."

"But what he had to do with Johnny Ray? I know you said he was his pops but I bet the muthafucker ain't never done shit for him," Man said.

"Yeah, I'm sho' you right. But some kinda way he found out 'bout his daddy and probably his uncles," June answered. He turned slightly, so that he could face Man. "You know how the Ray boys was living for years 'fore y'all finish 'em off," June said, as he shifted and looked at Eddie.

"What he shoulda knew was that he would be having a family reunion in hell. Fuck all of em," Eddie said as he stood up.

"Wait. There's a li'l mo'."

They looked at June, waiting. He filled them in about ShortDog and Jose's plan. Before he could tell it all, Man interrupted. "Shit, I ain't waitin' for them to make a move. I'm going to—"

"Hold up. Like I told ya', Kid and Pete was sittin' on Nicki's spot but they got tired of waitin' and—"

"And what?" Man cut in, iron in his voice.

June smiled, "Don't worry. You trained 'em right. They snatched both of 'em already."

"I knew there was a reason I liked them boys so much," Eddie said.

# CHAPTER FORTY-EIGHT

Kia pulled the phone away from her ear and smirked at it before continuing the conversation, "So, you got my beeps, but was too busy to call me back until now. Let me see, the first time I called was more than eight hours ago," she said incredulously.

Eddie held the receiver away from his ear and shook his head, he took a deep breath and put it back against his face, "Yeah, I was caught up in some shit and—"

"For eight hours? Eddie, I'm not stupid. If you don't wanna see me all you have to—" It was his turn to interrupt, "Listen, Shortie—"

"My name is not Shortie."

"Slow your roll for a minute, Kia, when I call you Shortie it's a term of endearment, and yeah, I couldn't call you right back. But that doesn't mean I wasn't thinkin' about you and it sure don't mean I don't want to see you. Think about it, have I done anything that would make you think I'm not tryin' to get with you. Think about the way I treat you and how we flow, Shortie."

Kia smiled at the phone, curled her legs under her thighs and leaned on the arm of the couch.

"Kia?" Eddie said.

Her smile grew as she heard the need in his voice. "Girl, what the hell is you doin'? You still there?"

Holding back the urge to giggle Kia said, "I was thinking and isn't that what you told me to do? And another thing, just because I let you call me Shortie, don't try callin' me no damn girl."

Eddie didn't hold back his laughter as he took a look in Man's direction. Man seemed to be wrapped up in a book, but Eddie turned his back to him anyway. Eddie's voice dropped and became deeper as he allowed some of the tension to drain from him. After a few minutes of easy conversation he hung up the phone.

He turned to find Man staring at him. "What?"

"I didn't say anything," Man answered, with a blank look on his face.

"Yeah, right" Eddie said, as if that was the end of the matter.

But when Man opened his book, as if he had nothing more to say, Eddie exclaimed, "What?"

Man smiled at Eddie.

"Man, you on some bullshit."

"Listen, homey, I was just admiring how you handled *Shortie*. That's all," Man said, easily.

"Yeah?" Eddie asked, unconvinced.

"Hell, yeah! I mean, the way you put your foot down and explained how shortie is a term of endearment was special"

"Aw, shit. I knew you was on some bullshit," Eddie said shaking his head.

"Nah, fo' real homey. You laid that down."

"Fuck you, Man. What? I pose' to just let her go off 'bout that bullshit?"

"Nah," Man said, setting his book aside as he stood up. "Especially since she important to you." Neither man carried the subject further, but both knew that Eddie returning Kia's call said a lot about his feelings for her.

Eddie shook images of Kia from his mind. He looked around the condo, rolled his shoulders and asked, "What time we goin' uptown?"

Man wondered if Eddie was as eager to get back to Kia as he was to get back to Nicki.

"Soon," he said, walking over to the sound system in the corner of the room. "The more time they lay there in the dark, duct-taped and gagged, the quicker they'll want to talk." He went through the albums and cassettes, before settling on Marvin Gaye's, *Trouble Man*.

"Sho' you right!" Eddie said, nodding his head to Marvin's message.

***

Nicki was beside herself. "You tell Man I am not leaving my house and that he needs to come talk to me right now!"

For the third time, Bigum failed to convince her that it would be safer for her to stay somewhere else for a couple of days.

Kid looked away, leaving Bigum with the job of responding to Nicki. After all, Man had talked to June and June had talked to Bigum. So it was only right that Bigum talk to Nicki, Kid thought smiling.

"Joseph!" The sound of his given name caught Kid off guard. "Would you mind letting me in on your little joke?" Nicki asked, turning away from Bigum to face Kid.

*Damn! Why can't she call me Kid,* he thought. "Ain't no joke or nothin'. You know, it don't take a lot to make me happy," Kid said, as he tugged on his ear and tried to look serious.

*Nicki shook her head, I refuse to call a grown man Kid and if he thinks it's okay to go through* life *with that dumb-ass look on his face...*

Kid hid behind his smile. He didn't want Nicki to bring up his mother. It was difficult acting a fool around people who watched you grow up. Although Kid hadn't felt much of a connection to most of the people who attended his mother's funeral, it was different with Nicki and a couple of the older women who were his mother's friends. Plus, the fact that she was Man's private stock lifted her even higher in Kid's eyes.

"Nicki, I know you gonna do what you wanna, but what you think we gonna do? Man asked us to make sure you was safe 'cause a bunch of stuff is goin' on right now," Kid said, then looked over at Bigum, before he walked over and took a seat beside Nicki's desk. "And you know we gonna do that on the strength of him, but also 'cause we peoples. Me and Bigum can't leave until we know you somewhere safe."

As Nicki stared at Kid, Bigum let out a sigh of relief and eased his back against the wall. She looked from Kid to Bigum and saw that they were serious. "Okay. So what now?" she asked in surrender.

***

Pete had Public Enemy playing as Kid entered the side door of the garage. Kid smiled and executed a quick dance step. "That's that shit, homey."

"For real... P.E. the truth." Pete said, laughing as he did a quick step of his own. They slapped palms as the sounds of Public Enemy bounced off the walls of the spacious garage. "Yo, what happened with Nicki? And when Man comin'?"

Kid laughed, shook his head and said, "Yo, you shoulda seen Nicki lettin' Bigum have it. Damn, I almost felt sorry for 'im. But, shit was funny. You had'da see that shit. Bigum ain't—"

"Wait up. What yo' ass was doin' besides laughing and actin' a fool?"

"Shit!" Kid said, twisting his face. "I'm the one that saved Bigum. I told her what Man said, and that we wasn't going nowhere until she did what Man said. And that was that," he added folding his arms across his chest.

Pete looked at his partner and arched his brow. "Was that before or after she called you Joseph?" he asked, smiling.

"Word. Why she always gotta go there."

"Probably 'cause she knew you since you was in pampers and had a runny nose and—"

"All right. All right. That's enough. She call you Peter and knew you just as long."

"Yo, Kid. You 'member Rita?"

"Yeah. I remember her and when all that shit happen with the Ray brothers. Fuckin' scum-dogs," Kid said, as he glanced toward the door leading to the basement. "C'mon, let's go get Ze and Dog ready."

Before Pete could answer, the side-door opened and Man and Eddie stepped inside. Kid and Pete smiled, taking their hands from their weapons as they crossed the room and embraced Eddie and Man. "Everything cool?" Pete asked.

"It's right as rain," Man said, taking a long look at his two young partners. "We took care of some things, and I gotta thank y'all for takin' care of some other things. Y'all done good."

"Ain't no doubt," Eddie said. "You li'l muthafuckers the truth."

Kid placed his hand on Pete's shoulder and nodded at Eddie. The praise meant a lot coming from two men he admired. "Shit ain't nothin'. You know how we go. We down for ours," Kid said, giving Pete's shoulder a squeeze.

"Down by law–Our law," Pete said as he held out his fist. Man, Eddie and Kid brought their fist to meet his, and they all nodded.

In a damp, musky, concrete corner room in the basement, Kid pulled the cord on the single bulb hanging from the ceiling. José and Short-Dog were strapped to metal-framed office chairs. Their ankles were taped to the legs of the chairs and their arms taped to the chairs' arms. Each had a black cloth bag over his head.

"Gentlemen, I have a once in a lifetime offer for you," Man said in his speaker's voice. "Well, actually, it's an offer that only one of you will be privileged to enjoy."

Though they couldn't speak with their mouths gagged, José grunted and squirmed, while Short-Dog nodded vigorously, as if his life depended on it. Which it did.

Man frowned at the pathetic efforts of the pair, before he continued, "I don't think you fellows fully understand the importance of my offer."

Short-Dog shook, then nodded his head with such force it seemed ready to fly off his tiny shoulders. José, unsuccessfully, tried to speak through his gag and started to choke. When Man went over and removed the black bag from Jose's head and the gag from his mouth, Eddie did the same with Short-Dog.

José threw his head back. He tried to speak, but only a hoarse croak escaped his mouth. He swallowed and almost gagged again on the dry fear that had taken root in his mouth. He closed his eyes and shook his head, as if that would wake him up from the nightmare he was in. Finally, he calmed down enough to shriek, "I swear, I wasn't gonna hurt her. I ain't even wanna do it. It was Dog that—"

"You a lyin' muthafucker," Short-Dog yelled. "Man, you know I wouldn't do no shit like that. I come from around the way. I was gonna tell you as soon as this bitch tried somethin'."

"You the one that come to me with—"

Bang! Man clapped his hands. Short-Dog and José jumped at the sound, neither one spoke or took their eyes off Man. "Okay. That's good y'all both got somethin' to say." Man held up his finger and shook his head to keep them quiet. "But, I want certain answers, and those answers is gonna decide which one of y'all leave this room alive," Man said, turning his back to them.

Kid looked at the two of them with disgust – strapped to their chairs, scared and willing to tell on their own mothers. He cut his eyes in Pete's direction and saw that Pete was disgusted also. It was chumps like these that had the game all fucked up.

Eddie stepped around Man and leaned down, his face inches from Jose's, "I just wanna know how much you paid Deacon?"

José gasped as he tried to move back. The chair balanced on its back legs before it settled down on all four. What little hope he'd had of getting out alive was gone that quick. Although he had no idea what Deacon had done, he knew that if Man knew about the fat crazy guy it was enough to guarantee his death.

Short-Dog didn't know what was going on, but took it as a good sign that José had done something that guaranteed his fate. He decided to take advantage of the moment.

"Man, this muthafucker wanted me to help 'im get in Nicki's house. I was gonna—"

"Dog, I told you I only want certain answers, right?" Man interjected, without turning around.

Short-Dog looked at Kid and then at Pete. What he saw on their faces told him that he wouldn't get any help from them, and that only quick thinking would save him.

Man turned around and faced them again. Eddie walked behind the chairs, out of their line of sight.

Short-Dog suddenly developed a tic in his left cheek. His face jumped uncontrollably, making him look comical. "Man, you know, Ricky workin' with the police. He got this fool here to help him pay off some police sergeant," he said with desperation in his voice.

Man smiled, "See, that's what I'm talking 'bout. You gonna be the one to leave this muthafucker alive, boy."

"Wait. I-I-I got money. I can get you $70,000 right now," José cried. Even though he had three times that amount stashed, he figured that'd be enough to get their interest. So, when Man stepped to the right and smiled, he thought everything was going to work out. That is, until Man said, "Is that how much you paid Deacon."

As the last glimmer of hope faded from his eyes, José turned his head toward Man, opened his mouth and started to speak. But before he could form a single word Eddie grabbed him under the chin and across the forehead and snapped his neck in one quick, powerful motion.

José never knew what happened as his left leg jerked and salvia ran down his chin. Man's smile never left his face as the sound of snapping tendons lingered in the room. Short-Dog screamed, and the smell of urine drifted from his body. Eddie released Jose's head and it fell in an unnatural position, his chin resting against the back of his right shoulder, Man was still smiling.

Kid stepped out of the room for a minute and came back with a large, heavy canvass bag. He and Pete cut José loose and dumped him in the bag. They glanced over at Short-Dog while they worked, making sure to step around the urine that was forming around his chair.
Each time Short-Dog tried to speak, Man silenced him with a wag of his finger. He was beside himself with fear.

With the knowledge that Eddie stood somewhere behind him, Short-Dog couldn't stop his body from shaking. He felt like a man with death standing over his shoulder.

Man walked over and lifted Dog up, chair and all and sat him next to Jose's body. "I told ya' only one of y'all would leave this room alive. And we know it ain't Ze punk-ass," Man said, as he toed the bag holding Jose's body. "So, that leave yo' scheming-ass. But since I lied..." he said and reached down with his gloved hand and gripped Short-Dog's throat, crushing his larynx and windpipe. As Short-Dog struggled against his restraints his body began to jerk and his eyes bugged. Man stared into Short-Dog's eyes as they grew, and watched the life drain out of them. Soon his body stopped jerking in the chair and he stopped straining. Still, Man kept up the pressure.

The look of surprise died on Short-Dog's face as his body went slack. His eyes were blank and his head sagged against his chest when Man finally released him.

"I got 'im," Kid said, who had watched the whole thing with a sour look on his face. He dropped an empty canvas bag on the floor and bent to cut the body loose.

Man stopped him, "Nah, you and Pete get the furnace ready. Me and E.K. gonna take care of this. We'll be down in a minute."

Kid gazed into Man's eyes, then glanced at Eddie, he knew they were still hurting from losing Born. After a moment he nodded and went to join Pete.

Man cut Short-Dog loose, and with Eddie's help, shoved him in the bag. Neither spoke until both bags were ready for the furnace. Before they dragged the bags down to that side of the basement, Eddie reached out and rested his hand on Man's shoulder, "At least when they bury the God tomorrow, it'll be over. We got the muthafucker who paid too," he said, as he gave the bag holding Jose's body a quick kick.

"Yeah. We got 'em both," Man said, without much enthusiasm.
Eddie gave Man a little shove and stepped in front of him. "Man, ain't no sense looking back, the God is gone and the muthafuckers who 'caused it is dead."

"Yeah."
Eddie sighed. "I know how you feel. It's hard to believe the God is dead, ain't it?" He held Man's gaze. "What you wanna do about Peto and Ricky?"

"Since we ain't hear Peto's name from nobody else, he got a pass on this one. And Ricky is mine. I got—"

"Wait a minute. We need to get on this, especially with him working with the pigs. He gotta go."

"Ain't no doubt. But you need to get back to—"

"I ain't going nowhere. We already lost the God and..."

"That's exactly why you gotta break out. I can handle shit here. You know how Kid and Pete get down. So I'm cool. *But,* just in case somethin' goes wrong, you'll be able to make it right."

 Eddie reluctantly gave in with a nod. "Okay, you got that."

"And, I 'on't think shortie gonna let you stay away too much."

"C'mon, don't start that shit," Eddie said with a grin.

"Let's get this trash burned. I got some Cuban cigars, and once the furnace gets hot we can light 'em right off the door," Man said, as he reached for the bag with Short-Dog's body in it.

"Oh, you left me the heavy one, huh?" Eddie said, shaking his head.

## CHAPTER FORTY-NINE

Ricky frowned as he stuffed the $1000 dollar stacks into the dark-blue Addidas gym bag. He hated having to transport money from the block to his stash crib, but it had been two days since Short-Dog made the pick-ups and the cash was piling up.

With the detectives pressing him about the payoffs and Man, the last thing he needed was to have to do Short-Dog's job. But he couldn't trust anybody else. Short-Dog hadn't even bothered to answer his beeps, not even after he'd used their 119 emergency code behind the phone number. Yeah, Short-Dog's ass was through, Ricky thought as he zippered the bag and went to the window.

He pushed the curtain back slightly–his eyes darted up and down the street. He hurried out the bedroom and shouted, "Freddy! C'mon, man, I ain't got all day!"

When his thirteen-year-old brother, Freddy, came out of the living room, Ricky handed him the gym bag. "You know where to go, right?" he asked in a nervous voice.

"Yeah, you told me like a hundred times already. Damn!"

"Your li'l ass don't mind askin' for money a hundred times though, huh?" Ricky told him, as he released all four locks on the door. "Grab the ball, and make sure you got your token ready for the bus."

Twenty minures later, Ricky pulled his BMW over in front of the P.A.L. gym on Webster Avenue. He watched Freddy get off the bus and dribble the basketball across the street."

"I coulda walked and got here quicker," Freddy said as he slid into his brother's $60,000 dollar car and handed over the bag with $41,000 in it.

"You too damn smart," Ricky said, taking the bag and shoving it under his seat. He reached in his pocket and brought out a knot with hundred dollar bills on top. He flipped through it – passing over twenty $100 bills and twice that in $50's – until he finally reached the twenties. He pulled four bills off the roll, thought for a minute and took one back. "Here," he said, as he pushed the three twenties in Freddy's hand.

Looking at the money, Freddy said, "What's this. I thought you said you was gonna buy me some sneakers and give me money for a haircut. This shit ain't enough." Freddy's bottom lip poked out and his nostrils flared and he wished, as he often did when he dealt with Ricky, that he could whip his ass.

Ricky's face changed into a display of what he really was inside, ugly. His small eyes drew together as he squinted and his mouth became a thin, mean line. "If yo' ass can't get no sneakers for that, you won't be getting' none. And go by the shop and tell Bucicy to cut yo' shit for you," Ricky said as he looked at the Presidential Rolex dangling on his thin wrist. "Get out. I got shit to do, and yo' li'l ass making my joint hot. In a minute, 5-0 gonna wanna know why yo' young ass up in my ride."

Freddy dropped his head. He hated the way Ricky treated him and his other brothers and sisters–especially the way he talked to their mother, as if she was worthless. What gave him the right? Freddy asked himself, but he knew the answer...because he had money? Well, fuck his money, Freddy thought as he threw the bills in Ricky's face and reached for the door.

Before he closed the door, Freddy leaned down and stared hard at his brother. "Fuck you. I hope your faggot-ass die 'cause you ain't shit," he said as he slammed the door and walked off.

Ricky laughed as he picked up the bills and pulled away from the curb. Maybe the little punk'll grow up to be something after all, he thought. Ricky knew that when you gave people shit they took it for granted. His family was the perfect example; always had their hands out. He wasn't going to support them. It was better for them, and him, if they earned what he gave them.

Maybe he'd let Freddy bottle up. Turning a thousand grams of coke into five-dollar capsules was definitely earning it. Three hundred dollars was paid for every key done. Shit, the punk could buy all the sneakers he wanted and pay for his own haircuts, Ricky thought with a smile.

His mind jumped to his meeting with Easy. He needed him to get down with the payoffs, and to help him give Man up to that crazy-ass albino detective. He felt the pressure that the cops were applying, and wondered if it hadn't been better when he worked with Man. Well, it was too late to go back to that. It was always something. Maybe it was time to get out, just walk away from the whole thing. Nah, only a fool would leave all the fame and fortune of the game, he thought, as he glided his ride onto the FDR Drive.

***

"Man, we need to talk," Nicki said as she dropped on the corner of her king-sized bed. She had spent the night at Ms. Nez's place, with Bigum checking on her every twenty minutes it seemed, and was glad to be in her own house. Man leaned back, laid his torso across the bed, yawned, and laced his fingers behind his head.

Nicki gave him a scorching look. Her hands went to her hips as a spasm of irritation crossed her face. "Man! I thought you said it wasn't safe for me to stay in my house."

When Man stretched his arms out, away from his body and gave her a blank look, Nicki looked skyward and her foot began to pat the floor in rhythm with her agitated breathing. "Oh, now, you don't know what I'm talking about?" she asked with her head moving in rhythm with her words.

Man turned on his side and stared at her. When a smile started to work its way to his face, Nicki's mouth opened, but before she could speak, Man said, "It wasn't safe."

Nicki looked at him, closed her eyes for a minute, and thought that little Jamel had more sense than Man did sometimes. "Okay, so, now...?"

"I want you to come to Brooklyn with me 'cause I still don't know exactly what's up," Man answered, as he sat up and ran his hands over his head. He was feeling the effects of the last few days. He needed more than the two or three hours of sleep he'd been stealing here and there. He tried to shake it off and focus on Nicki. Looking at her made him realize that he was in love with her.

"It's nice that it's all so funny to you," she said sharply, her eyes locked on him. "But while you don't know exactly what's going on, I don't know anything." She stepped over to the bed and knelt down, her face open and aimed up at his. "Why wasn't it safe for me before, and why is it safe now? I know you said you wasn't sure, so just tell me what you know," she said, taking his hands in hers.

As Man stared into her eyes he thought about choking the life out of Short-Dog and the sound of Jose's neck being snapped. He felt neither pity nor remorse. The punishment had fit the crime; they died for what they did or would have done. Man smiled, brought Nicki's hands to his mouth and kissed them. With his eyes locked on hers, he said, "Nicki, you said I didn't have to protect you that I just needed to love you..."

He stopped and thought for a minute... his mind went to a dark, sad place, he pulled it back and continued, "But for me, protecting you is the best way for me to love you sometimes. You gonna have to trust me." He took a deep breath and pulled her close. "I found out that somebody wanted to hurt you to hurt me, and I took care of it. I'd rather not say anymore. But if you feel that you gotta know, I'll tell you," he said, their mouths close enough to share each other's breath, as well as secrets.

Nicki's eyes took on a pensive look. Maybe, she didn't need to know everything he knew. She knew his heart, and that was good enough. She'd told him that she was a grown woman, one who knew what she was doing, and to prove it, she said, "No, I don't have to know." She curled up in his strong arms. "How much stuff should I pack for Brooklyn?"

*** 

Bigum held the shot-glass in his hand. He looked in it, searching for answers, maybe? He brought the glass to his mouth, turned it up and let the Scotch burn his throat and soothe his troubles. He poured another. Shine had left the bottle of Glenfiddich, after whispering something to the barmaid, and she'd left him alone– except for the one time she ventured to his corner of the bar to place a tall glass of ice water next to the full bottle of Scotch. The drink Shine had had with him, and the eight he'd had since had put a serious dent in the bottle of Scotch.

He stared into the empty glass. So, he poured again. He stared at the full glass. Then, he drank. Again, he narrowed his eyes at the bottom of the glass, reached for the bottle and poured. The drink stared up at him. With his elbows on the bar, Bigum rested his forehead in his hands and faced the drink down. He knew that he could outlast it and the next one, but wasn't so sure about the bottle.

He hadn't been drunk for more than thirty years, but when a man's dreams are threatened it could drive him to worse things than drinking. Look at Man–he'd been driven to the brink of destruction and had decided to stay. He had found Eddie and Born there, and they'd made a pact that the devil himself would fear. And, with Born's death, they had lived up to their covenant the only way they knew how — *blood for blood.*

Bigum knew that if Man was cornered, he would dig in and do battle to the end. That's why closing the game room had him worried. In his three-plus years, Badlands had never been closed. And as far as he knew, this was the first time since Man opened the place that it had been shut down. There had been days when Man'd just leave the kids in charge, telling them to close the door when they were finished, but today the door was locked and the gates pulled down.

The drink called him and he answered. It went down without the rough edge. Either it had aged and mellowed since Shine sat the bottle on the bar, or he'd drunk to the point where it didn't matter. He poured another one, dropped his head in his hands and eyed the amber colored liquor intensely, as if expecting a revelation—maybe an epiphany that would explain it all.

For the first time in years, Bigum thought about prison. He reached for the glass and it disappeared in his hand. As he downed the drink, he chased away thoughts of twenty-seven years behind steel bars and concrete walls. Then, he thought of Badlands being closed.

Without the game room, Bigum was lost. It was his life. He had finally found a place and, of course, someone wanted to take it from him. No, he hadn't found a place; it had been given to him. But now the very person who'd shown him the way was leading him into shadows he wanted no part of. Even with Nicki in the picture, Bigum knew that if pressed, Man would go out the way he'd learned to live...fighting. And that could mean the end of everything. In America, you didn't go up against the police, corrupt or not, and walk away unscathed.

He looked at his empty glass, pushed the bottle away, then stood. He gave a huge sigh that lifted and dropped his barrel chest. He focused his eyes, looking past the bottle. It was time to sleep it off. Man would need him, he thought, as he set his jaw and squared his shoulders.

Kid threw his hands up at Pete and playfully danced around, feinting and throwing jabs. "Don't let me do that Sugar Ray shit on you," he said.

Pete backed away, shaking his head. "I on't wanna play with yo' fool-ass, man."

"Aw, shit! So what you sayin', boy? You wanna piece of the Kid, huh?" Kid said, dancing around and laughing.

"Damn, yo' ass musta been bored like a muthafucker." "I know you ready to get back to work too, right?" Kid asked, as he rushed Pete and wrapped his arms around him.

They headed for Pete's BMW. "Yeah. I ain't do shit. It's been a lazy couple of days," Pete answered, as he slid behind the wheel.

After getting rid of José and Short-Dog's incinerated remains, they had taken a couple of days off and rested up. While Pete stayed close to home, Kid had gotten a few hours of sleep before searching for another reason to need some more rest. Her name wasn't important to him. If she was down for fun and games, she was the flavor of the month, or day, depending on how he felt. Kid loved the company of women. But now he was ready to get back to work and making the pick-up from Easy's was first on their list.

Pete parked down the block from one of Easy's stash houses. They had decided to show up an hour earlier than Easy expected. Working with Man, they learned to vary their routines – use different cars, cut through an alley, or over a roof, show up a hour early or late. Just don't become predictable.

As they entered the redbrick tenement, Kid fell back and waited for a few minutes as Pete went up the stairs. Once he was sure they didn't have company coming in behind them, he hurried behind Pete. He reached the third floor landing just as Pete knocked on the apartment to the far left.

As the door cracked open, warning bells went off in Kid's head. At the same instant, he saw Pete's hand reaching for his Ruger P85 ...9mm in the small of his back. Something was wrong. Alerted, Kid's arms were criss-crossing his body as he drew twin, Browning ...9mm's. Still, he was too slow. The shots rang out–five or six, he couldn't be sure. His ears were ringing.

As Pete stumbled back from the door, Kid was ready to fire but Pete was in the way. As another gun joined with the first one on the other side of the door, Kid's instincts kicked in, he took a quick step back, charged and went into a feet-first slide. He took Pete down, cradling him in his arms and letting the twin 9mm. sing.

While laying against Kid's body, Pete squeezed off shot after shot until his clip was empty before the gun fell from his hand and he slumped sideways. Kid crawled free of Pete, released the clip from one of his guns and threw in a fresh one. He put a few more shots through the door, grabbed Pete's gun, and the empty clip, and pulled Pete toward the stairs.

He saw that Pete was hit as least twice. "Pete," he whispered gently. At least, he thought it was a whisper, but with the ringing in his ears it was more like a shout. A whole lot had become distorted besides his hearing in the last forty-five seconds.

"Shit," he said, as he put his last clip in, and let loose at the door again. Walking behind the shots, he kicked the door open. A pair of legs stopped the door from opening completely– Kid riddled the body connected to the legs with bullets.

As Kid pushed against the door, Pete moaned and tried to stand, "Yo, we gotta get..." he said, leaning his back against the wall and reaching for the gun he no longer had.

Kid backed away from the apartment and rushed to Pete. Pete came off the wall and leaned against him, his face twisted with pain, "We gotta roll out."

"Can you walk?" Kid asked, sliding his arm around Pete.

Kid tightened his grip as he half carried and dragged Pete down the stairs.

Pete was in and out of consciousness in the three minutes it took to make it to the car. Kid heard the first sirens as he pulled away from the curb. He knew it would be close. He couldn't afford a run in with the cops. He had to get to a hospital, and he had to get word to Man.

*** 

Man looked up from the papers in front of him and reached for his beeper, his brow knitted together. "Ty, let me use your phone right quick?" he asked.

Tyrone pushed the phone across his desk, stood up and headed for the door, "Go ahead. I'll be right back. I want to check on the kids, they're too quiet."

Alone in the den, Man glanced at the papers he and Ty had been going over and looked from his beeper to the phone. He picked up the phone, the code following the number could only mean trouble, and punched in the number.

The ring had barely begun when Kid's voice rushed through from the other end, "Yo." His voice clipped, giving away nothing with that one word. Still, Man recognized the urgency there.

"Talk to me, homey," Man said in a low, steady tone. "We got trouble. Pete got hit. It was—"

Man cut him off, "Hold up, Pete been taken care of yet?" "Yeah, I dropped him at the hospital in—"

"Okay. Okay," Man said quickly. "That's good. Meet me at the warehouse as soon as you can. I'll be there in 'bout thirty minutes." He stood up as he dropped the receiver in its cradle. Man thought about calling Bigum and June, but decided to wait until he'd spoke to Kid. He looked around the room for a minute; pictures of Ty and his family reminded him of where he was– in the home of a family. He suppressed the memories, and decided he couldn't wait for Ty to come back.

He quickly signed his name to the papers on Ty's desk. Normally, he'd read them more thoroughly but he didn't have the time now and he trusted Ty. He left the den and followed the hallway toward the front door. Though it was his first time in the Jenkin's home, he had no trouble retracing his steps.

Ty was working out of his home for the time being. Man had been so adamant about Ty continuing to handle his business that he closed his account at Whitman, Brown, and Pauls and employed Tyrone as his broker. Man wasn't the only client that Whitman, Brown, and Pauls lost to Ty. But none of that mattered right now. As he neared the front door, the business that occupied Man's mind was far from stocks and bonds and the transferring of funds.

Whereas computers, contracts and conferences determined whether you made money or not, quick action with handguns usually was the difference between life and death in Man's everyday world. As he hesitated at the door, Ty's wife came into view. "What's wrong?" She asked.

The concern in both, her face and voice touched Man. "I apologize, but I have to go. Something came up," he said, in a manner designed to take the edge off his abrupt exit.

"Oh," she said, unsure of exactly what else to say. She'd been preparing dinner, thinking he was staying. Although she didn't know Man, she knew, how this man, whose background was surrounded by shadows had stood by the man she loved. And that meant more than anything else. "Let me get Ty, he'll want—"

"I'm really sorry, but I'm going to have to ask you to let him know," Man said, and smiled in apology.

From what Ty had told her, she knew that the man standing in front of her was from the streets, and though wealthy, had refused to leave them. While she trusted Ty when he insisted that all of their business dealings were legal, she could see trouble written all over Man's face. It showed in his slow, deliberate way of moving and speaking and in the savvy confidence that emanated from him. However, his sorrows couldn't be denied, either, they stood out like a mole on a super model's face. Sorrow drove this man, she thought as she said good-bye and watched his strong determined steps take him down the driveway to his car. As he drove off, she wondered about those sorrows.

Although Pelham Manor was an exclusive community, bordering the north Bronx, she realized it was a million miles from the world Man chose to live in. She'd been raised in an inner city neighborhood, but getting out had been the very first dream her parents gave her. And she'd grown up believing anyone worth anything shared that dream. But now, she wasn't so sure. What if seeing the hopelessness of life was what allowed you to know its true value?

"Sweetheart?" Ty's voice startled her out of her reverie. "What's wrong?" He asked, coming up behind her.

She gently closed the door. "Nothing. I was just watching our dinner guest leave," she said, turning with a crooked smile on her face.

"What..."

"I guess he heard about my cooking," she threw in, her smile widening as she looked at Ty. "Seriously, he said he had an emergency–to tell you that he's sorry."

"Yeah. Instead of your cooking, it was the call he returned," Ty said, knowingly. Ty thought for a moment, then slipped his arms around his wife's waist, and squeezed and just held on. "I love you, Mrs. Jenkins," as his mind dwelled on the realities of Man's life. He wondered if whatever was happening had anything to do with Man transferring and/or closing out and moving most of his holdings out of the country?

***

Ricky looked at Easy, he couldn't believe how stupid the fool was. "Let me get this shit right. Y'all opened up on Pete and Kid?"

"Word. You shoulda—"

"Muthafucker, is you stupid or just—"

"Fuck you, Ricky," Easy said, fixing him with a look of contempt. "I know what the fuck I'm doin'. What, you think putting po-po on Man is all it's gonna take to get rid'a 'im? Nah, that shit ain't enough. The muthafucker been duckin' the police for years, and he still here, ain't he?

"And, even if Man got knocked, you think Kid and Pete gonna retire? Hell no they ain't. They been runnin' with Man too long. Shit, them muthafuckers'll probably be worst than Man," Easy said, as he moved to the door and listened intently for a few seconds.

Ricky rubbed his hands together, thinking as he noted Easy's nervousness, "Did you lay 'em down?"

Easy looked away and ran his hand over his face. "Nah, they got away. But we hit 'em up. They know it's on. Shit gettin' ready to get buck wild. My boy Jerome got bodied and two more of my crew got hit, but bet them punk muthafukers know we ain't playin'. It's war now!" Easy said, as he reached under one of the couch's cushion and pulled out a big, ugly, bulky, ...9mm semiautomatic.

Ricky stared at Easy for a minute, with the Tech-9 and the other two guns stuck in his waistband. He wondered who Easy was trying to convince, because him and the four hoods crowded into the studio apartment looked more like men hiding out than men going to war. While two of them took turns peeping from behind the curtains of the one window in the room, another gazed at the door as if hypnotized and the fourth was more interested in reciting NWA's gansta lyrics than going to war.

As he stood up, Ricky said, "I 'on't blame you for steppin' to 'em, but you shouldn't of done it at your spot. Man gonna know—"

"Fuck Man!" Easy said loudly, his fear bouncing off the walls. He locked eyes with Ricky, "You think Kid and 'em was just gonna say, 'Okay', when I told 'em that shit 'bout po-po said not to pay them no mo'. Shit, they woulda' gunned my people down and came lookin' fo' me."

"Nah, Easy. We ain't paid Man in over a month. I'm tellin' you."

"I hear that shit," Easy said, leaning against the wall, hugging the Tech to his chest. "But, I also heard you askin' if anybody seen Short-Dog and José in the last few days."

Ricky shuddered at the thought, felt a wave of fear growing in his stomach, but said, "Man ain't do nothin' to them. Them fools somewhere fuckin' up money." But he couldn't shake the feeling of doom that came with the thought of Man coming after him.

"Whatever, homey. I'm gonna lay here 'til we ready to move on 'em. Don't nobody know 'bout this spot. 'Cept for you and us." Easy said, as his eyes went from the Tech-9 back to Ricky.

Ricky didn't back down, his eyes locked with Easy's. "If you feel that way, you should move somewhere that I 'on't know 'bout," he said, thinking of his co-op on the eastside that nobody knew about. "I'm out. I gotta see if I can get the white devil to get rid of Man and 'em."

Easy stepped back, let Ricky pass, and walked him to the door. "Yo, you know I been getting' mine too long to stop now. I'ma be on point and do what I gotta do, but if yo' people can take care of Man and 'em I got the paper for you. So, hit me on my beeper and let me know somethin'," Easy told Ricky, before turning the locks and letting him out.

Even if Ricky hadn't heard the fear in Easy's voice, he saw it in his eyes. He nodded, unaware that the look in his own eyes mirrored Easy's, and walked out. He was being pressed into a corner, the pigs wanted money, Dog and Ze were missing and Man was... Was what? He wondered as he climbed into his car. His hands shook as he dropped the Czech Star 9mm between his legs and put the key in the ignition.

Ricky froze as he noticed a car moving slowly up the street in his rearview mirror. He fumbled for his heat, but before he could get a hold of it, the gun fell to the floor, and the car stopped and made a u-turn. His whole body felt clammy, and he had broken out in a cold sweat. He was losing it. He had to make something happen. With his eyes darting like crazy, he decided that he had to play po-po into moving on Man.

*** 

"Yeah. I got Joe's li'l brother and his crew takin' baby sis and Mama-Duke up to the hospital," Kid said, his eyes never leaving Man's face. "They gonna make sure they there every day."

"Good," Man said, as he thought for a moment, then asked, "What's up with shortie and the twins?"

"The girls is staying with Pam's moms 'cause she gonna be at the hospital all the time."
"Okay. You got everything under—"

"Bullshit!" Kid said as he stood up and squeezed his fist into his other hand. "I left my fuckin' man bleeding in front of a hospital in Queens and the muthafuckers who shot 'im is still walkin' around."

Man got up and walked over to Kid. He felt the shit too. Remebering the God, he wondered if any of the street shit was really important. With Peter-Gun in stable condition, he didn't want to think about what could have happened. He pushed the thoughts away and focused his mind on what was about to go down – death!

Man and Kid were alone in the small office of the warehouse on Third Avenue–it was as quiet as Woodlawn Cemetery after dark. Neither of them was in the mood for music or conversation, for that matter. They had barely spoken in the hour they'd been there. Now, Man stepped into Kid's space, "You done good. You got Pete out and to a hospital where the police couldn't tie him to any bodies y'all might'a left in the Bronx." When Kid dropped his head, Man continued, "You made sure Pam and moms got there as soon as possible. And we 'bout to set it right."

"Man, I left my boy..."

Man grabbed him by the back of his neck and pulled him closer. With their foreheads touching, Man asked, "What you wanna do? Get knocked? 'Cause if you hada' stayed with 'im that's what woulda' happened. And like I was saying, we 'bout to make this shit right."

Finally, Kid brought his head up and their eyes meet; the grin on Man's face wasn't humorous. He had the look of a wolf about to invite the pack to dinner.

"That's what I'm talkin"bout," Kid said, in a rush as he started for the door. "Let's go put some heads to bed."

"Slow your roll. As soon as Black June and Bigum get here, we out. And guess what? We ain't got to find 'em," Man finished, his grin widening.

For the first time since Pete had gotten shot, Kid smiled his trademark smile. But the warmth was missing, replaced by the cold truth of his street code: *When crossed, gun 'em all down and let God sort 'em out.*

***

As he waited anxiously in the back of the van, Kid tapped his fingers against the toolbox. Sitting on the long, red, rectangle shaped box he was hidden from view, though he could still see the front of the building they were watching sixty feet away. He felt closed in as Bigum's huge body chewed up space like a pit bull on a steak.

His eyes narrowed into slits of sharp vision, like a high-powered scope. His jaw locked and his mind was set on taking care of business. But, Man's plan wasn't exactly what he'd had in mind. Sitting in the back of a van that said *Walker's Boiler Service,* backing up the move instead of making it, definitely wasn't his idea of stepping to business. As his jaw muscles clenched tighter, he thought of the AR-15 semiautomatic assault rifle and the Ruger Mini-14 submachine gun under the false floor of the van. "I should take a quick look and make sure shit is cool" Kid said.

Bigum didn't answer right away; he kept his eyes on the entrance of the red brick tenement three buildings away, "Let's do it like Man said. You know Easy and 'em'll recognize you."

Kid sighed. He was ready to move. "What? Y'all, think they ain't gonna recognize Man?"

Bigum took his eyes off the building and faced Kid, "You know better than me that Man know what he doin'?

Kid nodded. "You sho' ain't lied about that big man," he conceded, as he looked around the interior of the van, and turned up the police scanner.

Outside, a light drizzle had started to fall. His eyes cruised the street, dodging the tiny drops on the windshield. They lingered on an old bum digging through garbage cans. The bum could have been a hundred and twenty pounds or two-twenty, he had on one old, worn jacket over another, and at least three pair of old ripped up pants. On his feet, he wore a dirty, worn pair of combat boots that were so long they gave him a clownish look.

He treated every soda can he found like a rare discovery. He rubbed it against his already soiled pants leg, gazed at it, smiled and rocked his skully-capped head from side to side. The three or four, all different colored, wool caps hung at odd angles and covered most of his face. His scraggly, gray-flecked beard covered the rest. The beard was pretty much all there was of him, besides the old, dirty clothes, that is.

Once the soda can was placed gently into his homemade cart — two milk crates tied to a battered baby carriage–he'd dive back into the trash for another: digging in as if he was searching for his wife's lost wedding ring.

Kid watched the old man, stooped and broken, dig through the garbage with filthy work gloves covering his hands, thinking: *the garbage has to be cleaner than the gloves.* Just then, a red, fourdoor Pathfinder turned into the quiet street. Kid felt it. Once it stopped in front of the same building he'd spent the last forty minutes watching, he knew he was right. His eyes searched the area for Man. Damn, he thought, it's on and we ain't ready.

As Easy and three of his crew stepped out of the building, they scanned the length of the block, ignoring the old man digging in the garbage. Kid released the false bottom of the van's floorboard and reached for the Ruger.

"Wait," Bigum said, as his huge hand gripped Kid's forearm.

"Ain't no time. I `on't see..."

As Easy's boys positioned themselves near the driver's side of the truck and opened the door for their boss, the old bum came up out of the garbage can with a Heckler and Koch MP5 submachine gun, spraying first the two men closest to him, then sending a short burst of bullets through the windshield of the truck. The driver couldn't decide whether to put the truck in gear or dive down. It didn't matter–his time was up. The first slug tore through his chin and neck, killing him before the other two bullets hit him.

Kid followed the action; his eyes moving from the two men sprawled on the sidewalk, to the Heckler and Koch pumping bullets into the half open backdoor of the red Pathfinder, with the legs sticking out. Less than four feet away, two more quick bursts left the barrel and tore through metal and flesh. Then the H&K disappeared under the dirty, ragged jackets as the old, no longer stooped bum, crossed the street and melted into an alley.

The street was quiet as the five dead men that lay there. It was as if the last twenty seconds or so had never happened.

"Lock the floor down, Kid," Bigum said from the driver's seat as he started the van. "We rolling out."

Kid didn't remember the big man moving from beside him. "You see that shit? God damn!" Damn! I love this shit," Kid exclaimed, pumped up, as he fasten the false floor in place.

Bigum took a quick look at Kid in the rearview mirror, before focusing back on the scene in the street and slowly backing the van out of the street. At the corner, he spun the wheel to the left and headed toward Bailey Avenue.

Man stepped onto the next street carrying a large white canvas tool bag–dressed in blue overall. He swung the bag into the back of a pickup truck. Black June, also dressed in blue overalls, slipped the truck into gear as Man settled into the seat next to him. "I hear everything worked out just like you planned," June said, with a slight shrug.

Man leaned back, scratched under his collar, and tried to stop the adrenaline speeding through his veins–it was like a cocaine rush. Although he had never shot coke into his veins, right now he knew just what the hardcore fiends meant when they talked about bells going off in their heads and their stomachs flipping over. Too pumped up to speak, he rolled his shoulders and nodded.

"What? All them jackets got you itchin'?" June asked as a police cruiser rushed by, going the opposite way. When Man just grunted, put one foot up on the dashboard, tilted his head back and prepared to ride out the rush, June decided there was nothing else to say. Over the years, he had learned that there was a rare breed of men, no matter where life carried them, who didn't need to talk themselves down once they acted. Whatever came to them, they suffered it in silence. He turned on the radio: and fittingly, Miles Davis', *In A Silent Way,* filled the cab of the pickup.

June gripped the wheel until his aged knuckles ached. He wondered what it would take for Man to let go of what ached inside of him. He knew he was an old man, who'd lived the life and was fortunate that he would die before the game was totally shot to shit. What, with all the punks and snitches the life was dying with few to mourn its passing. Honor and strength were fading. Now, the life was lived-out in rap songs and videos. As he drove, he thought that Man's only chance was to get out.

***

Nicki walked over to Ms. Nez's window. "Girl, please sit down. You know Man gonna be here soon." Ms. Nez said.

Nicki looked over her shoulder and smiled at the two older women. It amused her, how delighted Ms. Nez and Ms. Mary were about her and Man. "How you know I'm looking for Man?"

"Oh, baby!" Ms. Mary said between giggles, "If I was you, I know I'll be looking for 'im."

"Ain't that the truth, Mary," Ms. Nez added.

"Y'all oughta be ashamed of—"

"Ain't nothing to be shame of when you in love, chile," Ms. Nez said, with her lips turned up.

With a smile that mirrored those of the two older women, Nicki shook her head and went back to her seat. Loving Man was what she wanted. She had made her choice and once he told her about Pete she knew there would be things she didn't need to know. Her choice was to stand by her man, no matter what.

Ms. Nez caught her eye and gave a little smile. Nicki returned the smile, and glanced toward the window. "Nicki, can you look out that window and see if the rain stopped?" the older woman asked, as she leaned back and crossed her legs.

## CHAPTER FIFTY

"Look here, we gotta finish this shit up. In a minute, we gonna be hotter than fish grease `cause muthafuckers gonna start snitchin'," Man said as he looked at Kid. He paused for a moment and looked out of the passenger's window at the moving traffic and crowded street. "See, it was cool when we was chillin' and muthafuckers was tryin' us. But now that shit is on..."

Kid glanced over at Man and nodded to what he said as well as to what he hadn't said. Now that the bodies were dropping the-wanna-be gangsters would do anything to stay alive. The light turned green as the wipers swept away the steady but small drops of rain and they moved along with the rest of the cars. "Yo, I think we laid all them bitches down. We just gotta lay low and stay—"

"Nah! Ain't nothin' happenin' with that," Man said, shaking his head. "You think Easy came up with that shit on his own? Hell, no! We need to find Ricky as soon as possible 'fore he can run to po-po."Kid's mind ran wild, as he turned onto Morris Avenue, "You think that faggot put all this shit together?"

"Nah. He just helped it along." Man said, motioning for him to pull over. "It was bound to happen. When you rollin' and stackin' paper, muthafuckers gonna wanna see you fall and when they ain't got the heart to step to you, they gonna put shit in the game."

Kid put the car in park and nodded, "I hear you. But I can take care of Ricky by—"

"Kid!" Man said, making a chopping motion with his hand. "Every move gotta be right. It's do or die, baby-bro. You know that punk fuckin' with po-po. It ain't like it gonna be you and him." Man's eyes locked on Kid's. "So, we gotta be right when we move, and end this shit with the quickness."

Kid was silent, he thought about Pete lying in the hospital bed. "Yeah, you right. We gotta be right and get this shit over with."

After they clenched hands, Man reached for the door, "After I pick Nicki up, we headin' to B.K., so hit me on my beeper as soon as you hear somethin'."

Kid watched Man disappear into the park, the hood of his Gortex rain jacket up against the wind and rain. Once darkness fell few people used the park, and with the rain and trees blowing it had a menacing look. It was a good bet that anybody in there was up to no good. Kid smiled as he pulled away slowly— if Man was mistaken for a victim, it'd be someone's last mistake, he thought, as he headed toward the Grand Concourse.

***

Shaking the rain off their coats, the two detectives made their way into the squad room, one lumbered while the other walked with a hard swagger. The pig dropped into the nearest chair, out of breath from the precinct's two short flight of stairs. The snake hung up his trench coat, ground his teeth and sneered at no one in particular.

Sergeant Gledhill watched his men, and waited. When neither of them acknowledged him, he voiced an impatient, "Well?"

True to his namesake, the snake shifted his eyes without moving his head and eyed the sergeant without speaking. The pig mumbled a few words into his chest, as if his head was too heavy to lift and he wasn't sure of the words himself.

Sighing with disgust, the sergeant asked, "What? You fuckers need a written request to tell me what happened?"

The pig started to mumble again, but the snake cut him off. He gave the doughy-looking detective a superior smile and shrugged, "Snider! I'll tell him. Not that there's much to tell. The game-room is still closed, and no one has seen our crooks on the street," he said, as he went over to his corner desk, sat down and examined his nails.

"Whaddya mean? Everbody knows this son of a bitch. He ran that god-damn game-room for years."

"Well, ain't nobody talking," the snake answered.

"Did you guys squeeze those jungle bunnies? It's bad enough we can't find that little snitch, now," the sergeant said. Pushing away from his desk, he stood and shoved his hands deep in his pockets. He looked from one to the other. "I want both of you's back on the street. We need that god-damn Man, or our fucking snitch. Homicide's got some bodies uptown and we don't have shit on 'em. Another thing, payment is due this week. So find that prick, Ricky," the sergeant commanded, as a cloud of irritation clouded his pinkish-white face.

As the sergeant considered his options, his light eyes held a hint of his fury. "Stop by that bar and put some pressure on that old coon. He knows more than he's letting on," he yelled, before the pig and snake could get out the door.

"Right!" The snake sneered and shouted over his shoulder with his back to the room. Not once did he take exception to the sergeant's racial slurs, he was blue and corrupt, and proof that black was a state of mind instead of the color of one's skin.

***

In his rush to escape the rain, he never saw Man until they were a mere foot apart. As he gasped in shock, and possibly fear, Mr. Sam recoiled as if physically struck. Man looked into the older man's face, a face telling a story while his own remained stoic. Man's expression was as empty as the eyes of an abused child.

"Wh...Wha...What?" Mr. Sam stammered.

Man shook his head and stared into Mr. Sam's eyes without speaking. His silence unnerved Mr. Sam even more.

"What do you want?" Mr. Sam muttered.

After a few seconds of silent staring, Man answered, "There's nothing I could want with you."

As Man turned away and started toward Ms. Nez's place, Mr. Sam regained his composure, "You in bed with damn drug dealers, but you can turn your nose up at an honest working man. I know yo' kind, you ain't—"

Man spun around, eyes blazing slits, "You might be a honest worker, but you sho' ain't no man. And 'cause you ain't, you can't even start to know nothing 'bout me."

Mr. Sam took an involuntary step back from Man's words, before steadying himself, "Who the hell you think you are?" he asked, pulling himself up to his full height and squaring his shoulders back. "I knew yo' mama and I—"

Man was on him as quick as a hungry alley cat on a pound of dropped porgies at the fish market. Their faces were inches apart; Mr. Sam smelled the raw garlic on Man's breath. Though heavier than Man, Mr. Sam seemed to shrink into his clothes as Man leaned into him, "Don't mention my mother, you coward mutha..."

He caught himself just in time to stop the words. Then, he stopped his hand from reaching for the four-inch, razor sharp knife he kept in his waistband. He took a deep breath and hurriedly turned away. He had to get control of himself. He couldn't lose it now. His pulse pounded in his temple and he felt the blood rushing from his heart to his head as he hurried to get Nicki. That was it, he had to focus on the present and leave the past behind.

Man tilted his head back, welcoming the raindrops that fell on his face. The rain calmed him as he walked into it, seeking its cleansing powers. After twenty feet or so, he turned and saw the sobs rock Mr. Sam's body. He felt nothing for the man; once again his expression was stoic.

By the time Mr. Sam got to Ms. Nez's place, Man had been there and gone. He tapped on the door and after a minute, tapped a little harder. Finally, the door opened. "Sam? I thought I heard somebody at this door. What you pecking on the door for? I declare, you..." Ms. Nez stopped in mid-sentence after taking a close look at him. "What's wrong, Sam?" When he leaned against the doorframe, she grabbed him and called, "Mary! Mary!"

Ms. Mary rushed to the door, "What's wrong, girl. I know that man of mine ain't..." Once she took in the scene, the words die in her mouth. "Oh, Sam, what is it?" They took him inside, his eyes unfocused and frightened.

After he was seated, Ms. Nez brought him a glass of water, "Drink this."

As he took the glass, his hand shaking, Mr. Sam said, "It wasn't my fault. I swear it wasn't. I...I...I wannn...I wanted to..." His head sunk to his chest as the glass tumbled out of his hand to the floor. His body shuddered and he began to sob uncontrollably at the sound of the shattering glass

Ms. Mary rushed to her husband and cradled his head against her body. "Oh, Sam, what is it? It's gonna be alright," she cooed as she rocked gently.

Ms. Nez was backing out of the room when Mr. Sam looked up in desperation and said in a strangled voice, "It's too late, Mary. I coulda' saved her. I coulda' saved that child, but..."

"Sam, what in the devil are you—"

He cut his wife off with a wave of his hand. Although the woman knew his deepest secrets, she knew nothing about the day he'd seen Fuddy Ray pulling Rita into the basement. He had lived with the pain of doing nothing to help her, the look in her eyes as she called out to him had haunted him ever since.

"Sam, what child?" Ms. Nez asked from across the room, her voice low and coaxing. He buried his face against his wife's body and sobbed uncontrollably. Both women waited while he tried to speak. Neither could believe their eyes. Ms. Nez was embarrassed by the collapse of a stubborn, proud man who could be just as ornery as he could be decent.

Finally, between sobs, he said her name — *Rita* — and told his story. It was a story of a man who had done what was right throughout his life and was forever haunted by the one time he failed to. Again, he heard the child's plea, *"Help me, Mr. Sam,"* and Fuddy's warning *"Mind yo' goddamn business, old man!"*

Now, he could add Man's words to those memories, Man knew all along, but remained silent over the years. Even tonight, it was as if Man could barely say it out loud, like he couldn't speak of such evil. And as Mr. Sam clung to his wife, he wondered if that's what had kept him alive–Man's refusal to acknowledge his cowardice. He had felt the danger radiating from Man and saw death in his eyes–eyes that claimed justice in every murder. Mr. Sam sobbed without shame.

Ms. Nez turned away; she just couldn't bring herself to look at him right now. Instead, she thought of Man and Nicki, and said a prayer to Oshun, the goddess of beauty and love, as she remembered Man's expressionless face when he had picked up Nicki. As she watched her friend stand by her man, Ms. Nez hoped it would be enough for both of them. She left the room as Ms.

Mary began the task of standing Mr. Sam up, not physically, but spiritually. "Sam, you know you shoulda help Rita, but…"

# CHAPTER FIFTY-ONE

Nicki reached over and touched Man's thigh –his body was tense as he concentrated on the road. With both hands on the steering wheel, he stared straight ahead, his face drawn. He'd barely spoken more than two words since picking her up and nodded and grunted in response to her attempts at conversation. Ms. Nez and Ms. Mary, who usually brought out his most charming side, had gotten little more than half-hearted smiles and nods. Other than the sound of the radio, the ride to Brooklyn was silent.

Now in the loft, the silence had a presence of its own– a dangerous presence. It hung in the air with the force of a volcano overlooking a village. Nicki watched Man pound on the heavybag he'd hang on the top floor, the muscles in his back flexing with each hook, and cross. He threw no jabs; just power punches, bulling his way in with no thought of defense. As sweat covered his body, ripples of muscles stood out.

Nicki repeatedly asked him what was wrong, but he told her over and over that it was nothing–that is, when he answered her at all. It was like he was some place else, and, at times, couldn't even hear her. Well, she wasn't going to let him shut her out!
She dropped the bathrobe to the floor. She'd been waiting for him to lotion her body up after her bath but now she grabbed the baby-oil and began applying it all over her body, taking her time. Once she'd finished that, she put on a pair of open-toe spiked- heels and pranced about the loft naked – doing a little of this and a little of that, making sure to bend and squat as often as possible.

Soon, Man's punches were less constant–one here, nothing, then a couple more with a longer wait for the next. With her back to him, she peeped over her shoulder and smiled when she saw Man watching her with his gloved hands hanging by his side. She went to him slowly, her tongue sneaking between her lips.

She stood on the other side of the heavy-bag for a moment, before stepping around it and pushing her oil-slicked body against his sweaty form. After grinding hard against him, feeling the strength of his body and his erection, she removed the gloves from his hands. Although neither of them spoke a word, their eyes and bodies shouted and screamed with passion and desire.

Man ran his hands through her hair, pulling and wrapping it around his hand. Sweat and oil mixed as Nicki pressed against him. Still, not a word passed between them. She licked sweat from his chest, reached in his shorts and held him in her hand. *My man,* Nicki thought, and it didn't matter if he ever spoke, as long as he loved her. She kissed from his chest down to his stomach, bending at the waist before squatting down in fromt of her. Man watched her, enjoying the visual as much as the physical warmth and wetness of her mouth. Finally, he guided her back up, lifting her off the floor and covering her mouth with his. He sucked on her bottom lip, on her cheek and neck, holding her against him.

She *was* turned this way and that, shifted over and around, before ending up facing the wall on her toes with him behind her–in her. "Oh, baby! Give it all to me. Yes, baby. I'm with you!"

Man did little more than rumble deep in his chest. "Goddamn, Nicki," he growled in her ear as he ran his tongue up and down her neck.

"That's it. Right there," she panted. "It's us no matter what, right?" When he didn't answer, she reached back, grabbed his head and turned her face to his, pushing her tongue in his mouth. "It's us, always," she said again, between kisses.

"Always," Man answered, with their bodies locked together.

Somehow they ended up in the bed, sheets thrown aside, and nothing but lust and love to cover them.

After they were physically spent, Man told her what he'd known all along about Mr. Sam. He told her about how he had changed his finances around and about the *We Raise Up Foundation*—the one that gave the daycare center its annual grant. He had started it in memory of his mother, Wilona, Rita, and his daughter, Utopia. He told her about the police hounding him and what he intended to do about it. Then, they talked about their future together.

By the time his beeper went off, his mind was clear and he was ready to tie up all the loose ends and get on with his life. At the door, he kissed Nicki and whispered, "I love you, always." Although she didn't want him to leave, she only held onto him for a moment before turning away so that he wouldn't see her tears.

***

Kid listened as Freddy talked about his brother's new place uptown. While Freddy bragged to his young homey, Kid turned his back on him and waved at Terry as she crossed the street from the center. His eyes were on Terry, but his ears snatched every one of Freddy's words.

As she got closer, Terry twisted up her face and said, "You ain't been waving at me." Kid smiled, looked her up and down, then leaned forward and peeped behind her. "You ain't been filling out them jeans like that either!"

"Yeah, right," she said with a roll of her eyes. "You just ain't been lookin'." Kid noticed the slight smile on her face and thought that if he didn't have to keep an eye on Freddy, he'd find out how Terry looked out of those jeans. "I been seen' yo' li'l ass since you was nine."

"Shit, boy, if you lookin' the last three years you know ain't nothing little about my ass," Terry said, jutting a hip out at him.

Kid laughed and shook his head, "Shortie, don't get yo' self in some shit you can't handle."

"Humph! I can handle—o"

Kid cut her off; "You just talkin', shortie." He got in his car with his eyes following Freddy, who had started down the block. He had not intentions of losing him now, especially after what he'd just heard.

As he started the car, he leaned his head out the window toward Terry and said with a wink, "You know you ain't hardly grown, but you keep playin' with me..." Kid left the rest to her imagination.

With her hands on her hips, Terry licked her full lips and said, "You the one they call Kid. So, I guess you know somethin' about playin', huh?"

Kid laughed as he put the car in gear and pulled away–Freddy had just jumped in a cab.

***

Ricky replaced the receiver. With Short-Dog and José missing, and probably dead, and the hit on Easy, he needed to get the sergeant to move on Man as soon as possible. And if Gledhill and his detectives couldn't get it done Ricky had decided it was time to make a deal with the D.A.'s office and turn state's on Man and the cop's. Although he didn't have any real proof about Man, he figured that what he did know would force an investigation, and at the least he could testify to the extortion from both parties. The feds would be happy to shut down dirty cops and a known murderer like Man.

Ricky dropped his head in his hands. He couldn't believe what had happened to his life in the last couple of months. He'd went from stacking dollars and chasing hoes, to ducking Man and being pressed by the police. While he saw nothing wrong with selling drugs, and taking advantage of all the young girls desperately trying to escape poverty, he couldn't see why anyone would prey on him. It never dawned on him that he'd become a snitch in order to get rid of Man. Nor would he admit, a life of crime usually ended with prison or death. He stood up and looked around his new crib. He'd ordered the hottest new styles from Seaman's– plush leather furniture in the living room and a King-sized bed in the bedroom. But, right now, none of it mattered. Ricky knew if he made a deal with the Feds he'd probably end up in prison for a couple of years. But, he thought, going to prison was better than ending up dead.

He looked over at the Adidas gym bag filled with cash that Freddy had dropped off, then at the large ornate cabinet against the far wall. He pointed the remote and pressed the on button. He listened intently and stared at the cabinet. He couldn't count the times he'd gone through the same drill and not once had he heard or seen anything.

Ricky hit the remote again, nothing. Since he'd painted over the tiny red light there wasn't anything to see, either. Everything was going according to plan–soon he'd be on top.

## CHAPTER FIFTY-TWO

With the rain and dark October sky, Kid went unnoticed by the few pedestrians as he watched the entrance of the tenement. He had checked out the alley behind the building, it was a direct route from Ricky's new stash spot to the next street over. The building was a small five-story, tenement on Stillwell Avenue, just off Eastchester Road, surrounded by colonial and Elizabethan style homes. It was one of only two apartment buildings on the quiet street.

It was easy to see why Ricky had chosen the place–a nice peaceful neighborhood, with mostly older folks tending to their own business, and just enough Blacks so he wouldn't stick out. And there were regular police patrols to make Ricky's punk ass feel safe, Kid thought as he checked his watch. He glanced in the rearview mirror of the old, but well kept Lincoln Towncar. The car fit right in. As Man would say, *"it was a grownup's car,"* and with Kid slouched down in the seat it hadn't gotten a second look from folks passing by.

With his eyes back on Ricky's building, Kid didn't notice the figure walking on the far sidewalk unitl it was only twenty feet away. His eyes narrowed and his hand moved toward his "Nine". He scanned the whole area while keeping the figure in view by pushing his head further back against the headrest and consciously expanding his line of vision.

Kid relaxed as he recognized Man crossing the street. He smiled at how easily Man had found him–even with the scant directions he'd given him an hour ago.

No interior light came on as Man opened the door and got in. "Nice car."

"I thought you'd like it"

Man took in the car's plush leather interior and light tinted window. He glanced over at Kid. "It's a li'l big for you, but it's just right for tonight."

"Yeah. I been payin' attention. Fit in, so you can get in and out without being noticed," Kid said, looking sideways at Man.

Man nodded, "That's right. Now, let's get outta here."

Kid looked puzzled, "Whaddya mean? I checked everything out"

"And you did good, but the car been here too long and we don't know who happened to notice me getting in. We gonna go a couple blocks over, then double back and leave the car by the parkway. I'll fill you in on how we gonna rock."

"So, what's the deal?" Kid asked Man, after parking on the service road along the parkway.

"First off; let's wipe the car down," Man said, as he pulled on a pair of deerskin driving gloves, and passed Kid a small white handkerchief. He took another handkerchief and began wiping the car himself. "Just in case somethin' go wrong and we gotta bounce without the car."

As they wiped the interior of the car, Man put Kid down with the plan.

\*\*\*

When he saw Man dip his head deeper into his jacket and walk by Ricky's building, Kid knew something was wrong. So, instead of turning and crossing the street he continued eastbound, knowing Man would catch up with him. As he slowed his pace, his mind seemed to make up for it by speeding from one thing to another. It wasn't often that Man wavered when making a move. He never lost his nerve, that's how Kid knew something was wrong.

After a block, Man caught up with him. Without slowing down or looking over, Man said, "Looks like Po-Po. Old, blue, unmarked, joint parked in front of the building." A few seconds of silence passed, before he went on, "Bet its them three pigs been sweatin' Bigum at the game room."

"Shit. Whadda fuck do—"

Man cut in, as they walked along, "Chill, knowin' the pigs, they came for some loot. And knowin' Ricky, he pressin' 'em to get at us. With Dog and Ze gone and that shit with Easy, he runnin' scared. But don't none of them know that we know all this shit. So it's a good bet that we can end all this shit tonight."

Kid licked his lips and took a quick look around, showing signs of a rare case of nerves. "So what we gonna do?"

"It's still cool. We gonna do what we came to do," Man said, finally looking at Kid. While Kid held his eyes, Man continued, "I'm a go through the alley you told me about. You go back to the car."

"C' mon, Man. I gotta—"

"Kid!" Man's voice was tight with tension. "We come too far to fuck this up. We can't both be moving around inside and the street is too empty for one of us to be hanging out. I'm a check the spot out on the Q.T., and in ten minutes you come back and if po-po is gone, then you come up. If they ain't, you go get the car and park where you can watch 'em."

Kid didn't like it, but he knew there was no use arguing.

Man entered the alley as if he'd done so a thousand times. His steps were deliberated and unhurried. In minutes he crossed over to Ricky's building and jimmied the basement door with the small crowbar he'd taken from the car. He stepped inside, closed his eyes, held his breath, and listened for a minute. When he was satisfied that no one had heard him, he headed for the stairs, bypassing the elevator on his way to the third floor apartment number Kid had given him.

As he stepped onto the first landing, Man heard the elevator start up. He eased back into the dark staircase and waited. He slipped his hand in his jacket, resting it on the butt of the sixteen-shot Browning .9mm that hung from his armpit to his waist. The shoulder holster was designed to accommodate the silencer attached to the gun, and gave him the confidence to fire on the cops if he had to

He knew that he'd be able to get off six or seven shots before they'd be able to get their guns out, and if it was three of them or less; they'd all be dead before they could get a shot off. But it would probably cost him his life, he thought. NYPD was ruthless when one of their own went down, no matter how dirty they might be. A cop once told him that no matter what gang or crew he ran with the police department the largest and most vicious gang there was was. Still, Man knew with the high-powered .9mm, he could lay the cops down. But, would he be able to get to Ricky in time? That was the key. If cops were dead in his lobby, Ricky'd be sure to give his name up.

As he eased the gun out and the elevator came to a noisy stop, he heard one of them say, "What's next, Sarge?"

"I'm not sure, but I wanna drop the bag off, then, we'd head back to the..." As the lobby door closed on the words, Man raced up the stairs.

***

Ricky held the tape in his hand as he sipped his drink —his nerves were on fire, sweat collected on his upper lip and in his palms. He looked over at the cabinet and smiled. The CD player pumped out En Vogue's, *However You Want It*. He couldn't believe he'd actually pulled it off.

As he sighed in relief, the door shook from a sudden burst of hard knocking. His stomach in knots, Ricky dropped the tape and looked, first at the door, then over toward the cabinet, then back at the door. Shit, he thought, what the fuck do they want now— he'd have run if he could.

"I'm comin', give me a sec," he said, as he kicked the tape under the sofa and moved toward the door.

"Let's go! Lets go!" Man said in a muffed voice.

Ricky was so unnerved; he released all three locks without looking through the peephole. With his head titled down and his shoulder pressed against the door, Man had crowded the peephole, blocking the view, anyway.

As the door started to open, Man crashed his weight against it. The door flung open...hit Ricky in the forehead, drawing blood. Man was inside before Ricky could react. He kicked the door close and caught Ricky with a left hook to the side of his head. Ricky used the floor for a quick punk-nap.

Man locked the door, stepped over Ricky and quickly patted him down. Once he was satisfied that Ricky wasn't armed, he went from room to room making sure they were alone. Then he dragged the unconscious Ricky into the living room, Man holstered his gun and took out his little knife. He went to the cabinet, turned up the volume, then he cut the cord off one of the lamps, and hog-tied Ricky. When he positioned Ricky on his side, he noticed the tape sticking out from under the sofa, and picked it up. He stood up and dropped it on Ricky's head and smiled when Ricky moaned. Maybe Ricky and the pigs were watching porno together, he thought.

Dazed and unsure, Ricky stirred slowly. Man nudged him with the toe of his boot. "Wake yo' ass up, Ricky. It's all she wrote time," Man said without emotion.

Ricky's eyes finally focused and the fear in them multiplied once they settled on Man's face and he realized that he was tied up like an S&M freak waiting to be spanked. "I-I-I-," Ricky stuttered uncontrollably.

Man shook his head, bored with the whole thing already. He stared at Ricky without speaking.

Ricky stalled for a minute—faking like he couldn't breathe– trying to compose himself. He felt a chill, but fought it off and swallowed the fear.

He forced his mind to be calm, now, if only his body would follow, he thought. "Look, Man, it ain't what you thinkin'. I can…"

Man put a finger to his slightly parted lips, "Shhhh." His eyes commanded Ricky to stop talking. "Now, how the fuck would you know what I'm thinkin'?"

When Ricky started to speak, Man stopped him, "Ricky, that was a rhetorical question. You dumb as a rock, ain't you?" Man asked as he pulled out the nine. His eyes poured into Ricky's. "Nah, you dumber than a rock, 'cause a rock got enough sense to lay low if ain't nobody fuckin' with. It's time to pay up."

With his eyes bugging out of his head, Ricky felt a brick-coldness settle around his heart. Although he didn't see his life flash before his eyes, he knew it was all over for him if he didn't think of something quick. "Wait, Man, oh-my-god, please," he said, in a childish whimper. When he saw the disgust on Man's face he raced on, "I got the tape. Yeah, that's it. I can make everything right. I swear, I can. Man, please, just listen for a minute. I got—"

"Ricky, shut the fuck up for a minute," Man said, shaking his head.

Fear forced Ricky to disregard Man's words. "I got the tape and I got paper. I mean, real paper. I swear."

"What the fuck I care 'bout yo' loot. And what the fuck you keep talkin' 'bout a fuckin' porno tape for," Man said, as he picked up one off the pillows from the sofa.

In a panic, Ricky looked down at the tape. "No, wait. Please, Man, it ain't no porno, it's that white-ass sergeant and 'em"

"What?" Man asked with interest. He snatched the tape off the floor and stared down on Ricky. "Now, tell me what's on this shit."

"It's like I told you. I got po-po on tape takin' money," Ricky said with hope as he saw Man's interest. "I can get 'im off yo' back, Man. I'm tellin' you we got his ass. Ain't shit he can do but what we tell him to do," Ricky finished in a mad rush to get the words out.

Man looked at Ricky and back at the tape in his hand. He was amazed how stupid Ricky could be. He really thought that pig was going to let somebody blackmail him. Man sighed,

"Okay, where your VCR at?"

Ricky told him, and in less than three minutes Man was back from the bedroom. "You got any more tapes?" he asked as he checked his watch– he knew Kid would show up soon.

"Nah, that's it. I just..."

Man shut him up with a wave of his hand. "I wanna know how you got this," he said, holding up the tape.

While Ricky explained, he made sure to leave the part of his plan to use the tape to force the cops to go after Man. Man went through the cabinet and the rest of the place. When he found nothing but a shoebox with a little over $20,000 he came back into the living room and picked up the pillow again. Ricky's eyes almost climbed out of his head.

"Wait. Man. I told ya' I got loot too. I got—"

"I found your stash already. It's time to—"

"No, Man, listen, please," Ricky begged. "I got over $800,000 stashed in the wall of my grandmother's basement over on Rosedale Avenue. She don't even know it's there. Don't nobody know. I swear..."

Man shook his head and grunted, "You ain't shit, Ricky." He raised the pillow and stood over Ricky.

"Awww, Man...please don't kill me. I got mo' money. Man, listen, I got money stashed in safe-deposit boxes too," Ricky pleaded. "Let me make this right, you know—"

Man silenced Ricky by bringing the pillow down on his head and firing two shots into his neck. Ricky's body jumped, did a little dance–both legs twitching—then went still. Man shot him twice more in the middle of the chest, just to the left. He put the tape in his inside jacket pocket, and grabbed the money out the shoebox. He slipped the stacks of loot in his jacket and pants pockets, but there was still three stacks left. He thought for a minute, then dropped them on Ricky's dead body. *Fuck it. It was blood money, anyway,* he thought as he searched for Ricky's keys.

# CHAPTER FIFTY-THREE

"Grant, bring his ass down here," Sergeant Gledhill ordered. 'I don't even want you to let him put on a fucking coat. Just get his black ass down here."

The skinny, Black detective, looked bored. "Yeah, got'cha, Sarge," he replied, as he pulled the unmarked police car to a stop in front of Ricky's building.

Beside him, the other detective snickered and rolled his little pig-eyes, "Want me to go too, Sarge?"

Gledhill snorted, "What? It takes both of you's to bring down one piece of shit? Goddamit! Maybe we should all go, huh?"

"Nah, I got it," the first detective said, as he killed the engine and slid out of the car, glad to be away from the sergeant's bitching. The sergeant had a bug up his ass about the money and something that he said was bothering him about the whole thing. So, after five minutes on the road, he'd demanded that they turn around and come back.

The detective pushed every bell on the first and second floors; somebody was going to let him in. I don't have all night for this shit, he thought, as he looked at his gold watch and straightened his silk tie.

\*\*\*

Kid made his way up the stairs, taking his time and listening for any sound. He'd waited almost ten minutes after the cops left before entering the lobby, using a picklock on the door. After a quick check of the basement, he made his way to the staircase, now he stood between the first and second floors. When he heard the intercom go off in all the apartments, he pushed his back against the wall and listened without moving.

Once inside the lobby, the Black detective couldn't get over how stupid people were. He had rung their bells and yelled, 'police', and they buzzed him in. They were like cattle, just waiting for somebody to herd them along, he thought as he waited for the elevator. No wonder the crime rate was so high.

"Shit," Kid muttered, as he saw the detective get in the elevator, before pulling his head back. He reached for his joint, a Beretta ...9mm, and held his breath, as he remained motionless. He heard the elevator start up, but couldn't chance a look. So he just listened with his gun ready. Since the cops didn't know he was in the building he had the advantage. If they caught Man sleeping, Kid would have them dead to right, he thought, as he waited and listened to the elevator going up.

\*\*\*

Man closed the apartment door behind him, but before he could lock it, he heard the elevator and rushed toward it. As the inner door of the elevator slowly slid back, he snatched the outer door open. The detective instinctively reached inside his coat, but Man was too quick—he stepped into the detective's body, caught his hand in mid-motion, inches from his service gun, while shoving his own gun under the cop's chin. "Move and die, muthafucker," he said, through clenched teeth.

The cop's free hand twitched, but the sight of the cocked hammer on the silenced nine-millimeter stopped it as effectively if Man had grabbed that hand too. The cop knew that the slightest move could mean death. It was a strange feeling for the detective—in his eighteen years on the force; he'd always been the one holding someone's life in his hands. The Black cop didn't like the feeling of helplessness, and he stared hard into Man's eyes, trying to regain the advantage he had grown used to since joining the force.

Man met the stare with one of his own, as he removed the cop's gun from its holster. "Press five, we going up."

* * *

Kid made his way slowly up the stairs; stopping every few steps to listen for signs of trouble when he heard the elevator stop, then start again. He waited, to see whether it went up or down.

* * *

On the roof, Man found the cop's second weapon, a small, six-shot, thirty-two automatic, in an ankle holster. "Now, what's this," he asked as he yanked the gun away from the spread-eagle cop.

With his face against the cold, wet rooftop, the cop was as helpless as the countless suspects he'd taken advantage of since he'd been on the job. He'd counted on his throwaway gun to give him the edge he needed–now it was gone. But, he knew the sergeant would come looking for him soon–he just had to stall this fucking hump, he thought.

"Look, buddy, I don't know what this is about," he lied; he knew exactly who Man was from the minute Man had caught him sleeping. "But, you know I'm a cop, and you ought'a know your best bet is to get away while you can. I mean, you know damn well if you—"

"Shut the fuck up." Man commanded, as he pulled the detective to his feet. He'd known right off that he'd bagged the snake Bigum had described. "What the fuck did y'all come back for?"

"I don't know—" the cop words were cut off by Man slapping him on side of the head with the butt of the thirty-two. His head snapped sideways and a small gash appeared on his temple.

"Where the other pigs at?" Man asked.

The cop stumbled, but somehow remained upright. He peered around wild-eyed, "I told you—"

Man hit him again, this time he dropped to one knee and screamed hysterically.

"Whaddaya—"

"Shut the fuck up," Man hissed, as he pulled his arm back for another swing. The detective pushed himself up and lunged at Man. The nine-millimeter fell from Man's hand as the cop grabbed him around the waist. Although Man was thrown against the ledge of the roof, he still had the presence of mind not to fire the thirty-two. As the cop tried to lift him off his feet, Man brought the gun down on the base of the man's skull, then swung his forearm around and elbowed him in the jaw. Still, the cop held on and pushed with a crazed strength born out of desperation.

With his top-half leaning over the roof's ledge, Man dropped his elbow into the cop's back. The blow stunned the cop for a second, Man seized the opportunity and grabbed him by the waist and yanked as hard as he could.

A horror filled scream escaped the detective's mouth as he went airborne. His arms flailed helplessly as the ground rushed up to meet him.

Man held on to the roof, his upper body threatening to send him behind the detective. With his breath coming in short gulps, a sharp pain running across his back, Man righted himself and looked down at the body in the alley below before grabbing his gun and moving to the fire escape.

***

Kid heard the scream as he stood outside the door to Ricky's apartment. He backed away, started for the stairs, listened for a few seconds, then started up toward the roof.

Gledhill and the fat detective rushed into the building, guns drawn. On the third floor, they found the apartment unlocked, and Ricky dead.

Kid found nothing on the roof, but after seeing the cop's body in the alley, he retraced his steps. Back in the lobby, he was stopped cold at the sight of a blue and white patrol car pulling up in front of the building. Kid slipped his gun in the middle of his back and headed for the stairs. "Shit."

Gledhill stood on the steps with his gun out and pointed right at him. "Don't move a muscle. Not if you wanna live."

Kid thought about going for his weapon, but then the elevator door opened and a fat cop with beady eyes stepped out. "Go ahead, you slug!"

Kid cracked his trademark smile, and thought: *"Shit, it 's only a gun beef "* just before he went out from the blow to the side of his head.

The fat cop laughed, "Sarge. You want me to read him his rights, now?" he asked, as he slipped the sap back in his pocket.

# EPILOGUE

Kid was arrested and charged with two counts of murder, plus gun possession. With nothing to place him at the scene of either Ricky or the cop's murder, he figured his only problem would be the gun. The first of the two messages he received from Man said: "Take it all the way. Right is might." Not that he had much of a choice; there were no plea bargains when it came to a cop's body–and without any physical evidence, he knew the State didn't have a case. Still, the word from Man was all he needed to hear. If Man had told him he could fly, he would have believed it and jumped.

So, it rocked him, two years later, when he was convicted of both murders. Man's second message arrived a few days after he blew trial: "Stay strong and in the end what is wrong will be right." Kid stared at the postcard — sloppily printed words under a postmark from Malaysia and a picture of a Buddhist temple on the other side. He tossed it aside and lay on his narrow bunk. The last thing he needed was more of Man's mystic bullshit, he thought.

Two months later, as the bus headed upstate on the Major Deegan Expressway, passing through Marble Hill, Kid thought about Man and the guy with the dog. In the reflection of the window, he saw the whole scene again — the swift action that cost a man his life, but saved a dog's. Man had just killed a human being with hands he gently comforted a dog with seconds later. Then he had turned to Kid, as if he felt Kid watching him, and said: "The man had a choice, the dog didn't. So, one just got what he got and the other got what he deserved." That was it. The only explanation Man had given about the incident, other than the fact that he loved dogs.

As the bus left the Bronx behind, Kid wondered what he'd gotten–just what he got or what he deserved? He wasn't guilty of either of the murders, but he wasn't completely innocent either. He moved his ankle from side to side to adjust the shackles, and looked over at the man shackled to him. Since it was his third bid, the man was fast asleep, without a care in the world. Kid shook his head, and tried to forget that the handcuffs were too tight and the waist-chain was digging into his side. He thought about all the spiritual shit Man was into and wondered how real it was and what good it was?

He watched the road slide by – taking his life with it. Like losers of Super Bowls, no one remembers who almost won. He shook his head again, but the fifty to life he'd been sentenced to refused to budge. It stayed right in front of him. What was the difference anyway, if he deserved it or not? Or whether he died on the street or behind the wall of prison? He'd have to ask Man. Yeah, he had some questions for Man, he thought as the bus rolled along, leaving his life behind.

Although Pete recovered from his wounds, they changed him. With his crew gone, he had little use for the street life. After Kid was convicted Pete moved his family to North Carolina, where he opened a plant nursery–it turned out he had a green thumb. So, with his knack for growing things, he enrolled at North Carolina A&T State University, in Greensboro. Nevertheless, he stayed in touch with Kid, and worked to free him.

Bigum became the sole owner of the Badlands, as well as two other buildings Man left him. He also worked closely with Tyrone Jenkins on the We Raise Up Foundation, creating scholarships and other charities. He also helped out at the daycare center now that things had changed over there.

Nicki? She hadn't panicked when Man didn't come back that rainy night. She went about her business of running the center. She poured herself into her work for the next four months. With Ms. Nez, Ms. Mary, and Bigum fussing over her, she stayed busy. Then, she took a vacation, and after a month, papers arrived turning the center over to Sara and Terry, with

Bigum, Tyrone, Ms. Mary and Ms. Nez as the board of directors. Though at first it had seemed as if she was hiding from the truth of Man's disappearance, in the end it appeared she was actually hiding a truth all her own.

Eddie took a fall –not with the law. Love dropped Eddie King like a bad habit. Kia decided that he was too much like her father, after all. She couldn't risk her heart with him. Especially, once he suggested breaking her father, who she finally told him about, out of prison after his latest appeal was denied. Shortly after Kia left, Eddie's young protégé was gunned down in the streets of Southeast D. C. Although he extracted vengeance, just as he and Man had done for the God, the deaths and everything else made him think too much and he realized that he was just as sad as Man.

Eddie drowned his sorrows in a river of debauchery that ran into an ocean of wasteful excess–the women and drugs made his old ways seem mild. Afraid to be alone at night, he partied until the sun searched him out. Then he slept all day and fought off the nightmares. Awake and sober, he thought of pulling off two prison breaks, in two different states, but instead he sent money and packages, and paid legal fees. Sober or not, he thought about Man, which made him believe in happy endings, and that tomorrow would be better, somehow.

Four hours after the detective hit the cold, wet ground in the alley; Man was getting off a plane at Dallas/Fort-Worth Airport. Seventy-two hours later he was out of the country and closing the accounts he had started setting up months ago. Although he was only wanted for questioning, he knew the police would hound him and force him to fight a war he couldn't win.

He also knew the few people he cared about would probably go down with him if he stayed. Since he couldn't take all of them with him, he left word with who he could, when he could and rode off into a moonlit rainy night in search of new Badlands–a land where outlaws roamed free. He felt just like he did watching the old western movies as a kid; he wanted the bad guy to get away for once. But in his heart, nothing was right as rain.